ALL I WANT FOR CHRISTMAS IS SANTA

SARA ELLIOT

CHAPTER 1

Merry's red bottomed heels reflected off polished white marble like warning lights signaling her approach. She eyed the plastic boughs of Fraser fir that had overtaken the reception desk of Kline & Associates Consulting over the Thanksgiving holiday, readying her defenses against the holiday spirit.

Henrietta, the very-blonde receptionist Merry had voted against hiring, wore cheerful earrings fashioned after Christmas ornaments and a hundred-watt smile. Clearly the spirit had claimed an early victim. "Good morning, Miss Claus. I have three messages for you."

"Email me." Merry barely slowed as she passed the second-rate receptionist. If she had her way and they'd hired the surly woman with thirty years' experience, she wouldn't have needed to repeat her preference for electronic communication over office small talk.

"Be a little nicer to Blondie. She made cookies," Deirdre said, falling into step at Merry's side.

She and Deirdre had met seven years ago at Kline & Associates' new employee orientation and been inseparable through the eighty-hour workweeks of their first two years. They'd set their sights at the very top and decided to become two of Arnold Kline's Associates—the capital "A" kind that came with a cushy title and seven figure salary.

Merry was close to achieving that goal. At just twenty-nine, she was already a Junior Partner with a ten-person team and her choice of mid-tier clients to boss around. Deirdre had gotten altitude sickness halfway up the

1

corporate ladder and defected to the Human Resources department, but she was still Merry's best friend.

As her best friend, Deirdre knew to offer a cookie in the shape of an innocuous snowflake rather than a Christmas tree. The name Merry Claus had given her hard-won immunity to holiday cheer, but she still took pains to avoid contamination.

Merry took the cookie and the coffee Deirdre seemed to pull out of thin air. "I need to schedule a meeting with Mike."

"Bringing you coffee doesn't make me your secretary, babe."

Merry forced a tight smile. "As a manager in HR, I'd expect you to use the term Administrative Assistant, and to know it's frowned upon to ask your admin to bring you coffee."

As usual, Deirdre only focused on the part of Merry's sentence that played into what she wanted to talk about next. "Speaking of admins, I'm thinking of hiring another one. You consultants are a needy bunch. I had to work forty-four hours last week."

"I remember my first part-time job," Merry said with a wistful sigh.

Deirdre knocked her shoulder, jostling her coffee but not spilling it. "Come take care of Rosie one weekend. A few days with a three-year-old will make consulting look like an after-school gig."

"No, thank you. But let me know if you need me to consult on parenting process improvement. Oh, or management. I'm sure I could wrangle you a little more power in the marriage."

Deirdre laughed. "Keep your corporate buzzwords out of my relationship. I'm content to let Charli and Rosie run the show. Now, we've spent the requisite two minutes on my stuff, what's going on with you? You look twitchier than usual."

"My grandmother died." They were nearing Merry's office, and she was annoyed to see the door next to hers already propped open, spewing fluorescent light and the sound of clicking keys. The optics were not good. Her office was dark and empty at six thirty while her rival was probably doing a crossword while he stuffed his face with Blondie's cookies, but it looked like he was working. Sneaky little suck up.

Merry was too distracted by Simon's open door to hear Deirdre's well-intentioned sympathies. "It's fine," she said, waving her friend off. "I never even met her. I just have to deal with the estate, which is a nuisance at year-end."

"Harsh, babe. Maybe fake some tears so the others won't realize you're a robot."

Merry snorted a laugh. "Let's talk more at lunch. I'll be leaving tonight to go sort it all out so a sympathetic ear and a noon glass of Reisling are just what I need."

"The Greek Grill?"

"Absolutely."

***

Merry's boss ran a hand through his thinning brown hair. It was a strange side-effect of the consulting business, losing one's hair. It didn't just affect the men. There was more than one woman with a bald spot on the thirty-seventh floor.

"You couldn't have picked a worse time to play the dead grandparent card. Norman's out with that heart stuff." A heart attack. "And Andrea has her baby thing." Just a baby. She was having a baby.

"I'm more than happy to help Merry," Simon The Suck Up said.

Merry hated his small, superior smile that implied a dead grandmother was a weakness.

"I don't have any family coming into town for the holidays this year, so I'm completely free." Of course he was. He'd made the mistake of thinking his paid time off was meant to be used one Christmas and never lived it down.

Now, Merry was unintentionally doing the same thing. At least it was only November 29th.

"I'll be available by phone and email. I just need someone to handle the Blue Arrow meeting on Monday," Merry reminded them. Like hell she'd let Simon steal all her clients while she was gone. "I'll be back in three days."

"No," Mike said with a sigh. "You get a week of bereavement leave. Plus, you haven't used any PTO for the past seven years. You know the partners are worried about the complaints to the labor department claiming we 'overwork' our employees. Take two weeks, minimum."

"I don't need two weeks. I—"

"I insist. Simon will handle everything while you're gone," Mike said.

Merry's arguments went unheard. She would be taking her first vacation since college whether she wanted to or not. If only she didn't have to spend it in Poleton, North Carolina.

CHAPTER 2

Christmas decorations looked ridiculous in Southern California but especially on the front of the Greek Grill. It was a white stucco building with a tasteful patio dotted with two-seater tables and wooden chairs painted in various shades of blue—or at least it had been the day before. Now, obnoxious red ribbons clashed with the terracotta patio pavers and boughs of cypress overpowered the aroma of fresh lamb.

Merry asked the hostess for a table on the back patio overlooking the sea and was horrified to find more of the same decorations there. It looked—and smelled—like a Michael's craft store had exploded in Santorini. The water decanters were sweating onto the red bows tied around their necks for goodness' sake.

But Deirdre was chatting with their usual waiter, complementing the decor, and he was proudly exclaiming that the whole staff had stayed all night to decorate. Merry liked these people, and this restaurant, so she ground her teeth, forced a smile, and ordered a bottle of wine rather than a glass.

"You've survived twenty-nine Christmases Ms. Claus, you'll survive this one too," Deirdre told her with a smirk once their waiter left to fetch their drinks.

Merry gave a self-pitying groan. "I'm not sure I will. Mike is forcing me to take two weeks off. If I didn't know about the complaints to the labor department, I'd think he was trying to force me out."

The waiter returned with their beverages and took their orders.

5

Neither Merry nor Deirdre needed a menu since they ate here at least three days a week. When he'd gone back to the kitchen, Deirdre leaned in. "You know the labor department won't do anything, even in California vacation time isn't a legal requirement. But our competitors would love to stir up shit in the media. Personally, I think some shit should be stirred, but you already know that."

"Yes, you're a communist, I know," Merry said with a teasing smile.

"Democratic socialist, you ass. You come back to work eight weeks after having a baby and then talk to me about the fairness of unpaid leave." Before Merry could argue, Deirdre raised a hand to stop her. "Yes, I know I was paid for parental leave, but a lot of people aren't. Then, daycare won't take a child under twelve weeks old, and there are waiting lists at most reputable childcare centers, and they cost more than a lot of people make. And on top of all that, we shame mothers who accept government benefits, and we shame mothers who don't accept them, and we shame mothers who work, and we shame mothers who don't, and—"

"And it's an all-around terrible system, I know," Merry agreed. "I'm on board. Raise my taxes and let parents stay with their children. Go ahead and pay for their healthcare too. Just don't force me to take time off and give my clients to Simon."

"I know you two have a Batman-Joker rivalry going on, but you have to admit he isn't terrible at his job. And you desperately need a vacation. You've needed one for years."

"Batman, really? You couldn't have made me Wonder Woman?" Merry interjected.

"Lasso of Truth and consulting don't really go hand-in-hand," Deirdre argued. "Maybe Batman-Catwoman?"

"Weren't they a couple?" Merry asked. Diedre just gave her a pitying look. Merry rolled her eyes. "How many times do I have to tell you that I hate him?"

"You can say it all you want, but I don't believe you. And you're intentionally missing my point. Whatever the reason, a vacation will be good for you."

Merry scoffed. "That's what you say now, wait until I tell you about the horror movie that is my inheritance."

"Oh, do tell."

The arrival of her watermelon and feta salad on a revoltingly red plate rimmed with gold holly delayed the terrifying reality of her predicament.

When the waiter accepted Merry's attempt at a smile and left, she filled her best friend in. "My grandmother left me a mansion in a small town in the Appalachian Mountains and a toy factory. A toy factory, Dee. Like creepy dolls whose eyes follow you wherever you go. And it gets worse. The toy factory burned in 1895 and was rebuilt on the same ground."

Deirdre shivered. "Just sell it. I'm sure some ghost hunters would love to get their hands on all that. It might actually be made into a horror movie or at least a crappy podcast."

"That's the thing—the lawyer says I can't receive it or sell it yet. He won't even send me a copy of the will. I have to go there in person."

"I see what you mean about the horror movie," Deirdre said. "Is that even legal?"

"No, but he was very adamant."

"What are you going to do?"

Merry shrugged and refilled her wine glass. "I'm going to go there tomorrow, get a copy of the will, and see it all for myself. Mostly the books. I want to know if I can sell the business or just the land."

"What about the funeral?" Deirdre asked.

"Already taken care of. Apparently, my grandmother had burial insurance and left specific instructions for a memorial service. It was two days ago."

Deirdre gave Merry *The Look*. She was very familiar with the nonverbal indictment of her character. The narrowed eyebrows and tightness around Dee's mouth clearly said *You're doing the selfish thing again*.

"The lawyer called me after the funeral. What was I supposed to do? Ask them to un-cremate her so I could meet her and pay my respects?" Merry defended.

"At the very least, yank a knot in that lawyer's behind for leaving you out of it."

"That I can do." Merry lifted her half-empty glass in salute to Deirdre's plan. "It will put him on the back foot in negotiations."

Deirdre rolled her eyes. "Just promise me you won't fall in love with the small-town, flannel-wearing lumberjack and his golden retriever. I need you here."

"I couldn't possibly do that," Merry said. "I'm married to my job, remember? We had a beautiful white wedding in the conference room when I made junior partner."

CHAPTER 3

Merry took a red eye and arrived in Charlotte just after five in the morning. She'd passed through every major airport in the country over the last seven years with little emotion, but the wide halls and stark white walls of Charlotte-Douglas International Airport stirred unwelcome feelings.

The airport had expanded in the past decade, but it was still the site of her tearful goodbye with her parents before college and the place where only her father had greeted her just two years later.

He stood in the arrival terminal in his usual khaki slacks, golf polo, and half-zip sweater. Merry grinned when she saw him, despite the pain in her chest reminding her there should be a dark-haired beauty in a sweater-set beside him.

"Hey, pumpkin." Her father opened his arms when she drew close.

Merry dropped her bag and accepted the hug. "Hey, old man."

Her father took control of her worn SteamLine carryon and steered her through the throng of yoga pants, sweatshirts, and pajamas toward the automatic doors. Merry would never understand modern airport attire. Sitting on a plane didn't require flexibility or sweating, so why did so many people forgo showers and wear athletic clothes?

She wore dark wash jeans that hugged her generous curves, a fitted oxford shirt, and a colorful silk scarf. Casual. Comfortable. Best of all, appropriate.

"You didn't have to come inside," Merry told her father.

"I know. But I didn't want to miss your reaction."

"My reaction to what?" The answer soon became apparent. The *weather* that had very nearly delayed her flight wasn't a thunderstorm, as she'd assumed, but a flurry of fat snowflakes that clung to travelers' clothes and turned the many, many parking lots white. "Yuck. I thought I was in the South."

Her father laughed. "I hope a little snow won't chase you back to California."

"It just might," Merry muttered, already shivering. "And this time I'm taking you with me."

"One day," her dad promised. "After I retire, of course. I can't leave the whole Southeast without power."

"And they can't possibly make electricity without their favorite middle manager."

"Exactly."

Merry wasn't sure what her father did at the local power company. All she knew was that he managed people, and he'd survived a dozen reorganizations over the years, so he must do it well. Maybe not so well that the Southeast power grid would fail without him, but she'd let him keep his pride.

They piled her bags into the four-door BMW he'd driven for the past decade and Merry immediately reached for the seat warmer.

Her father drove them to Waffle House where they ordered watery coffee, soggy waffles, and bland eggs. Each part of her breakfast was sub-par, but somehow the combination was delicious. Maybe it was just nostalgia.

"So, your grandmother left you the toy shop," her father began.

"She did."

He shook his head. "I wish I could go with you to sort everything out, but we're about to begin an outage. Today is my only day off for the next four weeks."

"I know." He'd said as much on their last weekly call. "I can handle it, don't worry."

"Your mother loved the shop once, but you know that," her father said. "She was so proud of her family's heritage that she talked me into taking her name. We were going to run the shop together after college, live in Poleton, and raise you to take over."

"What happened?" She'd never gotten a direct answer as to why her mother had left Poleton just before Merry was born and never looked back.

Her father shrugged. "She and your grandmother had a falling out. I never needed the details. All I know is that whatever your mother learned about the family business convinced her that it wasn't right for us, or for you."

It didn't surprise Merry that he hadn't asked for the details of the argument. Running a toy store was not his dream by any stretch of the imagination, and he hated small towns. He would have done it for Merry's mother, but it wouldn't have been the life he chose.

"I'll look into it, but whatever Mom didn't like won't matter for long. I'm either selling the toy store or shutting it down and selling the equipment, no matter what Grandmother Joy's will says."

"Just promise me you'll remember the people, Merry." He leveled her with an uncharacteristically serious expression. "There are not many job opportunities in small towns, and Poleton is an anomaly even by Appalachian standards. No Walmart, no chain restaurants, no real grocery store. It's like the town is frozen in 1957. I don't want to live there, but I'd hate to see all those people fall into the same trap as other small towns."

"A Southern town stuck in 1957? I hope you don't mean that."

"Not the racism and misogyny, but the way of life. They had a milkman the last time I was there," her father said.

"A sexy milkman with a dozen secret children?"

"Don't be crass. And no. Just a regular milkman."

"What a shame." Poleton sounded like the most boring place in America.

***

After breakfast, Merry spent the day helping her father with his Christmas shopping. She was an only child, but he had a dozen nieces and nephews that needed the latest gadgets.

For once, she didn't complain about the Garth Brooks Christmas CD in his BMW, the over-the-top Christmas decorations at the local mall, the lack of parking, or even the pushy crowds. The few hours with her father were worth the Christmas misery.

Mid-afternoon she hit I-85 in the beat-up old Chevy her father bought for a few hundred bucks from a neighbor for the sole purpose of hauling gardening supplies. The truck was stick-shift, it only got AM/FM radio, and the dry-rotted wipers made a screeching noise against the windshield.

She had plenty of airline miles to rent a shiny Prius, but her father had offered his truck, and she would only be here for a few days. Plus, there was something nostalgic about driving the old truck with a Sun Drop and a Styrofoam cup of boiled peanuts in the cup holder singing along to oldies hits. It reminded her of Sunday trips to Lowe's, and the inevitable return trip when they ran out of pine needles halfway through the back flower beds.

The only problem was the snow.

Southerners couldn't drive in anything resembling winter weather and the trip took nearly twice as long as it should have. It wasn't their fault, really. Cities didn't waste their money on plows and machines to salt the roads for one or two weeks a year. That meant slick asphalt, invisible spots of black ice, and nervous drivers who didn't know what to do with either of those things. Merry didn't know what to do either, so she couldn't judge the minivan driving thirty miles an hour in front of her with flashing hazard lights.

She turned onto the Blue Ridge Parkway just after seven PM and instantly missed the abundant lights on the interstate. It was dark, snow fell heavily, and the slush on the mountain road had begun to freeze.

After dark on a strange road in the middle of the Appalachian Mountains was a terrible time to remember her father's warnings about the truck's old brakes and bald tires. Merry considered finding a hotel for the night, but her GPS said it would only take another hour to reach Poleton, so she pressed on.

At eight thirty, she and the old Chevy limped into the light of a thirty-foot Christmas tree hung with big, vintage bulbs. It illuminated a wooden sign that said *Welcome to Poleton* in a font typically reserved for Old Time Photos shops in mountain tourist towns.

Behind the tree, a menagerie of wooden Christmas decorations draped in lights had overrun the town square. There were no fewer than three dozen reindeer, which at least made sense. The various bears, otters, dogs, and porcupines required more imagination. Merry couldn't see much else through the snow, but the decorations made the decision for her—she was selling the toy shop in the morning, getting out of this place, and never, ever coming back.

"Arrived," the authoritative voice of the GPS informed her.

"I have not arrived," Merry told the robot with all the sarcasm she could muster. She was in a field surrounded by wooden penguins and chipmunks. This was not an inn, even by small-town standards.

She scooped up the phone and checked the GPS app. Sure enough, the pin marking her location was directly atop the address the lawyer provided.

She pulled over to the side of the road and parked between a rabbit and a snowman. A circle spun in the center of her email application as it struggled to load. The one bar of service sputtered, then disappeared to be replaced by an exclamation point. Completing the trifecta of technological woes, her battery icon was as red as the lights draped around the nearby snowman's neck.

"Fantastic," Merry muttered to the empty seat beside her. "No cell service. It's 1957, just like Dad said."

She had two options: turn around, wait for service to return, and re-read the email from the lawyer to verify she'd copied the address correctly, or drive until she found the inn. Since she'd double checked the address before she left, Merry went with the second option.

How difficult could it be to find the only inn in a town of 6,000 people?

Six turns down increasingly narrow side streets answered her question. It could, apparently, be very difficult to find an inn when the world's most incompetent city planner had been involved in the town's layout.

She turned down yet another street, hoping to see the lights of an inn, but found herself trapped between stone walls, each a handbreadth from her mirrors. Those walls, and the road, seemed to disappear a few feet ahead of her.

Merry crept along, conscious of the snow obliterating her sight lines and freezing beneath her tires. The road didn't end, it just dipped down a slope so steep it could have been the side of a mountain.

With no other choice, she eased her way over the top of the hill, her foot on the brake.

Halfway down the slope, the old brakes gave out.

Merry shrieked as her foot hit the floorboard, and the heavy truck only sped faster down the hill. She scrambled to pull every lever she could reach, searching for the emergency brake.

She should have rented a Prius.

A shadow appeared through the snow, then headlights flashed off what were definitely eyes. A bear? A deer? It didn't matter; she was going to hit it.

Finally, one of the levers worked and the truck's bald tires locked, sending Merry skidding across as well as down the icy road. She laid on the horn, hoping to scare the animal into motion.

With her eyes squeezed shut, she waited for the inevitable impact. Miraculously, it never came.

The truck came to a rest at the bottom of the hill, facing the wrong way but intact.

Merry took a shuddering breath, still not ready to open her eyes. Her heart hammered against her ribs like it was trying to escape the terror of the last minute.

She was forced to confront her surroundings when the driver's side door swung open. Merry let out a little yip, already scrambling backwards to avoid swiping claws, but it wasn't a bear peeking into the dim interior of the truck.

Her mind whirled, trying to fit the person into any of the usual subconscious categories she tried her best to avoid. Salt white hair hung in loose waves past broad, flannel-clad shoulders. Honey eyes framed by long, snow dusted lashes were set in a face with high cheekbones and smooth dark skin. Delicate features, a strong jaw, full lips. The stranger was a beautiful contradiction.

"Are you alright?" Even his voice—because she was now sure the stranger was a man—was unusual. Smooth, deep, and steady.

"Fine," Merry squeaked.

The man rested his forearms against the top of the cab and leaned closer to Merry. "You sure? You're covered in peanuts."

Sure enough, her trip down the hill had scattered boiled peanut shells across the truck and her lap. "I am so sorry. I got lost and I couldn't read the street signs through the snow and then my brakes quit working halfway down the hill."

The stranger raised his white eyebrows but didn't ask any further questions. "Scooch."

"Scooch?" Merry repeated.

"Yes, I'm going to pull your truck off the road so no one hits it. You can call a tow truck in the morning."

Merry narrowed her eyes at the stranger, reconsidering her relief that she hadn't flattened him. She'd worked in a male dominated industry for the past seven years and she knew that condescending tone. He thought she wasn't capable of driving. Maybe her father had been wrong with his 'except the racism and misogyny' remark.

"What's next? Are you going to offer to cut my steak for me?"

"Are you inviting me to dinner? I don't normally date women who try to kill me, but I could make an exception. Only if you hurry up and scooch, though. It's cold out here."

Much to her embarrassment, Merry squawked with indignation. "I am not asking you on a date. I am pointing out how rude it is to insinuate that I can't drive."

"Can you, lovie? You drove the wrong way down a one-way street and almost hit an innocent, very handsome, pedestrian."

"One, I just told you I couldn't read the street signs through the snow. Two, I just told you that my brakes gave out. And three, don't ever call me 'lovie' again."

The insufferable ass grinned at her and had the audacity to make a shooing motion to encourage her to move. "As far as apologies go, that was terrible. Stick to asking me on a date, I liked that better."

"I have an invitation for you," Merry seethed. "Go stand in front of my truck again. If you survive, I'll take you to dinner and buy you something pretty."

"A tempting bargain, but no. You had your chance to kill me and date me. Unfortunately, you missed both." With another dazzlingly annoying smile, he pushed off the top of the truck and stepped back. "Try not to hit anyone else, and call Wayne in the morning. He'll come get the truck."

The stranger turned and faded into the flurry of snow after only a few steps. Gritting her teeth, Merry called after him. "Wait!"

"Yes, darling murderess?" The disembodied voice said from the shadows beyond her headlights.

Merry rolled her eyes. "Where is the inn?"

"So forward. Shouldn't we go on that date first?" He sounded farther away.

"I am cold and covered in peanuts! Just tell me where I can sleep tonight," Merry called into the falling snow.

His answer was almost too faint to hear. "Two blocks west, angel."

Merry hated that she'd leaned forward and strained to hear a useless direction and yet another pet name. West? Who gave directions like that? What was she supposed to do, consult the stars? Pull out a compass?

Her hands shook, half from cold, half from dying adrenaline as she closed the truck door and slowly turned the steering wheel. She was at the bottom of the hill, so gravity wouldn't be an issue, but it was still nerve wracking to move the brakeless truck. Plus, there was nowhere to move it on the narrow street with tall retaining walls on both sides.

A very small part of her wished she'd let the stranger help.

CHAPTER 4

Merry finally found the inn—no thanks to the stranger's directions—and slept trapped between too-warm flannel sheets. Despite her sleeping arrangements and ordeal the previous day, she woke at four-thirty sweat-drenched and restless.

The inn had an abundance of rustic charm, but no treadmill to work out her frustrations. Continued snow flurries prevented an outdoor run, so she had to skip her usual morning exercise.

Her room was also devoid of a coffee maker, so she wandered down to the empty lobby in search of caffeine. She found an old-fashioned drip coffee maker on an antique buffet table and a quick search of the drawers revealed locally roasted beans and a stack of filters. Perfect. If she couldn't run the jitters away, she'd drown them in coffee.

Returning to her room with coffee in hand, Merry settled cross-legged on the bed and thanked her lucky stars she'd remembered to get the Wi-Fi password the night before. She answered emails and handed out assignments for her team, then showered for her meeting with the lawyer.

She debated the contents of her suitcase for longer than she would like to admit before settling on dark bootcut jeans, a blazer, and leather calf-height boots with a small block heel. The perfect blend of professional and down-to-earth.

Evelyn, the inn's receptionist, arrived just in time to give her directions, a ceramic travel mug, and a blueberry muffin—elevating her to

Merry's favorite person in Poleton.

With her hands full of coffee and breakfast, Merry set out to meet her grandmother's lawyer. The long walk provided the perfect opportunity to study the town.

Poleton was charming in a made-for-tv-movie kind of way. Narrow, tree-lined streets and low stone buildings seemed pulled from a magazine offering a look at life in a quaint, mountain town. There were no neon signs, no billboards, no flashy advertisements, but—of course—there were plenty of obnoxious holiday decorations.

The snow had slowed to an occasional flurry, but ice still made the sidewalks treacherous. Merry took her time walking the eight blocks to the lawyer's office, since she wasn't sure there was a competent doctor to fix her ankle if she broke it.

She finally arrived at the small, stone house with cold feet, cold coffee, and cold, wet hair. Thoroughly miserable, she took a deep breath and walked confidently to the door—only to find it locked.

The clock app was one of the few that worked in this godforsaken town and it showed the time was nine fifteen. Any respectable law firm should be open at that time on a Friday, so she knocked.

"Just a moment!" a male voice called from inside the building.

Several moments later, the door opened revealing a wiry older man in an old-fashioned dressing gown. Merry glanced beside the door and confirmed that the sign said *Gray's Law Firm*.

"Mr. Gray?" she asked with a confidence she didn't feel.

"Call me Henry, please. And you must be Merry! Come on in, I'll have Dottie make some coffee while I get dressed." He stepped back and ushered Merry into what she was slowly being forced to realize was his home as well as his office.

A white-haired woman in a bedazzled tracksuit introduced herself as Dottie Gray and bustled Merry into a sitting room with shag carpet, a fraying sofa, and an upright piano. By the time she freshened Merry's coffee and offered her a variety of pre-made breakfast options, Henry rejoined them. He looked somewhat more like a lawyer in pleated corduroy slacks and a cardigan, but the effect was ruined when he excitedly accepted a cup of coffee and a plate of canned biscuits with apple butter from his wife.

Damn this cute old couple. They were throwing Merry off her usual corporate game.

"My grandmother's will," Merry prompted.

"Oh, yes I have it in my office," Henry said, setting aside his breakfast and pushing himself up by the arms of the chair.

His first attempt to stand was unsuccessful and Dottie laid a hand on his shoulder. "I'll get it, darling, you just enjoy your breakfast."

Henry patted his wife's hand and settled back into his chair, resting the plate on his lap. "Don't tell Dottie I said this, but I'm so glad she stopped trying to make biscuits from scratch. There's nothing wrong with Pillsbury, and there's no mess for me to clean up."

Merry offered a noncommittal smile. She had no intention of insulting either Pillsbury biscuits or Henry's wife since he seemed to be fond of both.

Dottie returned with a thick manilla folder, which she passed to Henry.

"Your grandmother owned quite a bit of property in Poleton. The toy store, of course, plus the mansion, her private residence, nearly all of Main Street, over eight hundred homes, and a three-hundred-acre tree farm just north of the town limits. She wanted you to have all of it, provided you planned to move here and keep running things as she had."

"That's not a legally enforceable request," Merry said gently but firmly. She'd done some googling on the plane and even consulted Graham, Deirdre's brother and the best lawyer she knew. "If she left me the land and company then I am free to sell it as I see fit."

"Ah yes, of course. The law doesn't favor overly complicated wills these days. That's why Joy named you the secondary beneficiary."

"Secondary? She didn't leave me anything, then," Merry said, annoyed that she'd flown and driven for a full day just to find out she *might* have inherited something if two people had died instead of one. Her grandmother didn't owe her an inheritance, of course, but it would have been nice to know the particulars before she booked a plane ticket.

"She did, just let me explain." Henry's serious expression was undermined by the biscuit crumbs dotting his cardigan. Still, Merry lent him her full attention. "Since most of her requirements for you to inherit are not legally enforceable, Joy named me the primary beneficiary of her entire estate. She asked me to greet you, explain her wishes, and see if you were willing to honor her requests. If you are, then I will disclaim the inheritance and it will pass to you, the secondary beneficiary. If you are not, then I will oversee her affairs to the best of my ability. But I do hope that you accept."

Merry stared at the older man, trying to make sense of what he'd just said. It was a lot of words that boiled down to: her grandmother hadn't been able to bully her legally, so she'd enlisted Henry to do it.

"What are her requirements? Specifically." There was no need to throw a tantrum before she had all the information. After the data-gathering was done, though, all bets were off.

"She wanted you to live in Poleton for at least six months so that you could get to know the people and the business. At the end of that time, she wanted you to agree to keep the toy store open, not to change it too dramatically, and not to sell it to anyone outside the family. It was her legacy, you see."

"I see," Merry agreed with forced calm. "But I can't do any of that. I have a job that I need to return to. I can't just move here and run a toy store."

"Joy did not stipulate that you must live here permanently, though I believe she hoped that would be your decision. She only wanted you to take the time to truly get to know the people that now rely on you before you decide. I'm sure you can understand that desire given your line of work."

People who would rely on her. She forced herself to ignore the swelling feeling in her chest that wanted her to agree then and there. Yes, being needed was nice, but she had that in California. In fact, she was sure that if she checked her email there would be dozens of messages from people that needed her. CEOs, CFOs, all the chief-something-or-others that needed her input to run their businesses successfully. Claus Family Toys was a small fish in a big pond of neediness.

"I can understand," Merry said after a brief pause to reorient her perspective. "The best companies I work with are those whose owners care about their employees and community. However, as I said, I can't stay here for six months. If that is my grandmother's requirement, then I will have to leave the business in your hands."

Merry stood to leave.

"The total value of the estate is one hundred and sixty-seven million dollars."

Merry sat back down.

Henry continued as if he hadn't just discredited all her progressive ideals with one sentence. "Your grandmother's real estate holdings produce about sixteen million annually. Plus, interest on her bank account balances is about four million. Claus Family Toys has hit a bit of a snag in profitability the past few years, but revenue remains over twenty-five million per year. I'm sure with your consulting experience you could turn that potential into profit."

Creepy dolls. Haunted mansions. She tried to scare herself with the facts. But, like so many horror movie victims, the possibility of financial gain was dangerously close to overruling her survival instinct.

"Why don't you stay a few days? Look over the financial statements, meet some of your employees, enjoy the parade. Then decide," Dottie suggested.

Her resolve couldn't withstand the financial temptation plus the grandmotherly tone. "I can do that. Do you have the financial statements?" She directed the last question to Henry.

The little lawyer nodded. "I'll fetch them for you now."

After three tries, he got to his feet and shuffled into his office.

A knock on the door drew Dottie away and Merry was left alone with her thoughts.

She could do both, couldn't she? What was the family business but one more client to add to her roster? She could manage it from California, keep her current job, and never have to update her budget spreadsheet again.

Oh, and charity. She could definitely give some of the money to charity.

She'd just managed to convince herself she was making the right decision for the right reasons when Henry reappeared with another manilla folder. Rather than being annoyed with or suspicious of paper financial statements, as she usually would have been, Merry found it charming that Henry had printed them.

"Ah, your escort has arrived," he said with a smile at the entryway.

Merry turned, with a mostly false smile plastered on her face, to find the last person she wanted to see.

He looked different in the daylight. For one, the contrast between his dark, red-brown skin, bright white hair, and honey-colored eyes was even more startling. For another, he was far taller than Merry had thought. He had to be at least six foot three.

As if his appearance wasn't unusual enough naturally, he'd taken care to make it even more so. His hair was braided on the sides and pulled into a bubble-braid-mohawk on top that showed a single golden feather dangling from one ear. He wore a worn brown leather jacket over multiple layers of light cotton fabrics in various shades of green and linen pants tucked into brown leather… boots? Moccasins? Something in between.

The stranger from the previous night froze for half a second, his easy smile faltering. Merry was sure hers did the same.

He recovered more quickly. "Hello, duckie."

Merry ignored him and turned back to Henry.

"Fantastic, you've already met Santa, the foreman," Henry said. "He will show you to the toy shop, it's on the north side of town so you'll have to drive. But don't worry, he's an expert at driving in snow."

As the words registered, the absurdity of the situation hit her, and Merry started to laugh. "His name is Santa? This has to be a joke."

"It's a nickname," the annoying stranger informed her.

Merry laughed harder. "You want me to follow Hippie Pirate Santa Claus to his workshop in North Poleton? This can't be real."

"Now you're calling me by your surname? As I keep telling you, there is an order to these things. Dinner, sharing a room at the inn, then marriage." Santa shook his head in mock disbelief. "I'm not saying I'm opposed to marriage, but I'd like to get to know you first."

"Nope. I am not going anywhere with him. You can keep the shop," she told Henry.

"Duckie," Santa chided. "don't hand over your inheritance because we had a tiff."

"I don't know you!" she nearly shouted.

"Santa," Dottie and Henry said at the same time, in the same exasperated tone. Henry relented and let Dottie continue. "What did you do? You promised to be on your best behavior."

"I did nothing untoward," Santa replied. "I found Ms. Claus in somewhat of a predicament so I offered my assistance. She refused but seemed to suggest we share a meal and a bed, which I declined, then she implied that she would like to kill me instead. Even after she nearly ran me over with her truck, I gave her directions to the inn. Like a good neighbor."

Both Dottie and Henry looked horrified.

"That is not what happened," Merry said. "That is not even close to what happened. And you have it all out of order."

"How can it be out of order if it is not what happened?" Santa asked with a quirk of his eyebrow.

Merry bottled up her anger, shoved it deep, deep down, and explained the previous night's events to the older couple.

When she finished, Dottie was once again glaring at Santa. He shrugged. "I like my version better."

With a sigh, Dottie turned to Merry. "Don't mind Santa, he can be mischievous, but he's a good man. Looks after the others at the shop. The whole town, really. Give him, and us, another chance."

How could Merry say no to the sweet older woman who'd invited her into her home and offered her apple butter? Plus, millions of dollars and an extensive real estate portfolio. If she could look past creepy, possibly haunted toys, she could also endure one uncomfortable morning with a delusional man who called himself Santa. "Fine. I'll tour the shop with Santa

Sparrow and look over the financials."

"Thank you, dear," the older woman said with a smile that suggested she'd known Merry's answer all along.

CHAPTER 5

Santa drove a vintage two-tone pickup truck in sage and white. In other circumstances, Merry would have thought it was adorable, but it belonged to an overly flirtatious stranger, so she settled for mentally describing it as 'cute.'

"You want to drive, duckie? I know how you get."

"You don't know anything about me, and yes," Merry replied, taking the offered keys.

She slid into the driver's seat and took a moment to admire the interior restoration. It looked completely custom in shades of green that hadn't been used in the 60s when the truck was manufactured. Her admiration dimmed when the truck's owner hopped into the passenger's seat, already smiling.

Merry slid the key into the ignition and the truck hummed to life. Unfortunately, the radio also woke and began belting "Santa Claus Is Coming to Town" sung by none other than Willie Nelson. She quickly found the knob and turned it down, but not before Santa turned it into a duet.

"You don't like that song? Or is it Willie?" Santa asked as if horrified by the concept.

"Love Willie. Hate Christmas music for obvious reasons."

"What reasons?"

Merry was momentarily frozen, watching the sunlight spark in his gold eyes. They were unnaturally bright, but she didn't see a ring around his irises suggesting contacts. She shook her head to clear the distraction and pulled away from Henry's street.

"My name is Merry Claus. As soon as people learn that they seem to think I'm obsessed with Christmas. No matter how many times I explain that my grandmother saddled me with the name, the assumptions—and worse, the jokes—just keep coming. So, I avoid all things related to the holiday."

Santa watched her for a moment, then opened the glove box and pulled out a handful of cassette tapes. "Makes sense. I have non-Christmas music. John Prine? Everyone likes John Prine."

She quickly glanced at his cassettes, trying not to get caught up on the fact that he'd taken her Grinchy opinions in stride or the even more unsettling fact that he had a cassette collection, and was disappointed to see her favorite John Prine album missing. "You don't have *Sweet Revenge*?"

"I did, it's a funny story actually—"

"Never mind, this is fine."

After a few minutes of uncomfortable silence, broken only by Willie Nelson's gravelly voice and a few simple directions, Santa asked, "Did you call Wayne about your truck?"

It was an innocuous question, almost normal conversation, so Merry rewarded him with a civil answer. "Yes, he said he'd tow it this morning and leave a message at the inn when it is ready for me to pick up. Thank you for giving me his name."

"You're welcome. While he has it, you might want to consider paint. And upholstery. The headliner was falling out. Plus, that hole in the seat probably has peanuts in it now." Santa pointed for her to take a right at the post office. "Actually, don't trust Wayne with cosmetic fixes, I'll do it for you."

"That won't be necessary," Merry said, unsure how he would turn this conversation into annoying banter, but sure he would find a way.

His list of problems with the truck concluded, Santa started to sing the chorus of "Frosty the Snowman." Despite her deep-seated hatred of Christmas music, she had trouble not humming as well. It was always that way with music, she couldn't stop herself from singing and dancing—much to her friends' enjoyment on rare nights out.

"Was the cap on the gear shift upside down or are the gears installed the wrong way? I can fix it; I just need to know what I'm working with." Oh, he wasn't done after all. At least that gave her an excuse to turn the music down further.

"How did you see all of that in the dark? And after you almost died?" Merry asked.

"You didn't hit me, remember? My eyesight was not impacted by the not-crash."

"Yes, but weren't you scared? And it was dark."

"More surprised than scared," Santa replied. "It's not every day that a Maui Blue '89 Chevy 1500 comes barreling down Elm Street."

"Now you're just showing off."

Santa smiled. "I am. I have excellent eyesight, and I know a lot about trucks."

"It was more effective when you let me infer those things," Merry told him.

"I'll keep that in mind. Now, how do I get you to infer that you need a paint job and a complete interior overhaul?"

"You don't," Merry said with a snort. "That truck belongs to my dad, and he only uses it to drive to Lowe's every few weeks. It doesn't need to be pretty."

Santa deflated. "Take a left here, then drive straight," he said morosely. He even refrained from singing along to "Silent Night."

A moment later, he perked up, his smile returning as more of a smirk. "When you take over the shop you can buy me a new truck. It doesn't have to be nice. Actually, it's better if it's not. I can fix it up and use it for deliveries and errands and other important things."

Merry glanced over at him, certain she'd misheard. Surely, this stranger, who'd only managed five minutes of semi-professional conversation with her, wasn't suggesting she buy him a vehicle. But he certainly was. "Are you...are you batting your eyelashes at me?"

"Is it working?" Santa asked.

Merry snorted and shook her head. "No, you crazy person, it is not working."

***

When they arrived at the toy shop twenty minutes later, Santa was still alternating between singing along to the radio and listing his top ten choices for the truck Merry was definitely not going to buy him. She'd given up telling him that and just let him ramble.

She'd expected a shop. A small, cute little store with a workshop full of sawdust in the back. Instead, she found a complex of old-style stone buildings next to a gargantuan house and surrounded by the charming equivalent of a strip-mall including a coffee shop, diner, clothier, and grocer. Claus Family Toys was a town all its own just a few miles outside of Poleton. And just like Poleton, it was drowning in Christmas decorations.

Santa led the way into the main office where a cute male receptionist wearing elf ears and a holiday sweater greeted her with a cheerful smile. Every horizontal surface dripped a thick layer of tinsel topped with garland, wooden snowflakes, bells, reindeer, and various other Christmas baubles. In short, Merry learned that hell smelled like wood polish.

A tall, slender woman with long black hair that faded to green at the ends stepped through the door leading to the main office and smiled at Merry, then rolled poison green eyes. They had to be contacts. No one had eyes that color. And the rest of her features put her ancestry somewhere in East Asia, so bright green eyes were even more unlikely.

"Do not buy him another truck, he has plenty," the woman said.

"Plenty?" Merry said, raising her eyebrows at her companion.

"Plenty is never enough, duckie," he replied with a wink.

"What does that even mean?" With a shake of her head, she turned to the new employee. "I'm Merry Claus, Joy's granddaughter."

"It's nice to meet you, Merry. I'm Faye, I manage the design department."

Oh good, the designer of the creepy, haunted dolls. Merry smiled anyway. "I'd love to see your department. Can we start the tour there?"

"Sure, I just need to discuss something with Santa first. Why don't you wait here and Jeraltan will get you a hot chocolate? Or a coffee if you'd prefer."

"Coffee would be great," Merry said with her blandest smile.

Faye seemed to get the message that Merry's smile wasn't the pleased kind, though she wasn't going to start pushing yet. The newcomer pulled Santa through the door to the main office space with an apologetic smile in Merry's direction.

The receptionist, Jeraltan, hurried out the front door and Merry watched him walk a few paces in the direction of the coffee shop.

She wasn't proud of what she did next. Alone in the reception area, Merry pressed her ear to the office door.

"You asked her to buy you a truck? Why? Why would you do that?" Faye hissed.

"She was going to give Henry the shop," Santa replied.

"How does that answer my question? And also, why?"

"She hates me," Santa said. "That's the answer to both questions. She hates me, so she was going to give Henry the shop. She hates me, so I got nervous and started talking about her truck, then that seemed to make her hate me less, so I kept talking about trucks."

"Every time you answer a question, another arises. Why does she hate you?"

"Remember the girl that lost control of her truck last night?"

"Oh," Faye said. "Oh. You were right, she is pretty. And I thought you offered to help her? You said you had a nice conversation and gave her directions."

"We did. I did. I'm not sure when things changed, but she definitely hates me today."

Merry backed away from the door, not sure whether to laugh or burst into the office and strangle the foreman of Claus Family Toys. She decided to do neither and wait patiently for her third cup of coffee of the day.

A few minutes later, she had coffee and a growing entourage as she was led through the design studio. Jeraltan had abandoned the front desk to join the tour. Pari and Rari, two women nearly as tall as Santa, had appeared from what Merry assumed was the workshop to follow her.

The design studio looked like an architecture firm from the 70s, or at least, what Merry assumed that would have looked like. There were no computers, just large flip pads that artists filled with detailed renderings, complete with measurements and notations.

"Santa, is this possible?" one of the designers asked, holding up a pad with the outline of an animatronic bear complete with callouts detailing the various gears that would be needed.

"No electronics," Santa replied immediately.

"It's all wood, I promise," the designer argued.

Santa stepped forward and took the drawing.

"Why don't you make toys with electronics?" Merry asked Faye.

"We don't have the equipment or the expertise," Faye replied. "All our toys are made completely of wood. Many of them are carved from a single block."

"So, no creepy dolls?" Merry asked hopefully.

"We make some dolls, but none of them are creepy."

Merry was not sure she believed that. No one thought their own creations were creepy, just like parents never thought their children were ugly. Statistically, some of them had to be wrong.

After the design studio, Faye showed her to the neighboring office building. Merry laughed out loud when she saw the massive sign above the door to a corner office. Each letter was the size of her hand and covered in a different color of glitter. Together, they spelled *Santa's Workshop*.

"He really leaned into the nickname," Faye said with a shrug.

The tour of the offices was quick. It was an office building, much like all the others she'd toured in her life, the only difference was a complete lack of computers.

They picked up a few more people in the offices and they trailed Merry as the group headed to the manufacturing building. All the employees were overly eager to meet her, shake her hand, and tell her about their job. It was a welcome change of pace. Most workers considered 'consultant' synonymous with 'layoffs' and either tried to suck up or avoid her notice altogether. These people just wanted to say hello.

The manufacturing building was even larger than it had appeared from the outside. As Merry entered, her eye was drawn first up to the second and third stories which overlooked the ground floor from balconies. It reminded her of the running track at her gym except bigger and noisier and not the same at all. From what she could see, each of those floors was as large as the ground floor, which was about twice the size of a football field.

Unsurprisingly, the manufacturing building was Merry's worst Christmas-themed nightmare. Not quite as bad as her nightmare of the bears with piranha teeth, but still bad enough to make her queasy. On the bright side, no one was making jokes about her name or saying that she should love the Christmas decorations because of it. She guessed that with a man named Santa in their midst, Merry Claus wasn't all that interesting.

As if summoned by her thoughts, Santa pushed his way through the crowd with a roll of paper under his arm. On second thought, he didn't push so much as he walked, and the crowd parted for him. Another day, Merry would have said it was further evidence that he was a jerk used to getting what he wanted. But the employees scurried out of his way with smiles and greetings, not fear or eye rolls. Maybe there was more to Santa than she'd initially thought.

Upon reaching her side, Santa took over the tour from Faye.

"This is where we make the toys. The first floor is carvers. We carve the toys, obviously. Then, we send them to Level Two for paint. After that, they go to Level Three for a final check and packaging. Level Three is the boring one. I assign people there when they annoy me." Pari and Rari huffed beside her but said nothing.

Merry assumed the last comment was a joke and laughed politely. That only made Santa grin. He was different here. Happier. It was a refreshing change to see him focus on work rather than devoting all his attention to making her uncomfortable.

She didn't have to ask questions as they toured the bottom floor. Many of the carvers were ecstatic to show her what they were working on and tell her everything from what type of wood was used to the intended age of the end user.

They were a strange group of people. Some sat at tables, as she'd expected, but there were young people scattered throughout the room sitting cross legged on rugs and carpets, bean bag chairs, and overstuffed armchairs.

Those youthful faces were the ones that captured her attention. Like Santa, they were of unidentifiable races with combinations of features and colorings she'd never seen before.

The toys they were making were as eclectic and interesting as the people. Complicated puzzle boxes that promised to take a year to solve, wooden hobby horses with carved manes that looked so lifelike Merry had to touch them to be sure they weren't real hair, chess sets with such excruciating detail Merry had to stare for a full minute to take them all in.

"These are wonderful," Merry said as she picked up a wooden Model T car with perfect detail down to the liftable door handle. She crossed to another table, this one empty of a carver, and reached out to touch one of a dozen fresh red roses. "A gift from a happy customer?"

Her eyes went wide as saucers as her fingertips brushed the petal. Instead of the softness of a flower, she felt fine grained wood. "This is wood?" she nearly shouted at Santa.

He laughed. "It was an idea I was working on, roses that never die. I thought we could sell them on Valentine's Day."

"You made these?" Merry asked, picking up one of the roses and admiring the painstaking detail of the leaves, stem, and thorns. They looked so lifelike that Merry's mind had trouble reconciling that they were made of wood.

"I carved them; Nerissa painted them. They're going in the reject room, though. Joy didn't approve."

"Why the hell not?" Merry said before she could think better of it. One of the leaves was so thin she could see the light through it. Not just the light, but each vein that it illuminated. It was worthy of being in a museum. And Santa had made it. The most annoying person she'd ever met was an incredible artist.

She pulled her eyes away from the rose to see Santa shrug. "She just said they weren't toys, so they didn't count. You can keep it if you like."

"No, I couldn't accept this, it's too lovely." Merry smiled wistfully as she put the rose back in the vase with the others. "Let's go see the second floor."

The painters were just as talented—and enthusiastic—as the carvers.

On the third floor, the quality control professionals were hard at work solving complicated wooden puzzles. Merry supposed the other toys were easy to audit, just requiring a glance and possibly a roll across the floor.

The packaging department was more interesting, at least to her consultant's eye. The toys were wrapped in paper and placed in red cardboard boxes that said *Claus Family Toys* in an old-fashioned script font, then hand-labeled with the type of toy and any applicable warnings. The process was painstakingly slow and left plenty of room for improvement.

By the time she finished touring the manufacturing center, Merry had seen enough of the toy shop for one day. Shutting it down wasn't an option. She still planned to sell it, or leave it in Henry's hands, but she couldn't do either of those things without studying the financial statements. Now that she'd met Faye and the others, she planned to at least offer her expertise on how to make the shop more successful for them and the next owner.

Santa drove her back to the inn where Merry planned to spend the rest of the day with a to-go sandwich from the diner and the manilla folder of financial statements from Henry.

CHAPTER 6

Sandwich in hand, Merry sat on the lumpy bed in the inn and called her best friend—on Wi-Fi, of course, since this godforsaken town didn't have cell service.

Deirdre picked up on the third ring. "Hey, babe. How's small town life?"

"Interesting," Merry replied. She hadn't planned what she was going to say—that was the point of having a best friend, after all. Best friends were responsible for picking through your addled thoughts and finding some sort of thread. Even knowing that, Merry struggled to find the words to describe her first day in Poleton.

"Give me more than that. How many heart-of-gold flannel-wearing hunks have tried to steal you from me?"

With a self-pitying groan, Merry pressed the speakerphone button and collapsed against the pillows. "Well, there's an idiot named Santa who told me I can't drive, then told me I wanted to take him to dinner, sleep with him, buy him a new truck, and marry him. So, none. No romantic prospects here."

Merry smiled at the ceiling, content knowing that she'd made Santa sound just as bad as he'd made her sound to Dottie and Henry, and he wasn't even there to defend himself.

"He must be either ridiculously confident or delusional. Is he handsome at least? Wait, his name is really Santa?" Deirdre said.

35

"It's a nickname. He's the foreman at the toy shop. I guess that makes him Santa." Merry added a few magical finger waves she was sure Dee would have appreciated if she could see them.

"Well, good. That's more cute than delusional. You didn't answer my other question, though. Is he handsome? What's his Instagram handle?" Deirdre was already typing.

"Do not stalk Santa or any of his elves. And yes, he's ridiculously handsome. Actually, let me rephrase, he's mostly ridiculous but also a little handsome."

"Obviously I can't find him based on 'Santa,' what's his real name?"

"No idea," Merry replied. "But he's not important. I need to talk to you about the business and the incredibly weird inheritance."

"Fine, but we're circling back to handsome men. You have twenty-seven minutes until my lasagna is done, so plan accordingly."

Merry laughed and launched into her tale, explaining her grandmother's wishes first then moving on to the business. "They don't make toys like you'd buy at Toys R Us."

"You're showing your age, babe. They went out of business years ago."

"Fine, Walmart. Target. Wherever people buy toys now. Anyway, these are wooden toys."

"Oh, Rosie loves her wooden kitchen set. It was three times as expensive as the plastic one, but totally worth it. I hate the thought of her touching nothing but plastic until she's a teenager."

"Send me a link to the one she has; I'll ask Santa if he sells any complementary products. Anyway, these toys are gorgeous. Intricate. More complex than anything I've ever seen. They're more like sculptures than toys," Merry said.

"That's super niche. And sounds expensive. What do the margins look like?" Even after years in HR, Deirdre still knew the first question to ask.

"Tight. Overall, the business had small losses the last seven years and broke even the three years before that. I only have summary income statements and balance sheets, so I can't really tell a lot about the potential from them. Here's the weird part though, my grandmother apparently didn't believe in technology. Like, at all. I didn't see a single computer on my tour of the office."

"That's sketchy."

"I agree. And the other weird part is this list of distributors. There are thirty-seven. The first thirty-six pay about the same per item—$80—but the last one bought half of all the toys made last year and paid half of the price. I looked up the company, Quinn Worldwide, but they seem to only sell Claus Family Toys on Amazon. That's it. No other products. No other sales avenues."

"That doesn't sound right. Is this all a front? Was your grandmother laundering money?" Deirdre asked.

"Weirdly, that was my first thought," Merry agreed. "No computers, no website, no online sales, printed financial statements. It's all fishy."

"Well, get to the bottom of it, babe. You don't want your name attached to anything illegal. That would be the death of your career."

Merry was relieved to have her friend's permission to dig. Even if she never took control of the shop, she needed to make sure everything was above board for the sake of her reputation.

A timer sounded in the background and Merry smiled, realizing that she'd talked long enough to distract Deirdre from asking more questions about Santa.

CHAPTER 7

The next morning, Merry woke ready to find out what was going on with her grandmother's company and turn it around. A second day without her morning exercise routine left her a little too sluggish to tackle such a large endeavor, but two cups of coffee helped restore her energy.

Wayne had called saying he had to order a part for her father's truck, so she would be without a vehicle for the day. She had blisters from so much walking in her heeled boots the day before, so she opted for riding boots she'd bought a half size too large to accommodate fuzzy socks. Dark jeans, an oxford shirt, and a cable knit sweater completed the casual look. She swept her long, dark hair into its usual clip at the back of her head and set off.

Surprisingly, or maybe not all that surprisingly, Santa was waiting for her in the inn's reception area wearing a knit Santa hat. It looked discordantly modern next to his worn leather jacket, green linen pants, and tall moccasins.

"Good morning, duckie," he said, holding out a to-go cup of coffee from the restaurant near the shop.

Considering the last time she'd told him she didn't like a nickname he'd chosen a worse one, she let 'duckie' slide. "Good morning, did we have an appointment?"

"No, but it's parade day and I wasn't sure you packed appropriate attire."

"I'm not going to a parade, I need to meet with the shop's accountant," Merry told him.

"Howard will be at the parade; you can talk to him there. Now, put this on." Santa held out a navy sweater with 'Treat Yo Elf' written in Grinch green down one side. Opposite the text, there was an elf that looked remarkably like Santa and a red pickup truck.

"I'm not wearing that."

Santa deflated a bit but kept his smile in place. "How about this one?" The next sweater had a white kitten in a Santa hat pushing a red ball of yarn and it said 'Meowy Christmas.'

"Somehow, that's worse than the last one."

"I told Faye that one was no good. How about this?" The third sweater he held up featured a string of old-fashioned Christmas bulbs that spelled 'Lit.'

"Nope. I'm not wearing a Christmas sweater. I am also not going to a Christmas parade. I'm here to learn about the toy shop, not learn the meaning of the season from Santa."

"You can do both," Santa told her. "All the employees will be at the parade. The whole town actually. Plus, you haven't voted for your favorite decoration. I snuck a peek at the results so far, and the race is close."

Merry wanted to tell him that he'd just described the number one item at the top of her *I Don't Ever Want to Do That* list, but he looked so stupidly charming in his Santa hat that she just sighed.

How long could a parade really take? She could drink her coffee, picture the ocean, muster a half smile, and be back to figuring out if she'd inherited a criminal enterprise by lunch.

"I'll go to the parade, but I'm not wearing a sweater. See, I can compromise."

"Everyone is wearing a sweater. It's a competition."

"I thought the competition was for decorations?" Merry said.

"There are two competitions. Well, two so far. I'm sure we'll think of more. What do you think of my sweater?" He unzipped his leather jacket to reveal a sage green sweater with 'Baby' written across the front and decorated with tasteful holly leaves and red berries.

"Baby?" Merry said, unsure how that related to Christmas. Santa looked at her expectantly and it clicked. She snorted and shook her head, "Santa, baby. I get it. Very clever."

"I thought so," Santa said primly. He stood a little straighter, practically preening.

Merry laughed and told him to hold still. He looked so silly she knew this was exactly what she needed to explain all that was Santa to Deirdre. She snapped a quick picture and sent it to her friend while she still had access to the inn's Wi-Fi.

Santa talked her into wearing an ice blue sweater with a single large snowflake. She considered it a compromise even though she knew he'd won. By the time she made it back to her room to change, Deirdre had responded to her text.

Holy crap, is that him? He's a giant hunk WITH a sense of humor. Kidnap him and bring him home! You can teach him manners from here.

Merry rolled her eyes and tucked her phone into her back pocket. It wouldn't be any use at the parade, but it was a force of habit to have her lifeline within reach.

***

Santa was right, the whole town had turned up for the parade.

It was a far cry from the spectacles that shut down city blocks and featured massive inflatable decorations. This one didn't even have real floats, just local groups who either walked or rode in the beds of pickup trucks.

It wasn't as awful as the big city parades either. Merry saw a few people she'd casually met, and it was almost nice to see them tossing candy and waving to their neighbors. Plus, there were only six thousand people in Poleton, so they couldn't drag the parade out for more than a half hour.

Jeraltan walked at the front of the Claus Family Toys procession wearing a bright red sweater that said 'HUNG' with several small stockings beneath it. Merry snorted when she saw it. She really needed to stop doing that, it was undignified, but how else was she supposed to convey the absurdity of the situation?

"Does Jeraltan's sweater say what I think it does?"

Santa followed her line of sight and, with a false look of confusion, said, "the stockings are hung by the chimney with care?"

Merry laughed outright as the man drew close enough for her to see the fine print of his sweater.

"Ms. Claus, are dirty jokes the way to your heart?" Santa asked with a mocking grin.

"Of course not, he just looks so proud of himself," she replied. Jeraltan strutted at the front of the procession, waving at various members of the crowd and throwing small items Merry could just make out as wooden Christmas ornaments.

"Ah, well, if pride is what you like then I can see why I'm your future husband," Santa said.

"Anytime you want to stop making that terrible joke, be my guest."

"Who says I'm joking, duckie? We'd be perfect. And I could finally be Santa Claus."

"Let me be very clear. I am not marrying you. I am not in love with you. We are not together in any way. You are an annoying stranger who I may or may not employ at some point in the future. Even if I wanted to date you, which I don't, it would be entirely inappropriate," Merry told him.

It was a challenge to summon her usual professional distance. Maybe it was just the flood of happiness all around her.

While she might hate Christmas, the children of Poleton did not share her feelings. They scrambled through the crowd, plucking up dropped candy and small gifts, shrieking with delight. It was infectious. Much like their runny noses. She tucked her hands into her pockets as another cute little germ factory passed.

Santa was ignoring her, as he usually did when she said something reasonable. He pointed to another pickup truck cresting the hill. "That's my favorite." The bed of the truck was full of children and the sign hanging from the window said 'Poleton Primary School Music Department.' Just when Merry was starting to soften, thinking he meant the float, he added "1949 Dodge Power Wagon."

Her momentary approval turned to giggles. Of course, he meant the forest green truck with a white stripe around each hubcap. And that sparkle in his eye? Also meant for the truck.

"Is it yours?" she asked, remembering Faye's comment that Santa had plenty of trucks.

"Ours, or rather, yours," he replied, his eyes never leaving his prize. "All of the trucks belong to Claus Family Toys; I just restore them and keep them running."

Merry had to look away from the sudden pain in his eyes. It was easy to pick out Santa's trucks interspersed with walking people and pickups of various other colors. His—or hers, she supposed—were all painted a shade of green and looked at least a decade older than the others. Each was a work of art in its own right.

She leaned closer and whispered conspiratorially, "Our trucks look nicer than everyone else's."

A day ago, she would have done anything to erase that cocky smile from his face, but now she was glad her comment had brought it back. "They do, don't they?"

There were only a few more trucks in the parade—none of them were Santa's. Merry took the final vehicle's departure as permission to leave, but Santa disagreed. Apparently, he had several more items on his morning agenda. First, hot chocolate. Second, Merry needed to cast her vote for the decoration contest. Third, getting reacquainted with the Claus Family Toy workers. The list went on and on.

Faye caught up with them as they accepted their hot chocolate from an elderly woman in a hand knit sweater. The older lady shot a disapproving look at Faye's demure nose ring and less demure studded choker but gave her a Styrofoam cup of hot chocolate anyway. Santa pulled a silver flask from his pocket and poured a generous amount into his beverage before offering it to Merry, who declined, and then Faye, who accepted.

"Everything makes sense now," Merry commented.

"What makes sense?" Faye asked.

Merry nodded in Santa's direction. "His entire personality. He's a drunk."

Both Faye and Santa looked aghast. "I'm just preparing for the after party. Everyone brought a flask."

"You're pregaming a town event?"

"No, I'm postgaming a town event. I'm pregaming tonight's party," Santa argued.

"Whatever you say, Santa baby."

Faye laughed; Santa just rolled his eyes. "Don't use my favorite song against me. I was hoping you'd serenade me with it at the party tonight." He pointed with his whiskey-laced hot chocolate to a squat, balding man drinking directly from a flask. "Your accountant is having a drink; now will you believe me that everyone drinks on parade day?"

"That's Howard?" Merry asked, snapping into business mode.

Santa confirmed that the man still guzzling the contents of his flask was indeed responsible for the finances of Claus Family Toys. Merry hurried over before the alcohol hit him. Santa and Faye followed close behind.

"Hi Howard, I'm Merry," she said in her best Boss Bitch voice. It was an octave lower than her normal speaking voice and as serene as a yoga instructor.

"Oh, hello! Did you enjoy the parade?" Howard did not make the same effort to control his voice. It was high and shrill—exactly the kind of intonation that would have undermined her authority.

"It was charming," Merry lied. "I was hoping to speak with you about getting access to more detailed accounting information for Claus Family Toys. As you know, income statements provide such limited data."

"They provide all you need if you know how to read them. You saw the line that said, 'net income', right? That's how much you get to keep."

"I understand how to read an income statement, but thank you for your concern," Merry said as neutrally as she could manage. "I don't need access to the accounting software, a spreadsheet would be fine. If you can just export the raw data for the last fiscal year, I can clean up the transactions."

"I'm sure you're a bright girl, but there's really no need to try to understand all those numbers, sweetheart, that's what your grandmother paid me for."

"Merry is a consultant. I'm sure she knows what to do with numbers," Faye interjected.

Howard pointed a wobbly finger at her. "*You* stay out of this."

Before Merry could regain control of the situation, Santa grabbed the accountant's outstretched finger and bent it back, pushing in close to his face. He had to lean down considerably to look the man in the eye. "I've heard enough of your condescension, Howard. Give Merry what she wants. It's her company."

"Actually, it's not," Howard said. Either he was a stupid man, or a drunk one because Merry could see the dangerous glint in Santa's eye, and she was much farther away.

She hadn't noticed the cold until then, but the temperature seemed to plummet. Strange. Anger usually heated her blood.

"Let him go, Santa, you're causing a scene," Faye said. It was true, all around them people were starting to whisper.

Santa released the accountant with a small but firm shove. He came to stand at Merry's side, looking very much like he wanted to cause an even greater scene.

Howard righted himself and sneered in Santa's direction. "She doesn't hold your leash yet. Her grandmother left the company to Henry. It's his choice whether it passes to Merry."

Beside her, Santa paled and drew back, his hands going slack at his sides.

Seething, Merry looped her arm through Santa's, reached for Faye with her other hand, and dragged both of them away from the awful man. Nothing like misogyny to turn acquaintances into friends. "Don't worry about him. I'll take care of it," she said just loud enough for the two of them to hear.

Santa was stiff next to her, his arm surprisingly chilly even through her sweater.

"Santa, you need to calm down," Faye said so quietly Merry could barely hear her over the wind.

One look at Santa and Merry knew Faye was right. He looked downright murderous.

Pushing her own indignation to the side, Merry forced lightness into her tone. "Now do you see why I thought it was so annoying when you started calling me pet names a moment after we met?"

"I'm sorry," Santa said. His voice was rough, like he was struggling for control. "I never intended to be like him."

"It's not alright but it's alright, if you know what I mean," Merry said with what she hoped was a reassuring smile.

Santa took over steering their little party—showing no signs of releasing her arm or allowing her to escape this conversation. "What did he mean about Henry owning the company?"

Merry sighed. "I never knew my grandmother, so apparently, she wanted me to prove myself before I took over her company. She left Claus Family Toys to Henry and if I follow her instructions, he will disclaim the inheritance, and it will pass to me."

Santa pulled Merry by their joined arms behind the hot chocolate stand. In the crowded square, it was the most privacy they could get. Faye, still gripping Merry's other hand, came with them.

"What are the instructions? What do we need to do?" Merry was surprised by the intensity in Santa's eyes.

"I—," Merry hesitated. How much should she tell them? Were Santa and Faye involved in whatever underhanded dealings her grandmother had been a part of? Is that why they were so intense?

She decided that the best way to judge that was to tell the truth and gauge their reactions. "My grandmother wanted me to live here for six months. To get to know all of you. Then she wanted me to promise not to change too much of the business."

"Six months?" Faye repeated, looking nearly as alarmed as Merry had felt when she heard the news. "You won't own the company for six more months?" She turned to Santa. "What does that mean? For us."

"I don't know," Santa said quietly. "Nothing good. We need to talk

45

to Henry, get him to give Merry the company now."

Faye nodded. Santa tilted his head. They seemed to be having a private, nonverbal conversation. One that Merry really should have been a part of considering it was her life they were discussing.

"I can't move here," Merry interrupted a little too loudly. "I can't just uproot everything I've worked for to run a toy shop in the middle of nowhere that loses money."

The moment she said it, Merry knew it was too harsh. Santa flinched and drew back a fraction. When he looked at her again, his golden eyes were pleading. "We'll do better. We can make more toys. Better toys."

Merry's frustration vanished. How could a grown man in his thirties manage to look exactly like a kicked puppy?

"That's not the problem," she said more gently. "You're all wonderfully talented and you seem like nice people. For the most part," she added, narrowing her eyes at Santa, recalling all the times he'd looked like a cocky asshole instead of an adorable puppy. "But I have a job, a home, a *life* in California."

"You can make a new life here," Faye suggested. Oh no, there were two of them. Two sad puppies that inexplicably needed Merry as a permanent playmate to cheer them up.

"I'll think about it." What else was she supposed to say?

Santa smiled and Merry's heart squeezed. "While you're thinking, come cast your vote for the decorations."

He had to be the most confusing person Merry had ever met. First, he was so angry she thought he'd hit the company accountant, then he was planning the rest of her life while pouting when he didn't get his way immediately, and then all of a sudden, he was back to being the Christmas spirit incarnate.

Hopefully, he wasn't also a criminal.

CHAPTER 8

Merry had never been to a Christmas party and she'd never wanted to attend one. But she needed answers about her grandmother's company and what better place to find them than a party where all the employees were drunk and loose lipped?

The party was held in what Merry assumed was once the ballroom of the mansion. At some point, it had been converted to a basketball court.

The combination of the crystal chandelier, candy cane painted poles, and basketball lines painted over the parquet floor was interesting to say the least. Merry simultaneously felt like she was entering a high school prom, a nineteenth century ball, and hell. Though, the last part had more to do with the Christmas carols than the decor.

Faye had picked her up from the inn and talked cheerfully through the twenty-minute drive. Merry had worried her red cocktail dress would be too fancy but Faye's sequined mini skirt and corset top matched well enough.

When they entered the party, Merry realized she couldn't have looked out of place if she'd tried. The attire was all over the place. Jeraltan was still wearing his 'HUNG' sweater, but he'd traded skinny jeans for black leather pants. He'd kept the combat boots, though. The twins, Pari and Rari, seemed to be wearing nothing but strategically placed tinsel. On the other end of the spectrum, one man she didn't know was wearing a full tuxedo and several more wore suits.

The entire scene was chaotic. Young people ground against each other, completely at odds with the subject matter of the Christmas carols, but perfectly on beat. Others used the candy cane poles for exotic dancing, which Merry tried to ignore. Just like she ignored a stranger's whispered instructions to "hide the mushrooms, the boss is here."

A couple danced like seasoned ballroom professionals right next to a group she recognized as carvers doing Jello shots. By the smell, someone was smoking in the middle of the dance floor.

There were only about a hundred people in the room, but they'd managed to create complete debauchery.

"If you're very nice to me, I'll talk Santa into wearing his Sexy Santa costume," Faye whispered to her as they entered the melee.

"Isn't that just his normal clothes?" Merry asked, still trying to take in the scene.

Faye's smile turned feral as she rounded on Merry with far too much excitement. "You think he's sexy all the time, then?"

"No," Merry sputtered. "I just meant that all his clothes are Santa clothes. Because his name is Santa. It was a stupid joke." Still not convinced Faye believed her, Merry pressed on, "I don't think he's sexy. His clothes I mean. His clothes aren't sexy. Not inherently sexy, anyway. I'm sure he could own sexy clothes, but they wouldn't be sexy just because they're his." She'd definitely made it worse. Merry clamped her mouth shut and vowed never to use the word 'sexy' again as Faye started to laugh.

"It's okay. We've all had a thing for Santa at one point or another."

"I do not—"

"Let's drink!" Faye shouted, dragging Merry toward the bar.

'Bar' was a strong word. There was a collection of old timey bar carts against the wall with dozens of liquors, wines, and one bottle that was possibly absinthe. Merry accepted a glass of champagne from an employee she didn't know, wishing she could drown her embarrassment in vodka but knowing she should keep a clear head.

The opening notes of "Santa Baby" began to play from a tinny boombox and Merry turned her attention to the front of the room which was acting as a makeshift stage. The tinsel-clad twins were swaying their hips seductively as they began the song. As one, they bent toward the crowd, revealing Santa sitting in what could only be described as a throne.

"Oh, he's already wearing it!" Faye said.

Merry froze, staring at the man sprawled haphazardly across the carved chair wearing very, very little in the way of a costume. He looked like the world's cheapest stripper. At the same time, Merry would have emptied her bank account to get him to remove the coat hanging rakishly off one shoulder.

She watched, unable to move, as the twins ran their hands along his muscled shoulders, asking him to buy them all sorts of things if they promised to be good. He laughed as if this sort of thing happened to him all the time. And it probably did when he looked like that. He was all long, lean lines and delicately cut muscle.

Merry's mouth watered, and she filled it with champagne, letting the bubbles distract her from the sudden bout of lust.

She didn't like him. He was rude and condescending. And overly excitable. And he talked too much. And he was *way* too into being called Santa. But he was also gorgeous. And getting up. And abandoning the tinsel twins in the middle of their serenade to approach her.

"You look stunning, duckie," Santa said, his honey eyes raking over her body, starting at her toes and lingering on her lips.

"You look… entirely inappropriate for a company party," she said, somewhat breathlessly. Up close, his tight red shorts and loose, flowing coat were even more obscene.

He winked. "I'm just getting started. Wait until you see the performance I have planned. It involves one of those pretty candy cane poles, a bottle of tequila, and—oh, wait, where's my hat?"

He turned accusing eyes on Faye, who shrugged. Without warning, he tore through the crowd, accusing anyone within reach of stealing his lucky Santa hat. At least his insanity cured her momentary lapse in judgment.

Merry could only laugh and shake her head. "It seems he hasn't lost the tequila."

"Nope," Faye confirmed. "He never loses that."

Jeraltan popped up from seemingly nowhere. "You don't like the Sexy Santa outfit? I made it."

"Made it?" Merry asked. It was an impressive feat.

"Yep." Jeraltan nodded emphatically. "100% wool with real mink and genuine leather. All ethically sourced."

"How do you ethically source mink?"

"You buy it from an estate sale. No additional minks were harmed in the making of that coat. And the leather is from the same place. I cut it from the bottom of these pants when I hemmed them. Hank had great taste. Too bad he died."

Merry talked with Jeraltan for a few minutes about his clothes. Not only did he sew, but he knit his own sweaters as well—which solved the mystery of where he'd found that day's attire.

The topic exhausted, she turned back to conversation with Faye.

"Since you're the only sober person I see, I'll ask you. What's the deal with Quinn Worldwide?"

Faye laughed and took a sip of her drink—which was at least ninety percent vodka. "Such a silly name. It's just Quinn. He lives in Red Bay."

"Oh?" Merry asked, utterly baffled. Quinn Worldwide—or Quinn, she supposed—had spent several million dollars on toys last year. That sounded more like a conglomerate than a man. Unless that man was involved with the mafia or mob or... some other crime organization that didn't sound like it had come from a 1940s movie.

"He buys everything we don't sell by the end of each year and resells it on the internet. He saved Claus Family Toys when our local distributors started cutting their orders a few years ago."

"Uh huh," Merry said. From what little she'd seen of their financial information, Quinn Worldwide was the sole reason Claus Family Toys wasn't profitable. But there was no reason to voice her suspicions.

"Henry argued with Joy every year about how much we sold to Quinn. I'm not sure if he wanted us to sell Quinn less or more, but Joy always told him it was none of his business."

"I see," Merry said. "And you said Quinn's office is in Red Bay?

That's the next town over."

Faye nodded. "Yeah, I've never been there, obviously, but I can get you the address if you need it."

"That would be great, thank you," Merry said. She wondered if Faye could also get her a gun. Though, her few trips to the gun range with her father wouldn't help all that much if she was going to confront a mafia/mob/other-crime-organization boss.

CHAPTER 9

The next morning, Merry woke to a pounding head and a pounding on her door. She stumbled to the door and groaned when she saw Santa on the other side, bright-eyed and bearing coffee. His long white hair was pulled into a casual bun, and he wore a cutoff sweatshirt that hinted at the vee of muscle above his hip bones.

"No," she said without hearing what tortuous activity he had planned for her Sunday.

"I am here to escort you to the gym, my darling truckless princess."

Too cheerful. Too loud.

"What time is it?" she asked, her voice still thick with sleep. The room was dark so it couldn't be nearly late enough to deal with Santa.

"Four thirty. You told me last night that you missed the gym, and you usually go at four thirty, so here I am. Right on time."

She should go to the gym. Plus, he'd driven all the way to the inn before dawn. But her head felt like it would explode at any moment and her stomach was not much better.

"Come in," she said with a sigh, taking the life-giving coffee from his outstretched hand.

Santa sauntered into her room, already chatting about gym equipment and possible partner workouts. Merry didn't hear much of what he said considering she was busy trying not to vomit into her suitcase.

A hazy memory from the night before surfaced. Jeraltan with his wide brown eyes and shaggy blond hair looking like a pathetic little bear cub as he pleaded with her to 'just try a sip' of the drink he'd made for her. He promised it tasted like chocolate, peppermint, and Christmas, and called the concoction 'his greatest achievement in this cruel mortal world.'

She'd finally given into his dramatics and three delicious drinks later her memories turned to a kaleidoscope of colors, glitter, and candy canes. At some point, she must have told Santa about missing the gym, but she couldn't remember the conversation.

Merry found her leggings and a compression half zip, then ducked into the bathroom to change and brush her teeth. When she reemerged, Santa had her Bluetooth speaker in hand, pressing every button until it made the little power up noise and connected to her phone.

Her music started playing automatically, a feature she'd never figured out how to turn off, and Bryce Savage informed her that she was in her "Villian Era."

Fortunately, the volume was turned down.

Unfortunately, Santa found the plus button easily.

"What is this? I thought you liked *good* music?" he whined.

"This is good music. It's motivation for my workouts."

He skipped to the next song using the controls on the speaker, played thirty seconds, and skipped again.

By the time Merry had finished half her coffee, wiped last night's lingering mascara from beneath her eyes, and found her concealer in the bottom of her makeup bag, Santa had finished his perusal of her playlist.

"These are the songs you listen to when you work out? Why are they all so mean?"

"Mean?" Merry asked, genuinely shocked he'd think so. It wasn't like they were listening to her heavy metal playlist or anything.

"They are all about men being addicted to or enslaved by or dying because of beautiful women. That seems mean."

Merry laughed and instantly regretted it as a pang went through her head. "Exactly, I just tell myself that if I run one more mile or do five more squats that I'll look good enough to have one of those songs written about me. It's the perfect motivation."

"You exercise so you'll think you're pretty enough to slay men with your beauty?" Santa didn't seem to understand the appeal.

"Yep," Merry confirmed. Belatedly, she added, "And health stuff. Endorphins, heart health, all that jazz."

Merry dabbed some concealer under her eyes and watched him in the mirror. He was still staring at the speaker like it held all the answers.

"You're taking the lyrics entirely too literally," Merry told him. "I just want to feel like a badass. Like the kind of girl that is so awesome that men write songs about how they will never get over her. I am aware that makes me sound completely shallow, but I can't think of a better way to say it right now."

Santa looked up at her in the mirror, his eyes bright gold even in the soft hotel light. "You don't need this terrible music for that. You're already a badass. It's obvious that you're the smartest person in every room you walk into. And I'm certain I'll never get over you, duckie. If you need that sentiment set to music, I will be more than happy to immortalize it."

What the hell? Santa had been flirty since the moment they met, but this was delusional. Or a joke.

Merry relaxed a fraction. Obviously, it was a joke. Not about her being smart—that was true—but his feelings… those were definitely exaggerated for comedic effect.

To distract herself from the conundrum sitting on her bed, she asked, "Well, what music do you listen to when you work out? What's your go-to song to get hyped up?"

"It's certainly not on here," he said, staring at the speaker like it was both disappointing and venomous.

Did he not understand Bluetooth? That was impossible. Merry assumed it was yet another joke that had gone over her head. She unlocked her phone, opened the music app, and passed it to him. "You can play your music, but don't go through my stuff."

He cradled the phone like a newborn baby and stared at it for a long moment. Slowly, he poked the 'search' button with an index finger. He tilted the phone away from her so she couldn't see what he was searching but she still saw that he typed with a single finger like an old man. His intense focus and general technological ineptitude brought a smile to her face.

Merry had time to apply mascara and ChapStick and find her hairbrush at the bottom of her suitcase before he finally found the right song. She froze with the brush halfway through her hair and started laughing at the familiar notes.

If she'd made a list of every artist Santa might have chosen for his 'hype' song, this band would have been near the bottom of that list, right between The Devil Wears Prada and The Wiggles.

Santa turned the music up but still drowned out the prerecorded voices of ABBA with his own surprisingly good falsetto. She felt every note of "Dancing Queen" in her skull but didn't ask him to turn it down, especially when he started spinning around her room pulling moves straight from a 70s disco.

She only rolled her eyes when he stole her hairbrush to use as a makeshift microphone. He was ridiculous. Absolutely absurd. But his insanity was infectious. When he held the hairbrush microphone to her lips, she finished the line about the tambourine without even thinking.

When the AI automatically played "Uptown Girl" next, Santa looked wide eyed at Merry. "How did it know what I wanted to hear next?"

He didn't ponder the question long. There were high notes to hit.

Merry showed him how to download a pre-made playlist on the inn's Wi-Fi so he would have music for the car, then grabbed her coat and followed him to the truck parked in front of the inn. He was still carrying the speaker, and she mentally prepared her defense if any townspeople arrived to yell about the volume.

He tossed her the keys, and she drove him to the toy shop while he proved unequivocally that he could give Freddie Mercury a run for his money when it came to theatricality.

He never broke the melody as he pointed for Merry to park in front of the mansion.

"The gym is here?" she asked.

He nodded, trying to guess her passcode since he'd let the phone go to sleep. She took it from him and unlocked it. As soon as he got his hands back on the music app, ABBA started playing. "Let's go wake everyone up."

Before she could ask what he meant, Santa was out of the truck, disco pointing his way up the front steps with her speaker on full blast. Shaking her head, Merry followed him.

Santa flitted through the halls of the mansion, singing to each door like a demented Disney princess. Grumbling, shouting, and complaints met him.

Jeraltan appeared from one of the doors, rubbing his eyes. "I thought I locked the boombox in the closet."

"You did. Merry gave me a new one!" Santa said, pulling a sleepy Jeraltan into the hallway by the hips and forcing him to dance.

Jeraltan turned to her, "Betrayal! I made you drinks, and this is how you repay me?" Before she could explain that she'd lent the speaker to Santa, not given it to him, Jeraltan started to dance.

By the time the second chorus started, Claus Family Toys employees were pouring from every door, filling the hallways with singing and dancing pajama-clad people. Faye looped her arm through Merry's and pulled her toward the ballroom.

"Did you all sleep here?" Merry asked.

"We live here," Faye explained. "Need coffee? Jeraltan should have it made in a few minutes. Oh, or aspirin? I can send someone to the store."

Merry shook her head. "I've already had both. I was told there was a gym? Or do you all just do Zumba in the hallways?"

"Sometimes, but there is also a gym."

The gym turned out to be the ballroom. The basketball court had been restored to its pre-party state—or at least what Merry assumed it had been—and there were two treadmills and a rack of mismatched free weights. It wasn't much of a gym by her standards, but it would work.

She'd done a lot of workouts in her life—both group and individual—but that morning's was the most chaotic. Seemingly all the Claus Family Toys employees piled into the ballroom-turned-gym not to exercise, but to fight for control of the music.

She shouldn't have bothered to bring her headphones because there was no chance of getting her phone back. Apparently, the Wi-Fi stretched from the closest coffee shop to the mansion, so they had the full Spotify catalog to choose from. They took full advantage of that and led her through a breakneck overview of every hit song from the last century, bouncing back and forth between the Bee Gees, Ariana Grande, Elvis, and NSYNC so quickly she couldn't keep a steady pace on the treadmill.

Not only did the music distract her, but the conversation jumped from interrogations on her life in California, her job, her childhood interspersed with random stories and tangents that she couldn't keep track of.

Santa stuck by her side for the first hour, doing something between tai chi, yoga, and interpretive dance on a mat next to her but he got bored quickly and started bragging about his basketball skills.

His comments were taken as a personal affront and a full game—complete with coaches, referees, and reserve players—broke out to the tune of Aretha Franklin's "Respect." They were all incredible but Merry stopped short of saying they could play in the NBA or WNBA since those organizations didn't usually allow sing-along breaks.

After a dispute over who would play point guard on Faye's team, Jeraltan abandoned the game to organize a makeshift Zumba class on the other side of the room. Merry gave up on her usual routine and leaned into the chaos, joining the Zumba class that quickly morphed into Pilates and then something else she didn't have a name for.

By mid-morning, she collapsed on a worn yoga mat, giggling as Jeraltan and Siofra settled yet another argument with a twerking competition discordantly set to Otis Redding. Jeraltan won by a landslide.

As an only child, Merry had always longed for siblings, and that's what this group of people acted like. They fought, cheered, and embarrassed each other with the closeness of family. For unknown reasons, they had immediately adopted her into that circle as well.

When her stomach started growling, Faye announced it was time for brunch. She explained that nothing in the town was open on Sundays, not even the grocery store, so they would have to make do with what they had. They had a lot.

Merry sat on the kitchen cabinet that looked to have been installed somewhere around the 1960s based on the avocado and gold color scheme while Santa fetched various snacks to tide her over until Jeraltan finished making pancakes.

He was like a magical golden retriever. Every time he disappeared, he came back with something new she hadn't considered they might have—like a bowl of puffy Cheetos and strawberries. Together. In one bowl.

It was her turn to pick a song, and she couldn't think of a single thing that hadn't already been played, so she surprised them with Skrillex. Santa hated it, of course. Jeraltan covered his ears with his spatula as if he was under attack. But Faye's eyes went wide with glee.

Just before the second drop, the relaxing jingle of an incoming video call cut off Sonny Moore's greatest achievement—"Bangarang"—and Merry saw her best friend's name on the screen. She answered immediately since Deirdre never called in the morning.

"Oh good, you survived. I was worried," Deirdre said.

"Survived what?" Merry asked.

"The party last night. You FaceTimed me to make sure I knew that none of Santa's clothes are sexy, and Faye's rendition of "Rudolph the Red Nosed Reindeer" is an—and I quote—absolute banger."

Merry began furiously tapping at the Settings app, blushing from hairline to collarbones. "Could you hold off on any more fun memories until I disconnect from Bluetooth?"

"Can't do it," Deirdre told her. "I'm conferencing in Graham; he was with me last night when you called, and he definitely has questions."

Merry managed to disconnect her phone from the speaker just in time for Deirdre's brother to appear on the screen. She tried to exit the room for a little privacy, but her path was blocked by curious eavesdroppers.

"Don't start, I know I drank too much," Merry pleaded.

"I don't care about that. You not being able to hold your liquor is old news. I want to talk about that man you were with."

"Which one?" Merry asked, delaying the inevitable. Graham had terrible taste in men so he no doubt wanted to gossip about the white-haired, honey eyed heathen that had been her shadow for the past two days. She refused to look at Santa after Deirdre's sexy clothes comment but could see him already grinning in her peripheral vision.

"The single most glorious bartender I've ever seen," Graham said.

"Wait. Who?" Merry asked.

"I don't know, that's why I'm asking. He had messy blond hair, big brown eyes, and all the sexual charisma of a teenage Simba."

"From *The Lion King*?" Graham nodded emphatically, so Merry added, "did we watch the same movie?"

Over the top of the phone, she saw Jeraltan jumping up and down and pointing at himself, mouthing 'me, me, me.'

Merry tried to control her smile. "And what should I do if I find this sexy bartender?"

Graham ran a hand through his messy curls, knocking his Clark Kent glasses askew. "Give him my number! Phone, credit card, Social Security. I don't care. Whatever he wants."

Merry couldn't hide her laughter any longer as Jeraltan was preening like a cat who'd received a big bowl of cream when his companions had been given water. "One more question," Merry said, already turning so that Jeraltan was in the camera frame. "Is this him?"

Graham gave a gratifying squeak of embarrassment and Merry decided he'd been punished enough for his comment about her being a sloppy drunk.

"I am so glad we did this on FaceTime but give me some warning next time! I should have recorded that," she heard Deirdre say.

Jeraltan ignored her. "Hello, Graham. I have questions. First, is Simba a particularly good-looking lion? I've never seen the movie." This was met with stammering from Graham and laughter from the other employees which Jeraltan quickly shut down. He sashayed his hips as he walked away with Merry's phone.

She turned to Santa. "I do need that phone back at some point."

She shouldn't have bothered.

Pari's war cry of "he took the music!" pushed the rest of the group into action. She ducked out of the kitchen just in time to see Jeraltan tackled and tickled until he gave up the phone and Skrillex started back up from the phone's speaker.

Jeraltan disappeared and reappeared a few minutes later with an ancient flip phone and a goofy grin. He tucked the phone in the pocket of his apron and threw the burned pancakes in the trash. As he started on a new batch, he said, "I need the phone. Forever. My new boyfriend lives in California."

Merry wasn't sure what she was more concerned about, that Jeraltan was already calling Graham his boyfriend or that the ensuing argument suggested the entire house shared one cell phone.

Once Santa presided over a vote to allow Jeraltan use of the phone for two hours a day, Faye confirmed that they all shared one phone—satellite, since the town had no regular service—and had no other connection to the world outside Poleton.

Merry stood in shock for a full minute, trying to wrap her mind around the self-imposed isolation. Then again, they were all artists—of a sort at least. Maybe this was some kind of commune? Surely someone would have mentioned that before. But did communes usually greet strangers by saying, 'welcome to the commune?' Or was it supposed to be implied?

It didn't really matter. They seemed happy in their Instagramless bubble, so who was she to judge? And she was starving. Ravenous. So hungry she joined the rest of the employees in begging Jeraltan to hurry up with the pancakes.

Merry spent the rest of the day at the mansion with the Claus Family Toys employees talking, laughing, and listening to music. Sundays in a small town were lazy and Merry had to admit that it was a nice change of pace.

When she got back to the inn, she changed her flight from Monday evening to the fifteenth—the last day of her allotted bereavement leave.

She told herself that it was a reasonable decision.

She needed to stay in Poleton long enough for her father's truck to be fixed and to find out what was going on with her grandmother's company. A small part of her knew, however, that she wanted to stay with her new friends a little longer.

CHAPTER 10

Monday morning Merry chided herself for her vanity. It was four thirty and she was blending a cream blush into her cheeks to create a natural fresh-faced look that involved several different types of makeup. She opted for ChapStick with a rosy tint and forced herself to stop. There was no one here to impress.

She jogged to the door when the knock sounded and found Santa standing with his hands in the pockets of his loose cotton pants. Like the day before, he wore a cropped hoodie and white converse. It wasn't a look that she normally would have called stylish, but it looked like the height of fashion with his lanky frame and snow-white hair.

"I don't have time to star in a musical this morning," she warned him. "Just a quick workout then I need to go to Red Bay."

"That's fine, everyone is getting ready for work, so they don't have time either. Do you need to borrow my—your—truck?" Santa said, already tossing her the keys as they approached his favorite pickup.

"If you don't mind. Wayne hasn't finished fixing my dad's brakes, so I am *without transportation*," Merry told him, scowling at the situation. She hated being dependent on someone else, even if Santa didn't seem put out. "Do you want to drive? I think you've paid your penance for insulting my driving by now."

He made a beeline for the passenger's seat and flashed her a grin as she slid behind the wheel. "Nah, I like being your Passenger Prince."

Her laugh was far more giggle than she'd expected.

"Do you want to come with me to meet Quinn?" She hated the note of hope in her voice, but she didn't like the thought of going to meet a possible mob boss alone.

"In Red Bay?" Santa asked, and Merry nodded. "I can't."

"Of course. You have to work; I shouldn't have asked. I wonder if Faye…"

"She can't either. None of us can go with you," Santa said. He looked genuinely upset by that fact. "You should take Henry. I don't like the idea of you going alone."

Even though Merry had just been thinking the same thing, it was annoying when Santa said it. "I'll be fine. Plus, I thought you didn't like Henry."

"Why wouldn't I like Henry?"

"You and Faye seemed adamant that you don't want him to run the company. I thought it was implied that you don't trust him," Merry said.

Santa shook his head, causing a few strands of silky hair to escape his bun. "I trust Henry. We all trust him. We just need you to run the company instead."

"Oh. Okay," Merry said. Santa's words were right, but there was still something off about his tone. An intensity that didn't fit with his statements. She didn't know him well enough to press, so she decided to take his advice. She could ask Henry to accompany her and get a good read on both him and Quinn. Two birds and all that.

***

At nine, Merry was showered and on her way to pick up the elderly lawyer. The trip was much nicer in Santa's truck than it had been on foot.

She tried not to be pulled in by Henry's grandfatherly charm since she still wasn't sure about his character, but it was really hard when he was waiting by the door in a tweed overcoat with a plate of cookies. Why were old people so cute?

Henry spent the entire drive sifting through Santa's extensive collection of cassettes and sharing his thoughts on the various ways music had been played during his life. Merry let him talk.

Her GPS started working once they left Poleton, and it guided them to the headquarters of Quinn Worldwide. She'd expected a warehouse, or second to that an office building. Instead, she and Henry found themselves outside of the textbook definition of a McMansion. It was monstrous with white columns, red brick, and a roofline that would make any sane roofer balk. If none of that was bad enough, the house was decked out in Christmas spirit.

Merry rang the doorbell and received another shock when Quinn answered the door. He looked like an accountant. Middle aged with rimless glasses and a slight paunch. Not at all the scary mafia boss she'd been expecting. Then again, someone had to count all the money from the... bad things that the mafia did. She wasn't entirely sure what those things were, but movies had told her they were lucrative.

Quinn was more than eager to invite her inside for a coffee—at least until he heard her name. By that time, he'd already extended the offer, so he couldn't take it back.

His kitchen was all yellow granite and maple cabinets. Merry assumed it would have been nice fifteen years before. Now, it just looked outdated.

"You buy a lot of toys from my family's business," Merry began.

Quinn stiffened where he was poking around at a stainless monstrosity of an espresso maker. "I do."

"And I was told that you resell them online," Merry prodded when he didn't seem inclined to continue.

"I do that as well."

"Is there a reason you pay half the price of the other distributors who buy our toys?" Merry asked politely.

Quinn turned with an espresso and a false smile. "Well, there is so much more to online retailing than many people believe. Advertising, of course, plus warehousing, shipping, customer service. Your grandmother didn't want to go through the trouble of managing such a complex and time-consuming task."

"I see," Merry said, keeping her expression and tone neutral. "And how did you and my grandmother become acquainted?"

Quinn turned back to the coffee maker, swapping the used espresso pod for a new one.

"He approached Joy fifteen years or so ago," Henry answered. "Her other distributors had cut their orders, and she had thousands of unsold toys. He gave her the same spiel about how difficult it was to sell toys online and convinced her that he was doing her a favor by buying her inventory at pennies on the dollar." His cheeks were flushed, and he was staring at Quinn like something nasty he'd found on the bottom of his shoe. "I argued against the deal, but in the end, it was Joy's company. In her mind, losing money was better than bringing computers into the business."

Quinn turned with the same false smile still in place. "I did her a favor. Selling toys is hard enough in a local store but it's nearly impossible online where there are so many options. It takes time and effort to move that inventory. Really, I'm not making much profit."

"Bullshit," Henry said, surprising even Merry. "You don't do anything but send the toys to Amazon and let them handle everything else. You make ten million a year without lifting a finger."

Quinn started to argue. "The customer service alone—"

"Is handled by your three employees in Mexico," Henry supplied. He turned to Merry. "Don't let him fool you like he fooled Joy. He is nothing but a leech."

Henry was serious. His shaking hands where he gripped his coat told her that. Merry started to laugh. "Oh, thank God! You're not a mobster, you're just an asshole."

"Mobster?" Henry said. Quinn looked equally baffled.

"You're not laundering money or shipping drugs in Claus Family Toys boxes?" Merry asked. Quinn was terrible at masking his expressions, so she believed him when he shook his head.

"That's great news, Quinn. Do I have your contact information?"

"I do," Henry interjected.

"Great." Merry stood, still smiling at the man who'd cost her grandmother—and by extension all the Claus Family Toys employees— more than a hundred million dollars over the past decade. "Thanks for the coffee. We'll let you get back to work."

She turned and left her untouched espresso on the counter. Henry trailed her out of the kitchen.

"So, what happens now?" Quinn called after her.

"We'll be in touch," Merry replied over her shoulder.

She made it out the door her friends had bought, down the front steps her friends had paid for, across the lawn her friends had paid to landscape without screaming. In fact, she kept a placid smile on her face until she pulled the truck to the side of the road a few blocks away.

"Merry, are you alright?" Henry asked. "You look like… well, not quite right."

"I am trying very, very hard not to turn around and wring his scrawny neck," Merry said. "But that wouldn't help us. What are our options? Our legal, non-neck-wringing options. Can we sue him? He clearly made false claims to my grandmother about his costs and profitability."

"I'm afraid not. All their communication was in person. If he lied to her, I can't prove it."

"How did this happen?" Merry said, bringing her forehead to rest on the steering wheel. At least money laundering made sense. It had a purpose, even if it was a nefarious one. But this was just negligence. Bad business. A waste of tens of millions of dollars.

"The first year that he bought from her, it was truly a godsend." Henry said. "It was during the financial crisis and money was tight for everyone. The distributors cut their orders, and Joy would have had to sell property to make payroll or lay off a quarter of the staff. But Quinn came along and offered to take the unsold toys off her hands at a price that would let her break even. He was just an opportunistic kid with a laptop then."

"Sure, I understand that. From both sides. He took a risk in an uncertain market. She cut him a deal to get rid of inventory during a recession. But what about after that? Why did she keep producing the same amount? And why keep selling to him at a loss?"

Henry sighed. "It was just easier for her, I guess. She got to keep her staff and her business the same even when the distributors cut their orders every year. She wasn't going in the red at first, then it was by such a small amount that I don't think she minded."

"All of this because she hated technology? That's the real reason, not a cover for something else?" Merry asked. It still seemed far-fetched to her that one person's fear could bring a business to the brink of collapse.

"It's the truth," Henry said. "I tried to talk to her about it. I'm no whiz on a computer myself, but I know when to hire someone to do it for me. She was old and stubborn and set in her ways. That's the only explanation I have."

"Okay," Merry said. "Okay. I can fix this. I can turn this company around."

She straightened, letting go of her frustration. What was done was done. Now, she just needed to do what she did best. The only problem was, she didn't own the company.

"That's great to hear, Merry. You'll be staying then?" Henry said. He looked genuinely pleased and a little proud.

"I can't live here for six months," she said with a frustrated sigh. "I have to get back to my job. If that means you need to keep the company, so be it. I will help you as much as I can."

Henry's expression fell. "I understand. Let's see what you come up with over the next few days to deal with Quinn and then we'll talk about next steps for the ownership of the company."

"I'll need access to the company's financial information," Merry said.

"Not a problem. I'll let Howard know."

CHAPTER 11

Howard was not pleased to be kicked out of his office, but Merry enjoyed it tremendously. She considered propping her snow crusted boots on his desk but decided that was overkill. She wasn't a movie villain. Watching Henry send him home for the rest of the day so Merry could have full access to his office was good enough.

The only part of the company's information she wasn't allowed to see were the employee files, including salaries. That was fine. She had the total cost of employee wages and benefits, so that was enough for the time being.

She pieced together a rough outline of the company over the past decade and found that Henry's version of events was true. Distributor orders had taken a steep hit during the financial crisis and continued to decline more slowly since then. Costs and output had remained pretty steady over that timeframe.

It was such a simple fix, Merry almost couldn't believe it. All she had to do was bring online sales in house and the company would make a profit. A decent one, given the industry and size of the company.

She checked the time, mentally converted to Pacific Standard, and called Deirdre during her usual mid-afternoon slump.

"Hey babe. I can't believe you've waited this long to call me back. Can you believe how embarrassing Graham was yesterday? I don't think he will ever recover."

Merry took a ten-minute gossip break before turning the conversation to the task at hand.

"I am knee deep in paper financial records right now, I feel like a time traveler. I need a blazer with shoulder pads and some man with a cigarette calling me 'sugar.'"

Santa chose that unfortunate moment to saunter in—without knocking, of course. He raised one eyebrow at her.

"Please don't get either of those things," Deirdre said. "You have enough problems at that company already. Any news on the crime front?"

"Yes, and it is a wild ride. I'll tell you about it later. I've got to run. Give Charli my love."

"Will do. You're coming home tonight, right?"

"I'll actually be staying a little longer. I'll fly back on the fifteenth," Merry said, earning a smile from Santa.

Deirdre's voice dropped to a whisper. "Does the mafia have you? Are they threatening you? My best friend would never agree to spend two weeks in a small town. Especially near Christmas."

Santa perched on the corner of Merry's—Howard's—desk and leaned in so close Merry stopped breathing. It took her a moment to realize he was getting close to the microphone. His voice dropped to a threatening growl which was at odds with his playful smile. "She's mine now. And I'm never letting her go."

Deirdre squealed. "I was joking Merry but now I'm genuinely worried. Who was that?"

Ignoring the warm, fluttering feeling in her belly, Merry forced herself to laugh. It sounded a little hysterical even to her own ears, but how could she not be a little hysterical when Santa was inches from her face, claiming her. "Just Santa. Ignore him."

"I've heard his voice and that didn't sound like him, FaceTime me right now and prove it."

Rolling her eyes at her friend's dramatics, Merry pressed the video call button, stood, and turned so that both she and Santa would be in the frame. Santa settled fully on the desk, pulling Merry backward with a gentle hand on her hip until her back hit his chest. He let that hand linger as the call connected and Deirdre's familiar office came into view.

"Oh, it is him."

"The one and only," Merry said as casually as she could under the circumstances. It wasn't very casual at all.

She felt rather than saw Santa smile at the camera. "Nice to see you again, Deirdre. We didn't get to talk much at the party. I'm working on—"

"And you won't get to talk to her today. As you can see, I am not being held captive by any crime organization, so I should really get going. Bye!" Merry ended the call before Deirdre could pepper Santa with questions.

"Are you embarrassed of me, duckie?" Santa asked, finally releasing her hip. Merry kept her back to him until she got her blush under control.

"No, I just have a lot of work to do." She turned her laptop to face him, keeping her eyes on the spreadsheet. "I'm manually entering every expense and sale from this year. I'm only in February."

"And how does the mafia play into this," he waved a hand vaguely at the screen, "jumble of numbers?"

"They don't," Merry said. She really didn't want to elaborate on the theory that now seemed ridiculous. "That was just a joke. Paper financial statements usually mean something shady is going on, hence the mafia jokes."

"So, the mafia doesn't use computers?" Santa asked. Merry finally looked away from the screen and saw a cute little wrinkle between his brows.

"I have no idea what the mafia does or even if they still exist. Paper records are just one of the things they teach us to look for in our classes on money laundering."

"You take classes on how to launder money?"

"No," Merry pinched the bridge of her nose and let out a frustrated breath. "I misspoke. Our *anti*-money laundering classes. And it doesn't matter. No one is laundering money here, for the mafia or otherwise. It was just a joke."

"That's good," Santa said. He still sat on her desk, seemingly content to hold March's expenses hostage with his perfect ass.

No. Merry mentally chided herself.

He was her employee, or something like it. She should think less about the anti-money laundering trainings and more about the anti-sexual harassment videos she and Deirdre always laughed at. "I had Pari and Rari recount this month's shipment. We made seventy-five more toys than last month. Will that help with the profits?"

"That's great," Merry told him. "You seem to be doing a great job as foreman. But you don't need to worry about the profits. I'm taking care of it."

"I trust you." Santa fiddled with the end of his emerald green scarf. If Merry didn't know better, she'd think he was nervous. "But we know we haven't been making a profit. Joy told us we've been losing money for seven years. Jeraltan's worried. We really need the company to do well."

"Jeraltan's worried, but not you?" Merry asked gently.

Santa dropped the end of his scarf and straightened. "We'll make more. Or something different."

"Just keep doing what you're doing. I'm taking care of the profits," Merry repeated in the soothing but authoritative voice she used with clients. Her confidence usually brought them comfort.

Santa nodded, but his smile was a little less bright than usual. "Okay. We can start working on Sundays if we need to. I haven't wanted to suggest it since it's our only day off but if that's what you think we need to do, we will."

"You work on Saturdays right now?"

Santa nodded. "Six to six, Monday through Saturday. Except last weekend because of the parade and the party."

Merry's eyes flew wide, and alarm bells went off in her head. They sounded a lot like they were tolling 'DOL, DOL, DOL'. She'd wondered how they managed to produce over four hundred thousand toys last year, and it seemed she had her answer—massive amounts of overtime. "That's completely unnecessary. I know it's close to the holidays, but you still don't need to work that much. Did my grandmother make that requirement?"

71

Santa shook his head. "We don't know what else to do. We need this company to be profitable. All our lives depend on it. So, we just keep working."

Merry wanted to tell him that it was just a job, there were plenty of others. But was that true in this case?

Her father had warned her to consider the people. There weren't many other businesses in town or close by. Plus, what other work was there for wood carvers? Not much. And they all seemed as close as family. Without Claus Family Toys, they weren't likely to find jobs together doing what they loved to do.

"How about this—I'll stop by after I finish here and explain everything that I know so far and my plan. I'll even make a presentation like I do for my clients. You'll all know as much as I do."

Santa agreed quickly. "I'm not sure we'll understand—," he pointed to the spreadsheet like it might bite him, "*that*, but we'll try."

"I'll make it pretty for you," Merry assured him.

With a final, more genuine grin in her direction Santa left to get back to his shift.

Merry spent the rest of the afternoon making a slide deck she hoped would assuage the employees' fear. She didn't exactly have the authority to share the information with them, but it was what was right. If Henry decided to keep the company, at least they would know what they were up against.

CHAPTER 12

That evening, Merry found herself in the ballroom of the mansion once again. This time, the Claus Family Toys crew was seated quietly in front of her. It was unnerving to see them all still and attentive since they'd been talking over each other in every previous interaction.

They'd dragged a variety of cushions, bean bag chairs, and mats into the space and they looked like a group of kindergarteners eager for story time.

Santa sat front and center with a kitchen notepad and red crayon in his hand. Beside him, Jeraltan had a fuzzy cheetah print diary complete with matching pen. Faye had a more subdued moleskin but paired it with a highlighter. Of more than a hundred employees, Merry didn't see a standard set of notepad and pen. At least they hadn't gotten too normal in the last few hours.

Luckily, she'd brought her full laptop bag to North Carolina, complete with a sleek mini projector. She set it up quickly, pointed it at a bare wall, and opened her presentation to a chorus of oohs and ahhs.

She began with the standard opening slides including her personal introduction, scope of work, methodology, and, of course, KPIs. These were met with crinkled brows from some employees and furious scribbling from others as they tried to absorb the valuable information.

After only twenty minutes, Faye stopped her with a not-so-delicately cleared throat. Merry turned, ready to address her concerns. Her eagerness quailed under Faye's dark expression. "We know you're smart. You don't have to speak incomprehensibly to prove it. If you have a point, get to it."

A sharp retort was on the tip of her tongue, but she swallowed it when Faye glanced sideways at Addie. His dark hair obscured the majority of his face, but Merry still saw his pale skin and the grim line of his mouth. It was strange to see him at the front of the room since he normally clung to the outskirts of the group, a quiet shadow hidden by glossy black hair and an oversized hoodie. Clearly, he wanted to resume his usual place, but Merry's presentation kept him seated beside Faye.

"I happen to like Merry's presentation so far. It's like a riddle." Santa chimed in. He turned from Faye to Merry with an eager smile. "I love riddles. Write down all these fun, confusing phrases for me."

She quirked an eyebrow in his direction, much to his delight. Arching only one brow was a skill she'd honed precisely for moments like this. "Just to ensure our goals are aligned before we expend valuable resources, you'd like me to cultivate a customized deliverable outlining the critical path to maximize verbal usage while minimizing intelligibility when communicating with internal and external stakeholders?"

He fanned himself with his notepad. "Say deliverable one more time and our goals are about to get very aligned, duckie."

With an eye roll and a chuckle-snort, Merry muttered, "absolutely ridiculous."

"I have received similar feedback from stakeholders in the past. It has not proved insurmountable," he returned. Then, he ruined the effect with a bright grin. "Did I do it?"

"You sure did, sweetie," she said as dryly as she could manage while holding back laughter. He preened. Merry turned back to Faye. "Sorry. I got caught up in presenting. I'll just skip over the introductory material."

"See that you do." No person had a right to sound so intimidating while sitting cross-legged on a beanbag chair, but Merry liked her all the more for it. If she could only find a way to get Faye and Simon in the same room, her rival would be defeated once and for all. That thought brought a smile to her face as she clicked through the next twenty slides and finally arrived at the meat of the presentation–last year's income statement.

Revenue rolled up to the top of the screen with a perfectly timed animation. "Last year you made four hundred and sixteen thousand toys. We sold them to distributors, retailers, and resellers for an average of sixty-one dollars each. That brings the total revenue to twenty-five point four million."

She scanned her audience and found them much more attentive now that she was discussing their work. Jeraltan raised his hand and Merry held back a smile as she called on him like a teacher.

"Is that good?" he asked.

"Wait until you see the rest and then you tell me," Merry replied.

He nodded impatiently and she pressed the button on her remote clicker to bring up the next number. "Labor was our biggest expense at just under twelve million. Materials were another three million. Shipping was one million. Utilities and other expenses were one million. Taxes, mostly on property, were eight million."

She brought up the final line of the abbreviated income statement. "That leaves us with a net loss of twenty-seven thousand dollars."

"So how many more toys do we need to make?" a woman Merry thought was named Melody asked.

"Twenty-seven thousand divided by sixty-one. She already told us how much we get from each toy." Pari said.

"Don't make us do math," Jeraltan whined. "Just tell us how many more we need to make."

"I'm getting there. That was just the overview," Merry said, quickly switching to the next slide with a nervous glance at Faye. Thirty-seven logos appeared on the screen. "Now, these are our buyers. They fall into three categories." At a click of a button, they organized themselves into three columns. "First, consignment sellers. These companies let us place our products in their stores and then they give us a percentage of the sales price once people buy them. We sold twenty thousand toys in these stores last year and received an average of eighty-four dollars from each sale."

She paused to let them write down the information before moving on to the next group. "The next group of distributors buy our toys and sell them to stores. Those stores sell them to people, but we get the money up front. We sold one hundred and ninety thousand toys to this kind of distributor last year for an average of eighty-one dollars per toy."

Jeraltan raised his hand again, waving it indignantly in the air. At Merry's amused nod, he blurted, "why are they paying us less? Can we take the toys away from them and give them to the people who pay us more?"

"When we sell on consignment, we accept the risk of a toy not selling. When a store buys from us upfront, they accept it. We have to give them a better deal to compensate for the additional risk."

"That's not a real risk. People will buy our toys," Jeraltan grumbled.

Merry chose not to argue with him. The next part was more important. "The last group is just Quinn. We sold him two hundred and six thousand toys at an average price of forty dollars."

Their reactions mirrored what Merry had felt when learning the truth of her grandmother's mistake.

"But that's half!" Faye said, her voice rising above the others. "That's half our toys and half the price everyone else pays."

"The other stores cut their orders, remember?" Santa said. "Joy said Quinn was our only option. We have to focus on making more toys so that we can make the same amount of money at the lower price."

"That would be true if Quinn was our only option," Merry said equitably. "But he's not." She moved to the next slide showing screenshots from Amazon's website for sellers.

"When you send toys to Quinn, you're not actually sending them to him. He doesn't have a warehouse or a physical store. He sends the toys to Amazon. They store them, ship them, and accept orders from customers. This is how much they charge to do that. Total, it is around twenty-five to thirty dollars per toy."

"So, it's expensive? Is it expensive? I can't tell," Pari said.

Merry gave up on her presentation and opened a new browser tab. She navigated to the Amazon site and showed them Quinn's page. "He charges an average of one hundred and twenty dollars per toy, about ten percent less than the physical stores that carry our products. He pays us forty dollars and pays Amazon twenty-five. That means he makes fifty-five dollars per toy—or eleven million dollars total. Every year."

Silence fell over the room.

"But…what does he do?" Santa asked. "We make the toys and package them. You said this Amazon person stores them and ships them. What does Quinn do?"

"Amazon is a company, not a person," Jeraltan said. "They sell books."

"Not just books anymore, but I'll explain Amazon later." Merry said. "The point is Quinn doesn't do anything that we can't do. He uploads pictures of the toys, writes descriptions, and then Amazon does the rest. If a customer has a problem, like the post office lost their package, then Quinn has three employees that handle their questions. Other than that, he just sits back and collects money."

"We can sell things on Amazon? We're allowed to do that?" Faye asked.

Bless their hearts. How had this entire group of people missed the soul-sucking joy of the internet?

"We are definitely allowed to do that," Merry confirmed. "And you don't have to be the one to do it, we can hire someone to manage the account. We can also get a website and sell directly to customers. We can build another warehouse and handle the storage and shipping on our own to avoid Amazon fees. There are a lot of things we can do down the road. But the first step is cutting Quinn out of the equation."

She switched the tab back to her presentation and skipped to the last slide which showed the projected income without Quinn in the mix, "If we do that, then we will make a six million dollar profit next year. That's after hiring more employees so you don't have to work overtime."

"So, we kill Quinn," a quiet employee Merry didn't know well said from the back of the room.

"What? No," Merry said. "His contract is year to year. We just won't sell him any toys next year. No violence required."

"That's it?" Santa said. "That's all we have to do?"

"Yep," Merry replied. "I'm sure there are a lot of other ways we can improve, but this is the easiest fix I've ever encountered as a consultant. You've all built a solid business with great products that people love. The only thing holding you back was a bad deal with an opportunistic jerk."

She'd never ended a presentation to a standing ovation, but there was a first time for everything. Clapping turned into excited chatter about how they would spend the profits and what they would do with their nights and weekends once they were no longer working so much overtime.

Surprisingly, Merry didn't hear Santa suggesting buying a dozen new pickup trucks next year. She searched for his white hair and lanky frame in the raucous crowd and found him grinning as he pushed past his friends. He swept her into a hug that lifted her feet off the ground and pressed her against his lean body.

She wrapped her arms around his neck instinctively, feeling the brush of his soft hair against her fingers. Her heart hammered as the scent of wood polish filled her nose. Beneath it, he smelled like cedar and snow.

"Thank you, Merry." His breath ghosted over the shell of her ear, sending a tingle down to her fluttering stomach.

She squeezed him a little tighter, not trusting herself to speak.

Their embrace was broken a moment later by an influx of other employees who wanted to hug and thank her. Someone found a bottle of tequila and an argument broke out over tequila versus champagne as a celebratory beverage. Merry just laughed and repeated that she hadn't done anything special by recognizing a bad deal.

When she finally had an opening, she pulled Santa away from the crowd and over to her computer. "I thought you'd want to see this," she said as she navigated to the browser tab still showing Quinn's amazon account.

"It doesn't have our name anywhere. Just his," Santa said.

"That's not what I wanted you to see," Merry said. She scrolled through the products and pointed out the star ratings. "A thousand people gave this puzzle box five out of five stars. I've never seen a perfect rating like that on any product. And this truck has three thousand reviews. Four point nine stars. That's incredible."

Since Santa could never manage to react the way she anticipated, she was only mildly surprised when he scoffed. "Four point nine? Who didn't like my truck? Wait, are all the toys on here? Can we see whose toys people like best?"

Merry laughed at the spark of challenge in his golden eyes. "That's the point of reviews," she told him. "Some people leave comments too."

"Show us," he said immediately. After a moment he added, "please."

"Sure. Just wrangle your staff and we can look at all of them together. I'll even let you click." It would be a good first lesson in computer literacy, even if it would take a while to work up to spreadsheets.

CHAPTER 13

Merry had relinquished Howard's office and officially commandeered Santa's instead. She would have preferred to keep using Howard's since it was clearly torture for the asshole accountant to be forced to communicate with the lowly employees who designed, carved, painted, and shipped the toys, but Santa offered and swore he never used his office anyway.

She had her personal MacBook open to Excel, a thousand paper order forms and expense reports to her left in the 'to be recorded' pile and... far fewer in the 'recorded' pile to her right. But she was making progress.

Slow, slow progress.

There were two reasons it was taking so long to make sense of the transactions. First, she hadn't brought her keyboard with the number pad, so she was having to use the keys at the top of her laptop like a peasant. Second, she was constantly being interrupted.

Jeraltan brought coffee. Faye brought coffee. Alastor, Pari's boyfriend who looked like the epitome of a frat bro, brought coffee. Chepi, the quiet man who'd suggested murder the night before, brought coffee. Naida, a freckle-faced young woman, brought coffee. And just when she was about to barricade the door to prevent overcaffeination—an affliction she'd never personally experienced—Santa breezed through the door with... a cup of steaming coffee.

Merry had to laugh. The alternatives were to jump out the window and run until her addled brain settled or scream at him to let her work.

She set aside her half-empty cup and took the fresh one. "I think I'm good on coffee for today," she said, gesturing at her collection of mugs.

"How about help?" Without waiting for an answer, he dragged one of the guest chairs around the desk and sat so close that she could smell wood polish and snow. Someone would make a fortune if they managed to bottle that scent. "What are we doing?"

Merry gave him her best side eye over the lip of her mug. "Same thing I've been doing all week—taking the numbers from those papers and typing them into this spreadsheet."

"I can type. I took a class once. Which form of shorthand are we using? Up." He gestured for her to stand. "I'll type. You read them out to me." As usual, all his thoughts jumbled together and poured out of his gorgeous mouth in a nearly incoherent stream of consciousness. She hated that she found it charming.

"You read, I'll type," she countered.

"But then how will I learn the spreadsheet thing?"

Damn. He had her there. He did need to learn Excel, even if she wasn't sure how he'd managed to survive into his thirties without such a basic skill.

With a sigh, she switched chairs with him and resigned herself to accomplishing absolutely nothing she'd set out to do that day.

It took fifteen minutes to explain how to tab from one cell to the next. Most of that was spent googling how the tab button got its name, then listening to Santa explain how a typewriter worked. She had no frame of reference, but still thought he was making it up as he went along.

Finally, she started reading numbers from the first expense report… and was interrupted by two tall figures crowding the open doorway.

Pari launched into a tale of stolen chewing gum, gesturing wildly as she tattled on her sister. Fortunately, she was directing her tirade at Santa. He listened patiently, then ordered Rari to share with her twin.

With an eye roll any teenager would have been proud of, Rari reached into her mouth and pulled out a golf ball sized wad of chewing gum, bit it in half, and offered it to her sister. *Gross.*

Pari accepted it and popped it in her own mouth. *Even grosser.*

Merry kept her thoughts to herself.

The twins left, both apparently satisfied with the outcome of Santa's mediation, and Merry returned to the task at hand.

They managed three invoices before they were interrupted again. Another dispute between employees, this one over a borrowed paintbrush.

Six invoices. A fight over a stolen snack.

Merry gently but firmly closed the door behind the latest interruption. "Maybe that will hold them at bay."

"I doubt it," Santa said. "They always find me."

Merry huffed a laugh to hide her annoyance. He'd been the picture of patience with every seemingly miniscule issue.

The closed door worked for an hour. Santa hadn't lied about his typing class, and they made quick work of the invoices. Not as quick as she would have alone, but it wasn't much of a hardship to share the work.

A tentative knock sounded on the door and Santa called for the person on the other side to "enter." Merry pictured an enormous crown on his head and an authoritative order for the petitioner to approach the throne.

The person on the other side of the door was Addie, Faye's friend who Merry had never heard speak. He was alone, white as a sheet, fisting his hands in the cuffs of his threadbare hoodie.

Santa's voice was softer than Merry had ever heard it as he asked, "overwhelmed?"

Addie nodded and Santa opened the bottom drawer of his desk. Knowing him, Merry expected to see a bottle of liquor tucked away. Instead, he pulled out a blanket.

"Merry doesn't mind," Santa said in that same gentle tone. She wasn't sure what it was that she didn't mind but chose not to chastise him for speaking for her. Addie was clearly upset.

That was all Addie needed to hear. He darted across the room and dove into Santa's lap. Merry's eyebrows hit her hairline as he straddled Santa and buried his face in his neck. But there was nothing sexual about it, especially as Santa unfolded the blanket and spread it over Addie's head. He wrapped the smaller man in his arms and squeezed him tight.

Santa gave her a sad smile over Addie's head and whispered, "Sometimes there's too much movement and noise. He just needs a few minutes."

"Of course," Merry whispered back. Reasonable accommodations were important and if Santa was comfortable with the situation, she wouldn't be the one to argue. "Do you want me to leave?"

Santa shook his head so Merry quietly brought the laptop to her side of the desk and kept working, glancing only once at the shivering blanket next to her. Fifteen minutes later, the blanket stopped shivering and Addie stood, gave her a small smile and a nod, and left.

Even though he'd shut the door behind him, Merry still kept her voice quiet as she asked, "Does he need to go home for the day?"

"Addie's fine now. And he's allowed two fifteen-minute breaks." It was as close to snapping at her as Santa had ever gotten.

"I know that," Merry replied. "I was only worried."

"In that case, you can stop. You don't need to worry about Addie or any of the others. I have it handled. Where were we?" He pulled the laptop back to his side of the desk.

Merry was sure he wanted her to let the subject drop. She was also sure she couldn't do that. "You do, don't you? You know what everyone needs. You know who needs tough love and who just needs love. That's really great."

She sounded like an idiot, but how else was she supposed to say that her heart felt all gooey watching him take such good care of his friends? It had gone even meltier when he'd gotten defensive about Addie.

"I'm not sure I always get it right, but I try to listen to what they need. I don't want to be my father. He—" Santa cut himself off and shook his head.

"He isn't a good listener?" Merry prompted. She realized a moment too late that she was prying and added, "You don't have to tell me."

Santa glared at the computer screen with an uncharacteristically serious expression. "No. He doesn't listen to anyone he believes is beneath him. Like me. And my mother. And all my friends." He shook his head again. "Let's not talk about my father, duckie. It puts me in a mood."

"Sorry I asked," she said with an apologetic half smile. "He sounds like a dick, by the way."

"He is. And never be sorry. You can ask me anything. I'm an open book when it comes to you. Just maybe not that chapter. Yet."

He finally met her eyes, and his gaze wasn't filled with anger as she'd expected but hurt so deep that she couldn't look away. She reached for his hand, her own chest aching in sympathy. Her fingertips met only soft cotton.

She tore her gaze away from his and looked down, horrified to find her hand resting on his thigh. Very high up on his thigh. She yanked the offending appendage back quickly, but it was too late, Santa was also staring down at his leg. Grinning.

"I swear your hand was there a second ago," she defended, her cheeks already heating.

His father forgotten for the moment; Santa locked both his hands behind the back of the chair so fast they blurred in her vision. "If sad stories are what it takes to get you to feel me up, duckie, I have a thousand. Want to hear about my pet turtle? It died."

"Is it too much to ask for you to let it go, just this once?" she whined.

"Absolutely," he replied, his usual exuberance surfacing. It felt forced at first, but he quickly fell into the old pattern of teasing her about how they were destined for a future together. It should have annoyed her far more than it did.

Fortunately, teasing turned back into working eventually. Merry's stomach was growling, but she kept pushing through the pile of paperwork, hoping in vain that a skipped lunch would make up for the rest of the time she'd lost that day.

Midafternoon, another knock sounded on the door. Merry hoped it was coffee this time. And a sandwich. Faye pushed into the room with an arm splayed haphazardly across her face. "Are you naked?"

She wasn't even trying to cover her eyes.

"Of course not," Merry said.

"If that's what you thought, why did you barge in?" Santa asked.

"What kind of question is that?" Faye replied, finally lowering her arm. "To see you two naked, of course."

"I have a better question. Why would we be naked? This is an office. We are working," Merry said.

"It's two fifteen," Faye said, directing this unhelpful statement at Santa. "If you're not getting busy in here, then you have no reason to be so late. Jake is doing me a favor."

"Who is Jake? What is the favor?" Merry began the lengthy list of questions that had formed since Faye's entrance. When Santa started rushing around to gather her coat and gloves, she added a few more. "Where are we going? Why am I coming? Or are you planning to squeeze into my pea coat?"

"So many questions, love. I know I said, 'ask me anything' but I didn't expect you to ask me everything all at once."

Santa shoved her knit hat down over her ears and brought his bright white grin right into her personal space. He hesitated a moment, then trailed his fingertips over her jaw. She meant to argue. She really did. But her traitorous heart decided to flutter instead.

"My questions still stand," she said instead.

Ignore her feelings and they would go away. A tried-and-true method. Sure, it was often tried and rarely true, but past results were easy to ignore.

"And they will continue to stand until we get there. It's a surprise."

Santa steered her through a crowd of employees who were definitely not doing the thing they were employed to do, then out to his truck. He rushed her into the passenger's seat so quickly she didn't have time to remind him that he usually let her drive.

"Sweet Revenge" started playing as soon as he cranked the truck, and he smiled expectantly at her. Who was she to deny his puppy-dog eyes?

"You found the cassette?"

"Anything for you, duckie."

She rolled her eyes but a small, secret part of her was dangerously pleased. He wasn't playing Christmas music for once and, on top of that, he'd remembered this was her favorite John Prine album.

The half hour drive passed quickly. Santa sang along with the radio, his voice so deep and clear that the artist on the track sounded like backup. Merry resisted the music's pull for as long as she could but only made it to the opening bars of "Please Don't Bury Me" before joining her voice with Santa's. Quietly, of course.

But quietness wouldn't stand with Santa. He sang louder, forcing her to do the same, until they drowned out the prerecorded music and relied solely on memory and each other's voices to recreate the album.

His nervous energy was back in full force when they arrived at the town square. Merry still had a hard time believing this town was small and old enough to still be centered around the large, grassy field.

Except, it wasn't a grassy field anymore. Barriers—dripping in Christmas paraphernalia, of course—cut a perfect circle into the open space. A large sign announced an ice-skating rink open for one week only.

A stocky middle-aged man in a flannel shirt and work boots stood behind the ticket table next to a petite woman in a fluffy coat. He met Santa's eyes and nodded once before saying something to the woman beside him. She set off, clearly on a mission.

"We're going ice skating?" Merry asked in disbelief. The question was entirely pointless because Santa was dragging her across the square to the ticket table.

Christmas music blared from travel speakers powered by orange extension cords, but Merry only spared it a passing thought. She was too busy being confused and more than a little relieved. She didn't know him well, but Santa seemed like the kind of person whose surprises should make her nervous. In the grand scheme of things, ice skating wasn't so bad.

"It will be fun. I promise," Santa declared. "And don't worry, I won't let you fall. I'm an excellent skater."

Merry snorted at his cockiness but she didn't have time to do more than murmur, "of course you are" before they were standing in front of the flannel-clad ticket taker. Or ticket-giver. Ticket-seller?

The ticket man grumbled as he handed over two neon pink wristbands. "Took you long enough, my shift ended a half hour ago."

"Sorry, Jake. We got distracted."

The man—Jake—harrumphed at that. "Got distracted, huh? While I'm waiting around to break the law."

"It's an ice-skating ticket, not bank robbery," Santa replied with a forced smile.

"Tell that to Jo. She's already saying we're behind on ticket sales. I told her no one would come while the kids were still in school, but the rental price triples next week." He fastened the wristband around Merry's wrist without looking at her. "If all we can afford is a rickety old travel rink that none of the kids will even get to enjoy, I don't know why we bother."

"Why aren't we paying for tickets?" Merry whispered to Santa. Not quietly enough, though. She'd caught Jake's attention.

"He doesn't have any money, sweetheart." Jake told her. The affectionate term didn't have the same effect as when Howard used it. She thought Jake meant it in the Southern way—as an actual term of affection for a stranger. "No one in this town has money except Joy. Especially her employees. That's the way she liked it."

Santa cleared his throat. "You really know how to kill a date."

"Just don't think you should be leading the lady on," Jake replied. "You can't even afford to take her ice skating. It's better she knows now that you can't take care of her."

Protective instincts she didn't even know she had roared to life. "Money isn't everything," she seethed as she reached for her purse. "And just so you know, *Jake*, I have plenty for the both of us." Not entirely true, but she had some money stocked away.

She slammed the cash down on the table. Fifty dollars a person. Skates not included. Ridiculous. Maybe the cost was the reason they didn't have enough visitors to pay for the rink. But did they consider that? No. They blamed Santa for not having a hundred dollars to spare.

She rounded on Santa, her annoyance only banking a little. "And this is not a date. Did you bring skates?"

His smile was back. "Of course. I hope you and Siofra are the same size."

He hadn't just brought skates. The bed of his truck was piled with blankets, cushions, snacks, and a thermos of coffee.

"Not a date," he defended before she had a chance to yell again. "I just wanted to show you that living here has its perks. Me, mostly. But the rest of the town is nice too. Even Jake. You caught him on a bad day."

Her annoyance diminished the longer she looked at him. Damn it. He was cute when he rambled. All confidence and teasing and just a little bit of unease undermining his bluster.

"Thank you. I haven't been ice skating in years. I'm looking forward to it."

She could see the tension leave his shoulders and he went right back to teasing her.

He insisted on checking the laces of her borrowed skates while she ate every snack he'd brought, then holding her hand for their first lap around the rink. She was almost disappointed when he let go to show off. Skating backwards, a few spins. Nothing worthy of the Olympics, but he was graceful and enthusiastic.

She had so much fun goading him into more theatrics that she didn't notice the afternoon slip away.

CHAPTER 14

For the first time since she arrived in Poleton, Merry felt like she was accomplishing something. She and Santa had fallen to a rhythm organizing financial transactions and the day had passed in a blur of paper and clacking keys.

She cast a discreet glance sideways and marveled at the little crease between his salt-white brows. His long fingers moved with more confidence over the keys, but he still hadn't mastered navigating the spreadsheet without using the mouse. She hid her smile by shuffling papers in front of her.

The barrage of complaints and conversation had slowed from the day before to a scheduled interruption at the top of every hour. Merry didn't know what Santa had said to the employees, but it had been effective.

At five on the dot, Jeraltan pushed through the door wearing an oversized hoodie and a bright red athletic bandana holding his blond hair in check. "I'm going to be late for Zumba. Hurry up."

Santa turned to her. "I need to drive him into town, but I can help more when I get back."

She shook her head and smiled. "I think we've made enough progress for the day. But I would like to hear more about this Zumba class. Is it open to the public?"

"Yep," Jeraltan confirmed. "And I've heard from multiple sources that the instructor is extremely talented. And handsome."

"It's him," Santa confided in a whisper. "Don't agree with him out of pity or you'll become another of his 'sources.'"

Merry rolled her eyes. "I loved dancing with you on Sunday, I'm sure I would love your Zumba class as well. Mind if I tag along?"

"Not at all if you hurry."

***

As Jeraltan had predicted, and then re-predicted every five minutes since he'd asked for a ride, they were late.

Santa had changed quickly into converse and a hoodie after inviting himself, and Merry had rushed so much at the inn she'd forgotten socks, but the two stops had cost precious time. Jeraltan was practically vibrating as he hopped down from the truck. He rounded on Santa—not an easy feat for someone a foot shorter—and said "you have to promise to be on your best behavior. I'm the instructor. I lead the dances."

Santa held up his hands defensively. "I'll do my best, but you know how hard it is for me. I was born to be at the front of a room with all eyes on me and all people following my lead."

Merry snorted. "So humble."

"It's true," Santa argued with a teasing grin.

Jeraltan was less amused. "Let's just go."

The community center was a far cry from the gyms Merry frequented in California, but it had the same promising scent of disinfectant and sweat. A handful of older women formed a rainbow of track suits and orthopedic tennis shoes in the dingy room set aside for group classes. Their faces lit when Jeraltan entered.

"It was Santa's fault," he said by way of greeting.

"A little my fault too," Merry added with a smile and a wave. "I'm Merry."

A chorus of half-hearted welcomes met her introduction. These women must not have been fond of her grandmother either.

They were much, much more excited to see Santa—especially when he stripped out of his hoodie to reveal a cropped tank top that flattered biceps, abs, and everything in between.

Jeraltan also removed his outer layers until he was wearing cotton

90

leggings, leg warmers, and an oversized long-sleeved t-shirt with what appeared to be hand-painted letters saying "it ain't gonna lick itself." It took her a moment to notice the small candy cane beneath the phrase.

She laughed, already pulling out her phone. "Can I take a picture of you for the group chat? They love your puns."

"Is Graham in the group chat?" Jeraltan asked.

"Yeah. It's just me, him, Dee, and Charli."

Before Merry had finished listing the members, Jeraltan had gripped one sleeve and ripped it clean off and was working on the other. She'd never seen anyone do that outside of the movies and startled herself with a laugh.

Jeraltan's ministrations had revealed biceps as big as Merry's head.

"Subtle," Santa commented. Merry started to laugh again but it died in her throat when he narrowed his eyes at Jeraltan's outfit. "Too subtle. Mary Ann, do you have scissors in your knitting bag?"

Five minutes later, Santa and the older ladies had Jeraltan primped to their satisfaction. They had cut the shirt from the neckline to hem, showing obliques just as toned as his biceps. His bandana had been adjusted to better show his wavy blond hair, and someone had even pinched his cheeks to add a little color.

Barely keeping her laughter in check, Merry lifted her phone for the promised picture. She lost the battle against her giggles when Jeraltan struck a pose any fitness influencer would have been proud of paired with a bright, boyish smile.

The photo sent, over Wi-Fi of course, the group finally focused on the class that had brought them all together. Jeraltan put a CD into an old school boombox and "Welcome to The Jungle" blasted from the speakers.

"Oh, we're starting off big," Merry commented as they gathered in a circle around Jeraltan for an instructor-led stretch.

"It'll only get bigger," Santa assured her. "This isn't my favorite music, but it's a lot better than when Pari and Rari lead the class. They're oddly obsessed with someone named Nicki Minaj."

Their conversation was cut short by a dark look from Jeraltan. So far, the playful animosity between Santa and Jeraltan was more entertaining than the class itself.

Jeraltan led them through stretches, then they started the class in earnest to "We're Not Gonna Take It." Merry settled into the familiar joy of movement, letting the steady beat and familiar lyrics drive away her stress.

She followed Jeraltan through the next two songs, but it wasn't until the opening notes of "Pour Some Sugar on Me" that she felt truly connected to him and the music. Her lips tingled with the familiar lyrics a heartbeat before they played through the speakers. Her feet itched with anticipation of Jeraltan's next move. She felt Jeraltan at the front of the room and Santa beside her, expertly gliding through the steps and adding his own flair.

This was what she craved. Why she begged her friends to find time in their busy schedules for nights out.

The music bloomed in her chest and spread through her limbs. She bit her tongue to keep from singing, but it was no use. The lyrics exploded from her in a joyful tide, her feet deviating from the prescribed steps, and she danced the way the song deserved—with her whole body, whole mind, whole soul.

Jeraltan grinned and beckoned for her to come to the front of the room. She locked eyes with Santa and power flooded her as he followed her steps, grinning at her with the same all-consuming joy she felt.

She and Jeraltan led the rest of the class, but Merry couldn't spare any attention for the people who'd paid to be there. She had no room in her heart for anything but Santa and upbeat hair metal blasting through the speakers.

When they reached the end of the CD, Merry was pleasantly out of breath and full of energy.

Her enthusiasm had won over the ladies, and they laughed with her about the difficulty of her class. Santa passed her a bottle of water and she took it gratefully.

"You couldn't help yourself, could you?" Jeraltan said. He was a lot less happy than he had seemed when they were dancing.

Merry shook her head and grinned, sure his sour mood had more to do with the end of the class than her. "No. That was great! I always forget how much I love Zumba."

Santa smiled at her; his honey eyes alight with the same energy buzzing through her. "You really are one of us."

CHAPTER 15

Merry pulled the size 10, "mid-rise" cotton panties out of the package and stared. They were twice as large as she'd hoped—both in length and width.

Who decided that 6-pack underwear should use a different sizing method than pants? And were they dead? If not, Merry had a few choice words for him. Yes, she was sure it was a man who'd made that decision.

Like any rational person, she'd packed six pairs of underwear for a three-day trip, but it was Day Seven in Poleton and her trip to the local drug store hadn't yielded the results she'd hoped for. She turned the white cotton monstrosities this way and that, trying to find a solution to her granny panty problem.

Rolling wasn't an option since that wouldn't solve the issue of bunching under her rear. There was only one solution. She needed to find a laundromat and wash the few pairs of correctly sized undies she'd packed.

Merry pulled on her loosest sweatpants, tried to forget that she was going commando, and stuffed all her dirty laundry into the spare trash bag for the wastebasket of her hotel room. Santa arrived just as the bulging bag started to rip.

With a frustrated huff, she threw the door open. "Do you have a laundromat in this town or does everyone go down to the creek, beat their clothes with rocks, and hang them on trees to dry?"

To Santa's credit, he didn't balk at her sour mood. He just leaned against the doorframe, smiled, and crossed his arms like he was posing for a rom-com movie poster. "No laundromat, and the creek is frozen. You'll have to settle for the washing machine at our house."

"Great. Perfect. Wonderful." She picked up the bag, careful to cradle the ripped side, and followed him to the waiting truck.

"You seem... out of sorts this morning." He swung into the passenger's seat with entirely too much grace for pre-dawn and passed her a cup of coffee. "I thought you had fun last night."

"Sorry," she took the cup and glanced sheepishly at him over the rim. "I did. There's just always a day when I'm traveling that living out of a suitcase becomes unbearable. I don't have my stuff or my pillow or the clothes I want to wear. I miss home and that makes me crabby. Plus, I hate not having a car. You're already chauffeuring me around and making my coffee and now I have to rely on you for laundry as well." She shook her head, knowing she was being moody and not having a good enough excuse for it. "Just, sorry. Put on your music, I'll be in a better mood soon."

"You can be in whatever mood you want, duckie. I'm not complaining about getting to spend more time with you."

Merry drove one handed, unwilling to let go of the life-giving coffee. Further adding to the list of habits her tenth grade driving instructor would be furious about, she took her eyes off the road to glare at Santa. He was smiling softly, sorting through his cassette collection, not even bothering to look ashamed of hitting on her again.

She took another sip of coffee and let his flirtation slide.

He chose George Strait to fill the silence and Merry hummed absently to "All My Ex's Live in Texas." It was a little too country for her taste, but she was proving that she knew all the words by the second chorus. She could never pass up an opportunity to sing.

The mansion was quiet, with only a few bleary-eyed employees wandering the halls in search of caffeine. Her workout partners had slowed from an onslaught to a trickle as the novelty of her presence wore off, but that was fine with Merry. In fact, it felt more like friendship for them to keep to their normal sleep schedules and trust that they would see her throughout the day.

Santa turned from a one-sided conversation with Faye—he talked, she blinked sleepily then shook her head—and his usually sunny expression was pinched with something like worry. "Jeraltan has a headache. He's sleeping in," he informed her in a tone that let her know this was an unusual occurrence.

"And that's not okay because…?"

"You need him to wash your clothes."

Now, Merry's brow crinkled to match Santa's. Clearly, there was a disconnect in this conversation. "I just need to borrow your washing machine. I am fully capable of operating it without assistance."

"Are you sure? I don't know if I'll be able to help if something goes wrong," Santa replied. By all appearances, he was completely serious.

Merry nodded, and he showed her to the basement door. "Just how often do things go wrong when y'all wash clothes?"

"Never. Because Jeraltan does all the laundry."

Santa pulled a string and bare bulbs hanging from ceiling joists illuminated the small, overpacked basement room. Most of the space was stacked concrete floor to exposed ceiling with boxes bearing scrawled labels that made no sense. There was one just labeled 'Feather Boas 1983.'

Several doors led from the room, which Santa explained were bedrooms for the more unfortunate employees.

One corner of the open space was cleaner and brighter than the rest. The bulbs were outfitted with mix-matched shades and a collection of vintage washers and dryers from at least three different decades stood proudly against the wall. Above them, a hand-carved and glitter-painted sign read 'Laundry is Loads of Fun!' In front of that, a large wooden table on a base of shelving with neatly organized baskets sat on a shag rug.

Merry smiled at the homey little laundry corner. If anyone could make a space devoted to the most boring chore look fun, it was Jeraltan.

She crossed to the most modern of the machines and found it empty of clothes, so she dumped her meager belongings inside. On a hunt for detergent, she didn't notice Jeraltan's light footsteps until he was beside her.

"What are you doing, Merry?" His words were slightly slurred and one look at his face told her the reason. He didn't just have a headache. His face was drawn and gray, even his gold hair had lost its luster. A migraine, maybe? Santa looked as concerned as she felt and had his hand wrapped around the back of Jeraltan's neck, making soothing circles with his thumb.

"Washing clothes," she said softly out of respect for his headache. "Go back to bed, you look awful. Or do we need to take you to a doctor?"

"I'm fine," Jeraltan replied in the same slurred, thick voice. "I just need to do something productive." He reached for a glass canister of powdered detergent. It was empty and he opened a cabinet for a refill. The box was an organic brand and boasted that it was scent-free and safe for infant skin.

Her expression must have revealed her confusion because Jeraltan clarified. "We all have sensitive skin. Especially Santa. I hope unscented is okay with you."

"It's fine, but you need to go back to bed," Merry said as she snatched it out of his hands and held it hostage against her chest.

Jeraltan shook his head slowly. "No. I need to wash clothes and cook breakfast. That's how I contribute to our goal."

"What do you mean?"

"I'm terrible at drawing and carving and painting so the others make the toys, and I take care of them. That's how I make sure Claus Family Toys is successful." He made a clumsy grab for the detergent. "I need to do this. I need to contribute. Then, I'll feel better."

Merry swatted his hand away and waited for his dull, scrunched eyes to meet hers. "Your job is just as important as everyone else's. Don't let anyone tell you otherwise."

Jeraltan gave a pained half smile. "Thanks, Merry, but lies aren't the answer."

She refused to back down. "You're the one who knows how to use the fax machine. You're the one who sends the invoices and paperwork to the distributors. You answer their questions when they call."

"They never call," Jeraltan argued with another tired attempt at a smile.

"That's not the point. If they called, you would be there. If they had questions, you would answer them. A business can't have customers without good customer service. And a business can't make money without sending invoices and collecting payments. Without you, Claus Family Toys would have a lot of great products and not a single person buying them."

The buzz of the exposed bulbs, the hum of the heater, even Merry's own breath went silent for a long moment, like the air around them had stilled, the world had paused. Before she could come to terms with that momentary strangeness, it snapped, and normalcy returned. She glanced around the basement looking for… something. Some reason to explain the shift. But there was nothing but cardboard boxes, outdated laundry equipment, and her companions.

Jeraltan's cheeks flushed, first bright pink and then settling into their usual healthy pallor. Santa smiled, his hand still on Jeraltan's neck. "Merry's explanation was heard and accepted." He spoke so softly Merry wasn't sure if she was meant to hear.

Jeraltan smiled, a true smile without any of the former pain. "Thanks, Merry. Let's get your clothes finished."

She was too stunned to argue when he took the detergent from her. Something was strange. Wrong? No, just different. It was…

"Can we have breakfast before we work out? I'm starving," she said, her growling stomach underlining her words.

"Of course," Jeraltan replied cheerily. "And I'll make you more coffee."

Coffee sounded perfect. Food too. Thoughts of those two things occupied every spare inch of her mind, until there was no room to consider anything else.

CHAPTER 16

Friday morning, a week after she'd arrived in Poleton, Merry finally got a voicemail saying that her dad's truck was ready to be picked up. The independent side of her was glad that she'd have transportation again. But there was another part of her that was disappointed she'd have less time with Santa since he would no longer need to drive her around. Despite her best efforts to hate him, she'd grown fond of their car rides filled with music and easy conversation.

The garage didn't open until eight, so Merry dressed in her freshly washed athletic clothes and waited.

When Santa hadn't arrived by five, Merry was starting to worry. He had picked her up each of the last five days at exactly four thirty. She knew he'd probably just overslept but called the Claus Family Toys cell phone anyway. It went straight to voicemail.

She started to pace. Should she ask the inn's receptionist to drive her to the mansion? Or was that overstepping? Did she even have a right to worry?

A knock on her door interrupted her racing thoughts. She ran to the door and threw it open, but Santa wasn't on the other side. Instead, she found Faye with her hands in the pockets of a bright blue parka.

"Where's Santa?" It wasn't the right way to greet a friend, but she was too worried to care.

Faye shrugged. "Haven't seen him since last night. There's no need

99

to look so worried, though. He disappears sometimes. We lost him for a whole week a few years ago."

"Oh," Merry said.

Faye laughed at the memory and ushered Merry to hurry up and follow her to the waiting truck. Merry grabbed her bag and followed. As Faye slid behind the wheel, she continued. "He came back with a hickey and a motorcycle. He gave me the bike, so I didn't ask questions."

"Oh," Merry said again. What else was she supposed to say to that?

"Shacking up is unusual for him though. Normally, when we lose him, he just went walking and forgot to check the time. That's what he was doing when he met you."

"I see," Merry said. She really wasn't holding up her side of the conversation. "So, he doesn't normally do relationships?"

Faye gave a knowing smile but didn't mock Merry for her not-so-subtle inquiry. "Nope. He's slept with pretty much everyone in the house—and in town—at one point or another but never found anyone special."

Merry thought she had a healthy relationship with sex, so she wasn't quite sure why that information made her stomach turn.

Once they arrived at the mansion, Merry went through the motions of her workout. But her attention was divided between the treadmill and Celestra's long, graceful legs as she stretched on one of the yoga mats nearby. Had those legs caught Santa's attention? Melody was flushed as she did jumping jacks. Had Santa noticed how pretty her cheeks looked with a little color? Alvar's biceps bulged as he curled massive weights. When Faye said everyone… did she mean every *woman* or every*one*?

Jeraltan made breakfast after her workout and then Faye drove her to the garage. It was a few minutes before eight, but the door was unlocked. Merry entered the empty waiting area and sat down.

Muffled shouts from the garage drew her attention and she peeked through the 'Employees Only' door.

Wayne was a tall, stocky man with a thick black beard and grease-stained hands. He was by far the most intimidating person Merry had met in Poleton and he was currently shouting at a much thinner, though equally angry Santa.

"How many times do I have to tell you this is private property, not your personal garage!"

"I didn't use any of your tools," Santa argued.

"You still broke in and tore a paying customer's truck apart! How am I supposed to explain this to Ms. Claus?"

Merry cleared her throat and both men turned to her. She leveled a glare at the Cassanova of Poleton as she entered Wayne's private space. "What did you do to my dad's truck?"

Santa normally looked hippie-chic but this morning he was a mess. His hair was falling out of a messy bun on the top of his head, his clothes were dirty and stained, and he had a smear of something dark across one cheekbone. Despite all that—or maybe because of it—he was still the most beautiful man Merry had ever laid eyes on.

"I cleaned it up a little," he said sheepishly.

"Oh no, don't you pout at me," Merry said, trying to convince herself that his puppy dog eyes weren't working. "What did you do?"

Instead of waiting for him to explain, she walked over to the truck and peered through the open door. The carpets had either been replaced or expertly cleaned. The bench seat that had once had a hole in it was reupholstered in fresh black fabric with a sky-blue trim to match the truck's paint. He'd fixed the upside-down cap on the gear shift, replaced the headliner, and cleaned every surface to a shine. A familiar red rose sat on the dash above the steering wheel—the one she'd admired from his workshop.

Merry stepped back and looked up at him, sure her expression had softened despite her best intentions to remain angry. "Lean down you giant," she said, closing the space between them and pressing her hand to his chest.

Santa did as she asked and Merry kissed his cheek. "Thank you. That was very sweet, and you did an excellent job."

His face split into a grin and he started to talk animatedly about everything he'd done. Merry ignored him and lightly slapped his chest. "But I asked you not to do this." She moved to his bicep and slapped that too. "You have to listen when people tell you no, Santa."

She pulled away, but Santa grabbed her hip and pulled her back, his expression serious. "I am sorry," he said slowly, holding her gaze so she could see he meant it. "I should have asked you, but I wanted it to be a surprise." She was certainly surprised when he brushed his knuckles across her cheekbone. "I waited as long as I could, but it was making me crazy to think about you driving a truck with problems I could fix."

"It's my dad's truck," she reminded him. "I'm only borrowing it."

"I don't care if you never drive it again, I just wanted it to be nice for you," he said. He pulled her closer until their chests met. Her breath caught. She couldn't look away from his honey gold eyes.

A little voice in the back of her head reminded her that they had an audience, and he was her employee, and he was a flirt who'd slept with the whole town. But that voice was too quiet. Santa smiled, "So, please accept my apology and go back to telling me how sweet and wonderful and sexy I am."

Merry forced herself to laugh and step away. "I only said sweet. And now I have to go pay Wayne for the great job I'm sure he did fixing the brakes and whatever extra he thinks is appropriate to compensate him for dealing with you."

She turned her best 'please don't call the cops' smile on Wayne.

He shook his head, admitting defeat. "I've been dealing with Santa for years, Ms. Claus. There's not enough money in the world to compensate me for that or to get me to turn him away. We're all good."

Merry headed back toward the waiting area and the ancient cash register. She didn't think she was supposed to hear Wayne slap Santa on the back and mutter, "It's about time you settled down, but the boss' granddaughter? Good luck to you."

Her heart really shouldn't have fluttered.

She would be back in California in a little over a week and, even if she took control of the company, she would likely only see Santa for company meetings. There was no future for them.

Wayne was all business when he got behind the counter. He gave Merry a lengthy list of problems he had fixed. Something was leaking,

102

something else was worn out, and yet another thing was cracked. She tuned out the specifics since they meant nothing to her but nodded confidently anyway. Wayne didn't seem like the kind of person to recommend maintenance that wasn't needed, but it was always best to look like she knew what was going on.

The final bill took her by surprise at fifteen hundred dollars. Before she could accuse him of taking advantage of her, Santa thanked him for the discount and Merry deferred to his superior knowledge. She handed her credit card over without argument and Wayne passed her an itemized receipt—which she still planned to confirm with her dad, despite Santa's opinion that it was fair.

The bell above the front door jingled and Wayne's beard shifted to accommodate his smile. Merry turned and snorted when she saw Jeraltan in a fuzzy blue sweater bearing the image of a cute polar bear and the phrase 'I ♥ Bears.' He was carrying a plate of iced Christmas cookies that smelled divine.

"Would anyone like a cookie?" he asked cheerfully. In a quiet voice that reminded Merry of fine print he added, "they're one dollar."

She dug around in her purse and came up with a twenty. "I take it you don't have change," she said as he tucked it in the back pocket of his white jeans. She took a cookie anyway and one bite told her she hadn't overpaid.

"Why are you swindling townspeople? You should be at work," Santa said.

"So should you," Jeraltan replied. He offered Wayne a cookie with his cutest smile. The big mechanic took it and opened the cash register to bring out a dollar. "And if you must know, I need more minutes."

"We just bought you more minutes," Santa said. "You're only supposed to have the phone for two hours a day."

It took Merry far too long to remember that prepaid cell phones existed and that they sometimes measured value in minutes.

"Yes, but text messages use minutes too. Not just talking," Jeraltan whined. "You can't expect me not to tell my boyfriend good morning."

"You mean Graham? You two are still a thing?" Merry asked. She'd thought the flirtation would fizzle out when Graham's shyness became evident, but she was happy to be wrong.

"Of course!" Jeraltan said. "Why? Did he say we weren't? Wayne, can I use your phone to yell at my boyfriend?"

"No, he didn't say that. I haven't talked to him," Merry said quickly. "No need to yell. I just didn't realize you were still dating."

"We are," Jeraltan confirmed vehemently. "And I didn't get to see his suit this morning because I ran out of minutes! The picture wouldn't come through. I have no idea which tie he's wearing and it's killing me. *Killing me*, Merry!"

"Oh, well we can't have that," she replied dryly. She pulled her phone from the side pocket of her purse, connected to Wayne's Wi-Fi, and handed it over.

Jeraltan abandoned his cookies on the counter and gently tapped the screen with an index finger. "Phone…contacts…search…" he muttered like he was reciting instructions.

A moment later, Graham's voice filled the waiting room. "Marshmallow! I tried to call you earlier."

Jeraltan bolted for the front door, taking Merry's phone with him.

"Graham Cracker! You wore the blue tie. It looks so good on you. But it would look even better wrapped around—" she was saved from the end of that sentence by the closing door.

He paced animatedly outside the building, going as far as the Wi-Fi would stretch.

"Marshmallow?" Merry mused. She'd never heard Graham use a pet name for anyone. She'd also never heard him sound so excited to talk to another person.

To her surprise, it was Wayne that offered an explanation. "No one can resist Jeraltan." He sounded almost sad, even as he reached for another cookie.

***

A half hour later, Merry finally got her phone back and headed to Target with a promise to buy Jeraltan more minutes. The closest one was nearly an hour away, so it was fortunate that cell reception returned as she left Poleton.

The holiday crowds were subdued since it was a weekday, but parking was still a hassle. Inside, she found more underwear to avoid another laundry debacle plus some casual and athletic clothes that would help her feel more comfortable in Poleton.

She made her way to the electronics section and found the prepaid phone cards. Depressing thoughts of the ancient flip phone the employees shared, and a conveniently placed sale sign convinced her to buy a new android instead—for Graham's sake. He shouldn't have to only see his boyfriend through grainy flip phone pictures.

But minutes were still a problem.

She considered adding Jeraltan to her phone plan and getting him unlimited talk, text, and data. But that would mean either keeping the employees on her phone plan forever or having to remove them if she didn't inherit the company. Neither of those were great options.

Another sale sign caught her eye, and she had a solution. For seventy dollars, she could buy Jeraltan a tablet. The whole town ran on Wi-Fi, so it would be as good as a phone in Poleton. She grabbed one and hesitated, thinking of all the other employees. They would either fight over the single tablet or resent Jeraltan for receiving special treatment. Plus, they'd all been so happy to borrow her phone and listen to music.

With a sigh, Merry began loading her cart. This trip to Target was going to cost her a lot more than she'd planned.

But her new friends were worth every penny.

CHAPTER 17

Merry called Henry from the road and asked if she could stop by to set up the new tablets at his house. He agreed easily and even said Dottie would put on a pot of coffee for her.

She called Graham next.

"I have a client meeting in twenty minutes, talk fast."

"Tell me I'm your favorite person," Merry said.

"You bought Jeraltan more minutes? If so, yes, you are my favorite person."

"I did better than that. I bought a tablet for every department of Claus Family Toys. Since he's the only person in reception, that means he has his own. You can talk to your little Marshmallow whenever you want."

"A tablet? I should have thought of that," Graham said. "I was going to add him to my phone plan, but I didn't want to scare him. That seems awfully permanent after five days, you know?"

"I do know, and I thought the same thing. You seem to really like him."

"I do," Graham said. "He's so smart and funny and strong. I can't imagine going through what he has and still being so positive."

"What do you mean?" Merry asked.

"He grew up in a cult. He hasn't told me much, he doesn't like to talk about it, but from what he's said there were two tiers. The dicks at the top who did nothing but boss everyone around and the people like Jeraltan who had to do whatever they said. There was no technology. At all. They didn't even have running water. Apparently, he and his roommates escaped a few years ago."

"That's why they don't know anything about the internet," Merry said. The pieces were coming together. "I thought it was something like that, but I was hoping for 'commune' not 'cult.'"

"Yeah. He didn't use the word 'cult' but that's the impression I got. I'm just glad Santa got them all out. Still feels weird saying that. You know I mean the Santa that works for you and not the mythical one, right?"

Merry laughed. "Yes, I know you don't mean a fat man in a red suit." The rest of what he'd said sank in. Santa got them out. He'd saved all of them and somehow brought them to Poleton where they'd gotten jobs they enjoyed. It didn't surprise her that he'd been the one to free them, but it did make her smile.

"I almost wish you hadn't told me about the cult thing, now I feel bad for buying off brand tablets. I should have gotten them all iPads," Merry said.

"Yes, you should have. So I could FaceTime my boyfriend instead of sending him a Google Meeting request like some sort of sexy business deal."

"Didn't need the word 'sexy' there," Merry told him. "But it's too late to turn around now, I'm almost back to Poleton. What's Jeraltan's favorite color? I got different cases."

"Red," Graham said without hesitation. "I'll Venmo you for his."

"Oh no you won't," Merry said. "If you pay for his, it destroys my whole 'one per department' thing and they'll fight like cats and dogs."

"You talk about them like they're children, Merry. You have to buy for all or none. They'll fight otherwise. They're grown adults."

"I know that," Merry said. "I'm not saying they're children, I'm saying they treat each other like siblings. If you and Deirdre still lived in the same house and shared everything, you'd fight exactly like you did when you were kids."

"Fine, that's true. But I still want to pay for his."

"I bought a lot of stuff, I'm sure there is something you can pay for that benefits everyone. He'll think you're even sweeter if you take care of his whole family."

Graham agreed and they talked for a few more minutes about which apps to add to the tablets and who should get what. He had to go to his client meeting right around the time Merry's service cut out.

She parked in front of Henry's house, and he rushed out to help her with the bags. Waiting by the door again. Just like a grandpa should. Merry grinned as she told him about her haul.

Dottie made cookies to go with the coffee and Merry was actually having a nice time while setting up devices. It had to be the first time she'd thought that in her life.

"It's so nice to see gifts for all those young people," Dottie said. She had pulled an enormous box of holiday wrapping supplies out of a closet and was tying bows for each of the gifts.

"That's true," Henry agreed. "Joy bought them things, but she was never happy about it. It's good to see you caring for them."

"I do care about them," Merry said. "I know I've only known them a few days, but they wormed their way into my heart quickly."

"Some wormed deeper than others, didn't they?" Dottie said with a knowing smile.

"You mean Santa," Merry said. "We're just colleagues."

"Sure, sweetie. I've known that boy all my life and I've never seen him so smitten."

"You mean you've known him since he moved here," Merry said.

"He's always lived here. The others too," Dottie said.

Merry stopped what she was doing to look up at the elderly woman. "You mean they grew up here?" Someone had their wires crossed. Either there was a cult in Poleton that Merry didn't know about or Jeraltan had lied to Graham.

"Grew up here? No. I don't remember knowing them as children. They've just always been here, right Henry?" Dottie said. She sounded as confused as Merry felt.

"I don't remember them moving here... but I don't remember..." Henry said. A deep wrinkle had appeared between his brows. All of a sudden that wrinkle disappeared. "Who wants another cookie?"

"I do," Dottie said. She, too, seemed to be over her momentary confusion. Merry smiled indulgently and nodded. She couldn't fault them for memory problems at their age.

Surely, what Graham had said was the truth. It was the only logical explanation for their eccentricities.

***

Jeraltan bounded down the front steps and was already asking about his minutes when Merry opened the truck door. She had Graham on FaceTime so he could watch the gift opening and put her phone in Jeraltan's hand. He walked away, too absorbed in saying hello to notice the truck bed full of gifts.

The rest of the employees were more observant. Siofra's shout of "Merry brought presents" called all one hundred and four of the mansion's residents to the courtyard.

Merry watched Santa hold them all at bay with a few strong words and laughed as he turned to her, tiptoeing with excitement just like the rest of them.

"Let's take them inside and split them up," she suggested. She might as well have said 'on your mark, get set, go' for the effect it had. They rushed down the stairs and carried the boxes of gifts into the ballroom.

Inside, Merry took her time studying the tags on the pile of gifts, relishing the impatient groans of her employees. She lifted the first one and said, "this one is for the design department." Faye bounded forward to accept it but waited to open it until everyone had theirs.

"Carving department," she said, pulling the next gift from the stack. Santa was at her side in half a second reaching for the candy-cane printed box. She slapped his hand away playfully. "Not you, let someone else open it."

"But I work in the carving department," he whined, turning his best puppy dog eyes on her.

"You're the foreman. You don't count as part of a department," Merry told him. Knowing she had a surprise for him was the only thing keeping her from falling victim to his pouting again. Honestly, how did a grown man manage to look so adorably pathetic?

"Okay," he said, his shoulders slumping as he handed the gift to Siofra.

She was glad she'd chosen to wrap everything individually. The employees were much more eager to open gifts than even she'd anticipated. Was this why people loved Christmas so much?

She had a tablet, case, Bluetooth speaker, stylus, keyboard, three sets of headphones, and a Google Play Store gift card for each department. The accessories had all come from a 'ten dollars and under' bin, so she wasn't sold on the quality, but they would do for now.

Santa looked close to tears—and not the happy kind—as he watched all his friends open gifts while his hands remained empty. Merry slipped a final box in front of him.

His face lit up and he tore into the wrapping with the ferocity of a golden retriever swallowing a dropped hot dog. His tablet was the same as the others, but she'd sprung for a sage green leather case rather than the brightly colored rubber ones the rest of the crew had. He lifted his new cypress green Bose speaker triumphantly.

"Don't tell anyone but I got you the nicest one they had."

"It's green! I love it," Santa said. He swept Merry into a bear hug that pressed the speaker into her back since he was unwilling to let it go. The hug was quick, and he stepped back to show her the gift card. "What is this? Can I buy music with it?"

"I'm not sure," Merry said. "I know you can buy movies, games, and apps. But I put Spotify on your tablet, you don't have to pay for music. You can play any song you want for free."

"Any song?" he confirmed. "Like on your phone?"

"Yes and yes. I thought you'd be most excited about that part," Merry said. His joy was infectious, and the excitement of the other employees was the cherry on top.

Jeraltan's voice rose above the others. "It has a camera! Can I video chat with you?"

"Yes," Graham said with nearly as much enthusiasm as his boyfriend. "I had Merry put a messaging app and a video call app on there. They should be good to go, if she did it right."

"I can hear you," Merry shouted at her phone across the room. "And of course I did it right."

The tiny image of Graham's face raised its eyebrows, and she supposed it was time to share the thanks with him.

"Did anyone not get to open a present?" she asked.

Half the room confirmed in forlorn tones that they hadn't gotten to unwrap anything.

"Graham sent gifts too," she said, stepping aside to reveal another box.

A crowd rushed toward her, and she started handing out more gifts. "Who wants to open the big one?"

"Me!" Jeraltan said. "He's my boyfriend, I get to open it."

There were enough small gifts for the rest to open that Merry didn't argue with him.

The small boxes held candy and popcorn. Pari opened the box containing a projector and immediately tried to trade it for a bag of M&Ms. "That projector is for the whole house," Merry told them. "So you can watch movies together. It's kind of like the one I brought for the presentation the other day." But much less expensive since she'd charged it to her personal rather than business credit card.

Jeraltan opened the big box holding the projector screen and Merry said, suddenly nervous, "I thought we could have a movie night tonight, if you want."

Her nerves were unwarranted because they quickly agreed and insisted that she join them—not just for technical support, but because they wanted her there.

***

"Raise your right hand if you want a movie with romance, your left hand if you want something funny," Santa said.

Hands went up all over the room.

It had been four long, tedious, loud hours since the Claus Family Toys staff had agreed to a movie night. Empty candy wrappers littered the floor between bean bag chairs, cushions, pillows, and blankets. The entire mansion smelled like burnt kettle corn.

"Stand on your left leg if you want to watch something with action, stand on your right leg if you want to watch something scary, and pat your belly if you want to watch something sad."

Merry giggled deliriously as she spotted a few employees trying to follow too many of Santa's instructions. It was almost midnight, well past her bedtime on a normal day. It felt especially late after the hectic week.

"But you already said sit if we want to watch something animated," Jeraltan said. "How am I supposed to sit and stand on my right leg and stand on my left leg and raise both hands and pat my belly?"

"You're supposed to pick one type of movie," Santa said.

"But *The Lion King* is all of those things!"

"We're not watching *The Lion King*," the rest of the group chorused.

"I'll watch it with you later, Marshmallow," Graham said from the tablet his boyfriend was holding.

"Merry, you haven't voted," Faye said. "What do you want to watch?"

"*Lord of the Rings*," Merry answered. "I've always had a thing for Legolas and his tight little pants." She must be tired, that was a completely inappropriate thing to say to her employees.

Santa quirked an eyebrow at her. Now that she thought about it, he reminded her a little of her favorite character but with darker skin and prettier eyes. There was something about the way he moved that carried the same ethereal grace Peter Jackson had tried to convey for the elves.

There was a collective groan. "We've already seen that one."

"How can you possibly like Legolas when Aragorn is right there, opening doors?" Faye demanded while still patting her belly and standing on one leg.

"I'm not saying Viggo Mortensen doesn't dirty up well but have you seen Orlando Bloom in that wig, come on," Merry shot back. "How do you not want to bite his pointy little ears? He's an elf. Aragorn is just a guy. Mostly."

"Interesting," Santa said with a delighted smirk. In fact, none of the employees seemed to mind that she was being more casual with them. "Merry bought the tablet, she gets to pick the movie."

"If that's the rule then Graham gets a vote too," Jeraltan put in. "He bought the projector. Tell them what you want to watch, sweet cheeks."

"How about the first *Thor*? It has action, it's funny, it has romance, there are hot guys for Merry to ogle and hot girls for those who prefer ladies. Plus, it will get you started on the Marvel universe."

"Yes, please. Idris Elba as Heimdall is perfection. Pass me the tablet, I'll pull up the trailer," Merry said.

Graham's laugh distracted her from her task. "Go to sleep, Merry. You only talk about hot celebrities when you're two seconds away from passing out."

"I'm fine," she argued and pulled up the trailer, pointing out the most underappreciated hottie for the rest of the group each time he came on screen.

They quickly agreed to the movie, which was a miracle given the length of their previous arguments, and she started it.

She sat at the front of the group on a couch cushion someone had brought from the living room. Santa sat beside her, wrapped in a pink throw blanket and fully engrossed in the movie. She enjoyed his reactions more than the movie itself. But by the time Chris Hemsworth slammed down his coffee cup and demanded another, Merry was struggling to keep her eyes open.

Santa looked over at her, probably because she was the only person not laughing. His eyes softened and he disentangled himself from the blanket. The next thing she knew, he was sitting behind her, pulling her against his chest and wrapping the blanket around both of them.

Merry tried to protest but he shushed her and whispered, "I've got you, duckie. You can sleep."

She shouldn't. She really shouldn't. But she nuzzled into the side of his neck. Her eyes closed as she breathed in his scent of wood polish, cedar, and snow. They didn't open again until he was tucking her into an unfamiliar bed.

CHAPTER 18

Merry woke between seafoam green sheets that were soft with age. The room she'd slept in looked like something out of a period movie. Heavy, ornate furniture against soft cream walls outlined by dark wood molding. It was definitely not her room at the inn. And she was definitely not wearing her pajamas. She pulled back the covers far enough to see a forest green t-shirt and flannel pants.

The door creaked open, and Santa peeked his head in. "You're awake," he said with a smile. He pushed the door open and entered, carrying two cups of coffee.

Merry eyed him skeptically, still too sleepy to rationalize why she was in his bed, wearing his clothes.

"I slept in the living room," he told her. "And you dressed yourself. You don't remember?"

A hazy memory of falling asleep in his arms watching an action movie resurfaced and Merry blushed. It wasn't as bad as she'd originally thought, but it wasn't great.

"Sorry, I guess the time difference and the busy week got the better of me. I didn't mean to kick you out of your bed."

"You could have been sleeping here all week if you'd made good on your promise to take me to dinner," Santa said as he sat on the side of the bed and passed her a cup of coffee.

"I don't recall making that promise," Merry said. She felt more awake the moment the coffee touched her lips.

"Recollection doesn't matter. You proposed a bargain the night we met. You told me to stand in front of your truck and if I survived, you'd take me to dinner and buy me something pretty. I declined an official agreement, but I still expected you to uphold your promises. Though, I guess the speaker counts as something pretty, so you're halfway there."

Merry shook her head and took another sip of coffee. She'd need the whole pot to find a way to say no to him. "It would be inappropriate for us to date since I might own the company where you work."

"You don't own it yet," Santa said. "And if we go to dinner and you are properly charmed—which I expect you will be—then we will already be dating when you take over. Problem solved. Scoop me up now before I'm against the rules."

"Idiot," Merry muttered, smiling against her mug.

"Not a very nice thing to say to your future husband. Have you been listening to those mean songs again?"

She ignored his commentary. "Shouldn't you be taking me to dinner, not the other way around?"

"How entirely sexist of you, duckie. Plus, you remember what Jake said, I don't have any money. You'll have to wine and dine me, I'm afraid."

Merry gave in, like she knew she would. "I can do that. But you pick the place."

Santa beamed.

***

Merry lay across her bed at the inn, willing herself to get up and go to the office. There were still papers to be sorted and files to be transcribed into a comprehensible spreadsheet. Instead, she reached for her phone and called Deirdre.

"I did something bad," she said as soon as her friend answered.

"Does that bad thing happen to look like Jesse Williams cosplaying as Geralt of Rivia?"

"Yes," Merry said. "I told him I'd take him on a date."

"Was that before or after the sex?"

116

"There was no sex! Agreeing to the date was the bad thing."

Deirdre sighed. A moment later she shouted, "No, she's still deciding. Let me deal with this existential crisis and then I'll do the dishes." She listened to her wife's reply and then relayed it to Merry. "Charli says, 'just do him already' and I agree."

"You are really the worst HR manager in the world. How can you say that? I'm going to be his boss. There's a total imbalance of power."

"Yes, but—"

"No 'but.' It's wrong. I have to cancel."

"BUT," Deirdre said, "there are degrees to these things. You're not abusing your power. You don't even have any right now. And if you did, you would never make business decisions based on personal feelings."

"I'm leaving in a week," Merry argued. "It wouldn't be fair to start something now."

"Graham is happy doing long distance. Plus, you have enough airline miles to fly back and forth every day if you wanted to."

"It's wrong, Dee. There are rules for a reason."

"He knows exactly what he's getting into. Don't throw away the only guy other than Simon I've seen you have actual feelings for because some HR person wrote a rule to keep interns from sleeping with each other in the breakroom."

"And CEOs from harassing their employees," Merry reminded her, ignoring the jab about her office rival.

"Are you harassing him?"

"No."

"So, you're not a CEO and you're not harassing anyone. What's the problem?"

"I... I think you should have followed Graham into law. You're making me question myself," Merry said.

"There is not enough money in the world to get me to do what he does. Oh, and if we're done with your love life, I'd like to know where Rosie's toys are. You've had plenty of time to ship them."

"Santa's working on them. He said the first ones 'weren't good enough for Deirdre's daughter.' You'll have to imagine the air quotes. I'm definitely doing them."

"That's sweet. And at least he knows better than to send me inferior products. Nothing but the best for my baby girl."

"Fine, fine. I'll go check on his progress now. But even without seeing them I can tell you they will be perfect."

Like him.

CHAPTER 19

Saturday was too soon to get a reservation at the only nice restaurant in town and everything in Poleton closed on Sundays so Merry had to wait until Monday for her date with Santa. She couldn't spend the entire day worrying about it because Quinn finally got back to her about a meeting. Because the jerk couldn't seem to do anything that didn't make Merry's life worse, he asked to meet at 4:30 on Monday afternoon.

Merry went alone to meet him. She had enough practice meeting powerful people that she rarely got nervous anymore. Quinn wasn't nearly as scary as the CEOs and board members she usually met with, but she was still much more anxious about this meeting than any of those.

In the past, she would embarrass her boss if a meeting went poorly. A strong motivator but not nearly as strong as the one she currently faced. If she failed in this meeting, she would let her friends at Claus Family Toys down. That wasn't an option.

She was halfway to Quinn's house when her phone rang, and she saw Simon's name on the screen. His comforting emails claiming he had everything under control at the office had grown shorter and less detailed over the past few days, so Merry answered immediately.

"I lost the Blue Arrow account," he said, not bothering with a greeting.

Merry ground her teeth to hold back her curses.

It didn't work.

"You changed my pitch, didn't you?"

"Of course. You were overpromising like you always do."

"I do not overpromise. I promise the exact amount I can deliver. You just play it safe."

"I don't play it safe. I live in the real world where 70% more risk isn't worth it for the possibility of 5% more return."

"You're making those numbers up."

"Like you did with your entire presentation? Every other slide had a note to 'look into this and add data.'"

"Which is what I expected you to have my team do! Not completely scrap my plan and pitch the exact same boring ideas our competitors offered."

They went back and forth for the entire forty-minute drive. She was passing the *Welcome to Red Bay* sign when Simon finally cracked.

"Fine! Fine. You win. You were right. You're always right, Merry."

She was shocked into silence. In their entire working relationship, Simon had never given up in the middle of a fight.

"Mike wants to meet with me to discuss my performance. Tonight. At seven."

Her heart dropped somewhere near her toes. "You'll be fine. Just kiss his ass like you always do. You'll be the golden boy again tomorrow."

"No. I won't." He swallowed audibly. It sounded painful. "This was the fourth straight pitch I've lost and three of my clients dropped me."

"Shit." She wasn't sure what worried her more, those troubling results or that Simon had shared them with her.

"Yeah," he agreed in the same tight tone. "If this meeting doesn't go my way, I just want you to know that you've made me better. Every time I feel like giving up and going home after fifty hours, I see you work sixty and it motivates me to stay. I thought I was keeping up with you, but after doing your work for a week, I realized I'm not even in the same ballpark. I don't know how you did all of this. I've spent more of the past week apologizing than working."

Just when she thought this conversation couldn't get any stranger, he said that. Silence stretched across the miles between them, and she felt every too fast beat of her heart.

Simon was her biggest rival at the firm. He brought in nearly as many clients and was fantastic at making sure the higher ups knew it. He couldn't just leave the firm. Without him…

"And, of course, if Mike just wants to yell at me for a while, then you can ignore everything I just said," he concluded with a rough laugh.

"He's not going to fire you," Merry said. Simon couldn't leave. She wouldn't let that happen. "Blue Arrow was always a long shot. And you're doing the work of two people, of course you're behind. I'll take care of it."

"There you go again. You'll *take care of it*. Even I believe you. No wonder your clients are antsy without you here."

"I'll take care of it on one condition. You have to stop with the compliments. They're freaking me out," Merry said with a huff of a laugh that did nothing to calm the fluttery feeling in her stomach. "Go back to hating my guts. I need this rivalry, Joker, or I'll never be Batman."

"At least tell me I'm Heath Ledger's Joker and not Jared Leto's."

"If that makes me Christian Bale then yes, you can be Heath Ledger," Merry said.

"Deal."

Merry hung up with her long-time rival and immediately called her contact at Blue Arrow. There was no time to waste on reliving the strange turn of events that led her to almost friendly terms with Simon.

The phone rang several times and Merry briefly wondered if she would have to leave a voicemail. It wouldn't be nearly as effective as a full conversation. But Ralph picked up with a sheepish "Hi, Merry. I guess you heard we went with Holstrom and Wade."

"I did," Merry said in her most soothing voice. "It would be hard not to considering Wade is your CFO's brother-in-law. I just wanted to see how things went with Simon, he's filling in for me while I'm away."

"Simon did well. His presentation was thorough, and his ideas were fine. He just doesn't have that spark that you do. The vote was close. If you'd been the one to speak to the board, I think we would have gone your way."

"Thank you, Ralph. And thank you for the opportunity to let our firm pitch our ideas. I wish we could work together, but I understand why you went with Holstrom. They're a solid firm."

Ralph made a noise that might have been an agreement but not quite. Good, he was still open to another option. "I saw your email, I'm so sorry to hear of your grandmother's passing. How are things going with her company?"

Merry smiled at the windshield. It was exactly the question she'd been waiting for. "I've been here ten days, Ralph, you should know me well enough to know we're projecting a twenty percent profit next year."

He whistled low. "Ten days and you've grown profits by twenty percent? That's impressive, even for you."

Merry's smile broadened. "Not by twenty percent, to twenty percent. There was a small loss last year but I'm righting the ship."

"Wow. Just wow. What industry did you say it was again? Logging?"

"Not quite, we make hand carved, hand painted wooden toys. You'd be surprised how many people are still willing to pay for expert craftsmanship. We had over twenty-five million in revenue last year and the latest projections show that increasing to thirty-five next year." They were her projections, based on nothing but hope, but still.

"You are truly something special, Merry. If I didn't know you so well, I'd think you were pulling my leg. I'm sure you'll do a case study on that company. When you finish, send it my way and I'll share it with the partners. If you can make a profit with wooden toys, I can only imagine what you'd do for us."

"I'll do that," Merry said, grinning. This conversation was going exactly as she'd hoped. Now she just had to cut it off before he asked too many questions. "I've got to run but keep a look out for a package from Claus Family Toys. I know how much Serena loved that Rubik's cube you got her; I want to see what she thinks of our puzzle boxes."

"Oh, absolutely!" he said. "She will love that. My little genius will figure it out in no time."

Merry got off the call as quickly as she could. She'd solidified their friendship, reminded him why his company should hire hers, and set up a reason to follow up in a few weeks to check on his daughter's progress with the puzzle box. One slight misstep from the consulting firm they'd hired and Merry would be at the top of their replacement list. It was the best she could do for now.

Quinn's house came into view with a shiny red Lexus parked in the driveway but Merry had one more phone call to make.

"You're supposed to be on vacation," Mike said.

"Yeah, yeah. You know I don't do vacations," Merry told her boss. "I just talked to Ralph at Blue Arrow."

"Simon really screwed that up."

"It was always a long shot," Merry reminded him. "We were competing with the CFO's brother-in-law. Ralph said the vote was close and he will keep us in mind for anything else they need. He wants a case study of what I've been doing in North Carolina."

"You mean the company you're selling?" Mike said.

"I'm not selling," Merry said. "That's what I wanted to talk to you about. I want to stay on and run my grandmother's company."

"You're leaving us?" Mike demanded. "After everything we've been through. All the opportunities we've provided for you."

He was winding up for a long list, so Merry cut him off. "No, I'm not leaving. I can do both. In fact, I want to hire our company to consult on the running of Claus Family Toys."

Mike was silent for a long moment, then he said, "You want to hire me to hire you to run a company you already own?"

"Yes," Merry said. "It will be great for the firm. Imagine the commercial. A cute little town, a feel-good product, a family connection. Plus, outstanding results. I'm thinking 'if this is what I can do for my family's company, imagine what I can do for yours.'" Thanks for the tagline, Ralph.

"I like that," Mike said hesitantly. "We could use some good PR. But I'm assuming you want to be compensated for using your company for marketing."

"Of course, I do," Merry confirmed. "I'm thinking it will be the difference between my salary and the fee the firm would charge for consulting."

Mike gave a bark of laughter. "You're something else, Merry. Get some results there and we'll talk about it. How long would you need?"

"Six more weeks now, then two weeks a quarter."

"One additional week now and three days a quarter. And those days count as your PTO."

"Four weeks now, one week a quarter that doesn't count as PTO, and I'll keep working with my other clients while I'm here."

"Get the results and I'll consider it."

"That's the plan, boss," Merry said. "And I'll need Simon to cover my meetings while I'm here. As much as it pains me to admit it, there's no one better."

Mike harumphed. "We'll see about that. I'm not sure he will have any availability going forward."

"I hope you aren't considering firing him."

"And I hope you aren't presuming to tell me how to manage my team."

"I wouldn't dream of it. I was just thinking about how noncompete and nonsolicitation agreements are unenforceable in California. If we leave…" Sometimes threats were best left unfinished. Especially when she was bluffing.

She wouldn't actually leave with Simon. Would she?

The pause was so long Merry had to double check that the call was still connected. "Did you say *we*?"

"Sorry Mike, I've got to run and wrangle a distributor. I'll take over all my duties that can be handled virtually starting tomorrow morning. If you need me in the meantime, you know how to get me."

Merry ended the call, pushed her flight out another week, and looked up at Quinn's monstrous house. It all hinged on this meeting. Her grandmother's company, her reputation with her current job, her future.

She'd thrown all her chips into this pot.

No pressure.

CHAPTER 20

Quinn was far from the nerdy accountant-type she'd met before. This time he was practically gleeful as he led Merry to his office. That did not bode well.

"I'll cut to the chase. We will be ending our current arrangement," Merry told him as she took the seat he offered. "Since you won't have any product to sell, we will buy the Amazon store you've established as a gesture of good will."

Quinn laughed. "A gesture of good will? No. You're offering to buy it because it is the only link anyone online has to your company. You don't have a website, an online store, or even social media accounts. You need this presence and the reviews I've accumulated to have any sort of reputation."

"We don't need it," Merry said. "But we would like to have it, yes. It's of no use to you without our products."

"That's where you're wrong, Merry," Quinn said with a gleam in his beady eyes. "No one knows the name Claus Family Toys, but they do know Quinn Worldwide. And I have thousands of product reviews to prove it."

He opened his laptop and turned it to face Merry. It showed a product page for a red train set with over three thousand reviews. "I've done you a favor by buying your products for so many years. I can have another 'red train set' made for a tenth of the price." He scrolled down to the fine print below the description and pointed to a spot halfway down the table of details. "All I have to do is change this little box from 'Manufacturer: Claus Family

126

Toys' to 'Manufacturer: Somewhere in China.'"

"Do that, then," Merry said with more confidence than she felt. "We'll open our own Amazon store. It isn't difficult."

"No, it's not difficult to open a store but it is difficult to get sales. Especially if I undercut your prices. Who would choose to buy a train set at one hundred and sixty dollars from a seller whose name they don't know with no past sales or reviews when they could get one for one hundred and fifty from someone that they know with three thousand five-star reviews to back up their reputation?"

"I see," Merry said. Her voice shook with barely contained anger. "I've dealt with enough men like you, Quinn. You don't want to go through the work of sourcing new products. This is nothing but a prelude to you telling me how much you want for the Amazon business."

He laughed again and the sound made Merry's vision go as red as the toy train still staring at her from the screen. Santa had made that one, she could tell from the exquisite detail.

Quinn had taken enough from Santa and all the others. He was the reason they worked seventy-hour weeks and still worried they weren't doing enough. She'd never been a violent person but, in that moment, she wondered how hard she'd need to smash his face into the monitor to ensure he never laughed at her again.

"Since you're so keen to 'cut to the chase' as you said. I took the liberty of working with an appraiser to value my business." He passed a sheet of paper to her with an unfamiliar company's letterhead. "I want ten million. That buys you the Amazon store and all the reviews. A foothold on the internet to build from."

Merry stared at the zeros in the number. She'd been prepared to offer five hundred thousand. It was all the cash she had, including her retirement accounts. She couldn't pay ten million without a loan or access to her grandmother's accounts—neither of which she could get until she dealt with Quinn.

She hummed like she was considering the offer. One thing she'd learned from working in a male dominated industry was that some men looked at her pretty clothes, wide eyes, and long hair and saw a pushover. An easy target. So, she let them underestimate her. That way, they were never prepared for her next move.

But this time, she didn't have a next move.

"I'll send this over to my contacts and we'll see if there is a number we can both agree to. Thank you for your time, Quinn."

Quinn followed her to the front door, puffed out and prancing like the world's most boring peacock. Her racing heart told her to run far away from the mess she'd made but Merry kept her chin high and her pace steady as she made her way across the driveway to her truck. Looking confident was the only revenge she could muster at the moment.

She drove five minutes before tears blurred her vision and she pulled over into an abandoned gas station parking lot. Her dad answered on the second ring, and she heard many overlapping voices in the background. "Are you okay, pumpkin?"

"I'm sorry," she said through her tears. "You're at work. I didn't mean to bother you."

"I am at work, but you're not bothering me. What's wrong?"

Merry didn't bother to hide her frustration. She told him everything, including how unprepared she'd been walking into that meeting. "I don't know what's wrong with me. I never would have made a mistake like this for one of my clients. But now I've put everything on the line for this and I screwed it up. *I screwed it up*, Dad."

"You didn't," he told her in the calm, steady voice that had always brought her peace. "You haven't agreed to anything yet. You got blindsided, so you stepped away to regroup. That's good. Now, regroup."

"How am I going to face them? They all trusted me to fix this. I told them I would. And now I have to tell them I messed it all up."

"Merry," her father said in the voice she imagined he used with insubordinate employees. "You didn't mess anything up. The only thing that has changed in the last hour is you learned what you're up against. I've never known you to back down from a fight, pumpkin. Don't start now."

"It's never mattered this much," Merry told him. "I care about these people. So much. I know I've only known them for a few days, but they matter to me. I don't want to let them down."

"You won't. You're going to cry it out where none of them can see, you're going to go back to your company, put on a brave face, and let your employees know you can handle it. Then, you're going to handle it. I believe that with my whole heart. And if you need backup, I'm only three hours away."

"You're in the middle of an outage. I couldn't ask you to leave."

"There is not a job in the world that would keep me from you. I think you can take care of this on your own, but if you need me, I'll be there."

"Thanks, Dad. I can handle it though. Go back to work, I'll need electricity to do it."

He gave a little chuckle that was more worried than amused. "I'll call you later, sweetheart. I love you."

"Love you too, Dad."

Merry sat in the truck for a while longer. She knew she had no reason to cry, but the tears kept coming. She'd dealt with worse men and far worse situations before. This should be nothing but a small setback.

But then she pictured Faye's face, grinning as she walked into the design department and announced that they could make more creative things next year, since a product flop wouldn't tank the budget.

And she pictured Jeraltan bringing her hot cocoa with whipped cream and a cherry just as a midday thank you for bringing them into the conversation.

Then there was Santa. He'd been so relieved that his friends' jobs were safe. How could she tell them all that it might take a few more years to be profitable?

Under promise and over deliver. It was the first piece of advice Mike had given her when she started as a consultant. She'd thrown it and everything else she'd learned out the window when it mattered most.

She wasn't ready to face her employees, so she stopped at the next gas station she saw and bought a bag full of candy and a pint of ice cream. She ate it in an empty parking lot.

CHAPTER 21

Merry pulled into the inn's parking lot at eight fifteen, feeling slightly sick from all the sugar but a little better emotionally. At least until she saw the two-tone pickup truck parked out front and the handsome white-haired man leaning against it tapping furiously at a tablet.

Oh no.

No, no, no.

She'd gotten so caught up in feeling sorry for herself that she'd forgotten about their date.

Santa looked up and saw her, relief spreading across his face. He ran to her as unselfconsciously as he did everything else.

She barely had the door open before he was wrapping her in a hug. "You're okay."

"I'm sorry," Merry said. The tears she'd managed to keep at bay for the last hour resurfaced as his tweed sport coat scratched her cheek. He'd dressed up. Like her *Intro to Philosophy* professor, but he'd still dressed up. "I'm so sorry. I forgot about dinner. Just give me five minutes to change and we can go."

"Absolutely not." Santa pulled back and wiped the tear from her cheek with the pad of his thumb. "Duckie, what happened? Why are you upset?"

"Quinn is being a bigger jerk than I expected," she told him. There was no use in delaying the inevitable. "I'll fix it, I just need a minute to wallow."

"Okay, come inside. If you can show me how to use this stupid tablet, I'll call the restaurant and order us food to go. We'll eat and plot his demise. Or if you're not ready for plotting, I'll sing to you until you feel better."

"You're not mad?" she said. "I should have predicted this. I should have been ready for anything he threw at me. And I definitely shouldn't have forgotten about our date."

"Oh, I'm mad. Very mad. I'm not sure exactly what I'm mad about yet, but I'm sure it's not directed at you."

Merry followed him into the inn and told him about the meeting with Quinn.

"You know I don't know anything about the internet. I couldn't even figure out how to call you. So, you'll have to back up a little bit and explain why this Amazon thing is so important," Santa said. He was sitting cross-legged on the floor, and she sat with her back against the footboard. Both of them seemed to know without speaking that the bed was off limits. That left only the questionable hotel carpet.

Merry racked her brain for a way to explain twenty years of internet evolution. "Imagine Amazon as the biggest shopping mall in a city and each seller's account as a store. Each store has a big sign out front with their products, prices, and numbers showing how many people are happy they shopped there. Quinn's store has been there for fifteen years, and his sign looks really great."

"Okay, I understand that."

"Now imagine we open a store next door. No one knows who we are. Our prices are higher than his and we don't have any numbers to show that people are happy they shopped with us."

"So, we put up signs saying why we are better than him. Our signs can say 'Quinn's a jerk.'"

Merry shook her head. "We can't do that. We can only put up signs inside the store to say why we're better—those are the seller description and product description. But most people don't come inside to see them because they're already next door."

"We won't sell anything online? He'll take all the customers?" Santa asked.

"Not all of them. Some people will come inside and see our descriptions, or they'll like our pictures better, or they'll be local and recognize our brand. We can make a website, run ads, sell other places. But all those things take time and money. It's not that we won't be successful selling online, it will just take longer than what I originally said."

"That's why you were so upset. You think you made us a promise and Quinn is preventing you from keeping it," Santa said, and his eyes softened.

Merry nodded. "I never get attached to clients like this. I stay objective, that's the whole point of hiring an outside consultant. It's never my job to care about the people, only the business. This—caring about all of you—is new for me."

"We care about you too," Santa told her. "That's why no one will be mad when we tell them it will take longer. Quinn has been a problem for years; we just didn't know it. Now, we know, and we just need to come up with a plan to fix it."

"Yes, and to do that, we need Charli."

"Deirdre's wife?"

"The one and only. She's the best marketer I know."

"Can we call her now or is it too late?" Santa asked.

"Too early, actually. With the time difference it's only six there. That's dinner time for Rosie. We can call her after bedtime, so that gives us an hour and a half. Are you hungry? We can go get dinner. Probably not at the place we planned but there's Ida June's on Main Street."

"See, I knew talking about it would help. We have a plan. Dinner, talk to Charli, sing karaoke, save the company."

"You're not sneaking karaoke into tonight's plans, but I will buy you dinner. Especially since you look so handsome in that jacket." Her cheeks heated as she said it. Flirting didn't come naturally to her, and she hadn't had many chances to practice over the past few years.

Santa grinned at her and straightened his lapels. "I thought you'd never notice. It's very itchy."

"So, take it off." His grin widened and she realized her mistake. "Dang it, that's exactly what you wanted me to say. Do not start with the 'always trying to get my clothes off, duckie.'" Her impression of his voice was terrible, but he laughed anyway.

"You see straight through me. Let's go. You can buy me an ice cream sundae before you start taking my clothes off."

"I just said don't start," she grumbled as she stood and grabbed her coat.

A half hour later they were back in her room with a massive bag of takeout—most of it for Santa. He'd ordered a cheeseburger, two types of fries, a salad, and dessert. Merry nibbled at her fries, still full from her earlier meltdown-fueled binge.

She'd sent Charli a text asking for a 'non-emergency phone call ASAP'. Clearly, she hadn't conveyed the non-emergency part well because Charli called her during Rosie's usual bath time.

"I said not an emergency," Merry said as Charli's freckled face came into focus. She was wearing a t-shirt with a faded band logo and sitting in her home office.

"But you also said, 'possible job opportunity' so I let Deirdre handle bath and bedtime."

Charli had started her own marketing firm six months before and business was slow despite her previous success at a large agency.

"Hi, Charli," Santa said. He was gathering his considerable supply of food and ferrying it next to Merry. When he got situated, Merry made the introductions and explained their situation.

"So, this human turd only sells on Amazon? That's fine, we can get a website up in a few weeks and start running ads on Google. You'll get more business there anyway with a niche product."

"I considered that first," Merry said. "Margins would be way higher selling direct, but we don't have the warehouse space or staff to ship thousands of toys per month. Normally, I would say hiring would be the easy part but, in a town this small, there isn't exactly a line of people looking for warehouse jobs."

"That's tricky. I can look into other ecommerce platforms that offer those services. But our first step is getting a website. Very few people are willing to pay a premium for a product that they can't get any information on."

"Agreed," Merry said. "I have a few more ideas to run by you in the meantime."

Santa was surprisingly quiet, letting Merry take the lead. Now that she had someone to bounce ideas off and some real food in her belly, her hopeless mood had lifted. She was in full problem-solving mode.

"We could offer better bulk discounts for distributors to encourage them to buy more. That would take some of the burden off online sales."

"Yes. From the pricing information you gave me, I'm surprised anyone is willing to buy with such tight margins," Charli said.

"Okay. I'll look into pricing strategies and get back to you on that. I can also contact more distributors. There have to be some that are outside the box. We already sell at Mast General stores but think more like that."

"That would be good for brand recognition as well as immediate sales. How long would it take to cross train the carvers to make something other than toys? I'm thinking Christmas decorations like those tabletop winter towns but made of wood."

"That's a question for Santa. I know he can make anything, but I don't know how versatile the others are."

"Oh good, I was starting to think I was here just to feel stupid," Santa said with a self-deprecating grin at Charli. "We can make anything you want. I have a room full of cast offs right now if you want to see any of them."

"Yes, let's look at those. And would you be willing to put your face on any of them?"

"My face?" Santa asked, surprised. "Like a carving of my face? I've never tried a self-portrait."

Charli laughed. "No. Would you be willing to be the metaphorical face of a new art department. You're hot. I can sell that."

Deirdre chose that moment to breeze into her wife's office. "What exactly have I walked into, darling?"

"Just me trying to sell handsome men in-store and online."

"Ah, as long as it's omnichannel that's fine." Deirdre plopped down in her wife's lap so she could see the phone screen. "Hello, my dear friend and her boy toy. What are we talking about?"

"Boy toy," Charli said. "Write that down. It goes with my sex appeal angle."

"Let's reel in that angle. We make toys, remember? For children?"

Santa was preening as if the entire conversation wasn't demeaning. He scooted a little closer to her. "I like marketing meetings," he whispered in her ear.

"You only like them when we're talking about you," she whispered back. He shrugged.

"Stop being adorable and fill me in," Deirdre demanded.

Merry told the story for what felt like the thousandth time. She'd already told Deirdre most of it, but the latest conversation with Quinn warranted a full discussion.

"You should call Graham. Mergers, acquisitions, and assholes are his thing. I'm sure he has a few tips for talking this Quinn person around."

"He's on my list," Merry said. "I just called Charli first to see how upset I should be if we don't get the Amazon account."

"Short answer: moderately. Enough to toilet paper his house, not enough to set it on fire."

"Those are terms I understand," Santa said. "Though, I'm still in favor of setting it on fire since he was rude to Merry, and he's been stealing our work for years."

"Wait," Merry said, something niggling at the back of her brain. "You said that the other day too, but I was too distracted to think about it." She pulled up the Amazon page and scrolled through the product description, a relieved smile spreading across her face. "Charli, I'll call you back."

She hung up and turned to Santa, "You brilliant, beautiful man. Do you have a key to the office?"

"I would break down the door if it meant you'd say that again. But, alas, I do have a key."

CHAPTER 22

Three cups of coffee later, Merry sat on top of a rusted file cabinet and watched Santa flit around the records room like a nerdy dragonfly. Her talents lay in numbers. His, by all appearances, were better suited to words.

"You should have been a lawyer," Merry told him.

His black slacks were covered in dust and his jade green oxford shirt was rolled at the sleeves. He would have looked like a character from *Suits* if it wasn't for the dozen tiny braids with gold beads holding his hair back.

He didn't hear her. "Sections 11.2 and 11.3 cover the copyrights, trademarks, and patents. We need those documents."

Merry just shook her head and watched him work. Legal documents made her eyes cross, but Santa had no problem deciphering all the 'hithertos' 'notwithstandings' and seemingly random capitalization in the distribution agreement. He'd even held his own on the video call with Graham, a Stanford educated lawyer.

Santa was elbow deep in a file cabinet labeled '1967' when he suddenly stopped and turned to her. "Are you tired? I forget other people need more sleep than I do. I can find these papers and bring them to you in the morning."

"It's already morning," Merry told him. "The rest of the staff should be here in less than an hour."

"Then we have time for pancakes," he said with a grin. The overhead lights illuminated the dust kitty stuck in his hair and Merry hopped down from the file cabinet to fix it.

"How about a shower first, then I'll buy you all the pancakes you want."

His eyes seemed lit from within when he tilted his head down to look at her. "My shower isn't very big, but we can make it work."

She slapped his bicep to distract from her blush. "Alone, you idiot. You have dust in your hair."

His hand slid around her waist. "You're so mean to me, duckie. First, you cancel our dinner date. Then, you cancel our shower date. Am I ever going to get to kiss you?"

"I—I'm sorry about dinner." Merry's heart was beating against the bars of her ribcage. A bird ready to take flight.

He brushed a strand of hair away from her face and let his fingertips trail across her cheek. She must look awful. She hadn't showered or changed since the morning before and, ugh, she hadn't even brushed her teeth. This was not the time for a first kiss. "A joke, darling. I have all the time in the world, and I'll spend it waiting for you."

Merry turned away, partly because she couldn't look at the earnest expression any longer and partly because she didn't want to subject him to her coffee breath. "I bet you say that to all the girls. Faye told me you have… history with a lot of them."

"Just passing time until I found you," he crooned.

It was so clearly a line that Merry should have had something clever and biting to say in response. Instead, she smiled like an idiot, keeping her face turned away so he wouldn't see.

"You'd better hurry and change if you want those pancakes. I'm going to go do the same."

**

After breakfast with Santa, Merry retreated to her office. Even though she had a plan for dealing with Quinn, she wasn't ready to face her employees and their questions about her previous meeting with him.

Her concentration was broken a few times by cheerful friends stopping by to say hello. It was a touch too much to be normal and she wondered if Santa had encouraged them.

Her stomach was starting to remind her that she'd missed lunch when an inhuman shriek made her jump and spill her coffee. She ran to the reception desk in time to see Jeraltan sprinting toward the door. With his oversized sweater billowing around his arms, he looked like a flying squirrel. The likeness only grew stronger when he jumped with his arms outstretched and wrapped himself around a man in a sweater vest and Clark Kent glasses.

"Graham?" Merry asked, astonished.

No one heard her over Jeraltan's excited, "you're here, you're here, you're here."

Three more figures pushed inside the office behind Graham—Deirdre and Charli with their hands on their daughter's shoulders.

Deirdre shook her head at the very warm greeting between her brother and his boyfriend. Merry was surprised she didn't shield her daughter's eyes.

"I think he decided against a handshake," Charli mused.

"I don't think Graham got a say," Deirdre countered.

Merry didn't bother trying to puzzle out what they were talking about, she was already moving to hug her friends. "What are you doing here?"

"You needed help, so help is here," Deirdre said.

Merry's eyes filled with tears, and she squeezed her friend harder. "You flew all the way here? I thought you had plans. Pictures with Santa, baking cookies, decorating ornaments. You had a whole special Christmas month planned for Rosie."

"What's more special than visiting a toy shop in a snowy little town?" Deirdre replied. "She'll remember this forever."

Merry couldn't believe how lucky she'd gotten.

She watched Jeraltan sweep Graham off his feet and carry him out the front door. From the astonished smile on Graham's face, he felt as lucky as Merry did.

Santa slid an arm around her waist, and she made the introductions. He greeted both Deirdre and Charli with hugs before inviting Rosie to tour his workshop.

The little girl was gleeful as she took his hand and skipped forward, Merry and her friends following a step behind. At least two of her friends. She didn't want to think about what Jeraltan and Graham were doing.

Santa had made wooden foods and cooking tools to complement Rosie's current kitchen. He'd also made an entirely new kitchen—complete with walls, appliances, and cabinets to store them in.

"Sorry," she whispered to Deirdre and Charli as Rosie darted around the child-sized room they definitely wouldn't be able to fit in their apartment. "He doesn't know how to do anything halfway."

"It's sweet," Dee said.

"And really well-made," Charli said, already assessing the rest of the half-finished toys. "I can sell this. Not only can I sell this, I will feel good about selling this."

"Thank goodness. Because we need you. So much. Please save me from the endless list of marketing acronyms I don't know." Merry was exaggerating and they all knew it, but Charli only rolled her eyes instead of calling her out. "How long can you stay?"

"Two weeks. We fly back on the twenty-sixth."

Merry would have preferred to keep them forever, but ten days was a start.

CHAPTER 23

It took a day to coax Graham out of Jeraltan's bedroom, prepare their arguments, and get Quinn to agree to a meeting. Of course, Merry let Quinn believe they were prepared to agree to his terms. Because of this ill-conceived belief, Quinn agreed to come to them.

Merry took a deep breath and studied her reflection in the mirror while Bryce Savage assured her that she was a 'bad chick.' She looked it in her black turtleneck, blazer, and red bottomed pumps. Santa slipped inside her room at the inn and laughed. "I thought this music motivated you to exercise."

"ABBA won't get me in the mood to slay my enemies," she replied.

"Fair enough. As long as it's Quinn you're hyping yourself up to kill and not me, I can live with this terrible music."

Merry laughed and paused her 'get psyched' playlist. "You sure you want to be there?"

Santa hadn't bothered to dress for success. He wore head-to-toe brown leather so rough it looked like tree bark. Interesting choice, but Merry chose not to question it. "If you're triple checking that I can keep my mouth shut for five minutes, then the answer is yes. If you're asking if I want to be there to watch you save us all, then also yes. I already know you're incredible Merry, I can't wait to see you prove it to Quinn."

"Don't get too cocky," Merry replied. "He's a devious nerd with no morals. I wouldn't put it past him to keep fighting just to make this difficult for us."

Even without his usual green, he looked every inch the quirky Tinkerbell and his smile was nothing short of vicious. "He won't make anything difficult for you again, duckie. I swear it."

With that final vote of confidence, Merry was ready to take on Quinn. Then, finally, she would take Santa on a date.

***

Merry, Graham, Henry, and Santa sat across a thick wooden table from the jerk wearing an ill-fitting suit and a cocky grin. Out of sheer arrogance, Quinn hadn't brought a lawyer.

"Thank you for agreeing to meet with us," Merry began and nearly laughed when she caught Santa muttering something unintelligible and shooting a death glare at Quinn out of the corner of her eye. She managed to keep it together and continued. "There are just a few things we need to clear up."

"Of course," Quinn replied, his grin still firmly in place.

Merry pulled a thick stack of yellowed papers from her briefcase and one newer document. She pushed that one toward him. "This is your distributor agreement. I had Henry look it over and we decided to call in a legal consultant as well." She nodded at Graham. "We found a few interesting lines that I've marked for you."

She pointed at the first flagged line. "Here you agreed to act as a middleman between Claus Family Toys and the general public, providing online sales of Claus Family Toys products according to the procedures laid out in the *Distributor Policies and Procedures Manual*." She flipped to the next page and pointed to another flagged line toward the end of the document. "And here you agreed to do nothing that would jeopardize the goodwill associated with product design, trademarks, and the Claus Family Toys name."

Quinn's brows scrunched together as he looked over the marked lines of text. "I have done nothing to harm your business. And this contract expires at the end of the year. On January 1st, I am free to do as I please with my Amazon store since it will no longer sell your products."

142

Merry nodded in agreement. "That is true. What I am concerned about is the final line I've marked." She flipped the page again and read, "'Distributor agrees to pay reparations if the terms of this contract are broken according to an independent assessment by a third-party expert.'" Both Henry and Graham had agreed that the line was an odd one, but fortuitous, nonetheless.

"I've done nothing wrong!" Quinn burst out. "I listed Claus Family Toys as the manufacturer of the toys, I held to my part of the agreement. You won't strong-arm me with your fancy lawyer."

Graham pulled the *Distributor Policies and Procedures Manual* from the stack of papers. It hadn't been updated since the mid-80s, but he'd assured her that it was still valid since Quinn had been given a copy.

"I'm consulting, not acting as a lawyer, but even in my current capacity I can read. Page seven, paragraph four says, 'The Brand name, all applicable trademarks, and taglines will be clearly visible in any display.' As you've said, you mentioned Claus Family Toys as the manufacturer, not the brand."

He pulled out a screenshot of Quinn's Amazon seller account and pushed it across the table before continuing. "Here, you've listed Quinn Worldwide as the brand." More screenshots, this time of the product images and descriptions. "You were provided photos of the toys to use in your product listings. Each of those images included the box labeled 'Claus Family Toys'. You chose not to use the branded images. Then, we can see that you neglected to use our trademarks and slogans in any of your product descriptions."

"Those photographs were taken using a camera from 2002. I took higher quality pictures that better displayed the products, as was my right," Quinn argued.

Graham nodded without a hint of emotion on his face. Merry once again had to stop herself from laughing. She'd seen this man twerking to Beyonce on more than one occasion, drinking tequila out of no less than a dozen belly buttons, and belting out Celine Dion on road trips. He had no right to look so professionally intimidating now.

"You intentionally left the brand name out of the photos, the description, and mislabeled the products under your own brand. It is my recommendation that Henry sue you for the goodwill you so graciously had calculated by a third party," Graham concluded.

Quinn sputtered something unintelligible, his face going red and splotchy. He turned to Merry, seething. "You set me up! You're twisting everything I've done to squeeze money out of me."

"We discussed privately and are willing to accept one million dollars, full ownership of the Amazon seller account, and a signed agreement that you will not sell competing products for a term of ten years," she replied.

He huffed, furious white patches appearing between the red on his cheeks and neck.

"I wanted to take you for all you're worth," Henry interjected mildly. "You took advantage of Joy. You took money away from her hardworking employees. As far as I'm concerned, you couldn't find your way through an open doorway with your moral compass. But Merry is kinder than I am."

"A million dollars?" Quinn repeated. "And my business? I'll have nothing left."

Merry laughed for the first time in the meeting and it had nothing to do with amusement. "You made tens of millions off my grandmother's naivete. You have enough money to fund your lifestyle until you find another elderly woman to screw over."

Quinn's face had gone eerily white, but his neck was redder than ever. He'd come to this meeting expecting to leave with ten million dollars and a profitable business. Now, he was leaving either with a lawsuit or a lighter wallet.

"Fine."

Merry's heart soared. She hadn't been sure it would work.

Santa surprised her by slamming his hands on the table and leaning in close to Quinn. There was a manic gleam in his eyes that reminded Merry of molten gold, and it was only the more terrifying combined with his trickster's smile. She was so startled that she didn't move to pull him back.

"You'll deliver the check in person to us at the Bank of Poleton in four days' time. Then, you'll spend the rest of your miserable life as the impotent, fangless, snake you truly are. Do we have a bargain?"

"Yes. I've already agreed. There is absolutely no need for this level of animosity." Quinn tried to sound confident, but his voice had gone squeaky.

Merry pulled Santa back with a hand on his arm. She knew people had a tendency to go overboard during their first corporate victory, but this was too far. Then again, it was Santa. 'Too far' was not a measurement he knew.

After signatures on the documents Graham and Henry had prepared and strained but polite handshakes, Quinn left looking tightly wound and more than a little bewildered.

Merry turned to Santa and couldn't help but laugh at his wild grin. "I think I'm good at this business thing. You should promote me."

CHAPTER 24

Henry pulled Merry aside as the others filed out of the conference room. The elderly man had a twinkle in his eye as he said, "I was very impressed with how you handled this entire situation. You've put the employees first at every turn. Protected them. Befriended them. And you've done it all with a poise and professionalism that your grandmother would have admired."

Merry's chest constricted. She had come to Poleton certain that she would never take over a company in the middle-of-nowhere North Carolina. But in two short weeks, she had fallen in love with the town, the people, and even the company. It was beyond gratifying to hear that she lived up to the lawyer's expectations, even if he was exaggerating her success.

Henry continued. "I know that your grandmother wanted you to stay here for six months, but I believe that the spirit of her request was to give you time to build a bond with the company she loved so dearly. You've done that. So, I am comfortable passing the company and all your grandmother's assets to you."

"Thank you," Merry replied, surprised to find unshed tears thickening her voice.

"No, thank you, Merry. I have always been fond of the team at Claus Family Toys, and I am thrilled to be leaving them in such good hands. I brought the initial paperwork so we can get started immediately." With a chuckle, he added, "Now that Santa has set such an aggressive timeline, we'll have to hurry to get things sorted. Fortunately, I have a friend in the local probate office."

Merry snorted at the mention of Santa's antics. "He took it a little far, didn't he?"

"I'm not sure he knows how to do anything halfway," Henry replied with a fond smile. Merry smiled because she'd said the exact same thing to Deirdre.

He beckoned for Merry to join him at the conference table and pulled innumerable sheets of legal documents from a tattered briefcase.

The first document he passed to her was short and handwritten. The lettering was old fashioned cursive, all slanting lines and smooth transitions. It reminded Merry of the photos she'd seen of the Declaration of Independence, though with fewer flourishes.

Merry,

In exchange for ownership of my company, you agree to make no changes to current employment agreements for a term of five years, except as required by law or voluntary separation. You also agree to retain the spirit and purpose of Claus Family Toys.

I hope that this time will open your eyes to what I aim to accomplish and the choices I have made.

Sincerely,

Joy

"Is this legally binding?" Merry asked dubiously.

"No, but she insisted I have you sign it anyway," Henry replied.

With a shrug, Merry signed her name on the appropriate line. A zap of energy flowed through her, like a dozen cups of coffee taking effect at once. Her mind went fuzzy as the feeling drew in from a tingling in her fingertips to a weight in the center of her chest.

She shook her head to clear it. By the third shake, she'd forgotten the strange feeling and moved on to signing the rest of the papers.

Henry had already signed his own name, so the process was fairly quick. Merry was certain Graham would berate her for skimming the documents without proper time to vet them, but she was eager to be finished.

Within half an hour, the paperwork was signed and all that was left to do was have the probate office verify everything. Then, of course, the tedious process of having accounts transferred and renamed, plus the headache she imagined it would be to take over a company. And taxes. She would definitely owe those.

Henry was confident that she would be able to deposit Quinn's check in the Claus Family Toys account when the time came, so the rest was a worry for another day.

***

Santa and Graham—and, of course, Jeraltan, who was eavesdropping during the meeting—were waiting for her when she left the conference room. Henry patted his briefcase, winked at Merry, and took his leave.

She quickly explained the delay and all three of her friends broke into ear-splitting grins. Santa, not to be outdone by Graham and Jeraltan's heartfelt congratulations, swept her into a bear hug and spun her around until she was laughing with him. He paused and she forgot their audience as her gaze caught his. She felt breathless and it had nothing to do with the tightness of his embrace.

"We did it," she said lamely.

"You did it, you smart, beautiful, terrifying creature. I am so proud of you."

She slapped his bicep lightly as a segue to less blush-inducing topics. "Speaking of terrifying, we're going to have a talk about professionalism later."

He kept smiling, unperturbed by her threats. "I look forward to it. But first, we must hasten to the party!"

"You're such a dork." Merry's laughter turned to a squeal as he tossed her like she weighed nothing and caught her in a bridal carry.

"Just so you know, we would have planned something bigger if we'd had more time to prepare," Jeraltan said as if it was completely normal for Santa to carry people away from important meetings.

Graham shook his head, a besotted expression on his face as Jeraltan

148

swung their interlocked hands and rambled about the upcoming party.

CHAPTER 25

If this party was 'thrown together at the last minute' Merry shuddered to think what her employees could do with more time. Twinkling lights, thin silver streamers, and wooden snowflakes covered the walls of the ballroom. There was a disco ball hung beneath the chandelier (and attached by an orange extension cord that looked like a fire hazard) plus several piñatas. Tables with an artfully haphazard assortment of tablecloths and centerpieces dotted the space. Against the far wall, the projector was displaying the lyrics to music played at a volume reminiscent of Merry's distant clubbing days.

The best part of the party was the people. Her new friends from Claus Family Toys shouted their excitement and her old friends rushed to hug her.

Deirdre and Charli had brought some of her clothes from home and she'd decided on a green backless dress with a pleated skirt that made her feel like Marilyn Monroe when she twirled.

She wasn't the only one who'd dressed up. Graham was, unsurprisingly, wearing a boring charcoal suit with no tie. Deirdre and Rosie wore party dresses and Charli had gone with sleek black trousers and a collared blouse. It was easy to spot her California friends among the local guests, as the locals were all dressed to the nines, but on a scale she wasn't quite sure of. Some wore long gowns, others miniskirts. Some bared all the skin they could legally show, others were covered from neck to ankle. They were as delightfully mismatched as the decor.

Merry smiled as Graham headed toward her, pulling Jeraltan by the hand. As the shorter man left the crowd of people he'd been speaking with, his idea of formal wear became apparent. Tight leather pants and a fuzzy pink sweater cropped to show toned abs.

Santa appeared at her side and all the other party guests faded into the background. He wore something akin to a vest but made of green and gold silk that dipped between sculpted pecs. His white hair was a magnificent array of braids and gold dipped feathers that formed a crown around his forehead and hung from the soft waves. If she wasn't mistaken, he was also wearing eyeliner in a very sexy-pirate-esque way. The overall effect was strange yet devastating.

He looked at her like the feeling was mutual. "You are the most beautiful woman... person... thing. You are the most beautiful thing I have ever seen."

Merry blushed and slapped playfully at his exposed bicep. "You were doing so well until you called me a thing."

His soft smile made her blush even deeper. "Let me try again," he said, his voice a bit raspy. "I've seen waterfalls and wildflowers. Paintings and sculptures. Eagles soaring through clear blue skies, lightning illuminating stormy seas. And you are more beautiful than all combined."

Her muttered curse was not an appropriate response to his sudden bout of poetics. She fought the urge to fidget under his intense stare. Men never said things like that to her. Sure, they complimented her, but never in such a specific—and if she was being honest, overkill—kind of way.

She was saved from having to find something equally kind to say by the arrival of Jeraltan and Graham who'd finally made their way through the thick crowd.

Jeraltan grabbed her hand and, with surprising strength, dragged both her and Graham toward the projector. "Our music app has karaoke, remember? We have to sing."

Merry and Graham's objections were so loud they were heard over the music. Jeraltan stopped and dropped their hands to place his hands on his hips as he rounded on them. It was not intimidating. He was all big brown eyes and fuzzy pink sweater. "You have to sing. You're the guests of honor."

"Sorry Marshmallow, I don't do karaoke," Graham said.

"Me either," Merry agreed. As a united front, they just might be able to resist Jeraltan's pout. Graham was a wild card in this fight, though. On one hand, he was enraptured with the blond cutie. On the other, his shyness was legendary, especially in front of crowds. For once, Merry hoped the shyness won.

She hadn't considered the other wild cards that had followed them. Deirdre's laughter sent an icy tendril of foreboding into Merry's heart. It was confirmed when she said, "Oh, you two don't do karaoke? Are we supposed to forget the Summer of Heartbreak? Otherwise known as the *Summer of Shania?*"

"Drinks!" Graham said. "I need a drink. And I've been wanting to try your signature cocktail, Marshmallow."

"Don't 'Marshmallow' me, mister. And don't try to distract me. What is this about a summer?"

Santa's gentle smile was replaced by a dangerous smirk. "Yes, Merry. Do explain."

Merry desperately glanced around for a distraction. Rosie was happily riding on Pari's shoulders under the watchful eyes of Faye. No immediate childcare needs, then. She was on her own.

"Nothing. There was no summer. Dee doesn't know anything. She doesn't remember anything. And she's not going to say anything." She leveled a glare at her best friend.

Her point made, Merry ducked between her friends and darted as quickly as her heels would allow toward the alcohol. She'd just finished adding lime to two vodka sodas—one for herself, one for Graham—when she heard Deirdre ignore her warning completely.

"It was 2018. Both Graham and Merry had gone through terrible breakups and they decided to drown their sorrows at a country karaoke bar. Yes, for some unknown reason, that existed in Southern California."

Merry considered making a run for it before her humiliation could be completed, but her loyalty to Graham won out. She headed back toward the group and pressed the drink into his hand. It was gone before she had a chance to taste her own.

"Stop talking," Graham begged his sister. As usual, she ignored him.

"They drank whiskey and sang duets. Mostly Shania Twain. By the end of the summer, they even had matching rhinestone cowboy hats."

"And we never sang karaoke again," Merry rushed to put in.

"Also false," Charli put in cheerfully. Why did Merry make friends who enjoyed embarrassing her? "We've all sung karaoke together several times since then, including at our bachelorette party where Merry and Graham teamed up for 'Bootylicious' if I remember correctly. And before you ask, yes, they dance too. Even Graham once you get a few drinks in him."

Jeraltan was looking at Graham like he'd hung the moon, the stars, and several planets. "Really? This is such good news! I'm even willing to overlook the lying if you sing and agree to dance with me all night."

Graham looked slightly green, so Merry passed him her drink. He downed it as quickly as the first.

She hesitantly turned to the person she'd been avoiding since this conversation started. Santa looked just as pleased as Jeraltan. "Merry, Merry, Merry. I didn't know you were capable of lying to us. That's very good to know. Almost as good as knowing you can't help yourself when it comes to karaoke."

She regretted giving Graham her drink as the familiar mischievous glint appeared in Santa's eye.

"Don't worry, duckie. You don't have to sing right now. You can just watch us."

Jeraltan beamed. "Yes! We will sing for you. Just give us five minutes to prepare." He gave Graham a quick peck on the cheek and scurried off, already shouting orders for the rest of the Claus Family Toys employees to convene in an adjoining room. The twins passed a sugar-high Rosie back to her moms. Despite her dread of what was to come, she couldn't help but laugh. Jeraltan sounded like he was readying troops for war, not a performance.

Santa brushed his knuckles along Merry's cheekbone and leaned in close. Her heart skipped and rattled in her chest, as it always did when Santa touched her. "We are all glad you're staying, but none so glad as me."

His smile was soft when he pulled away, his eyes a hazy burnished gold. Then, he transformed into her favorite attention-loving fiend and followed his friends from the room.

Merry finally caught her breath and turned a glare on her friends. Deirdre and Charli were both smiling like they knew all her secrets. "I hate you both" she whispered, hoping to keep her words from Rosie's little ears. She hadn't even gotten the chance to tell Santa she wasn't moving to Poleton, even though she'd taken control of the company.

"I second that," Graham said. He was already turning toward the bar for a refill.

"Oh, come on," Dee complained. "If there was ever a group of people that won't judge your terrible karaoke, it's them."

"And you saw how happy your boy toys were," Charli added. "Really, we did you two a favor."

Both Merry and Graham scoffed at the term boy toy, but let it go. The damage was already done.

Merry sighed and tried to find a silver lining in the situation. There were so many silver linings to this day that it was nearly solid. So what, she might get talked into doing something embarrassing? She had her grandmother's company and a room full of friends—both old and new. Nothing else mattered.

"You might want to record this," Merry told Charli. "If their karaoke is as good as their Zumba, you'll have incredible social media fodder."

Charli sprang into action, commandeering cell phones and setting them up around the room to capture different angles of the makeshift stage.

Five minutes later, the familiar first notes of "Dancing Queen" started to play and Merry rolled her eyes. Clearly, Santa had laid down the law when it came to song choices.

Her employees filed out onto the stage, Jeraltan at the front of the procession. They took up positions reminiscent of a church choir and began to sing, melodious voices overlapping in a rich harmony. She would never be able to listen to ABBA again, it would seem thin and underproduced compared to this performance.

Not only were their voices angelic but they moved like individual streams of water, clashing and merging across the stage. Their dance moves were stolen from the days of disco but performed with the restrained poise of a professional ballet.

As the first verse progressed, their voices grew stronger, and their dance coalesced into a beautiful maelstrom. Jeraltan danced and sang front and center with an unadulterated glee that brought a smile to Merry's face and tears to her eyes. They were all so talented, but there was still one missing.

Never wasting an opportunity for a grand entrance, Santa's voice overpowered the others as he leapt onto the stage, jumping and spinning like a gorgeous cross between a ballerina and an over-caffeinated chihuahua.

Jeraltan faded into the background, letting Santa lead the performance. He belted out the lyrics of the chorus without a hint of shyness, grinning at Merry as he danced.

He hit his knees and slid halfway across the stage at the line about the tambourine and Merry was openly laughing, forgetting to mute herself for the sake of Charli's recording.

As the next verse began, Merry had the feeling that the entire company was singing to her. Their dancing queen.

Santa alternated between meeting her eyes as he shook his hips and disco pointed and riling up his friends until they were dancing as if their lives depended on it. She was moving from foot to foot, a desperate yearning to join the dance seeping from her bones out into her limbs.

At the start of the third chorus, Santa held out his hand to her and she didn't hesitate. She loved to dance, but knew she wasn't as good as the rest of the employees. That didn't matter when they all so obviously wanted her to join them.

Santa pulled her onto the stage and didn't give her a moment to feel self-conscious before twirling her around the makeshift stage. Soon, she was singing with them and dancing without a care in the world except the glimpses of gold eyes that she got between spins. Santa was in his element, brighter than the stars, and Merry wanted nothing more than to dance with him until the sun rose.

The song ended too quickly, but Santa pulled her to the middle of the ballroom, and they kept dancing while Claus Family Toys employees took their turns at karaoke. It didn't matter to her whether they danced to Barry Manilow or TLC—and they were graced with renditions of both. Her aching feet didn't matter either. There was just Santa and the insatiable need to keep dancing.

CHAPTER 26

Merry woke the morning after the party with a clear head and aching feet. She vaguely remembered singing "Any Man of Mine" with Graham in the wee hours of the morning, complete with line dancing and wolf whistles from Jeraltan. No embarrassment followed the memory. She had been too happy to be embarrassed. These were her people; she was surer of it now than she had ever been.

Santa had driven her home as the sun rose. A quick glance at the clock showed her that car ride had been only a few hours before. She didn't feel tired, though. That was probably because she'd been having too much fun to drink heavily.

A coffee from the lobby rejuvenated her enough to tackle a few hours of consulting work. Mostly, she emailed clients to assure them she was alive and on top of their projects. Then, she emailed her assistants and colleagues for updates on what those projects entailed. Any actual work would have to wait.

She drove to Henry's at nine and he greeted her with a crinkle-faced smile and yet another cup of coffee. She was so grateful for the old man's approval that she felt her heart would burst. How had she gotten so lucky?

They rode to the neighboring town to visit his friend at the probate office and made small talk along the way. Merry had the feeling he was leading up to something, though she didn't know what it could be.

Thirty minutes outside of Poleton her good humor was getting a serious test. To preserve her morning bliss, she asked, "is there something you want to talk to me about?" *Please don't tell me you've changed your mind.*

"Your friend Graham seems awfully fond of Jeraltan," Henry said. Merry changed her mental tune to *please don't be a homophobic jerk.*

"He is," she said instead, forcing a smile through her nerves. "I'll admit I was surprised how quickly things between them progressed, but if anyone is worth jumping on a plane for, it's Jeraltan."

"So, you think it's serious, then?"

"I do," Merry said. "Graham is an overthinker—a hazard of his profession, I assume—but he didn't have to think at all about Jeraltan. It's adorable." *Say they're adorable*, she mentally begged the lawyer.

Henry laughed, and Merry belatedly realized it was at her joke about lawyers. "That's wonderful to hear," he said. Merry relaxed. "Graham is also very competent from what I've seen."

"At his job?" She clarified. At Henry's nod, she continued, "He's the best. He's not too fond of courtrooms, but there is no one better at finding loopholes in contracts or making sure they don't exist in the first place."

"Excellent. I have been thinking of cutting back on my hours…" He left the statement unfinished and Merry nearly swerved off the road when she realized the implications.

"You want Graham to take over your practice?" she asked. She had to be sure before she mentioned it to Graham.

"I would consider it," Henry said. "He'd have to pass the bar in North Carolina, of course, and I would have to see how he handles a broad array of cases. I'm the only lawyer in town, so I have to know a little bit about everything."

"I can bring it up, feel him out a little," she suggested. It would be a big step down from his current high-profile cases, but Graham was an interesting person. On one hand, he loved the convenience of a big city and the challenge of corporate law. On the other, he was profoundly lonely in a giant law firm, hated company politics, and mostly hated his clients.

Would he be happier with a quiet life surrounded by people that he loved? Merry pushed the question away because it hit far too close to the doubts that were creeping up in her own mind.

Henry agreed to let her broach the topic with Graham and Merry settled into her own thoughts. She wasn't Graham. She loved the cutthroat business she'd chosen. She liked outsmarting and outworking her colleagues. She liked her clients and wanted to help their businesses succeed.

But she was also beginning to like being in Poleton. Wearing comfortable shoes. Smiling at employees because she liked them, not because she wanted something from them. Knowing the names of the people she passed on the street.

At some point, she would have to choose, but not yet.

The visit to the probate office took just shy of forever but she left with the documentation she needed. It was a miracle—or a fine example of a good-ol-boy system—that Henry had been able to have their case heard on such short notice.

Either way, Merry had everything she needed to start contacting banks, other government offices, and a thousand places that would need her to retitle assets and debts. The to-do list was daunting, but she could get started on it the next day.

When she dropped Henry at home, he gave her the key to her grandmother's home and an address. Strange, all the time she'd been in Poleton she hadn't considered asking where her grandmother lived. Or maybe she had considered it, but it just slipped her mind when it came time to ask the question.

***

Her grandmother's house was modest, especially compared to Merry's expectations. Then again, Joy was only one person, how much space did she really need?

The answer, it seemed, was four bedrooms. The house was a tasteful mixture of gray stone and cedar that felt at home in the mountains. Lingering snow collected on the edges of the roof and lent a cozy feel to the exterior.

Inside, the home was traditional but clean. Everything felt old, but somehow not outdated. Like the decor transcended fads and settled straight into antique.

Merry crossed a worn entry rug and looked into a tidy dining room. An envelope sat on the table. On closer inspection, her name was written across it in the same old-style cursive she recognized as her grandmother's. Creepy. How had Joy known to leave her a letter? Or had Henry placed it here and forgotten to mention it?

Merry read the letter and set it back down. Her pulse was hammering but she couldn't remember why. In fact, she couldn't remember a word she'd just read.

She tried again.

Merry,

If you've gained entry into my house, then you have earned Henry's trust. There are a few things you need to understand, and lessons I need to impart. First,

Merry's gaze drifted to an oil painting on the wall. It was a massive, lovingly rendered duck. Her eyes fell to the signature, trying to puzzle out who would waste such talent painting waterfowl.

She couldn't read the messy scrawl, and her mind wandered back to more immediate needs. Why were her breaths so shallow? Why did her head feel so fuzzy? And why was she suddenly ravenous?

She glanced down at the table and picked up the letter. Hadn't she already read this? If so, why couldn't she remember what it said?

Three more attempts to read the letter went the same way. She started, then her mind drifted and she couldn't recall what she had been reading. She tucked the letter into her jacket pocket with a shake of her head. The sleepless night was definitely getting to her. A quick tour of the house and she would leave to catch a quick nap before meeting Faye, Deirdre, Charli, and Rosie for dinner.

By the time she reached her grandmother's study, she'd forgotten the letter in her pocket and her heartbeat had slowed to a steady thump. All four walls were lined with file cabinets, but that was not surprising given her grandmother's feelings about computers.

Merry opened a drawer at random and flipped through the files. Birth certificate, marriage license, Social Security card, death certificate. All for a man named Barnabus who'd died in 1972. Behind those documents were ten folders full of bank statements, tax returns, and paystubs for the same man.

Next, she found the same detailed records for a woman named Helen. Vital records spanning her entire life until her death in 1973. Who were these people and why did Joy have so much information about them?

Merry turned from that cabinet and opened the drawer closest to the door. These documents were older, handwritten, but they too spanned a person's entire life from birth to death.

She thumbed through the documents, finding weekly paystubs from 1866 to 1902, all issued from Claus Family Toys. Merry felt foolish. These were employment records. She hadn't known that she needed an original copy of legal documents for employees, or their personal tax returns, but she supposed things might have been different before the advent of the internet.

It was growing darker and colder by the moment so Merry abandoned her search for the day and went to meet her friends.

CHAPTER 27

Merry arrived at the Poleton Community Bank at exactly nine in the morning, knowing that there would be paperwork to sign before she could deposit a check in the Claus Family Toys account. Henry met her there, dispelling the idea that he couldn't drive. Maybe he just liked being chauffeured most of the time.

Like with the probate office, Henry's presence smoothed the process immensely. The bank was tiny, and Henry knew all the higher-ups that would need to sign off on Merry's takeover of the account.

By noon, she was sipping coffee in the waiting room, officially a multi-millionaire. Not only had Henry gotten her added to the Claus Family Toys account, but her grandmother's personal accounts as well. She didn't feel rich in her snow-crusted boots and dark jeans.

Merry scrolled through the local area of Facebook Marketplace, not sure what she was looking to buy. With her new bank balances, she should have been scrolling the Louboutin site instead. But she kept sorting through other people's discarded items, sending a few bids for the thrill of negotiating alone. She had just enough time to send one on a box set of Graham's favorite book series before the bell above the main door of the bank signaled Santa's arrival.

Merry tucked her phone into her pocket and flashed him a smile a little too bright for a Monday in the middle of a bank, but he returned it just as brightly. Behind him, the cavalry poured in—meaning Jeraltan, Graham,

Pari, Rari, and Faye. Merry briefly wondered how they'd all gotten there in one of Santa's trucks, but the snow dusting the three women told her she didn't want to know the answer. She could lecture Santa on the dangers of letting people ride in the back of a truck later. At the rate she was filling up her 'poor decisions to discuss with Santa' list, she was going to have to set aside a full week for the conversation.

Greetings and hugs all around took up the next few minutes and Merry was smiling when Quinn entered the bank. The man looked awful. There were dark circles under his spectacles and new frown lines around his mouth. Surely, the last few days hadn't been enough to add wrinkles.

The teller was speaking to Henry about his personal account, tapping away at her computer. With her head tilted down, she held up one finger to let Merry know she would be with her soon.

Jeraltan had positioned himself between her and Graham and Merry jumped when he pinched her arm. Judging by Graham's bewildered expression, Jeraltan had done the same to him. But Jeraltan didn't offer an explanation or an apology, he just stared at Santa. Merry and Graham followed his gaze.

Santa always looked strange with his loose, natural clothing, dark skin, white hair, and gold eyes, but he looked downright feral as he approached Quinn. His soft-soled boots made no sound as he moved with a dancer's grace across the linoleum floor.

Merry's heartbeat picked up, but she couldn't say why. Maybe it was the manic flash of his eyes, the grin that was a touch too wide to be friendly, the way his hair seemed to blow in a breeze that she couldn't feel.

Was she worried that Santa would attack Quinn? That didn't feel like the right explanation. If anything, she felt anticipation. Goosebumps skittered along her skin. He was magnificent.

Quinn held out the check. "As promised."

Santa left Quinn with his hand outstretched for a long moment while he studied the other man's face. "Yes, you would have found it quite difficult to ignore our bargain, Quinn. I'm glad you made the right decision."

The goosebumps rose to a shiver that wracked Merry's body as

Santa laughed. It was a cruel, dangerous sound, lacking the warmth of his usual chuckle. She locked eyes with Quinn for the briefest moment and all her instincts screamed for him to run. A visceral reaction that had no place in reality.

She was being absurd, reactive, downright crazy, but she couldn't stop the voice in her mind that screamed Quinn was in danger.

Santa's hand closed around the check and Merry felt like the whole scene was in slow motion, dragged out by her strange rush of adrenaline.

A flash of white light surrounded Quinn and through it Merry could just make out an open mouth, screaming soundlessly. His body collapsed in on itself, shrinking until it disappeared entirely.

Reality rushed back in. The clicking of the teller's nails on a keyboard. The hum of fluorescent lights. The warmth of Jeraltan's arm against hers. But there was nothing real about what she was seeing.

Santa bent and reached into a pile of discarded clothing on the floor. When he rose, he was laughing and holding a green garden snake in one hand. He turned to her, holding the snake out in front of him like a prize.

Merry's blood ran cold.

How had she not noticed that his cheekbones were abnormally sharp? His jawline too defined. His coloring more like a sci-fi character than a human.

Everything that she had ignored came tumbling back into her mind like the broken pieces of a dam that could no longer deny the river pushing against it.

An unexplained cult that spawned one hundred of the most talented artists Merry had ever seen. A toy shop in the middle of nowhere that employed them all. No knowledge of the internet or computers. Strange clothing. Strange appearances. Strange familial bonds.

Her grandmother at the center of it all.

Odd inheritance rules reminiscent of a b-rated movie plot. A cabinet full of too much information. Letters that she read and couldn't remember.

Then, there were the other things she'd ignored since coming to Poleton. Headaches, memory loss, townspeople who remembered her employees but didn't remember the basic facts of their lives.

Graham spoke first. "What the ever-loving f—"

"I wanted to tell you, but I didn't think you would believe me," Jeraltan said quietly.

"Wanted to tell me what?" Graham squeaked. "That your friend can turn people into snakes? That I'm losing my mind? That we are on a prank show? Please tell me we are on a prank show."

Merry glanced around at her employees. The people she had considered friends just a moment ago. Faye, Pari, and Rari were staring expectantly at her. Santa was still holding the snake. It reared back, opening its jaws, and clamped onto his hand. Merry jumped forward to stop it, but it was too late.

Santa just laughed. "Remember when I said, 'fangless' and 'impotent', Quinn?" He turned his too-bright smile on Merry and it was discordantly familiar but also completely alien. "I never promised how long the rest of his life would be. Would you like to kill him? Or would it be more fitting to keep him like this? A trophy of our triumph."

It was too much. Too much information. Too much casual cruelty that she didn't even understand.

Merry vomited on the floor of the bank.

Henry rushed to her side and the teller made her way around the desk, scolding Santa as she did. "You can't bring pets in here, Santa. And why have you thrown clothes on the floor of my bank?"

The teller didn't know. She hadn't seen. Her mind was probably struggling to come up with a rational explanation for what had just occurred.

Henry's warm brown eyes met hers as she straightened. "Are you alright, dear? Have you eaten something that didn't sit well with you?"

Merry stared into the old man's eyes and couldn't understand how he could be worried about her reaction and not the massive, earth-shattering, worldview-changing event that had caused it.

Graham was behaving rationally, at least. He was just muttering curse words and staring around the room like he'd never seen normal bank decor.

Henry straightened. "Where did Quinn go? Wasn't he here just a moment ago?"

"I have the check," Santa said instead.

Henry tilted his head to the side, studying Santa from head to toe. Then, his expression smoothed, and he smiled. "Excellent. Let's get it deposited and then get Merry home. After that, maybe some lunch? I'm suddenly starving."

Merry started laughing. Uncontrollable, body wracking laughter that squeezed tears from her eyes. Henry and the teller both looked concerned, but Faye stepped in to offer explanations. Merry was too far gone to know what she said.

The teller brought a mop, then something for Merry to sign. Before she knew what was happening, she was being led out of the bank with Pari and Rari on either side of her.

CHAPTER 28

Merry didn't remember the drive back to Claus Family Toys. Nor did she remember walking into the ballroom and being directed to a beanbag chair. She finally recognized enough of her surroundings to grab Graham's hand, a solid piece of wood to cling to in the storm of insanity.

Her employees were gathered around, whispering and casting nervous glances at her and Graham, except Faye who was busy chastising Jeraltan. She was trying to be quiet about it, but her words still made their way to Merry's ears. "We discussed telling Merry, not your boyfriend."

"I can't help that he saw," Jeraltan argued. "I have no control over his eyes."

"You brought him to the bank, and I saw you pinch him."

"Maybe Santa should have picked a more discreet show of power if he didn't want anyone other than Merry to see."

They fell silent—all of them—as Santa entered. For once, he wasn't smiling.

Worry looked wrong on his face. Or maybe it was just him that was wrong.

He peered down at her, tall, imposing, with inhuman gold eyes. Her pulse skittered, her skin crawled, and her muscles tightened with an ancient, intrinsic need to either bow to the predator before her or run as fast as she could in the opposite direction.

Another, equally subconscious but no less insistent part of her demanded that she fight with teeth and claws and raw power—all things that she did not possess—to prove herself as his equal. That part of her was a fool.

She didn't know what he was, but her conscious mind told her that she was something else. Something lesser. Something that needed to listen to the flight instinct and completely ignore the fight alternative.

Graham crushed her hand in his, making her bones grind against each other. The sudden pain grounded her. She was being fanciful. Santa wasn't a predator. She wasn't prey. There was no need for such dramatic instincts.

Still, her pulse didn't calm as she stared up at Santa.

"I put Quinn in a terrarium with food and water. I am sorry for suggesting we kill him; I got carried away." Santa's voice was gentle. Coaxing.

Merry made a gurgling noise that could have been the precursor to laughter or tears. No amount of gentleness would disguise the fact that he was talking about making a snake that had once been a man more comfortable. How would he ever be comfortable again?

"What did you... How did you... What happened?" Merry struggled to find the right question when her mind was filled with buzzing static and competing instincts. Some part of her felt like the answer was right in front of her, but she couldn't grasp it.

Santa knelt before her. "Let me start at the beginning. My name is Santerralesium, son of Granterralesium, the Unseelie king, and Alfiva, a fawn of the Wild Realm."

"Unseelie? Like fairies?" Graham asked, his voice strained to the point it was unrecognizable.

Santa nodded with a tentative smile. "A common mistranslation, but yes. The land is called Faerie. The creatures that inhabit it—like all of us—are called Fae."

Another one of those strange sounds escaped Merry's lips but she had exhausted her supply of words. This was madness. Utter madness. Yet, a small part of her relaxed, already accepting his explanation.

But Faerie wasn't real. Santa was just a man. Just a man who jumped on her bed and sang ABBA into a hairbrush. Just a man with a quick smile and a cassette collection. Just a man who turned other people into snakes...

"There are two... tiers of Fae," Santa went on, oblivious to Merry's inner turmoil. "The High Fae who rule Faerie, and the Lessers who serve them. We are all Lesser Fae, at least in part."

"You're all... Fae," Merry managed to say. "You're not human?"

"No, we are not human," Santa confirmed. Merry glanced around the room at the sea of very human-looking faces. Well, she'd thought they were human-looking. Now, she noticed Faye's poison green eyes, Pari and Rari's unusual height, Addie's unearthly beauty.

But humans came in all shapes, sizes, and colorings. None of them looked Fae—or at least, none matched the descriptions of Fae in popular fiction.

"This next part will be difficult for me to say, and probably difficult for you to hear," Santa said. Merry gave a derisive little snort. He was suggesting that 'we're not human' was an easy thing to hear? Santa ignored her outburst and pressed on. "I hope that you will remember we were all very young. My antlers were little more than points."

"Your *what*?"

Santa waved a dismissive hand. "Half fawn, remember? I don't have hooves if that matters to you."

Did it? She would love to be the kind of person who could say it didn't matter what body parts her lover had, but now that he'd confirmed he didn't have hooves, Merry could say with certainty that 'no hooves' was a requirement for a romantic partner. Even the thought made her want to laugh. Hysterically. Forever.

She nodded to show that she was listening. Not comprehending but listening.

"We found each other because we each wanted a different life than our parents had. We didn't want to serve the High Fae, cleaning their castles and polishing their cutlery. We wanted to enjoy life."

That's not so bad, Merry thought. They were once lazy, entitled teenagers. So what? Most people were.

"So, we decided to find another workforce; a race that would happily do our chores so that we could live freely."

Oh, now that was bad. And Merry had a sinking suspicion that she knew which race he meant.

"Humans." Graham confirmed her thoughts.

Santa nodded solemnly. "You have to understand, Faerie has been separated from the human lands for many years. All our knowledge was old and outdated. It said that humans lived to work. They enjoyed it. So, we thought it would be a mutually beneficial arrangement. They would get to do what they loved and in the most beautiful land of all."

"But they didn't want to go with you," Merry suggested. Her voice sounded dead to her own ears. Santa had tried to enslave humanity. He was a comic book villain. With antlers.

Santa shook his head. "No, they did not want to go to Faerie."

"How did you end up here? Not the human lands. I mean here, here. In Poleton." Merry asked.

"In the now, now," Graham added. This was not the time for *Space Balls* references, so Merry ignored him.

A small, sad smile turned the corners of Santa's lips. "Magic, duckie. And a push from the Fates. I asked them to show me the path to a better life. And they did, just not in the way I was expecting."

"I don't understand."

"I know. There is a lot to explain. The short version is: We came to the human realm, fought, lost, and your grandmother offered me a bargain. We would repay our debt to her in exchange for our lives. I agreed and we have been working here ever since."

Jeraltan came to sit beside Santa. He looked so innocent with his messy blond hair and big brown eyes. Merry's chest ached. She'd thought of him as a cute little brother just a few hours ago. Now, Santa was saying he was part of a plot to enslave humans and then had subsequently been enslaved. Was the punishment just? What did that make her? An enslaver? Or a savior of humanity?

"Bargains, like what Santa made with Quinn and what we made with Joy, are unbreakable. They're enforced by the magic of the Fates. No Fae or human can break one once the agreement has been struck," Jeraltan explained. "The only way for us to be free to return to our natural forms is to fulfill the bargain. Until then, we are stuck in these human bodies, driven to complete our task. We have to work, whether we want to or not. The bargain demands it. And if we put off the magic's pull for too long, we get sick."

"Your natural form?" Graham said. "This isn't your true body? Do you have antlers too?"

Jeraltan smiled nervously. "No antlers. I'm a brownie. We're the second most powerful Fae race," he said, like that would make a difference to Graham.

"Pixies are the second most powerful Fae race," Faye interjected from across the room.

"The fact that you can say that just shows that brownies not only have more magic but also more intelligence," Jeraltan argued.

"None of your magic matters when a troll tosses you into the nearest tree," Pari put in.

"Pixies can fly away from the tree," Faye argued.

"Brownies can disintegrate the tree," Jeraltan added.

"We will throw you so hard that you won't have time to work your puny magics," Rari said.

"Enough," Santa commanded. The room fell silent.

Trolls, pixies, brownies, Merry felt like she'd fallen headfirst into a book of fairytales. And hit her head very hard on the binding.

Jeraltan turned back to Graham. "Anyway, I look pretty much the same in both forms. I'm a little shorter, my eyes are a different color and my ears are pointier, but you would still recognize me. I would still be me if the bargain is fulfilled."

Graham looked like he was going to be sick, but then he slowly nodded. "Okay." He kept nodding. "Okay," he said with more vehemence. "I can live with pointy ears."

"What?" Merry said. "You're just going to accept this? That they tried to enslave humans?"

"I know Jeraltan," Graham said. "He truly believed it was something the humans wanted, otherwise he wouldn't have done it. And they failed, so does it really matter what they tried to do... what, a decade ago?" He directed the last statement at his boyfriend.

Jeraltan and Santa shared a look. "We came here in 1895," Santa said finally.

The last shred of Merry's sanity snapped. "No, no, no. I can't. I can't listen to any more of this."

She stood and turned toward the door. On second thought, she started pacing instead.

If what they said was true, she couldn't leave them. Yes, they'd tried to do something awful, but they'd been dealing with the consequences for over a century.

She knew these people. At least, she knew what mattered. They were kind and goofy and welcoming. They worked hard and enjoyed their jobs.

Or was that just the compulsion of the bargain?

She stopped pacing and turned back to Santa. He still sat cross-legged in front of the beanbag chair she'd vacated. He looked worried, even hurt. And it broke her heart. Whether he was human or Fae or something else altogether, she cared about him. Maybe even loved him.

"What was the bargain? Specifically."

Santa's cheeks flushed. "Erm..."

"He doesn't remember," Faye supplied with an annoyed look in Santa's direction.

"Everything was on fire!" Santa argued.

"Maybe you shouldn't have set it on fire," Jeraltan muttered.

Santa heaved an exhausted sigh. Clearly, this conversation had occurred before. Many times. At least that explained the story of the toy shop burning.

"We have to make a ten million dollar profit in a single year, I remember that much," Santa said. "That was the amount Joy decided she was owed for the inconvenience of dealing with us."

"And the fire. Don't forget the fire," Faye added dryly.

"So, you want me to help you make ten million dollars so you can go home? That's why you've all been so happy that I'm here."

"We're glad you're here because we're glad you're here," Santa said. "And if you can help us fulfill the bargain, we would appreciate it. We would like to take our true forms again, to be able to use magic, to truly mate and have children. But we do not want to return to the Unseelie court, or to any part of Faerie. We like it here, we like our jobs, and if you'll have us, we would like to stay and keep working for you."

A chorus of agreements went up around the room.

"You want me to set a bunch of dangerous, magic wielding fairies loose on the world? After you tried to enslave us once? How do I know this isn't another ploy to... do something bad?"

"Fae cannot lie," Santa said simply. "You can ask each of us our plans after the bargain is fulfilled and we will tell you the truth. You can even require a new bargain from us, hopefully one that allows us to take our true forms."

Merry thought about that for a moment, searching for the loophole in his words. How could she prove whether he could lie? Lying about not being able to lie was the perfect lie. Even that sentence made her head hurt.

"I need some time to think about all this," she said instead. Defer a decision, the hallmark of management. She just needed time to understand the problem fully, make several pro-con lists, and then she could decide what to do about the fairies—no, Fae—she employed.

No one stopped her as she left the house and walked over to the office building. The human staff asked her where all the other employees were, but Merry brushed off their questions and retreated to her office.

CHAPTER 29

This was an HR nightmare. She wished she could ask Deirdre what to do. But did HR have a manual for dealing with Fae employees under the compulsion of a bargain? Probably not.

Free them. It was the obvious choice. The business was viable, she could make a ten-million-dollar profit. Then, Santa, Faye, Jeraltan, and the others would be free to do whatever they wanted with their lives.

But what if they wanted to steal her and take her back to Faerieland? Worse, what if they took Deirdre? Charli? God forbid, Rosie? It was a risk. A massive risk to the entire world.

What if they took some humans and it went well? Would more Fae, worse Fae, come into the human lands? What if they were no longer satisfied with ruling Faerie and decided to take her world as well? Then again, what if she'd seen too many movies?

Merry still couldn't understand what she, and by extension her grandmother, had to do with this. Joy had tricked the Fae into a bargain to grow her business. But how had she known that Fae existed or how to make a bargain bound by fate or whatever Jeraltan had said?

And the timeline. Her mind could not comprehend the timeline.

She pulled her grandmother's letter from the pocket of her coat. Maybe this time she would be able to remember what she read.

Merry,

If you've gained entry into my house, then you have earned Henry's trust. There are a few things you need to understand, and lessons I need to impart.

First, do not trust the Unseelie. They are tricksters, and worse, they are children. They came to this world as little more than toddlers throwing tantrums because they didn't want to work. They have not improved.

I am forced to manage everything for them. I tell them what to do at work or they would spend all day singing and carving instruments. I manage their money, or they would spend it the moment they got it. I know this first-hand because for several years they bought clothes and music and had no money left for food. I tell them when to cook and when to clean and how to care for themselves.

I keep their existence hidden and I keep them safe. It has not been easy. I regret passing this burden to you, but it is necessary. You must keep things the way they are. Do not allow them to fulfill the bargain. Do not unleash powerful, temperamental children on the world. Even I cannot foretell the destruction they would cause.

I know they are charming, sweet even, but never forget what they are. They are not like us. Unseelie are the dark mirror of our kind. They are wicked and cruel, selfish above all things. They do not know the true meaning of empathy, only self-interest.

She stopped reading when the office door opened and Graham entered, Jeraltan on his heels. Jeraltan placed a mug of coffee in front of her with a tentative smile. "Coffee, and if you don't need any more caffeine right now, my famous cocoa." He set the second mug down and whipped cream spilled over the edge. How could he be the monster her grandmother described?

"Thank you," Merry said.

Jeraltan gave her another small smile and glanced at Graham before leaving them alone in the office. Graham collapsed into the chair across from her and rested his head in his hands. "I said I was fine with pointy ears, but I don't know if I am. I don't know if I'm fine with any of this."

"I know," Merry said.

"I mean… just what? It all came out of nowhere. I met this sweet, hot, funny guy who inexplicably liked me. And now what? He's not even human?"

"It appears not," Merry said. "But I do think he cares about you. He wanted you to know the truth. That counts for something, right?"

Graham ignored her attempt at comfort. "And he's old. Like, really old. And he's not going to age any time soon. He'll look like that for another nine hundred years, so he says. *First gray hair at eleven hundred for brownies!*" Graham laughed a little hysterically.

Merry winced, she hadn't even thought of that. If the stories were true, Santa would outlive her by several lifetimes. That fact was worse than the antlers.

"It's going to be okay," Merry soothed. "We'll figure out what to do with our faerie boyfriends."

Graham snorted. "Fae."

Merry rolled her eyes. "Oh yes, that's the important part to focus on."

She pushed the cocoa toward Graham, and he took it, wrapping his hands around the warm cup but not drinking. A sip of her coffee told her that some things had not changed. Coffee still tasted divine. Graham was still in her corner. Two things that remained the same. That was a start.

"I was just reading a letter from my grandmother telling me what monsters the Unseelie Fae are. There are no specifics other than they don't know how to manage a bank account and they don't clean their rooms," Merry said. "I really don't think those are good reasons to keep them enslaved. Budgeting is hard for everyone."

Graham snorted, shook his head, and snorted again. "Fair point, Merry," he said sarcastically. "A better point would be, you shouldn't keep anyone enslaved for any reason, ever. Period."

"I know that, jerkface," Merry countered. "But surely these are extenuating circumstances. Like keeping Loki in that plastic prison bubble so he didn't destroy the world."

"We are not the Avengers, and this is not a movie," Graham said. "Our only options are to help them or be terrible people."

"You're right." Merry shook her head. "Of course, you're right. I'm just scared. I never thought I would have the fate of the world depending on my business consulting skills."

"So dramatic." Graham finally sipped from his cocoa, a little bit of life returning to his eyes.

"How are we going to tell Deirdre and Charli?" Merry asked after a moment of silence.

"We can't. Apparently, they won't remember if we tell them. Something about a 'glamour.' I didn't understand exactly what they were saying, but it seems like some sort of perception shield around the town. Everyone who doesn't have irrefutable proof of the existence of Fae will come up with some other explanation of events, decide not to remember at all, or suddenly get very hungry. They don't know why the last part happens."

"Distraction," Merry said automatically. "Biological need overrides conscious thought. I don't know, that's just a guess."

"That makes sense. Well, as much as any of this makes sense." Graham scrubbed his hands over his face. "That's it. I've decided. No more moping. I'm going to go tell Jeraltan I love him even if he's two inches tall and glows like a firefly."

"Adorable. It's like one of those weird relationship questions—you know, the 'would you love me if' ones—but real. Also, I hope he's not two inches tall and glowy."

"Me too." Graham pushed to his feet and turned to leave. The door opened before he could pull, revealing Santa on the other side. Graham cast a glance over his shoulder to make sure Merry was okay being left alone. At her nod, he left.

"Hi," Santa said, shoving his hands in the pockets of his loose pants. He seemed nervous, but even his nerves made her heart sing.

"Hi," Merry parroted. "I'm sorry I freaked out. I'm going to help you."

He smiled, just a little upturn of his full lips. "I'm glad. But there is more I need to tell you."

"Noooo." Merry brought her forehead to rest on the desk. The papers there muffled her next words. "No more, my brain is going to explode."

Santa laughed and slowly crossed the room. She knew he was making an effort to let her hear his footsteps so he wouldn't scare her. His hand was warm where he rested it on her tense shoulder. When she didn't protest, he started to rub soothing circles across her back.

"Your grandmother is Fae. She never confirmed which court she belonged to, but her gift for glamour and the fact that I never heard her mentioned in my father's court led me to conclude she is Seelie."

"What?" Merry sat bolt upright as his words cut through the temporary calm his hands had given. But then again, Merry shouldn't have been surprised. What other explanation was there for the fact that her grandmother had lived well past the normal human lifespan?

"I don't know how she came to the human realm or why she was inhabiting a mortal body. All I know is that she is definitely Fae, probably High Fae, and she has excellent control of her magic."

"But I'm human," Merry protested. "My mother was human. Oh, no. Did you know my mother? You didn't… date her, did you?"

Santa laughed softly. "Let me answer those questions one at a time. I suspect that you are not fully human, nor are you fully Fae. I don't know your grandfather's identity, so I can't say with any certainty if your mother was full or part Fae. She always appeared human to me. And yes, I knew her. No, I did not have a romantic relationship with her. And before you ask, neither did the others."

Merry nodded, her thoughts in disarray. No one should be asked to digest this much information so quickly.

Santa resumed rubbing her back, allowing Merry a silent moment to collect her thoughts. A moment turned into minutes. When she reached for her coffee, she found it ice cold.

"Let's go for a walk," Santa suggested. His voice was too gentle, like he was coaxing a frightened animal. "We'll get you more coffee on the way."

Merry nodded dumbly, it seemed all she was capable of at the time. Santa found her outerwear and a fresh cup of coffee. It was nice to be taken care of for a change. It reminded her of Santa fixing her dad's truck, making sure she ate, and all the other little things he did to make sure she knew she was treasured. Or to convince her to stay. She still wasn't sure of his motivations.

He led her to the woods bordering the manufacturing complex and Merry followed him without question. She relaxed further when he wrapped his gloved fingers around hers.

"I—"

"Will—"

They spoke at the same time and Santa smiled and nodded for her to speak first.

"All the flirting…" she began, unsure how to ask the question. She didn't want the answer, but she knew she needed it. "All the times you flirted with me. Were you trying to get me to stay because of the bargain?"

Santa didn't hesitate. "At first. Then it was genuine."

Her face must have shown her disbelief because he continued. "When I first saw you, after you tried to kill me, I knew that you needed to stay in Poleton. I didn't know who you were or why I needed you here, but I knew I did."

"You knew… magically?" She resisted the urge to put the last word in air quotes.

He nodded. "I felt the Fates' hand guiding me only one other time in my life. Before we came to the human realm. This felt the same. I knew that I needed you here. Once I found out who you are, I realized you must be important to fulfilling the bargain. But the more I got to know you, the more I wanted you to stay. Not because of the bargain, but just because I want you here."

"Okay. So, if I said I don't want to help you fulfill the bargain?"

Santa glanced sideways at her, his mouth pulled into a tight line. He took a long moment to collect his thoughts before answering. "I would love

179

to say that wouldn't matter to me, duckie, but it would. The others are my people, I have sworn to protect them. I would not look forward to the choice between you and my duty, my family."

"I understand that, and I believe you. You've always put the others first. Well, in the time I've known you. It's what I admire most about you."

"Not my incredible sense of humor?"

"Calling me pet names that haven't been used in a century isn't my idea of a good joke," she said with an attempt at a teasing smile. It faded too quickly as the dire situation demanded the lion's share of her attention. She shook her head, praying that she wasn't about to make a mistake. "I'll help with the bargain."

"I know you will, duckie." His smile was just as tentative, but it lasted longer. "Your compassion and competitive nature are what I admire most about you."

"Great. We can admire each other while we make a ten-million-dollar profit." She had healthy self-confidence, so why did she always shy away from compliments? Maybe sarcasm was just easier. "Before we do that, though, I need to know about my mother." Merry needed all the uncomfortable answers at once. Then maybe, maybe she could make sense of it all. "She hated my grandmother. What happened?"

Santa swallowed hard. "It was my fault. I slipped up and used magic in front of her. Not like today," he rushed to assure her. "There was an accident in the warehouse and Pari was injured. Your mother saw me heal her and could no longer deny that magic existed, or that we were not human. She didn't take it well and demanded that your grandmother release us. As Jeraltan explained, once a bargain is struck it is enforced by the Fates. Joy couldn't release us, even if she'd wanted to. They had a falling out and your mother left. After that, I don't know. I never saw her again."

"You said you healed Pari. So, Fae can use magic to heal?" Merry's stomach was a lead knot. She didn't know if she would be able to bear hearing that her mother could have been saved from her illness.

"We can heal some things," Santa confirmed. "Jeraltan, Faye, and I are the only ones with enough residual magic to heal now, and it is very limited. I slept for two days after the incident I just mentioned."

"Can you heal cancer?" Her voice was barely more than a whisper.

"Not easily. Like human treatments, we can cut it out and heal the damage from surgery. But if that isn't an option, then no. Is that what happened to Noel?"

It was strange to hear him use her mother's name so casually. Merry nodded. "It was everywhere by the time they found it. She was going to try radiation to slow the growth, but she had a heart attack during the first dose."

Santa made a sympathetic noise. "That may have been due to her Fae heritage. We are more sensitive to many things, including medicines."

"Wouldn't she have known that?"

Santa glanced sideways at her, his golden eyes bright in the winter dimness and full of pity. "I do not know for sure, but I suspect that Joy altered her memories of us and Poleton to keep the secret of the Fae alive. Joy could not have predicted that outcome, though. The Fae rarely get sick, and most mild medications do not cause lasting harm."

Merry fought a surge of helpless anger. Her mother's memories had been erased. It was a violation she couldn't imagine, but it wasn't Santa's fault. It would be unfair to unload her anger on him. Instead, she squeezed his fingers and kept walking.

"I am very sorry that you lost your mother, and that the world lost Noel. I remember her as bright, happy, and kind. All attributes that the world needs more of."

"She was," Merry agreed through a too-tight throat.

"My mother is one of the only things I miss about Faerie," he continued. "I wish you could meet her, though I would never risk bringing you to my father's court."

"You said she is a fawn, what does that mean?" Merry welcomed the subject change.

"There are many races of Fae, though species might be a more appropriate term. High Fae are what you would consider elves. They look nearly identical to humans except for pointed ears. Fawns are a type of Lesser Fae with some characteristics of deer or other similar animals. My mother has furred legs, hooves, and ears that resemble a deer."

That wasn't so hard to imagine. "She sounds beautiful."

Santa smiled, a real, genuine smile. "She is. But I hated seeing her tie her hair back for work and her hands reddened from laundry. She was the king's Fated mate, she should have been sitting on a throne, being served, not working in his house."

"Fated mates are real?" At least fantasy novels got that much right.

"They are. But probably not in the way you think. It's a push from the Fates toward the strongest offspring and bond with the land, so those types of bonds are typically reserved for the High Fae."

"So, your mother is unique."

Santa shook his head. "She is certainly that. She felt the pull and followed it from the Wild Realm all the way to the High King's palace. Even though he can't mate anyone else, he rejected her and put her to work because of her Lesser Fae status." Santa practically spit the last words. "But the pull was strong for him as well. Hence, my existence."

"That must be so difficult for your mother," Merry said. "I can't imagine knowing I was meant to be with someone and being forced to serve them instead. It seems cruel of the Fates to push her toward him. And, no offense, your dad sounds like an ass."

"He is." Santa's tone said the subject was closed. Merry wanted to delve into his relationship with his father, but let it go for the time being.

She looked up at the barren treetops, still crusted with snow in the places the sun didn't reach. Sunlight sparked off each icy branch, creating a ceiling of diamonds.

Santa had been right to suggest a walk. His hand in hers, the crisp day, and the natural beauty around them calmed her frazzled mind. There were more questions she needed to ask, and she was sure they would arise over the coming days, but for now she just had to put one foot in front of the other.

The snow took flight from the branches, swirling overhead in intricate patterns seemingly unaffected by gravity. Ice crystals coalesced into the form of a bird with wings outstretched, then scattered like stars across the blue sky before reforming as a cartoon heart.

She turned wide eyes on Santa and saw him directing the snow with graceful flicks of his wrist. He sent the flakes falling down on them in a gentle flurry and turned to smile at her. "I wanted to make it snow for you, but this is all I can manage right now."

"It's beautiful."

His smile was tentative as he pulled her to a stop, facing him with snow still falling around them. "I have little magic in this form. I have no home to give you except a room in a house that you already own. I have no money, no family name. I am bound by a bargain and cannot leave this town. I have nothing of value to offer you, except myself. But I am yours if you want me, Merry."

"What are you saying?" Merry asked, hope rising in her chest and bringing tears to her eyes.

Santa reached to run a hand through his hair, but his gloves only allowed him to smooth it. He looked more nervous than Merry had ever seen him.

"I have waited to speak to you about my feelings. It didn't seem fair when I was keeping such a secret from you." He turned to face her and took the coffee from her hands so he could hold both of them. Looking into her eyes, he continued, "And I should probably wait a little longer, at least until you are more comfortable with everything you learned today, but I can't. I think I want to be with you."

"You think?" she pressed, stepping closer until she had to crane her neck to look up at him.

He smiled down at her, more comfortable now that she was challenging him. "I'm sure. I love that you never let me off the hook. And I love how incredibly smart you are. And I love the way you get that little dimple in your cheek when you're trying not to yell at me. I love everything about you, duckie."

"I think I want to be with you too," she whispered.

If this were a movie, he would cup her cheek in his hand and kiss her slowly. But it wasn't a movie, and he wasn't a human man. He pecked her lips quickly, excitedly, then peppered kisses across her cheeks. When she started giggling, he picked her up and spun her around until her legs flew behind her. She squealed. Laughing, he hefted her higher and she wrapped her legs around him to discourage any further spinning.

"Kiss me properly or I'm taking it back," she demanded, still laughing.

"You're the boss," he said cheekily. Her protest died as his soft lips found hers.

He kissed her so thoroughly it stole her breath. Merry wasn't entirely aware of her actions as she removed her gloves and tangled her fingers in his silken hair.

Santa was all heat and restrained strength, peppermint and snow as he pressed a hand to the small of her back, drawing her as close as their thick coats would allow.

No matter what he was or where he was from, Merry knew that this was right. They were right together, and they would figure everything else out later.

CHAPTER 30

A fantastic, earth-shattering kiss with a nearly immortal magical being didn't solve as many problems as Merry hoped. Yes, it solidified her relationship with Santa. And yes, it felt good to have the weight of indecision off her shoulders—at least as far as romantic partners and HR violations were concerned. But there was still a Fates-enforced bargain that she didn't fully understand, and a heap of marketing tasks needed to break said bargain.

"We need a to-do list," Merry said as she and Santa entered the Claus Family Toys main building hand-in-hand.

"I thought I knew what was going to be on this list, but now we're heading back to work so I'm less certain."

Despite her worries, Merry laughed. She was still a little fuzzy brained from their kiss and not even Fae bargains could dim the glow of their private little bubble. "I'll make a second to-do list for later. Just one item."

"Is it me? Am I the item? Please tell me I'm the item," Santa said with his teasing smile—the one Merry used to think was pure arrogance. Now, it just looked like bliss with his kiss-swollen lips and honey-colored eyes.

"This is a workplace, Santa. Don't be crass." She lightly swatted his chest with her free hand. To soften the admonition, she gripped his hand tighter and whispered. "But yes. As soon as we finish work you are at the top of my 'absolutely-needs-to-be-done-immediately' list."

"I've always been at the top of that list," he replied. She'd been wrong. That smile was pure arrogance.

She pushed thoughts of later to the back of her mind as she noticed the crowd of anxious Fae standing behind Jeraltan's reception desk. For once, they were silent. Still. It was unnerving and entirely her fault.

"I'm sorry I overreacted," Merry began. A small voice in the back of her mind told her she'd *under*reacted to the information she'd been given, but she pushed that voice down as well. "I will help you fulfill the bargain or find a way around it. You'll all be free as soon as possible. And in the meantime, I will do everything I can to make you more comfortable."

Small nervous smiles met her impromptu speech. Her employees didn't look entirely at peace with the situation, but they relaxed a fraction. Fortunately, Charli's arrival saved her from further explanations of how genuinely thrilled she was to learn that half her employees were not human. It would have been too easy for them to see through those lies.

Charli gave the team a quick wave and smile before letting Merry know they needed to speak in private. Merry's heartbeat kicked up a notch. Does she know? Is she going to quit before we've even gotten started?

But that was ridiculous. For one, Charli was as far from a bigot as any person Merry had ever met. And there was no way she could know. Because of 'glamour' and 'magic' and all the things Merry didn't understand.

Merry refused to let go of Santa's hand, so that meant he joined them in Merry's office. His office. Their office?

All thoughts of office ownership flew out of her/his/their window when Merry closed the door and saw Charli's serious expression and nervous hands clasped in a white-knuckled grip in front of her.

"What is it?" Merry asked in her calming, professional tone. She'd never used it with Charli, and it earned her a small smile in return.

"Contract. Budget." Charli said and color rose to her high cheekbones. Merry sighed with relief then grinned.

"We need to work on your sales pitch for your next big client," Merry told her. Charli's gaze dropped to Merry's nose as she squared her shoulders and nodded once. Horrified that her careless words had caused that change in her usually unflappable friend, Merry continued. "But for now, yes, we can talk 'contract' and 'budget.' I'm sure you have standard terms. I can have Henry look over them and get back to you within 48 hours."

Charli perked up but Santa spoke before she had the chance. "Do we really need a lawyer? It's Charli. She's your friend."

Merry chose not to point out the consequences of the last time Santa had agreed to something without checking with a lawyer. Though, were there lawyers that specialized in what to do if a Fae offered you a bargain to save the lives of the other Fae you'd brought to enslave the human realm? Probably not.

"She's not my friend right now," Merry explained. "She's the best person for this job. And it is a job that I will pay for with the money my employees create. So, yes, for your sake, I will have our lawyer look over the terms."

Her words only caused a crease between Santa's brows, but Charli broke into a smile. It seemed she needed this to be a professional arrangement as much as Merry did. Their friendship was the reason Merry had paid attention to the work Charli had done, but it didn't skew her perception of that work. Charli was, as she'd said on multiple occasions, a marketing genius, a hard worker, and the best person to bring Claus Family Toys into the digital age.

"And as far as the budget goes," Charli began more confidently. "We have options depending on how much you want to do in-house and how quickly you want sales to take off."

Merry hid her smirk. "I assume those things are inversely related."

"Of course," Charli countered, her smile widening. "I'm Queen Midas. The more you put into my hands, the more gold you'll have."

Merry actually let herself laugh. There was a balance between friends and colleagues, and they would find it. "I knew you'd say something like that. I've put together a list of top priorities, let me know when you have a chance to do the same and we can compare notes."

"It's like you don't know me at all," Charli said, smile still firmly in place and looking more natural by the second. She pulled a tablet from her satchel and opened a lengthy checklist.

Merry motioned for her to take a seat in the chair across the desk from her own computer and turned to Santa, "You're welcome to stay but I can already tell you this is going to take a while."

His gaze ping-ponged between Merry and Charli, clearly trying to understand the dynamic. He gave up, shrugged, and flopped into Merry's chair. She raised her eyebrows at his choice of seating until he patted his knee for her to sit.

"Absolutely not," she said with another of the unprofessional snorts she really needed to stop. She took the chair beside Charli and turned her laptop around. As it booted up, she said, "You have to tell me what app you're using for checklists, I need to add this situation to my never-ending list of 'unprofessional things to discuss with Santa.'"

Before Charli could reassure her, Santa was around the desk again, sinking to the floor at her feet and resting his head against her knee. "Is this professional enough?"

Despite herself, Merry smoothed her hand over his braided hair, luxuriating in the feel of the silky strands. He looked up at her with bright, golden eyes and she didn't want to be away from him either. "Somehow this is worse. But we'll make it work."

***

It took an hour and a promise to double Charli's payment to get her to agree to let the Claus Family Toys employees help with the branding, website, text, and imagery. She knew it would be a hard sell since Charli was the expert and no one wanted to answer to a hundred more people than they had to.

With that out of the way, they made it through all Merry's list and half of Charli's even more thorough one before Charli reluctantly ended the meeting to go meet her wife and daughter for dinner. She invited Merry and Santa, but Merry had consulting work to do. So. Much. Consulting. Work.

It was almost like she'd agreed to take on two full-time jobs. Wait, that's exactly what she'd agreed to do. She just couldn't remember why.

Santa couldn't sit still for more than ten minutes at a time, nor could he stand to be away from Merry for even half that time, so she'd accumulated a desk full of little gifts from his multiple trips to the coffee shop, workshop, house, and other places she couldn't even guess based on what he'd returned with.

She was sipping yet another coffee, feeling both jittery and exhausted, when her team meeting began. Simon logged on last, which was unusual in itself. Then, he was almost silent during the two-hour meeting, which was unheard of. There was none of their usual professional jousting to control the meeting or to one-up each other on the off chance a team member mentioned them to the higher-ups.

Simon's off mood extended to how he'd been managing her team while she was out. They showed her multiple presentations that were polished but lacking direction and substance. Then, they filled her in on which of her clients were unhappy. Which was all of them.

She thought the team would be disheartened by the re-work she requested for nearly everything they showed her, but they only seemed relieved. They knew their work was sub-par, but they hadn't known how to fix it. Now that they did, she expected they'd be ordering takeout to fuel their all-nighter.

When she finally finished reassuring them and handing out tasks, the meeting concluded, and Simon was the first to log off.

"Time to go home?" Santa asked hopefully, setting another silver-wrapped candy bar in front of her. He'd said he was part deer—or something like that—but Merry suspected there was some raven heritage mixed in. He sure knew how to collect shiny things, and he was making significant progress in turning her/his/their office into a nest.

"I'll meet you out front in ten," Merry said, frowning at her computer screen.

Santa left her alone with her thoughts and ten thousand shiny gifts but neither of those things helped her decide what to do about Simon. He'd admitted that he was in over his head days ago. She'd offered to help. And she hadn't followed through in a meaningful way. This was on her. But it was on him too. He was a professional. There was no excuse for the shoddy work she'd seen in that meeting, or his blase attitude about it.

She didn't get the chance to decide whether to call him out or let it slide because her phone lit up with her boss' image.

"Hey Boss."

"I need you back tomorrow," he said without formality or greeting.

"We agreed on a timeframe for my return," Merry hedged with a sinking feeling in her gut.

"And now that timeframe has changed. Book a red eye on the company card. First class."

"I can't do that. I have back-to-back meetings lined up tomorrow." It wasn't exactly a lie. She did have to meet with Henry to give him Charli's contract and then she had to meet with Charli, but both could be handled virtually in a pinch.

Mike harrumphed. "Do I need to remind you that outside work activities have to be approved by the board?"

Merry narrowed her eyes at her boss' name on her screen. It wasn't as satisfying as doing it in person. "Claus Family Toys is a client. We discussed this."

"I haven't seen a signed agreement saying as much," he countered. "And now I'm not sure I will support bringing on a new, non-paying client when your existing ones are threatening to leave, no matter what PR opportunities you're trying to sell me."

Mike's name blurred in front of her increasingly narrowed eyes. "I'm on PTO." Her tone was sharper than she'd intended.

"All PTO must be approved in writing and is subject to change with business need. You were approved for two weeks. By that standard, you were due back last Friday. The business needs you here. Get back tomorrow and I will consider not giving you a written warning for job abandonment."

The lump in Merry's throat prevented her from speaking. Which was good, because she wasn't sure what she was going to say. This job was all she'd wanted for so long. It was her life. Her family. Her friends. Her future. Everything.

But she thought of Santa and her new friends in Poleton. Their dedication and quirkiness. Their singalongs and beautiful art. They were family too. It had happened so quickly she hadn't even felt the shift. Kline & Associates wasn't her whole identity anymore.

And they needed her. Santa needed her.

"I'll consider my options and get back to you in the morning," Merry said, matching her boss' pushy tone with one of cool detachment.

He started to say something, but she ended the call before he finished.

A month ago, she would have been on her way to the airport, proud that she had made herself indispensable. Now, she was only disappointed that she hadn't realized she'd also made herself a doormat for Mike's own ambition.

She'd worked eighty-hour weeks to impress him. She'd given back PTO every single year. She hadn't been home to visit her father in seven years and had made him fly to her for holidays. After the holiday, of course, so she could be at the office while Mike spent time with his family.

Her team brought in more profit than any other with fewer people. That used to make her proud. Now, it only made her feel used. They brought in more profit because they worked themselves to death doing the job of two people to save on salaries. Literally worked themselves into sickness. Norman's heart attack. Whatever was going on with Simon. Her own empty life outside of work. The tradeoffs didn't seem worth it anymore.

Mike was an ineffective leader. How had she never seen that before? He didn't hire enough people and bullied his staff into accepting guilt over that fact. Then, he went to the partners and bragged about their success. No, he bragged about *his* success. His team. His success.

She'd thought that was just the way the world worked. Hell, she'd even emulated him—taking credit for her team's work. That changed when she came to Poleton.

Her employees did things that she couldn't do. They were incredible artists and people, and it was so blatantly obvious that she had nothing to do with their work product that she should have drawn comparisons to the other people she managed.

Now, when it was too late, she did. And she didn't like what she found.

Her dad picked up on the second ring, sounding exhausted but happy to hear from her.

"I think I hate my boss," she told him.

"Welcome to corporate America," he joked. "I was beginning to think you were lying about having a job."

"Wait, do you hate your boss? Your job?" she asked.

He laughed in a way that reminded her he'd been working non-stop for two weeks. "Would I rather be playing golf than being asked to come in early before a twelve-hour shift for a safety meeting about—I'm not joking—the dangers of checking your email while walking? Of course. Do I also recognize that this job put a roof over your head and paid for your college? Same answer."

Her heart sank. All his jokes about living to work seemed a little emptier than they had before. Then, she perked up. "You know we're rich now, right? Like let-me-call-my-accountant-and-move-some-money-around rich."

"So, Joy did all right with the toy shop, then? I'm happy for you. But that's your money."

"Like hell it is! What am I going to do with thirty million dollars in cash and over eighty in property?"

He gave an impressed whistle before suggesting, "Private plane?"

Merry huffed an incredulous laugh. "How about early retirement for my dad?"

"While you work two jobs? No thank you. I appreciate the offer, pumpkin, but I wouldn't be able to look myself in the eye."

"What if I only worked one job?" she said in a small, unsure voice. Kline & Associates had been her identity for so long. Could she really give it up? Did she have a choice? Santa and the others needed her. Kline would hire someone else before the end of the week. Someone inferior to her skill, but still.

"That's up to you," her dad replied. "I won't push you in one direction or the other. But I will tell you that you've pushed yourself to the limit for the last seven years. I'm worried about you taking on even more."

"Would you still be proud of me if I just owned a toy company instead of making partner at the most prestigious consulting agency in California?" She was being needy, but that didn't stop the question from haunting her. Would people think she'd given up? That she couldn't cut it? Worse, that she'd given up her dreams for a man? Shit, she hadn't told her dad about Santa...

"I'm proud of you every day, no matter what job you have," her dad said with uncharacteristic seriousness. Thankfully, the moment passed quickly. "But would I be embarrassed to tell my golf buddies that my daughter is the CEO of a company with a private plane? Nah."

"No plane," she said with a chuckle. "Dee would kill me over the carbon emissions."

And that only brought up another wrinkle in her plan. No more lunches with Deirdre. No more drunk shenanigans with Graham and their little group. No more beach days and city life and having everything she could ever want with same-day delivery. She could live without the conveniences of California, but not seeing Deirdre every day was another story.

"You're a CEO now, time to come to the dark side politically. Leave all that socialist nonsense to the underlings."

"I sincerely hope you're joking."

"Half joking. Half interested to see how your opinion of corporate taxation changes when you're the one paying it," he admitted.

"Well, you were no help at all," Merry said. "You've only given me more terrible possibilities to consider."

"You'll make the right choice, Merry. I know it."

With that final reassurance only her dad could provide, she let him catch what little sleep he could before his absurd early morning safety meeting.

Merry pulled on ear warmers and gloves and walked out of Claus Family Toys at almost midnight. Fresh, cold air and twinkling holiday lights greeted her. It smelled clean here. Like mountains and snow and small-town nostalgia. Even the mashup of Christmas decorations seemed charming rather than overwhelmingly cheerful. And then there was the man waiting for her.

Santa was all the things she hadn't realized she loved about Poleton wrapped into one gorgeous, over-the-top package. He was the smell of Christmas trees and friendly smiles and easy warmth that thawed the frozen parts of her. He was everything she didn't have in California and everything she wasn't sure she could live without.

Beaches and delivery service seemed inconsequential compared to the arm he wrapped around her waist and the musical timber of his voice as he whispered, "Ready to go?"

"Yes," Merry said, the weight of the decision lifting off her shoulders, at least for the night.

CHAPTER 31

"Quinn is a snake!" Merry shouted, sitting bolt upright in bed. Santa was beside her, his hair lying like a perfect silk banner across the pillow.

He was wide awake, as he had been when they arrived at the inn last night. She, on the other hand, had fallen asleep on his shoulder on the drive over and then mumbled apologies and promises of 'tomorrow' before falling asleep again the moment her head hit the pillow.

"He is," Santa agreed with a vicious smile. It faded as he got a better look at her expression.

She was a mess, and she knew it. Yesterday's mascara was gluing her eyelashes together and she knew it was probably smeared under her eyes. Her hair was a rat's nest since she hadn't brushed it the night before and she was still wearing jeans.

Her groan probably woke the entire town, but she dragged herself out of bed and started pacing. "He's a snake. A literal snake. In an aquarium."

"Terrarium," Santa corrected.

She rounded on him. "Fix it!"

For the first time since she met him, Santa looked uncertain. "He made a bargain. He has to live with the consequences."

"Unacceptable," Merry said. "Let him out of the deal. Change your mind. I won't date a murderer, Santa."

"He's still alive," Santa pointed out.

Merry shook her head violently, making the rat's nest of her hair even more obvious in her peripheral vision. "He. Is. A. Snake. That's too close to murder for me."

"I… He… I had to protect you and my family." Santa was paler than usual as he climbed out from under the covers and sat cross-legged on the bed. He was unnaturally still as he watched her, and Merry briefly wondered how she'd ever thought he was human.

"Undo it," she demanded.

"I can't," Santa admitted quietly. "The bargain was made. It is enforced by the Fates. Magic itself. I have no power over it now."

She'd backed herself into a corner and true fear gripped her heart—for all the wrong reasons. She didn't want to lose their fledgling relationship, but she couldn't date a person who turned another person into an animal as punishment.

Sure, she could understand his motivation. Quinn had threatened his family's well-being. He'd effectively extended Santa's enslavement by a decade. But at the end of the day, it was a business deal. One that Joy had entered into. Like all their problems, the blame for this one rested firmly on her grandmother's shoulders.

"There must be a way," she nearly begged. She wanted nothing more than to crawl into his lap and hide from all the problems she had to solve today. It was a new feeling, but not one she could succumb to.

"The only way out of a bargain is to find a loophole the Fates will accept. They are very nit-picky about wording. Like when Jeraltan was feeling the bargain's pull, and you convinced the Fates that his normal duties were satisfying the bargain."

So that's where all the stories came from about Faerie bargains and riddles. A loophole. She could do that. Or, better yet, she could ask the hundred and four Fae and one lawyer at the mansion to find one.

"We're fixing this. This morning. I want Quinn back to his human self by lunch."

She didn't give him time to argue. Just grabbed her toiletry bag and slammed the bathroom door between them.

Was this their first fight as a couple? Or was it the first time she'd threatened an employee? Both?

***

Merry felt a little more human after a shower, but she was still a bundle of nerves as she climbed behind the wheel of Santa's truck. They couldn't build a relationship on the foundation of murder. She wouldn't let that happen.

She visualized her to-do list for the day.

1. *Find a loophole in a Fae bargain to return an annoying man to his human form.*
2. *Make life-changing career decisions.*
3. *Legal meeting.*
4. *Marketing meeting.*
5. *Find a financial advisor who knows something about estate tax.*
6. *Convince Graham to move to Poleton so she wouldn't be alone.*

It was a decidedly eclectic list, but that didn't make it any less challenging.

Santa was silent on their drive to the mansion. He didn't even turn on the radio.

Merry shouldn't feel bad about Santa's mood. She hadn't forced him to turn Quinn into a snake. But she hated seeing the light that usually surrounded him so dim.

Another problem arose when they arrived at the mansion.

Graham, wearing only a pair of plaid boxer shorts, was standing in the doorway of Jeraltan's bedroom which had once been some sort of closet, shouting at the other inhabitants of the house.

"Just because he is a brownie, doesn't mean he's your maid!"

"Yes, it does," Pari argued.

Rari nodded. "Brownies live to care for their families. We're his family."

"Have any of you ever considered taking care of him? Anyone? No?

You're just using his race as an excuse not to see him as a person, and I won't have it."

Jeraltan peeked his head under Graham's arm and beamed up at his boyfriend. Like Graham, he was wearing only underwear, but Merry didn't find it as strange as she should have. If anything, she was happy that Graham was losing some of his characteristic shyness. Graham met Jeraltan's eyes, and his expression softened in an instant. "We're going back to bed. Make your own damned breakfast."

Jeraltan had just enough time to duck back inside the bedroom before Graham slammed the door on a hundred stunned Fae.

"Merry, make your friend stop being mean," Pari said, turning bewildered eyes on her and Santa. There were nods of agreement all around.

"Graham's right. I know Jeraltan loves doing things to show he cares but you can't rely on him for everything. That's not fair. You all know how to cook, so do it. I need to talk to you, anyway."

The Fae traded glances and once again it was the twins who spoke up. "We don't know how to cook, though. Jeraltan doesn't let us touch the stove."

"I'll show you while we figure out how to turn Quinn back into a person," Merry said. She really didn't have time for a lesson on basic household skills, but if these centuries-old people couldn't even feed themselves, it would need to move near the top of her list.

"You can't undo a bargain. It's enforced by the Fates," Faye said.

"Rule number one of talking to your boss: bring me solutions, not problems," Merry said. Crap, she sounded just like Mike. Finding a balance between friends and professionals was hard. "You can bring me problems, too, of course, but right now we need solutions. Creative thinking. You're all good at that." Too far in the other direction? She couldn't tell.

Faye raised her eyebrows, a smirk playing on her lips. If there was one person who could handle her snappishness, it was Faye.

A mass of uncertain Fae followed her into the kitchen with Santa sticking close to her side but not touching her. That was a problem too, but one that didn't have a solution yet. She'd only had one day to hold his hand,

and she already missed it.

"What do you want for breakfast?" she asked. And received two dozen different answers.

Merry held up a hand. Boundaries. She could set those. "Pick one thing and I'll show you how to make it."

Santa presided over the vote with none of his usual good humor. She barely had time to make coffee before they'd decided on oatmeal. No one seemed particularly happy about that choice, but they'd made it in record time.

Merry found a half-full container of oats, thankfully with the instructions printed on the back. She'd never made them without a microwave. It was straightforward—pour boiling water over them and stir.

She handed out orders to gather bowls and showed each person how to use a measuring cup—something she'd never thought she'd have to explain to a full-grown adult. But, then again, her grandmother had treated them like children and Jeraltan had kept them from learning basic skills by doing everything for them.

While they were busy painstakingly measuring dry oats into their bowls, Merry found four kettles, filled the first, and showed Faye how to light the gas stove.

"That's it?" she asked.

"Yep. Now we just wait for it to boil. You can fill the other three kettles and put them on as well."

It was more sad than cute how carefully her friends handled the kettles and stove.

"So, we need a loophole in Santa's bargain," she announced. The clattering of silverware and measuring cups paused. She glanced at Santa who was looking sheepish.

"What exactly did you say?" Faye asked.

"Umm…"

"You don't remember? *Again*?" Faye said, eyes wide. "Santa, you can't make bargains on a whim! They are the most sacred form of Fae magic. The Fates are not pleased with those who abuse them."

Oh, goodie. Another worry to add to the list. The universe could turn on her boyfriend at any moment.

Nope. There was no reason to borrow trouble. Merry had enough of it already.

"You told him to deliver the check in person at the Bank of Poleton in four days. Then, you said he would spend the rest of his life as an impotent, fangless snake," Merry supplied. She remembered his outburst well. "Then you said 'do we have a bargain'"

Muttered curses filled the crowded kitchen. "That's too simple. There's no loophole." Merry couldn't see which of the Fae had voiced her biggest worry. She'd been racking her brain all morning and had come to the same conclusion.

The mood was subdued as the kettles began to whistle and Merry showed them how to use the large measuring cup with the handle to transfer boiling water for their breakfast. The kettle and cup made their way around the room with only a few hisses of pain from spilled water and too-hot bowls. The rest of the group quietly repeated Santa's bargain, searching for a loophole that didn't exist.

"Actually, he said Quinn would spend the rest of his 'miserable life' as the 'snake he truly is,'" Graham said from the doorway.

"What?" Merry said, though she'd heard him perfectly.

The mood lifted considerably as Jeraltan hip-checked Merry away from his stove and put on more water to boil. "I've got this. Let Graham solve your other problem."

Merry chose not to notice the flush in Jeraltan's cheeks, the sweat darkening the hair around his ears, or the bite mark on Graham's neck.

"Miserable life," Faye repeated. "So, if his misery ends, the bargain is fulfilled?"

Siofra nodded enthusiastically. "His happy life doesn't have to be spent as a snake. Or his indifferent life. His scared life. Any emotion other than misery."

"What about the 'snake you truly are' bit?" Merry asked. "He isn't truly a snake, so wouldn't that be a loophole?"

A hundred and four Fae heads shook. "The Fates like metaphors. They don't like imprecise language. 'Miserable' is our loophole," Faye said. She and Merry turned to Santa. He didn't outright agree but his expression was less pinched than before.

"So, we just need to make Quinn happy," Merry summarized.

"I think that will work," Santa agreed.

On the surface, they'd found a loophole, but how would she make a man-turned-snake happy? Or anything other than miserable?

Once again, it was time to delegate. "Everyone think of an idea to make Quinn happy and go through them one by one until it works." She turned to Graham, "Thank you. Your lawyering is a literal lifesaver."

He just shook his head, bed-head curls flopping around his ears. "I didn't mean to help. I personally think Quinn got what he deserves, but I can't help remembering details."

Merry chose to ignore this murderous side of Graham as well.

CHAPTER 32

Santa didn't follow Merry to the meeting with Henry, so she had a half hour car ride to think about her future. The choice was more difficult than it should have been.

The previous night, she thought she had it all figured out. Santa was here. Her new friends were here. They needed her. That should have been the end of the story.

But in the early morning chill, Merry remembered the warmth of Southern California. The beaches. The food. And mostly—the satisfaction she got from kicking ass at a very difficult job.

She loved her high heels and designer suits. She loved walking into the challenge of a new company and a new set of problems. And she loved walking out knowing that she'd helped turn things around. For the most part, she loved her coworkers, the fast-paced lifestyle, her apartment. It all seemed exciting and bright in her memories.

There were downsides, of course. Every job and life had them. She was lonely in California, even with Deirdre, Charli, Rosie, and Graham. They had their own lives, and she spent too much of hers alone, shoulders hunched over a spreadsheet.

But was it worth it?

Could she give up everything she'd worked for? Focus on one company for the rest of her life?

If she changed her mind... if she freed the Fae from their bargain and they chose to leave… if she and Santa didn't work out. What then?

She pulled over in the parking lot of the grocery store and watched the people of Poleton go about their day. There were holiday sweaters and sneakers all around. Unfashionable haircuts. Kids with sticky faces and roll-down socks. It was quiet. Comfortable. Homey. All things Merry had tried to avoid when building her life in California.

She called the one person who she'd sworn to never go to for advice.

"'Ello?"

"Simon. Sorry, I forgot about the time difference."

He sighed. "At least let me make coffee before you start yelling." The shuffle of bedding let her know he was dragging himself upright.

"I'm not calling to yell," she told him.

"Well, you're the first person this week, then," he said. Water ran in the background as he filled the coffee pot. Or maybe a cup if he was a Keurig man. He probably was. Laziness, even in his coffee preparation.

"Has it been bad?" she asked.

Simon grunted in response. "I'm so tired of it. Everyone needs something *right now*. And they're all mad. All the time. It's not that serious. I mean, the world isn't going to end if the social media campaign kicks off a day later than planned. I can't believe I spent six years in college just to tell CEOs that the graphic designer I recommended is a day late with the sixth revision of the cartoon puppies they asked for."

"Richard?" she asked.

"Yep."

"He needs a firm hand. I told you to tell him he only gets two free revisions. He won't spend money on a third. Or a sixth."

Something ceramic hit something plastic with a bang. Keurig. She knew it. "Yeah. I get it. You have all the answers. None of this would be happening if you were here. I've heard it all from Mike and every single client."

Merry tried to interject, but Simon cut her off. "My grandmother cried when I told her I couldn't come home for Christmas again. She *cried*, Merry. And the doctor told me that she—the woman who raised me when my parents died, who never asked for anything in return—might not get another holiday. That's what I'm missing for you. For this job. For these ungrateful clients. So, sorry that I'm not living up to your expectations."

"I'm so sorry," Merry said. She hadn't known any of that. In fact, she'd learned more about Simon's life outside of work in the last thirty seconds than in the seven years she'd known him.

The stress in his voice, the sacrifices he was making, even the fact that he was talking to her about work at five in the morning like it was the expectation, made the decision for her. She didn't want to go back to that life. She wanted time with the people she loved, while she still had them. No job was worth giving that up.

"I'm quitting," they said at the same time.

"Wait, what?" Simon said at the same time Merry said, "Good."

She stayed quiet and let him explain first. "I'm moving home to Tennessee. I don't know what I'll do for work, or where I'll live, or anything else, but I won't miss this last year with my grandmother. I've given enough to Kline. Too much."

"Where in Tennessee?" she asked, a possibly awful idea forming.

"Near Doe Valley. Why? Know any small-town consulting firms looking to hire a CPA with no recommendation from his previous employer? Shit, what am I doing?"

Merry pulled up a map on her phone and laughed, despite his bitter tone. "I can't get away from you Joker. You'll be forty minutes from me."

"Great. We can have coffee, and you can remind me I'm unemployed while you're a CEO."

"It wouldn't be a fun commute, but…"

"Don't you dare offer me a job," he said but his voice had lost the hopeless edge.

"I hate my current accountant and, like you said, you're a CPA. Our financial records are a mess and a half. The business is about to go through major growing pains. I need a CFO I can trust."

"So, you want me to recommend someone, then? 'Cause I know you don't trust me."

"That's the strange thing. I do. Plus, I'd be your boss, so that's the ultimate win," Merry joked.

"You inherited the company, doesn't count," he shot back. "But if you're serious, I'm in. Provided you meet my extensive list of demands."

"I'll send you a reasonable and only-slightly-lowball offer this afternoon," Merry replied.

Simon was silent for a long moment. "We're really doing this? Quitting?"

"Yep. It's the only thing we've ever agreed on, so it's either an idea so great it surpasses our mutual dislike or so terrible we'll be glad we can blame each other in a few months."

"If it gets me close to Nana, I don't really care which of those it is," Simon said.

"Go drink your coffee. Book your flight. Find a place to live. Have a relaxing morning," Merry suggested.

"So you can call Mike first and I'll have to deal with the yelling? No thanks." He hung up before Merry could get in another word.

"Damn you, Simon," she muttered to her empty car. And started typing a resignation email.

***

Henry skimmed Charli's contract and gave a tentative thumbs-up. That was good enough for Merry who considered the lawyer's input just a formality. She knew Charli was hungry for her new firm to succeed, but not enough to harm a friend. He also agreed to write Simon's employment offer. Merry threw numbers together based on gut feeling and quick searches on her phone. Simon would let her know if she was truly low-balling him.

She made her way back to the Claus Family Toys complex just before lunch and just in time to see her current accountant storming up the front steps of the mansion. She followed him without a second thought.

The tail end of his tirade included the word 'lazy' more than once and concluded with "Get to work!" He turned on his heel and came face-to-face with Merry.

"I wasn't aware that you were the foreman or the CEO, Howard," she said coolly.

"Someone has to keep them in line. Joy never would have stood for this. She knew what trouble they get into when left unsupervised."

Merry cocked her head at him. Did he know about their heritage or was he just a jerk?

"I asked all of them to work on something for me today," she looked up until she found Santa's eyes. "I apologize for not being more specific, Santa. You can tell everyone else that Claus Family Toys will be closed the rest of the week. With pay for everyone scheduled to work, of course."

"I didn't authorize that," the accountant snapped.

"You're overstepping, Howard. In fact, I don't think—" *your services will be necessary anymore*. The words wouldn't come.

You're fired. She tried to say instead. The words lodged in her throat.

Howard watched her, oblivious to her inner turmoil. "You don't think?" he prompted after a too-long moment.

"I was going to say, I don't think I told you I hired a CFO," she said. Whatever magic or curse or Fates-something was holding her tongue let her get those words out.

So, she couldn't fire him, but she could hire someone above him. That was good to know, even as her mind spun trying to remember how she'd gotten herself into this position in the first place.

Howard's expression fell. "You did what?"

"Hired. A. CFO." Merry repeated, her even voice at odds with her pounding heart.

"I have managed this company's finances for ten years! You can't do this."

"Sure, I can. Now, go home and enjoy your days off. I'll see you and the rest of the team on Monday."

Howard gaped like a fish before storming off.

Merry looked up to see her employees looking at her like she'd just slayed a dragon. She didn't see Santa at first, but quickly found him where he belonged—at her side.

She hadn't heard or seen him move, but she should have known he wouldn't let her face an uncomfortable conversation alone. He hadn't stepped in, but he'd been there in case she needed him.

"Kitchen," she whispered.

Santa nodded and followed her, motioning for everyone else to stay where they were except Faye, who went to spread the word about the closure. It was a spur of the moment decision she hoped wouldn't delay any important shipments.

Graham and Jeraltan followed them into the kitchen and Merry was thankful for old houses and their lack of open floor plans as she shut the door behind them.

"You should have fired him," Graham said. When had he grown a mean-streak? Merry guessed it happened right around the time he fell in love.

"I tried," she said, then explained the choking feeling that kept her from speaking the words. "That was magic, right? But how?"

Do not panic. She told herself. It wouldn't do any good. Sure, she was magically tongue-tied. Sure, she'd somehow entered a bargain with a dead woman or been affected by some other spell. But those things could be dealt with. Right? She just needed to think calmly and rationally.

"Bargains can be oral or written. You've said before that you never met Joy, so did you sign something?" Santa asked.

Merry thought back to her strange experience in her grandmother's home with the letter she couldn't read, then managed to. But she'd never signed it.

The memory hit her then, just a blip in an otherwise stressful day. The letter Henry had put in front of her with the ownership transfer paperwork. The one that he said wasn't legally binding, but her grandmother insisted she sign anyway.

"I did. I can't remember what it said. I didn't think it would matter since it wasn't a legal document," Merry said.

Graham groaned. "I'm stealing all your pens until you learn the number one rule of life: Don't sign anything. Ever. Without a lawyer's approval."

"Oh, and you would have been able to tell that it was a magically binding document? In that case, I'm so sorry I didn't run it by you first," Merry snapped.

Graham rolled his eyes. "Where is the contract? I'll do my best to get you out of it."

Merry still had the paperwork in her laptop bag in the truck so Graham went to get it, and Jeraltan followed since they couldn't be more than a foot apart at any time. That left Merry alone with Santa.

"We haven't been able to make Quinn happy yet," he admitted quietly. "I'm sorry."

Merry closed the space between them and did what she'd wanted to do since she woke this morning—she buried her face in his chest and breathed in his unique scent of wood polish and cedar. "We'll figure it out. All of it."

His arms wrapped around her, tentatively at first. When she didn't pull away, he sighed against the top of her head and tightened his grip.

They stayed like that for a silent few minutes, just leaning against each other, hoping their combined strength was enough to deal with the monumental tasks ahead of them. Merry pulled away, needing to get started on those tasks, but Santa held firm. "Just another minute. If I'm going to lose you, just let me pretend for one more minute."

She'd never heard him sound so broken and never wanted to hear it again. This time, when she tried to pull away, he let her. She didn't go far, though. Just enough to look up at him with her hands resting against his chest. "You're not going to lose me. I quit my job in California. I'm staying."

His smile was a dull replication of his usual grin. "If that's what you want, then I'm glad. It will be good to see you every day, even if we can't be together."

"Why wouldn't we be together?"

"You said we couldn't be if I didn't fix Quinn."

Merry let out a relieved breath. "I was being dramatic. We will fix Quinn. We are together, as long as you still want to be. We will free you from this bargain and then we will still be together. Okay?"

There it was. His beautiful smile. The one that turned her heart mushy and her knees to Jello. "Okay. Yes. Let's do all of that."

He leaned down and brushed a soft kiss to her lips. It was sweeter and more restrained than their kisses the day before, but she liked it even better because it was a promise of a million more to come.

CHAPTER 33

"I hate your grandmother," Graham said. He and Merry were sitting in uncomfortable chairs beside the only playground in Poleton. The chairs, like the playground equipment, had seen better days. And those better days had been decades ago.

"She was Fae, according to Santa, so she probably had a lot of experience with bargains." Graham had gone over the document Merry signed, vowing not to change any of the current employment contracts with no success in finding a loophole. "I haven't had a chance to grill him about that yet. Remind me to put it on the list."

"That list is getting pretty long, isn't it?" Graham said sympathetically.

"Too long," Merry agreed, turning her attention back to Rosie and her moms. Charli was behind her on the swing pushing, Deirdre was in front of her, grabbing her feet and lifting her further into the air with each swing forward. Rosie shrieked with infectious joy every single time.

Merry smiled. She loved her new friends in Poleton, but she was going to miss these friends more than she could say.

"Let me scratch one thing off my list—Henry wants you to stay and take over his practice."

Graham let out a long, whistling breath. "There is no bar reciprocity between California and North Carolina."

Merry glanced sideways at him, raising her eyebrows. That was his

ALL I WANT FOR CHRISTMAS IS SANTA

only objection? "You passed the bar once; you can do it again."

"I—" He stopped and shook his head. "I think I'm in over my head." He turned to Merry, brown eyes pained behind his glasses. "It's only been three weeks. I've only known him for three weeks, but I'm already thinking of who I can get to sublet my apartment. I've lost my mind, haven't I?"

"Did we smoke something we shouldn't have? I know Faye isn't growing daisies in that greenhouse." Merry asked. "Oh, or is this an *Alice In Wonderland* situation? Did we fall into some alternate reality where hot Fae men love us?"

Graham quirked a half smile. "I think I've read that book. But however we got here, I don't want to go back. Jeraltan makes me… probably not altogether sane, but braver. And happier than I've ever been. He's just so… real. He has such a big heart, and he's never embarrassed of anything he does, or I do. I've never felt free like I do when I'm with him."

"And he's gorgeous," Merry added.

"So damned beautiful. And the sex…"

"Playground. Children," Merry reminded him.

Graham laughed. "Fine. I won't give details, but it's as amazing and unique as he is."

"Unique? We're going for drinks later so I can get those details."

He laughed and stood, shaking his head with a blush creeping up his neck. "On second thought, I'll take the drink, but you're not getting details. I'm keeping this one all to myself."

Merry stood and rubbed her gloved hands together. Dee and Charli were looking tired, but Rosie was having the time of her life. Who knew kids could be so enthralled with an old swing set? It had been over an hour of the same push and pull, and she wasn't bored yet. But her cheeks were redder than Merry liked to see them and it was much, much colder than she'd ever experienced in her short three years of life.

"Hot chocolate break?" she shouted in her friends' direction. The distraction worked and Rosie was already clambering to be let down so she could start her next adventure.

"We need to tell them," Graham said quietly as Charli and Deirdre disentangled their offspring from the child-proof swing.

"That you're staying?"

Graham shook his head. "I'm not sure about that yet. But we need to tell them about the Fae. And magic." After a moment he added, "Can't believe I just said that with a straight face."

"We can't. The more people who know the more danger Santa and the others are in. They're stuck in this town and don't have much magic to defend themselves."

They were running out of time to have a private conversation as Dee and Charli approached with Rosie in tow.

Graham sighed. "You're right. I can't stand keeping a secret from Dee, but I also don't want to be the reason the CIA kidnaps my boyfriend. His safety has to come first."

"The CIA doesn't operate inside the country."

"Tell that to Kennedy."

"Not this again. I swear if you go off another rant about conspiracies…"

"What are you two whispering about?" Deirdre asked with a tired smile. Jet lag always hit her hard and between that, the time difference, and a toddler suffering from the same afflictions, she was barely staying on her feet.

"Boooys," Merry said, drawing the word out in a sing-song voice. "The same thing we're always talking about."

"Yuck," Charli joked, in keeping with the theme that they were all twelve years old.

"Cooties," Deirdre chimed in, like she hadn't dated multiple men in the past.

"What's cooties?" Rosie asked.

Merry left that to her parents to explain as they walked the short distance to Main Street. The lamp posts were all wrapped in faded red ribbon and hung with fake poinsettia wreaths that had turned pink with age. Normally, the Christmas decorations would make her skin crawl, but this time Merry only wondered if it would make the town happy to have new ones. She had plenty of money, after all.

The coffee shop/ice cream parlor/used bookstore was a charming mix-match of sofas and old-fashioned booths stuffed to the brim with people escaping the cold. Their little party waited in line chatting quietly amongst themselves. But good ol' Southern Hospitality reared its charming head.

People complimented Rosie's outfit, asked her name, joked with her about ordering an espresso. Others introduced themselves to Merry, complete with their street name and job title. A few more asked invasive questions about the toy shop and Merry's plans. It was a bit overwhelming, but—like the Christmas decorations—not as bad as Merry expected.

The giant mechanic pushed his way out the front door as they finally got a chance to enter, and Merry smiled and said hello. Wayne was friendly enough until she introduced Graham, then his mood shifted as he looked the lawyer up and down.

With a gruff and unexpected, "Take care of him." Wayne walked away with a coffee that looked tiny in his beefy hand.

"I will," Graham called after him, a little too possessively.

Merry, Deirdre, and Charli exchanged a look. Then, started laughing at the fist Graham had balled at his side.

"Okay, who are you and what have you done with my brother?" Deirdre asked. "My sweet, innocent brother who has never gotten jealous in his life."

"I'm not jealous," Graham argued. Again, too sharply.

"We all know he's willing to start a fight over things he cares about," Merry said to lighten the mood.

Even Graham cracked a smile at the shared memory of a hazy night over six years before.

"Never tell Jeraltan," Graham said.

"About which part? You fighting a DJ over playing TLC at a Destiny's Child dance party? Charli dragging you out of the bar by your sequined top and falling in love with your sister? Or the more recent development of you considering fighting a man twice your size over a completely innocuous comment?"

"Those are all great starts to the list of things we will never tell my boyfriend," Graham said. "I should have you all sign NDAs."

They finally made their way to the counter and ordered coffees for the adults and a hot chocolate for Rosie. The poor thing was fast asleep against Charli's shoulder.

"Are you here for the festival?" the barista asked excitedly.

"Festival?" Merry asked.

The young woman nodded enthusiastically. "The Christmas Festival. We have it every Christmas Eve. We've been trying to attract visitors for years but mostly it's just locals."

"I thought the parade was weeks ago," Merry said.

"What does the parade have to do with the festival?" the girl asked, obviously confused. A cleared throat from the line behind her forced Merry to move to the side while they waited for their drinks.

Her friends took the opportunity to laugh at her. "You look like you're going to be sick. Is it the Christmas Spirit making you green?" Deirdre asked.

"Yep. Gets me around this time every year. Luckily, I've built up a tolerance, but I'm not sure Santa has," Merry replied.

"His name is Santa," Charli pointed out, quietly to avoid waking her daughter. "You're definitely getting dragged to the party."

"At least I know Graham will be dragged along with me. Probably wearing one of Jeraltan's suggestive Christmas sweaters."

Graham didn't look nearly as upset as Merry expected. Either he had it bad or he hadn't seen the worst of the sweater collection yet.

CHAPTER 34

Merry drove back to the mansion for the third time that day, wishing she had enough money to have the entire Claus Family Toys complex moved closer to town. The afternoon with her friends had settled a lot of her anxiety, but also created an ache in her chest that wouldn't go away no matter how many times she rubbed the spot.

They were flying back to California the day after Christmas and Merry wouldn't be with them. She would have to go back at some point to pack her things, but other than that she was finished with California. It was sobering. And scary. But those feelings faded as she parked in the gravel drive, spotting the squeaky-clean taillights of Santa's favorite truck peeking around the side of the building.

Jeraltan was waiting at the bottom of the stairs, his wide brown eyes searching the truck then the drive behind her for Graham.

"He'll be back in an hour or so, he had to run an errand," Merry said. Graham was actually talking to Henry about taking over his firm, but he'd asked her not to share that news yet.

"I like errands," Jeraltan said.

Merry shrugged, trying her best not to smirk. Graham was going to break and tell him everything before dinner. She could barely hold out against his sad doe eyes, and she wasn't in love with him. Speaking of men she was in love with. "Where's Santa?"

The pleading expression quickly changed to a guilty one. "Inside.

We still haven't been able to make Quinn happy enough to break the bargain."

Merry nodded, because what else was she supposed to do? She couldn't say it was okay. It wasn't. It was definitely not okay that there was a man-turned-snake in the house she owned. And it was definitely not okay that the man she loved was responsible.

"He feels really bad," Jeraltan said, falling into step beside her.

"I know."

There was nothing else to say, so she and Jeraltan made their way inside. The team wasn't gathered in the ballroom for once. First, they passed a group carrying boxes of Valentine's Day decorations down from the attic entrance in the foyer.

"You're decorating for Valentine's already?" she asked.

Jeraltan shook his head. "We're looking for anything we can use for a booth at the Christmas festival. We used all our decorations for the workshop and office again."

"Again?"

He shrugged. "We always mean to save some for the house, but we run out."

Merry hid a smile. There were plenty of decorations to tastefully adorn both the business buildings and the mansion, but they'd chosen to *dis*tastefully drown the workshop in tinsel instead.

Faye carried a pinata Merry recognized from the last party down the ladder. She grinned at Merry. "We never get to go to the festival. We're all so excited."

"Why not?" Merry asked.

Faye set the pinata down out of the way so Addie could climb the ladder next. "We get to choose either the parade or the festival and every year we say we're going to choose the festival, but parade day comes, and we just can't miss it."

It was a good thing Merry's grandmother was already dead or Merry would be facing a murder charge as she looked at her exuberant employees. She might hate Christmas celebrations, but she would never keep other people from enjoying them.

She opened her mouth to say that they would never have to work festival day again, but the magical choking sensation came over her.

Okay. Apparently, it was in one or more of their employment contracts that they had to work that day. How had she gotten around the bargain earlier?

"Claus Family Toys will now be closed December 23rd through the 26th every year with pay for all employees scheduled to work."

You forgot to take away my ability to close the company whenever I want, she thought with a mental bird flipped to her dead grandmother.

Their faces lit and Jeraltan actually squealed with excitement. She handed over her credit card to buy actual Christmas decorations and left them to celebrate the paid time off.

She found Santa sitting on an ugly floral sofa with little ruffles around the bottom in the living room with a block of wood in his hand. He stared straight ahead, but his carving knife slid through the wood like butter. The side panel of a toy truck appeared in a single swipe. It was unnatural, probably magical, and definitely how the Fae were capable of making a hundred toys in the time it would take a normal human to make one.

Across from him, the ancient box TV had been moved, and a terrarium complete with green garden snake sat on the console table. Siofra held a terrified white mouse above the snake's enclosure. She grinned at Merry. "This is definitely going to make him happy!" Merry didn't have time to point out that Quinn the snake was curled into a decidedly unhappy ball in the furthest corner of the terrarium before she dropped the mouse directly on top of his green scales.

Snake Quinn panicked. The mouse panicked. And for the first time in the history of snake-mouse relations, it was impossible to tell which was more terrified. Both animals tried to climb the glass walls to escape the other.

"He doesn't like it," Merry said as she crossed the room.

Siofra's face fell. "Why not? It's food. He hasn't eaten all day."

"Maybe because he's a person, not a real snake?" Merry suggested. She didn't actually know how the bargain's magic worked—whether it

217

altered Quinn's mind or just his body—but it seemed as good of a guess as any.

She stood beside the terrarium trying to remind herself that the snake didn't have fangs and there was nothing inherently scary about a mouse. It didn't help. She still couldn't force her hand to reach into the enclosure.

"Merry's right, I'll get it," Santa said, sounding disappointed. Quinn gave up on escape and curled into an even tighter ball when Santa drew near. His scales actually began to quake when Santa scooped the mouse out of the terrarium.

"Have you been here all day?" Merry asked.

"Of course," Santa replied. "You want him free. I'll do everything I can to make that happen, even if the Fates decided I have to work while I supervise this."

"The compulsion to work is acting up?"

"Yeah, but it's fine, duckie. Don't worry about me."

"Why don't you go for a walk, and I'll try," she suggested.

"I'd rather not leave you alone with him, even if he is a harmless snake."

"Just give me five minutes."

Santa watched her for a long moment, then chose to trust her. He took Siofra and closed the living room door behind them. She didn't need to listen all that carefully to know his footsteps stopped right outside the door.

With a half smile at his overprotectiveness, Merry turned to the terrarium.

"Quinn, can you hear me?"

Nothing. The snake stayed in a tight ball, half hidden under moss.

"I'm trying to help you, Quinn. If you can hear me, lift your head."

Slowly, the snake lifted its blunt head a fraction of an inch, eyeing Merry as its tongue darted involuntarily out of its mouth. She shivered. Snakes were creepy, even little green ones like this.

"You made a magical bargain with Santa," the snake's head tucked all the way under its belly and the trembling resumed. She hadn't known snakes could tremble.

"He's not here right now," Merry soothed. "It's just us."

The snake showed its eyes once more. "As I was saying, you made a magical bargain, but Santa left a loophole. He told you you'd spend the rest of your miserable life as a snake. So, if you are no longer miserable, you will no longer be a snake. Does that make sense?"

Merry was aware that she was talking to him like a child, but she wasn't sure how much of his human mind he'd retained.

The snake lifted its head enough to give a shallow approximation of a nod.

"Good. So, try to be happy."

If a snake could look like it was concentrating, Quinn would be doing that. Nothing happened.

"Maybe happy is too hard. How about calm? Calm isn't miserable."

Still nothing.

Calm. She could help with calm.

Merry began a lullaby her mother had sung to her when she had trouble sleeping. Her voice was not as beautiful as her mother's, but she could carry a tune.

Quinn began to slowly, slowly uncurl from the tight ball, so Merry kept singing. Then kept singing some more until she'd exhausted the typical lullabies and moved on to The Beatles.

She poured more of herself into the music, making sure to keep her voice upbeat but soft and reassuring. *You will be calm, damn it*, she thought as she moved through the greatest hits album she'd had on CD in her first car. *Calm, calm, calm.* She repeated the mantra until her head hurt and she'd made it halfway through another album.

Finally, there was a flash of blinding light and the sound of glass shattering. When the light faded, a very naked Quinn was standing before her, glancing around the room like he'd just woken up in a Saw movie.

She tossed him a blanket from the couch but didn't have time to do more than that before the living room door burst open and… no that couldn't possibly be right. Graham was holding a sword. An honest-to-God sword. It was made of wood and looked a bit like a thorn, but still. It was a sword.

Jeraltan entered behind him carrying a stack of papers, and Santa filed into the room after them.

How long had she been in here? Seemingly long enough for Jeraltan to return from his decoration-buying errand and everyone to lose their collective mind.

Quinn hid behind Merry, but Graham stepped around her and held the wooden sword against his ribs. "Sign the NDA and you're free to go."

Merry turned just enough to see Quinn shaking his head so violently it looked like it would pop off and go rolling across the floor.

"No." His voice was raspy, panicked. "No more agreements. No more...*bargains*."

"Sign. It. Or we'll leave you here with Santa." Graham replied tonelessly.

Quinn swallowed. "Pen."

Jeraltan stepped forward with an unusually serious expression, a lengthy legal contract, and his favorite fluffy leopard print pen. Quinn signed quickly and that zap of energy she'd come to associate with magic ran through the room.

"You good, Marshmallow?" Graham said.

Jeraltan nodded, his face pale and drawn.

Graham finally put the sword away and Quinn ran. No questions about what had happened to him. No threats of retribution. He just ran.

Maybe he was smarter than Merry gave him credit for.

Once she followed him to the front door and watched him awkwardly run through the public street with just a ratty blanket around him, Merry started laughing. First out of relief that she could finally, truly forgive Santa. Then, out of humor at the details of the situation—sword, fuzzy pen, Graham acting like a lawyer-in-shining-armor.

"An NDA? Seriously?" she said, wiping a tear from her eye.

"You gave me the idea earlier. And I've seen a lot of movies. I won't let this be his villain origin story so he can go start an anti-Fae hate group and target Jeraltan."

"Bargain disguised as an NDA," Jeraltan added sleepily. Clearly, it was his magic fueling the bargain because he looked a second away from collapsing in Graham's arms.

Merry's humor disappeared. "Are you alright? What can I do?"

Jeraltan waved her off, "I'll be fine in a moment. There were a lot of words to wrap magic around."

"More words mean more magic, why didn't you tell me?" Graham chided, already sweeping his boyfriend off his feet.

"I'm a brownie. I can handle it. Second most powerful…" The rest of their conversation was inaudible as Graham carried him to his bedroom to rest.

"Will he be okay?" Merry asked Santa.

He nodded. "He'll be fine by morning."

Good. Jeraltan would be fine. Quinn would be fine. With that track record, it was easy to believe that everything would be fine. That mentality had to be one of the common logical fallacies—she couldn't remember the name of it—but that didn't matter. Sometimes fallacies were comforting.

She nestled against Santa's chest and let his strong arms protect her from the rest of the endless list of tasks she had to complete that evening.

She'd spent the better part of a decade carving all distractions out of her life, but she was more than happy to let his warmth keep her from work for a little while.

CHAPTER 35

The day felt like it would never end, but Merry had one more stop to make and then she could fall asleep in Santa's arms. That promise was the only thing keeping her on her feet.

Joy's house looked different after dark. The antique charm was gone, replaced by shadows and chill. Merry shivered as she stepped up to the door and her reaction had nothing to do with the lack of central heat.

Now that she knew about magic, she could feel it in her grandmother's space like it had leaked out of her and sunk into every surface. It was a slight heaviness in the air, raised hairs on the back of her neck, goosebumps up her arms. It felt like being watched, though she knew the house was empty.

Santa's hand in hers kept her steady.

"The house doesn't like me," he said in a near whisper.

Merry would have laughed if she wasn't so uncomfortable with her newfound magical awareness.

"It's a house. It doesn't get an opinion," she said instead.

"It would be just a house if Joy had not built it. But this is an extension of her. It remembers." His voice sounded nothing like a character from a horror movie approaching the haunted house. Absolutely nothing.

She slid the key into the lock and another shiver shook her. "It's just a house," she repeated, more to herself than Santa. Where was this wariness the last time she'd visited? "And she's dead. Shouldn't the magic have evaporated or something?"

Santa gave her a professional-grade side eye. "If it worked like that then the glamour protecting our true identities would have also evaporated."

"Stop making sense. It's disconcerting," Merry said, only slightly embarrassed at her lack of logic.

All thoughts of embarrassment and logic fled when they entered the house. The step across the threshold felt like treading through water, but she made it and dragged Santa along with her. Inside, the feeling intensified from pushing through water to trudging through mud.

Merry shut the door behind them and every window in the house shook. It reminded her of a cat that had been sprayed with a garden hose. Irritated, but unwilling to attack. For now.

"Hurry," Santa said. He didn't need to encourage Merry; she wanted to spend as little time in this place as possible.

She pulled him behind her, holding her hand straight out like she could physically part the magic. They headed directly for the office and the dozens of file cabinets it contained. It seemed to take an hour to make it there, but it was probably only a minute.

"I hope no one is looking through the windows," she forced herself to joke. "We probably look ridiculous."

Santa only grunted in response.

This was supposed to be a quick errand before they headed back to the inn. Just a stop along the way. But it was turning into an ordeal. Though, that seemed to be a running theme when it came to her inheritance.

Even the file cabinet resisted when Merry pulled out the bottom drawer. Santa came up behind her and reached for the handle to help. The magic in the house was so unnerving, she didn't even stop to marvel at his lean body pressed against hers.

Santa pulled his hand back with a grunt of pain and cradled it to his chest. His fingertips were singed black.

"That is enough!" she said to the house. Oh good, now she was talking to the magical house. She didn't feel ridiculous enough to stop, though. "This is my house. He is my guest. Behave!"

Disproving Santa's previous comment, the oppressive magic evaporated like a popped balloon. She still felt it wiggling along the baseboards and ceiling, but it stayed well away from them.

"Now," she said, more baffled than proud. "I'm going to open the file cabinet and get my files."

The cabinet relented and let her pull open the drawer.

Not trusting the tentative truce with the house, Merry grabbed a handful of folders from a few different cabinets and pulled Santa through the dark house and out the front door as quickly as possible.

"As you can probably tell, Joy didn't have us over for tea very often," Santa said as they hurried down the sidewalk toward his fourth-favorite pickup parked in the driveway.

Merry gave a breathless laugh. At least he was attempting to joke, even if it was halfhearted.

He finally smiled as he opened the driver's side door and slid behind the wheel of his truck. Merry didn't question it even though he always let her drive. If anything, she was glad he was behind the wheel since she was still shaky from the magic.

She chided herself for being a baby. Nothing had *happened*. There were just uncomfortable feelings. She was fine. Santa was fine, even if he was still looking paler than usual.

The old-fashioned streetlamp cast a warm yellow glow across the leather seats and Santa's tight-jawed expression. Of course, there was no backup camera in the vintage truck, so Santa draped his arm across the back of the seat, smoothing Merry's hair absently as he turned to check for oncoming traffic. His touch soothed her scattered thoughts, but adrenaline still coursed through her veins.

There was magic in Poleton. Undeniably. And she'd felt it. Argued with it. Controlled it?

There were too many questions, too many conflicting feelings, and too little information. But it could wait. It could all wait until morning. She'd deal with it then.

For now, they were alone, the rest of the houses on the quiet street darkened for the night with just a few porch lights left burning by absent neighbors. Santa's salt white hair glowed bright, the rest of him a study in shadows and angles.

Merry watched, transfixed, as he put the truck in reverse and steered with one flattened palm against the wheel. Whatever had happened to his hand when he touched the file cabinet was gone now. He was truly okay.

The warm glow of the streetlight illuminated the long column of his throat, and she watched his throat bob as he swallowed. She had trouble doing the same, her mouth suddenly too dry.

All the adrenaline from the past hour—hell, the past week—had to go somewhere and her body had decided it should narrow her focus to Santa alone.

They pulled away from the cursed house and the foul magic residing there. He rested his hand casually on her knee and she let out a strangled sound. "This is why you always let me drive," she said.

He turned to her and quirked an eyebrow in question.

"You know how sexy you look behind the wheel. It's putting us in imminent danger."

His full lips curved as they passed under the glow of another streetlight and Merry was treated to a brief flash of color—gold eyes, pink lips, white hair. A combination as strange and wonderful as the rest of him.

"I'd never put you in danger, duckie." He squeezed her thigh.

And since her body always knew how to ruin a sweet moment, she snorted. "You are, though. We could be in the middle of the interstate, and I'd still want to crawl in your lap."

"Should I pull over?" His hand drifted higher, then inward. His thumb teasing her sensitive inner thigh. The fear she'd felt at her grandmother's house was long forgotten. This was a different kind of magic. One Santa fully possessed, even in his mortal body. Especially in his mortal body, since it was the only one that she'd ever known.

His smile took on a feral edge as he glanced over and noted her shallow breaths. Damn him, that was even sexier. But two could play this game.

Merry slid across the bench seat and nestled against his side, placing her hand on his knee. With no room to maneuver, he was forced to let go of her leg and reposition so that his arm was wrapped around her, thumb rubbing semicircles across her waist, her ribs.

She trailed her hand up his thigh, relishing the feel of his tense muscles and the smooth glide of worn cotton under her palms.

"Patience, duckie." He sounded as breathless as she felt.

"I don't want to be patient." She wanted to be bold. And she was. Heart ricocheting off her ribs, she let her hand wander over his body, memorizing every hard plane.

She'd worried about being intimate with him. She loved his teasing, carefree attitude but she'd worried that he couldn't be serious when the time came. That it would be wrong to ask him to focus for once.

All those worries were in vain.

His smile had faded from sunshine to smoldering embers as his hand continued its steady ascent up her body, never faltering, never hesitating as he learned her curves with a single-minded focus that should have made her worry about their safety.

She slid her hand under the hem of his t-shirt and dipped her fingertips into the hollow above his hip bone. "You're killing me, love," he groaned into her hair as she followed those grooves lower, beneath the waistband of his loose cotton pants. "I need to get you in my bed. Your bed. Hell, I'd settle for the bed of the truck, but you deserve better than that."

His smile had disappeared completely, replaced by lips parted to accommodate too-quick breaths. She knew her needy expression matched. His hand slid higher, his thumb brushing the sensitive underside of her breast, and a soft moan escaped her lips.

Luckily, Poleton was tiny, and they were parked in the inn's gravel lot before her pent-up desire put them in any real danger. She climbed into his lap before the truck was even in park, capturing his lips and every stilted breath. He tasted like peppermints and snow and magic. The good kind.

Their kisses thus far had been sweet, playful. But this was all heat. Santa's hand knotted in her hair, holding her steady as his other arm pulled her flush against every inch of his hard, lean body.

Their hips ground together and Merry stopped thinking. There was no paperwork in the passenger seat. No spreadsheets or emails from angry ex-bosses waiting for her. Just Santa's tongue claiming every inch of her mouth.

She canted her hips, and he growled into her open mouth, a sound so inhuman that it sent a delighted shiver down her spine. Santa grabbed her ass in a bruising grip that forced another groan from her.

Cold air hit her a moment later, and it felt like bliss against her overheated skin. He lifted her from the truck easily as Merry wrapped her legs around his waist, unwilling to let him go for even the short walk to her room.

It must have been after midnight because there was no one at the front desk to tell them they were being inappropriate.

They made it to Merry's door and Santa broke their kiss long enough to say, "Key."

"In my purse," Merry whispered, her voice as rough as Santa's. "In the truck," she added with a groan that had nothing to do with pleasure.

Santa grunted. "Too far. You're rich now, right?"

Before Merry could question what her money had to do with a key, the antique brass door handle exploded, falling in ice-crusted splinters to the carpeted floor.

Santa carried her through the door and kicked it closed.

CHAPTER 36

Merry woke alone in her bed at the inn. Her heart sped at the implication that Santa had left before she woke. Then, she heard his carefree laughter somewhere inside the inn.

She dressed quickly and went in search of that laugh, pausing briefly to survey the metallic remnants of her doorknob.

It was barely morning, but she should have known that Rosie would already be awake, tearing through the small lobby of the inn. Charli and Deirdre watched over twin cups of coffee as Santa chased their progeny.

The front desk attendant looked more amused than annoyed so Merry shot her a smile and joined her friends on the sofa.

"I heard you quit," Deirdre said by way of greeting. "*By email.*" That earned her two sets of raised brows.

"I've been dodging Mike's calls since then," Merry admitted. "He threatened my job, now he's mad that I called his bluff."

"I would say his anger pales in comparison to the partners'. Word on the street—and by that, I mean the group chat—is that Mike is basically begging for his job right now."

"As he should."

Deirdre shrugged. "I don't care about Mike. I care that my best friend did the one thing I asked her not to do."

"What's that?"

"Went and fell in love with a small-town man and abandoned all her hopes and dreams. Seriously, what happened?"

"To be fair, he rarely wears flannel, and he doesn't have a golden retriever," Merry argued.

"He is a golden retriever," Dee said, pointing at her boyfriend who was currently fetching a toy Rosie had thrown.

"Leave her alone," Charli said. "Plus, I'm happy with the way things worked out. We have somewhere to visit for vacation."

"No one in their right mind goes from California to backwoods North Carolina for vacation," Dee shot back.

"We do, apparently."

Before they could settle into loving bickering, Merry dragged the conversation back to the topic at hand. "I will miss you. Terribly. But I have responsibilities here. And I do have people that I love in Poleton. Not just Santa."

"Not just?" Deirdre repeated, heavy emphasis on the *just*.

"Exactly what I said," Merry replied without hesitation. "I love him and all his family. And... Actually, I should call a doctor to be on standby when I tell you the rest."

"Tell me right now. Are you pregnant?"

"No! But I hired Simon. He'll be here later this week."

Dee didn't laugh. She didn't even yell. She just stared at Merry with her characteristic *You've Messed Up* expression. "Merry..."

"I promise I'll be nice." She shook her head, messy ponytail smacking her cheek. "I promise I'll *try* to be nice."

"That's not the problem, babe." Dee checked their surroundings. Rosie was happily playing, and Santa was distracted by distracting her. Dee leaned in. "I know what I just said will make this hard to believe but I like Santa. And I like who you are with him. You're happy. You're free."

"What does that have to do with Simon?"

"You know exactly what it has to do with him. You've been in love with him for seven years."

"I have not! We hate each other."

"Yeah, you *hate* him. You hate him so much that you talk about him all the time. You hate him so much that you compare every guy you date to him. And you hate him so much that no one ever lives up to the standard he's set."

"That's…" Merry gaped at her best friend, unsure how she could have the situation so wrong. "That's not even close to true."

Dee exchanged a look with her wife and sighed. "Okay, Merry. I'll be here for you when this all blows up, but just know that I won't be happy about it. Santa is sweet. I hate to see him dragged into… whatever it is with you and Simon."

Deflect. She had to deflect from this conversation. She wouldn't hurt Santa. And she certainly wouldn't hurt him over Simon. "Graham's moving here too."

"You're stealing my brother?" It worked. Dee's attention was immediately diverted from the topic of Merry's love life.

"That was mostly Jeraltan," Merry hurried to shift the blame.

"Between all the trips we'll have to make to visit both of you and the fact that you're my only paying client, maybe we should move here too," Charli said equitably.

"Absolutely not!" Deirdre nearly shouted.

Even Santa couldn't distract Rosie when her mother was upset. She ran over and crawled into Deirdre's lap with huge brown eyes and a worried, "what wrong, Momma?"

Dee reined in her temper and told Rosie what was happening.

"Uncle Graham too?" Rosie asked with tears welling in her eyes.

Merry winced, she really should have let Graham tell them he was planning to move. As if sensing she'd stolen his thunder, Graham and Jeraltan bounced cheerfully through the front door of the inn. Well, Jeraltan bounced, but Graham at least looked happy.

"You're mooooving?" Rosie cried. She ran at Graham like a linebacker, and he scooped her up before she could face plant against his knee.

Graham glared at Merry. "Yes, sweetheart. I wanted to be the one to tell you. Won't it be exciting to visit? I'll have a big house with a swing set in the backyard for you. And you'll be able to visit the toy shop and test all the toys before they're shipped."

He was doing his best to distract Rosie, but she was still crying. "What 'bout pancakes?"

"I make excellent pancakes," Jeraltan assured her while smoothing her golden curls. "And I'll make them for you every time you visit."

It took a while to convince Rosie that the move was a good thing, but eventually she stopped crying and started planning for all the consolations Graham and Jeraltan had offered. Merry hid a smile against Santa's shoulder. Rosie had negotiated like a champ.

They spent the rest of the morning carting Rosie around to various child-friendly stores, the playground, and every display of Christmas decorations they could find.

She should be miserable shoved in the backseat of the rented minivan with Rosie's car seat between her and Santa, but she wasn't. The cheerful displays, the upbeat music, and, most of all, the company brought a sense of warmth she'd never expected.

She reached under Rosie's wildly swinging feet and gripped Santa's hand. Christmas wasn't so bad.

CHAPTER 37

While the morning had been devoted to family, the afternoon was all work. Graham tore himself from Jeraltan's side long enough to pick up the photography equipment Charli had chosen. Charli oversaw the transformation of an empty office into a small studio. Santa created an elaborate competition with far too many rules to create new product descriptions. And Merry had the joyous task of creating a spreadsheet of every available product and a link to each store that sold it.

While she was in Excel, she tallied units sold the previous year and the profit margin of each item. A few commonalities started to take shape, and she occupied half her mind with how to broach the topic of cutting low performing products for the upcoming year.

She checked in on the photography progress mid-afternoon and found Pari and Rari still putting together the massive setup while Charli read from a list of instructions. No wonder the cost had been measured in thousands—there were six stationary cameras, even more lighting equipment, and the base turned at the click of a button to capture panoramic video.

She swallowed her protests and reminded herself that the cost would come out of the current year's budget and have no bearing on their profit the following year—the one that mattered for the bargain.

"Looks great," she said instead.

Charli turned to her, sleek blonde bangs falling in her eyes, and grinned. "You want to yell at me so bad, don't you?"

"No. I trust you. If you say we need all this, then we need it."

Charli explained anyway. "I could have gotten good photos with my regular camera this time, but with this setup anyone can recreate the exact images. You won't be able to tell which pictures were taken today and which ones were taken next month or next year. And all you have to do is put the product on the mark and press a button. Easy-peasy."

"So, we won't have to fly you out every time we make a new product," Merry said.

"Exactly. You're saving money in the long run."

"I trust you," Merry repeated more confidently.

"And if we get the lighting right, I won't have to do much editing at all."

Merry laughed. "Oh, you mean to tell me you weren't looking forward to editing six angles of over nine hundred different toys?"

"I was not," Charli replied. "It should take about three days to photograph them all, then we can upload the images to Amazon and send them to the distributors. If you're done with the spreadsheet and Santa is ready with the descriptions by then, we should be up and running by the new year, like you asked."

"Then I'd better get back to my part."

She hit row 1000 in her spreadsheet by dinner time and was only a quarter of the way through the products. Santa was finding his task equally time consuming, but it would be worth it when they had brand new product photos, descriptions, and a comprehensive website.

***

That evening, once Rosie and her moms were tucked into bed, Merry, Santa, Graham, and Jeraltan crowded into Merry's room at the inn. Jeraltan immediately plopped down in the middle of the bed, but Graham eyed it skeptically. "I'll stand. I have a pretty good idea of what you two have been doing on those sheets."

"Prude," Merry said, settling beside Jeraltan. Santa sat behind her with his arms around her waist. She snuggled back against him, relishing the ease with which their bodies fit together.

She spread the papers she'd taken from her grandmother's house across the duvet, seeking out employment contracts. Luckily, her mad grab of random folders had yielded results.

Graham took the oldest folders and Merry the newest. She triple checked the name, and yes, she was holding the birth certificate of one Carlo Santana.

"That's me," Santa said with a proud smile. "We get to pick our names."

"Maybe we should back up a step and you can explain what you mean by that," Merry suggested.

"Sure. The government doesn't like people who live over a century, so we had to 'die' and be 'born' a few times. That's my most recent name for obvious reasons." Merry must have looked skeptical because he explained those obvious reasons. "Santana because it sounds like Santa and Carlo after Carlos, the third best guitar player in the human realm. Behind me and Faye, of course."

"I take offense to being considered the fourth best," Jeraltan added.

Graham sidled up to Merry and peered over her shoulder, ignoring Santa's explanations and Jeraltan's complaints. "Please tell me that isn't a fake government document."

Santa shook his head. "Joy had an arrangement with the doctor in town. We aren't sure if she used magic or money to convince him, but every year he signs a piece of paper saying someone died and another saying someone else was born. Then Joy sends that paper somewhere and gets these official documents back. Something about numbers needing to be put in a database…"

"So, they're real birth certificates and Social Security cards based on falsified medical records." A vein Merry had never seen was throbbing prominently in Graham's forehead.

"What is the alternative?" Merry asked him. "Tell the government that we have a hundred people who have been doing the same job since 1895?"

"You're right," Graham said. "But I just don't know how we will keep up this ruse. You don't have magic, and it seems like a bad idea to waltz into the doctor's office and offer him money to risk his medical license."

"Merry has magic," Santa said. "Like I told her, she appears to be stuck in a human body, like her mother was. Once the bargain is fulfilled and I can access my magic, I should be able to tell how Joy did that—and undo it. Plus, I will have enough magic and Merry has enough money to convince the doctor to sign whatever we need." Santa said.

"What? I was wrong. Back up several steps. What do you mean I'm trapped in a human body? This is just my body. The only one. And magic?"

"We talked about this, didn't we?" Santa said.

Merry shook her head vigorously enough to dislodge the clip holding her hair at bay. "We did not."

"Oh. In that case, I'm pretty sure you're trapped in a mortal body. Like your mother. I can't really be sure without full access to my magic, though."

"Trapped how?" Merry asked.

Santa shrugged. "Joy's magic was beyond my comprehension. I don't know how she maintained her own human body, much less yours or Noel's. I initially assumed some sort of curse or bargain, but that would only apply to her, not her children. Well, as far as I know. I didn't pay much attention to my tutors."

Merry let out a huff of breath through her nose. "Did anyone pay attention in school?"

Santa and Jeraltan shared a look. "None of us had much schooling. Maybe Faye? She's the most likely to have been offered an education. I think." Merry gave him a hard look and he shrugged. "She never talks about her past. I don't even know her real name. When we met, she said, 'I am Fae, that's all you need to know.' That's how she got her nickname."

Merry nodded. And nodded again. And kept nodding until the movement triggered a Pavlovian response that made her agree with the current lack of knowledge. "Okay. So, we'll ask Faye about my... human body. And we'll worry about government records after you have your magic back. No one will 'die' or be 'born' this year, and we will figure everything else out eventually."

With a sympathetic grimace, Graham reluctantly agreed to the terrible plan, and they turned back to Carlo Santana's paperwork. "At least everyone pays taxes. We won't have to worry about the IRS."

"See, we are solving problems already," Merry said.

"Well, they don't pay taxes since your grandmother was paying everyone minimum wage, but they file taxes."

Merry shouldn't have been surprised. Everything her grandmother had done made her stomach turn but hearing that her employees made so little caused her hands to ball into fists, crinkling the paper between them. "She only paid them $16 an hour?"

"Minimum wage is $7.25 in North Carolina," Graham informed her. Merry could tell he was trying very hard to not yell in front of Jeraltan.

Apparently, Merry wasn't doing as good of a job holding her emotions in check. Jeraltan patted her hand. "We're fine, Merry. Joy worked it all out. We even get spending money every month."

She forced a smile and flipped the pages in her hands. Santa's bank statements with Joy listed as an authorized person. Each month, twelve hundred and fifty dollars were deposited on the first and nine hundred was withdrawn the same day and paid to Poleton Property Management. Another three hundred was transferred to an account titled 'CFT Grocery Fund' and the remaining fifty dollars was withdrawn in cash.

Merry started to speak, but her voice shook so badly she had to clear her throat and try again. "Fifty dollars in spending money?"

"Yep! Isn't that nice of her?"

"No. *No.*" A deep breath did nothing to calm her. "It's not freaking *nice* of her to charge you nine hundred dollars for a room at the mansion. It's not freaking *nice* of her to hold your money hostage. And it's definitely not freaking *nice* of her to make it seem like charity to give you a few dollars of your own money every month." Merry seethed. She stopped looking at the papers and pinched the bridge of her nose. "Graham. Tell me I can pay them more."

He was silent so long, Merry had to look up to make sure he was still there. Graham was white with fury. "No. Pay is part of the contract. Minimum wage. No overtime pay."

She met Graham's eyes, and they held their anger in the taut space between them. But Santa and Jeraltan didn't need their pity. They just needed the situation fixed.

"I own the mansion," Merry said after a long, tense moment. "I can at least do away with rent."

Graham nodded once. "You will."

"I know I will, I just said that," she snapped.

Jeraltan's smile had faded into confusion and Santa squeezed her tighter. "Are you okay, love?"

She couldn't meet his soft gold eyes, so she nodded. "Outside business activities?" she asked Graham.

"Prohibited."

"Hobbies that happen to make money?"

"Gray area."

"Gray areas are good," Merry replied. She turned to Jeraltan, praying that the magic would let her get the words out. "You should sell your cookies at the festival." Thankfully, the words were easy to speak.

"Which ones? Snickerdoodle?"

"Whatever you want," Merry said with a forced smile. "They're all delicious."

Jeraltan's returning smile was hesitant but genuine.

"What else do we need to know about the bargain?" Graham asked. He was right, it was better to get all the unpleasant truths out in the open at once.

"We can't leave Poleton," Santa supplied. "I can't remember exactly what Joy said, but something like 'you'll stay here and work as humans'. The magic seems to have defined 'here' as the Poleton town limits."

It was too much. They had been trapped in this place for over a century. No vacations to the beach. No skiing in the Rockies. They'd never seen the Grand Canyon or New York City.

Merry buried her nose in Santa's neck. "I'm so sorry this happened to you. We'll fix it."

"Don't feel bad, love. We are happy here." He kissed her temple. "And we are even happier now that you're with us."

She wanted to cry. Scream. Break something. Instead, she leaned against Santa and started a new mental list. This one was all the places she wanted to show him once the bargain was fulfilled.

Maybe he would see those places and never want to return to making toys in Poleton. Maybe he would meet other people and leave her behind. But he deserved the chance to decide for himself where he lived, what he did, and who he loved. She would just have to hope he chose her.

They went through the rest of the paperwork and confirmed that all the employment contracts were the same and all the employees were equally broke thanks to said employment contracts. Her mood didn't improve much throughout the evening, but her anger morphed into a clawing sadness as Santa and Jeraltan did their best to be helpful and upbeat.

***

Graham looked as exhausted as Merry felt when he and Jeraltan finally left around midnight.

The room was silent without their voices and Merry was all too aware that Santa was still here. Still in her bed.

"Should I go?" he asked.

Merry shook her head and climbed into his lap. "I'd prefer if you stayed with me tonight. Is that okay?"

"Yes, duckie. There's nowhere I'd rather be."

The awkwardness of gauging each other's mood and expectations passed surprisingly quickly. Santa let Merry take the lead and she kissed him softly, reverently.

The night before had been all passion, broken doorknobs and ripped clothing, but tonight she needed something deeper. A soul connection that reminded her they were in this together.

She pulled back far enough to look into his eyes and found them full of the same emotion she was too cowardly to name. Instead of putting her feelings into words she reached for the intricate braids that held his hair flat against the sides of his head.

He held still, watching her face as she slowly unwound each braid and ran her fingers through the silky strands. "Beautiful," she murmured against his lips.

Merry slid his shirt over his head and took a moment to marvel at his smooth red-brown skin, broad shoulders, and flat stomach. "Absolutely beautiful," she whispered, bringing her lips to his collarbone.

He understood without words that Merry needed to take care of him, so he let her touch and taste every inch of his body. She took that permission as the gift it was and slowly, teasingly, learned all the things he liked and the reactions they elicited.

***

Hours later, she lay draped across his chest drawing sleepy patterns against his skin while he smoothed her hair in gentle, loving strokes.

"How old are you?" she asked. Her voice was whisper soft after having gone unused for so long.

"One hundred and sixty-seven. Does that bother you?"

He let her think for a moment, still running his fingers through her hair. Finally, she shook her head, "No. Mostly because I have no idea what that means in Fae terms. Give me the human equivalency equation."

He laughed softly and pressed a lazy kiss to the top of her head. "We age differently than humans. Faster at first, then much, much slower. We're children for about a decade then teenagers for a century. After that we're just adults for a few millennia depending on the type of Fae."

"So, you're a hundred and thirty-eight years older than I am, but also not older at all?"

"If you want to think of it that way."

"I do." Merry replied. "And I can live with that. I mean, it doesn't bother me that you've lived so much longer than I have. It does bother me a little that you will live so much longer than me, though."

Santa pressed another kiss to the top of her head, the only place he could reach without jostling her. "That might not be as much of a problem as you think."

"How so?" she asked.

"We don't know what will happen when the bargain is fulfilled. Fae have never survived long in the human lands. Even in your human form, you may outlive me by several decades if I don't figure out how to replenish my magic in this realm."

Merry sat up to look at him, the hazy warmth between them snapping to be replaced by sharp panic. "What do you mean?"

Santa gave her a sleepy, unconcerned smile. He, at least, was content to continue basking in their own personal glow. "It will be fine, love, but there is a reason my people live separately. In Faerie, magic is abundant. The High Fae bond the land and all the Fae in their territory bond them. Through those bonds, the Fae and land become one, sharing magic."

"And the magic is what gives you such long lives?"

"Yes. The High Fae are tethered directly to the land, so they can draw the most magic and live the longest. Brownies bond to houses and homesteads, and pixies bond to orchards and farms, both of which are permanent parts of the land and give them a stronger connection to magic. There are many other types of bonds, but those are the strongest."

"And what happens if you don't have a bond?"

Santa shrugged. "Unbonded Fae can't replenish their magic. Once it is gone, so are they."

"Can't you... you know, bond here?"

"Other Fae have tried to bond the human land in the past, but it has never worked. Some have written that they feel magic in the land here, but they cannot reach it. Others wrote that there is no magic here at all. I haven't been able to draw my own conclusion trapped in a mortal body."

"Are you saying that you could die? Once the bargain is fulfilled, if you stay here, and you can't bond, you will die?" It was unthinkable. She wouldn't let it happen. She didn't know what she would do about it, but she would do something.

"I don't think so," Santa said slowly. "I felt the Fates' push to come here. They wouldn't have sent me somewhere I couldn't survive. I don't know how else to describe it other than I know in my soul that this is where I am supposed to be. The others too."

Merry wrapped her arms around his waist, squeezing him tight. As far as she was concerned, the Fates had done nothing but cause trouble in his life thus far and she was unwilling to trust them with the rest of it. "Promise me that you will go back to Faerie if you can't bond here. Promise me you'll live."

"Let's just see what happens, love."

That was as good of an answer as Merry was going to get, so she let the conversation drop and held him close while she still could.

CHAPTER 38

Another day passed and Merry was no closer to understanding her possible Fae heritage, the bargain that kept her new friends enslaved, or how to move forward with her new life. At least Santa's sheets smelled divine. Like snow and the woodsy scent of his hair products. She smelled like those things too since she'd borrowed his shower after their morning workout.

She hid her sappy smile in his pillowcase, glad she'd agreed to split their nights between the inn and the mansion. The inn was great for privacy, but there was definitely something to be said for waking up to the noise of a big, happy family just a few doors away.

Her peaceful mood evaporated when her phone buzzed on the nightstand, and she saw the last name she'd expected.

She cleared her throat and straightened the blankets around her even though he wouldn't be able to see her. "Mr. Kline."

"Well, you certainly have my attention, Merry." Arnold Kline was a ruthless man, and his voice carried a threatening edge even when he was being conversational. Merry felt like a child being called to the principal's office.

But she wasn't a child. She shoved those feelings down and matched his tone with an icy one of her own. "I would have preferred your attention while I was busting my ass bringing you clients instead of after I quit."

To her surprise, he laughed. "You had my attention then too. Especially when you promised more than I ever thought you could deliver—

and then followed through. In a few years, I think you can be the best of us. Now, tell me what I need to do to make that happen."

She'd never heard a word of praise from Kline, and it took her a moment to recover from the shock. When she did, she explained the situation—the non-Fae parts—and that no amount of money could change her mind.

"Disappointing, but I understand. I still expect you to train your replacement and oversee the transition of your clients. Your quarrel is with Mike, not with me. Don't ruin my reputation over a petty squabble."

Harsh but fair. That phrase could adorn his headstone.

Merry could have pushed back, but she still had lingering guilt over abandoning her clients. They'd put their faith in her, and she couldn't turn her back on them.

She agreed to continue working for Kline for ten hours a week for the next three months to be paid at a frankly exorbitant rate.

When the call ended, Merry sat staring at the blank screen. She should have been feeling grief over the loss of her dreams, anger over Kline's abrupt tone, or even annoyance at having her old life drag on into her new one. Instead, she felt nothing. Her thoughts were background noise, drowned out by Santa singing in the shower.

She smiled at the closed door, picturing him using his bottle of super-special, Fae-friendly organic conditioner as a microphone while he waited the requisite five minutes for it to permeate his hair. The song was unfamiliar, something reminiscent of black and white movies and men with slicked back hair. Had Santa given into that trend?

The idea of Santa with a pocket watch and a patterned waistcoat was much more entertaining than thoughts of consulting. Still, she couldn't spend all her time questioning him about his past. She had practical questions that needed to be answered and a company to save.

Her workout clothes were still sweaty, and the rest of her wardrobe was in the wash, so she pulled on a pair of Santa's soft, drawstring pants and a flannel overshirt. Both were tight across her curves and a good six inches too long, but she wasn't as self-conscious as she expected to be. She'd seen the mansion's residents in much odder attire.

Santa paused his rendition of the unfamiliar song long enough to hear her explain that she was going in search of coffee… and to invite her to join him in the shower instead. As much as she wanted to accept that offer, his shower was tiny, and she was already getting a headache from lack of caffeine.

She found Jeraltan in the kitchen frying eggs with an apron and a boyfriend wrapped around his waist. Both moved with him as he poured Merry a cup of coffee without her having to ask.

"Faye wanted to see you," Jeraltan told her as he handed over the steaming cup. "She's in the greenhouse."

"Where's that?"

"I'll take you. It's a little hard to find."

Merry had a thousand things to do, but none were more important than gathering answers to the questions that haunted her. Plus, Faye did not strike her as the type of person who would ask for her frivolously.

The morning was crisp and overcast and Merry wished she'd also stolen one of Santa's jackets as Jeraltan led her from the mansion into the woods that bordered it. The bare, clawing branches above them and the stillness of the morning reminded her of a horror movie. And like the typical victim, she followed complacently, trusting Jeraltan to lead her to safety. She calmed her fanciful thoughts by remembering that horror movie villains rarely wore hand-knitted sweaters that said *I Have The Prettiest Balls* surrounded by Christmas ornaments.

A frozen, torturous mile down a well-worn path, the weak winter sunlight glinted red, blue, and gold. A little further and Merry found herself in a clearing facing a conglomeration of old wooden windows.

Around the outside, stained glass depictions of biblical scenes dominated the structure. Between and above them, wooden windows of various sizes that appeared to be pilfered from homes completed the makeshift greenhouse. Faye's dark head was just visible through the glass as she bent over an unidentifiable plant.

Jeraltan headed back to the warmth and safety of the house, leaving

Merry to figure out which of the windows doubled as a door. Faye saved her from an hour of trial and error, and she followed the pixie into her private space.

Addie sat scribbling in one corner, his dark hair shielding his sketchbook from view. He looked up just long enough to meet her eyes and make a few quick movements Merry recognized from her ASL courses.

"He says good morning," Faye supplied.

"He also said 'go away, we're busy'" Merry replied with a smirk in Faye's direction.

"You know ASL?"

"A little," Merry replied. "It's been a while since I had anyone to practice with." She turned to Addie, speaking and slowly signing, "Do you read lips?"

He pointed at his ears and gave a thumbs up, then at his mouth and turned his thumb the other way.

"He can hear, but not speak," Faye explained.

"Ah," Merry said and didn't press further. If Addie wanted her to know the details, he would share them. "I'll brush up on my ASL, I'd like to be able to talk to everyone."

"Good. Let me know if you have questions or need someone to practice with." The implication was clear—no one got to Addie except through Faye. It made sense. The only time she'd seen Addie alone was the afternoon when Faye was scamming free ice-skating tickets from the town council.

"I will," Merry promised with a reassuring smile. "What did you want to see me about this morning?"

"Have you had any luck accessing your magic now that you know it's there?" Faye asked. Merry followed her through the narrow aisles of potted plants. It didn't take a horticulturalist to determine that three-quarters of the plants were marijuana. The remainder were mushrooms and Merry had a sinking feeling none of them were legal. But that was a worry for another day. A very distant day since her calendar was overflowing with worries passed to a future date.

"I bossed my grandmother's house around, but other than that I don't feel any of the things Santa says a Fae should feel. No connection to the land or anyone else. No tingles or sparks. I'm pretty sure I'm more human than Fae."

"Hmm," Faye replied, nose still buried in a plant. "That could be true. Or you could be trapped as we are in a mortal body, unable to access your magic."

"My grandmother was trapped in a human body as well and she could use magic," Merry pointed out.

"Was she?" Faye asked. She kept her face turned away from Merry, cradling a wilting plant between her palms.

The unmistakable feeling of magic filled the space between them. It wasn't something she saw, heard, smelled, or perceived with any of her usual senses. Yet, she felt it all the same. Hairs rising on the back of her neck, goosebumps across her skin. Like a memory of a touch.

"How would I know? I never met her," Merry said. "Santa said she was *inhabiting* a mortal body. Whatever that means."

Faye hummed again. Under her fingers, the brown tips of the leaves retreated, replaced by vibrant green.

"Should you be doing that? Santa said Fae can't replenish their magic without a bond to the land, which we don't currently have."

"I have been rationing my magic for over a century. Even if Santa can't form the bond, I have enough magic to last another three centuries at this pace." The whole plant seemed to preen, eager for more of her magic. "It's him you should worry about. Santa is not overly accomplished at rationing—or being patient. But to get back to the topic at hand, I do not know how Joy came to be in these lands or why. Nor do I know how she maintained her human body."

"So, all we do know about my grandmother is that she was an evil bitch and Santa might die because of her?"

Faye turned with a startled expression. "Joy is the kindest High Fae I've ever met."

It was Merry's turn to be surprised. "Kind? She enslaved all of you.

She paid you barely enough to survive. She made absurd rules like banning you from making instruments. That's cruel."

"Ah, I see the issue." Faye turned to the next plant in need of her attention. Again, magic rose thick in the air between them as Faye called on her dwindling gifts. "You are judging her based on human standards, not Fae."

"We can't be that different," Merry argued.

Faye's laugh was the hollowest sound Merry had ever heard. "They are monsters. If you don't believe me, ask Jeraltan. His mother made the mistake of saying aloud that she was the best healer in the Unseelie court. The king blinded Jeraltan's father and dumped him on her doorstep saying that if she was so powerful, she could heal him."

"Did she?" Merry asked, her voice barely more than a whisper with bile burning her throat.

"She did. The king killed him because she didn't thank him for the opportunity to showcase her skill."

Merry couldn't think of a single thing to say. The monster Faye was describing was Santa's father. If he'd been that terrible to Jeraltan's family, how had he treated his own son?

"There are more scarred and maimed Lessers in Faerie than those that are whole," Faye continued. Merry stared at the sliver of Faye's face that was visible with her nose tucked into the pungent flower. Her hands were steady, her voice emotionless, but a muscle ticked in her delicate jaw. "The High Fae do not care who they hurt, or how badly, as long as they are entertained. Joy was different though. Maybe that's how she ended up here."

"What you just described is… unspeakably cruel. But what my grandmother did is bad as well. You don't have to diminish what you've been through just because others have it worse."

Faye ran her fingertips over a perfect green leaf, but Merry didn't think she was marveling at its beauty. Her jaw slowly unclenched, and she turned with a smile that didn't meet her eyes.

"Put yourself in Joy's shoes. Imagine the son of your worst enemy appearing in the middle of your workplace with a small army, smiling while he claimed your employees were now his."

Merry gladly tore her mind from the horrors Faye had described and tried to picture it. She snorted.

"Why is that funny?"

"My worst enemy has dimples," Merry explained. "They're kind of adorable and probably hereditary... sorry. Not the point. Please continue."

"You're not supposed to find your enemies adorable. Choose another one to picture. Your worst enemy."

"I just have the one," Merry replied with a shrug. "And I don't think he's adorable, just his dimples. You'll understand when you meet him, he's flying in tomorrow."

"The person you hired to work with us is your worst enemy? Why..." She shook her head. "Stop distracting me. Forget the enemy part. You're in your office in California. An army appears, attempts to kidnap your employees, then burns the building to the ground."

"That would be less than ideal," Merry agreed.

"An understatement," Faye replied. "Now, to prevent the aforementioned kidnapping, you strike a deal with them in the heat of the moment. Because of that deal, you inadvertently become responsible for over a hundred people who are essentially pre-teens with their very first taste of freedom."

Merry shivered. "Teenagers are terrifying."

Faye nodded. "All the rules you think are unfair were born from the others being very, very annoying. Like when Santa sang the same Elvis song over and over for a full week. Or when Jeraltan bought an entire cow because Pari and Rari wanted steak for dinner. Or when Melody accidentally enchanted the milkman, and he left his wife."

"Okay, not touching that last one with a ten-foot pole, but I kind of see what you mean. There's still no excuse for her paying you minimum wage or keeping you from fulfilling the bargain. It's unfair."

Faye shook her head. "You say you understand but you don't. We remember enough of the bargain to know that she didn't promise food or shelter or even safety. But she provided all those things anyway. I'm not saying she was a saint, but Joy wasn't all bad. She was even nice for a little while after Noel was born. I'd never seen anyone so happy."

Faye finished with the row of plants she was helping and settled cross-legged on the floor with her back against a planter. Merry mirrored her pose, more confused than ever.

"Noel was perfect. A wonderful little terror. We all loved her, even though Joy kept us away from her for the most part. Then, she learned the truth. By that time, she was pregnant with you, and she worried for your safety. So, she left. Presumably, she also asked Joy to hide her. Make her fully human. Make you human. And remove all memories of the Fae."

If her mother had asked to have her memories erased, did that make it better or worse? And if she'd asked to be made human, then whose fault was it that she died?

It had been so easy to lay all of the blame at her grandmother's feet. But if what Faye was saying was true—and it had to be since she couldn't lie—then at least some parts of the current situation were caused by circumstance rather than cruelty.

Before Merry could puzzle out what to do with that information, Faye continued. "It broke Joy's heart when Noel left. Then, she learned Noel died and it destroyed her completely. She stopped caring about the business. She stopped caring about the town. Spent most of her time alone in her home. I'm not sure she was even aware of anyone else."

"That's why she agreed to the deal with Quinn," Merry said, the puzzle finally solved. Her grandmother was so careful with everything else, so that one piece had never seemed to fit.

"Probably. Like I said, she stopped caring."

"How did she die? My grandmother."

Faye contemplated for a long moment. Merry didn't think she was pondering Joy's death, she had surely thought about that before, but rather she seemed to be choosing her words.

"The official report said she had a heart attack," Faye said finally.

"Do Fae have those?"

"Not usually," Faye admitted.

"Then how did she die?"

"She could have run out of magic. She could have been poisoned. She could have simply gotten tired of living in Poleton with the memories of her daughter."

"You think she died by suicide?"

Faye only stared at her. The other meaning for Faye's last statement clicked.

"You don't think she died at all."

"I don't know what happened. All I can say is that she is no longer here. And since she passed her business and wealth to you, it doesn't seem that she plans to return. But let's focus on your magic. That is what's important now."

Merry sat among the illegal plants, trying to focus on Faye's demonstration of summoning a flame when her mind was still turning over the pieces she had just learned and trying to find how they fit together. For a fourth time, Faye demonstrated summoning a tiny flame, no larger than a candle wick. There were no words to accompany the feat, no hand movements to direct the magic. It just appeared, floating above her outstretched hand.

Faye patiently explained once again how to look within herself and find the fire burning in her soul. But Merry couldn't feel her soul—aflame or otherwise.

After a frustrating few minutes, Merry asked. "How do I know if I even have magic or if I'll be able to bond?" It was a delicate way of asking how soon she would die. She'd never thought much about the human lifespan. It was the same for most people, so there was no use dwelling on it. But now that the possibility of a long life was presented, Merry found that she wanted it.

"We don't know much about half-Fae or quarter-Fae, whichever you are. There are only a few stories. Some inherited their Fae parent's gifts. Others did not. As far as bonding, there is as much hope for you as the rest of us. There are more stories of Fae trying to bond the human land. None were successful. Santa will have as much of a challenge creating the bond as you will accepting it, if not more since he is only half High Fae."

"What a cheerful thought."

Faye gave a slash of a smile. "You can lie, that is a human trait. But you can also feel music and compel others to follow you. Those are Fae traits. High Fae traits, to be specific."

"What do you mean? Everyone can feel music. It's vibrations and sound waves... and stuff."

"Yes, but you feel it in a way that humans don't. I've seen you sing and dance. You understand it as we do."

"I still don't get what that has to do with magic." Merry began fiddling with the leaf of one of the plants. Exhaustion, mental and physical, was taking their toll. Maybe if she'd had more sleep or less stress, she'd be able to follow Faye's train of thought. Then again, maybe nothing could make magic comprehensible.

"Music is a form of... worship isn't the right word, but it's close enough. The Fates love it, so we love it. Those that are more closely tied to the Fates have more ability to understand and make music. High Fae, those most closely bonded to the Fates, can even compel those around them to make or enjoy music."

"Compel? I've never tried, but I don't think I can do that."

"You already have. I saw you compel Graham to sing at the victory party. And Jeraltan says you stole his Zumba class. Santa certainly can't help himself when he's around you, though that may be for a different reason."

"I compelled Graham?" Merry asked, horrified. "He didn't want to sing karaoke?"

Faye shrugged, apparently unperturbed by mind control. "I have no idea what he wanted. You wanted him to sing, though, so he did. Based on that alone, I am hopeful you will be able to bond. It doesn't take much magic, as evidenced by the fact that trolls do it. Let's worry about that when the time comes, though. Right now, I am more concerned with finding out what type of magic you may have inherited."

"Sure. Why not? Let's just push one more worry to later. We definitely don't have enough to deal with."

That quicksilver smile flashed again. "I envy your ability to use sarcasm."

"It is pretty useful when you have nothing worthwhile to add to a conversation," Merry replied.

That earned a laugh from Faye. "Let's start by seeing if you have an affinity for any of the other elements. Fire was our best bet, since most Seelie have an affinity for it, but that doesn't seem to be working. We'll try water next."

A few frustratingly unproductive minutes later, the greenhouse door opened, and Santa emerged, bringing the promise of snow and the radiance of the sun with him. Merry beamed at him, her frustrations calming at his mere presence.

He ruffled Addie's hair like an annoying older brother before sinking down beside Merry. "I thought you were looking for coffee."

"Shoot. Sorry. I should have told you where I was going."

He kissed the side of her head. "How could I be mad at you when you look so delicious in my clothes."

She grabbed a fistful of his shirt and pulled him in for a real kiss. "You look pretty delicious yourself."

"Less flirting, more magic," Faye interjected.

"Any magic would be more than I've managed so far," Merry explained to Santa.

"That's okay, duckie. You'll get it. And if not, you can share mine."

"Is that possible?" Merry asked. Surely, it had to be if he'd been able to suggest it truthfully.

Faye seemed to be stunned into silence. After a moment, she cleared her throat and said, "It is. In very select cases."

Santa just smiled and pulled Merry against him. "We'll see, love. For now, just keep trying."

They tried every exercise Faye suggested. Meditation to connect with her magic. Feeling for the lifeforce of the plants. Reaching for still water in a nearby can. Pushing the air around her.

Nothing.

Merry felt no stirring in her soul or her, apparently, nonexistent, magic. Santa finally coaxed her out of the greenhouse after dark. She trudged behind him, frustrated and tired, with absolutely nothing to show for it.

CHAPTER 39

Merry's alarm sounded at three and she considered texting Simon to rent a damn car. Santa was a warm weight at her back, his strong arm wrapped around her middle and holding her flush against him.

As much as she wanted to stay cocooned with him all day, she couldn't. Simon still hadn't signed the employment contract, and she had a three-hour car ride to convince him or risk losing the only CFO she trusted.

So, Merry dragged her exhausted body from bed and dressed respectably in dark jeans, heeled boots, and a chunky sweater over a collared shirt. She did the bare minimum with her hair and makeup, then grabbed her keys.

Three and a half hours later, the sun was valiantly trying to rise over the airport. Her palms burned but she had nowhere to sit the coffee cups with their too-thin paper sleeves in the crowded baggage terminal.

Simon finally appeared in black sweatpants with his college logo down one leg, a matching hoodie, and headphones around his neck.

"You're one of *those* people," Merry accused as she held out one of the coffees to him, mentally begging him to hurry up and take the cup while her palm still had skin.

"Black, you mean?" he said as loudly as humanly possible. "I didn't think that would be a problem."

His baritone voice carried, and several people turned to shoot disgusted looks at Merry. That was not what she meant, and the twitching corners of his lips showed he knew it.

Well, two could play at the embarrass-your-frenemy-in-public game.

"A catfisher! You look nothing like your online profile," Merry replied, equally loudly. Thankfully, the judgmental eyes moved from her to him. "Are you even a veterinarian for wounded squirrels?"

He was trying not to laugh as he grabbed his bag from the carousel. "I look exactly like my online profile. Are you confusing me with one of the many, many other men you offer to fly out for a weekend?"

"Really?" Merry hissed at him as they started for the door. "Slut-shaming is the best you have?"

His reply was cut off when a stunning blonde stepped up to Merry's side and asked after her safety. A few bumbled explanations later, the woman shook her head and informed Merry that catfishing was serious, and she shouldn't joke about it.

After that humbling exchange, Merry and Simon quickly found their way through the automated doors.

As they passed into the short-term parking deck Simon started laughing. "I really don't know whether to be impressed that she stepped in or offended that she thought I would need to catfish you."

"She wasn't planning to say anything when she thought I was racist, so I think we can safely ignore everything else she said."

Simon shrugged like the concept of someone sticking up for him was too ridiculous to even consider. They didn't have the kind of relationship where she could question that look, so, she said, "I'm driving. Don't even try to argue."

He not only tried but succeeded in arguing. He did not, however, win that argument. After all, the old truck was not much to look at, but it belonged to Merry's father, not Simon's.

The airport was confusing to navigate, and they held off on further conversation until she was safely out of the throng of cars all rushing to their destination.

When she pulled onto Billy Graham Parkway, Simon said, "Are you finally going to tell me what you meant by that 'those people' comment?"

"Sweatpants on airplane people," Merry told him, which only made him laugh, look over her outfit, and laugh again.

"I'm uncomfortable enough on planes, even with that fancy first-class ticket you bought. I'm not going to wear a suit and make it worse."

Merry cringed at the thought of Simon squeezing into a tiny airplane seat. Then, cringed again at the hell his neighbors had undoubtedly endured. He was massive. A D1 linebacker in college—as he liked to remind everyone at every possible opportunity.

"Fine. But it wouldn't have killed you to wear jeans."

"Better not to risk it. I have injured squirrels to heal."

Merry snorted a laugh. "That wasn't my best lie."

"It was more believable than the salary you offered me," Simon replied.

"Oh, we're just going to jump right into the negotiations? No 'how have you been, Merry?' or 'thanks for the coffee, Merry?'"

"Nope. And I need breakfast. I'm starving. I assume you'll pay."

"Of course," Merry demurred. "Please allow me to escort you to one of the many fine dining establishments that allow sweatpants and hoodies."

They continued to bicker through the drive thru at Bojangles and as she turned the truck east and headed to her dad's house. Despite his constant stream of other complaints, Simon didn't put up a fuss when she said she needed to run a quick errand.

They got back on the road shortly after breakfast, but their arguments never stopped—starting with his ridiculous expectations for salary quickly followed by his equally absurd schedule requests.

Around the Gaston County line, Merry called a truce and turned on her innocuous pop playlist. She'd pilfered an ancient cassette adapter from her dad's garage and added a dongle to plug in her phone just because she'd known she would need these upbeat songs to put her back in a good mood. Pop wasn't her usual go-to genre, but there was something soothing about the repetitive beats and simple, catchy lyrics. It reminded her of Santa and his ABBA obsession.

Merry hummed along, never able to resist the pull of the music, for a few miles until Simon let out a groan of annoyance. "I can't listen to this anymore."

"It's literally a Top 100 playlist. I didn't pick the songs," Merry countered, reflexively snapping at Simon. She let out a huff through her nose and reminded herself that they were friends now. She handed over the aux cord. "You pick."

He tried to plug in his Android much to her amusement. She saved herself from another of his lectures about the superiority of anything-but-Apple products and handed him her unlocked phone.

Simon didn't hesitate to take her up on the offer and it took all her willpower not to make a snide comment about the golden boy being way too comfortable getting his way. At least his taste in music wasn't bad. Surprising, but not bad.

"Who is this?" she asked as the soothing electronic music filtered through the speaker on the dash.

"Pretty Lights."

"Oh, I've heard of them. 'Rainbows and Waterfalls', right?"

He huffed a laugh. "Him, not them, but yeah that's one song."

"Well then why did he choose a plural sounding name?"

"How would I know? I'm not him." Merry's phone pinged with an incoming message on the app she'd installed for the Claus Family Toys employees, and she asked Simon to read it since he still had her phone. He did, then thrust the phone away with a muttered curse. "Too far. You did not need to get someone to send you nudes as a prank."

"I'm sorry, what?" She reached for the phone, ignoring the little voice in her head that said texting and driving was a bad idea. She spared a single glance at the mouthwatering abs, sculpted chest, and pouty lips and felt unwelcome heat pooling deep in her gut. Santa was still in her bed, apparently, *very apparently*, missing her.

He answered her voice call immediately. "Hello, beautiful." His voice was gravelly, seductive, and not at all appropriate given the company.

"You're on speaker. I need both hands to drive," she told him quickly. "I just called to say what the hell are you thinking. It's nine in the morning and Simon had my phone."

"I'm trying to be a good boyfriend. Jeraltan says sexting is the key to a long-distance relationship," Santa replied.

Merry stared straight ahead to avoid looking at Simon. If the burning in her cheeks was any indication, her face was red as a tomato. "We're not in a long-distance relationship. I've been gone for five hours."

"But we are dating. And you are a significant distance away from me right now," Santa argued.

"I'm on my way back!"

"Now you are," Santa said with smug satisfaction.

Merry let the silence drag on for one beat, then two, waiting for him to give any indication that he was joking. When he didn't, she started laughing. "Yes, babe, you've convinced me. I'll come straight home."

"You're finally warming up to pet names. I'm so glad. But you have to be more creative than that. I'm thinking Lollipop would be a good start. You know, because—"

"I'm hanging up. See you in three hours when I strangle you. Did you not hear the part where you're on speaker phone?"

"Oh, I'm being rude. Hi, Simon."

The combination of wordless sounds of annoyance and genuine laughter that escaped her were entirely inarticulate. She shook her head, but still risked her life to take him off speakerphone long enough to whisper. "You look gorgeous, babe. I miss you. See you soon."

She hung up before he could say anything else embarrassing.

"Don't say a word," she warned Simon.

"I'm still trying to find words," Simon replied. A quick glance at his expression showed the same mix of confusion, amusement, and reluctant charm Santa brought out in everyone. "New boyfriend, I assume."

Merry huffed another laugh and hated how gooey her heart went at the label. "Yeah. That was Santa. You'll meet him soon."

"Santa? I was right. I'm being pranked."

With more nerves than she expected, she gave Simon the overview of Santa and the rest of the town. She decided that the 'grew up in a cult' explanation would be best. He certainly wouldn't believe the truth and it gave him enough warning that there would be quirks to overcome with the employees.

Simon took it in stride, for the most part, then directed the conversation to the financial situation of the company and his role in turning it around. Either her grandmother's glamour extended much further than Merry had thought, or Simon was desperate for a job.

They finally agreed to the terms of his employment contract as they crossed the boundary into Poleton. Merry held firm on the salary but agreed to a flexible schedule, lots of PTO, free housing, and a frankly ludicrous signing bonus.

Since Simon thought he'd won the negotiation, he relinquished the aux cord as they crossed the Poleton town line. Merry knew she'd actually won since she'd only offered perks that could be paid for before the new year but accepted the peace offering anyway.

She shuffled her downloaded music since she couldn't stream anything without cell service, and all her favorite songs played in quick succession. With all their arguments either settled or set aside for the time being, she could focus on the music. It built inside her like water pressing against a dam.

A little before the usual lunch hour, Merry parked in front of Ida June's, a meat and three vegetable restaurant on Main Street. Santa's two-tone pickup was already there and far more people than would comfortably fit in the cab were crowded around it.

The pressure inside her burst. She cranked the volume, threw open the door, and ran.

Santa met her with open arms, already singing along to Survivor's "I Can't Hold Back." She launched herself at him and he caught her easily, turning a clumsy leap into an elegant spin.

They finished the song together at full volume, dancing and generally making fools of themselves in the parking lot.

When the final notes sounded, she turned sheepishly to Simon who

259

was leaning against the truck with his arms crossed, dimples fully on display. "Batshit."

"What did you call her?" Santa said, taking a step in Simon's direction. Simon just kept smiling.

Merry pulled Santa back with a laugh. "He says that every year at the Christmas party."

"I say that every year when one of the partners comes to tell me to 'get Merry off the bar' or 'get Merry off the buffet table' or, my personal favorite, 'get Merry off the stage, we paid good money for that band.'"

Merry shrugged. "I like to have the high ground when I dance."

Santa cradled her cheek in his hand, grinning at her. "Of course you do, duckie. You deserve to dance on a throne that's on a pedestal that's on a stage." His smile faded into a threatening glower he aimed at Simon. "And if they don't know that then they don't deserve you."

"You get me. I'm so glad I brought you a present." It was quite possibly the only thing she could have said to keep him from starting a fight in the parking lot.

"Dibs," Faye said somewhere behind her. A quick glance told her Simon hadn't even finished unloading the off-brand electric guitar and amplifier before Faye had pounced.

She moved to the bed of the truck and pulled an acoustic guitar case to Santa's immediate, "Dibs. Mine. It's for me. Merry got it for me. Mine." He took it from her and hugged it like he expected to have to fight for it.

She shook with laughter. "I love it when you ramble. And just so you know that—"

"DIBS!" Pari and Rari appeared from nowhere and shouted in unison.

"—guitar is bubblegum pink," she concluded, then turned to the trolls. "I only had the two guitars."

"We want him," Pari said, pointing to Simon.

Rari nodded her agreement. "He looks like he can carry a lot of boxes."

Simon chuckled, dimples popping in both cheeks. "Thanks, I think."

"Simon is our new CFO," Merry explained.

"We don't know what that means. Is he part of the packaging department?"

"Chief Financial Officer. Simon will make sure we all stay on budget and help us make a profit."

"He controls the money?" Jeraltan asked, proving that the trolls weren't the only ones who could move abnormally quickly as he sidled up to Simon. "You're very handsome."

"I'm right here!" Graham shouted, abandoning his niece to pull Jeraltan against him with a not-very-menacing glare at Simon.

Jeraltan cackled. "I was joking." Graham's expression relaxed, then hardened again. Merry could almost feel the moment he remembered Fae couldn't lie. That meant Jeraltan truthfully thought Simon was handsome and he was joking. Merry didn't waste time trying to puzzle out how neither of those things were a lie.

Luckily, Simon thought it was funny. "Thank you, I'm straight though. And I'm sure there's a rule about fraternization?" He sounded surprisingly hopeful that wasn't the case when he turned to Merry.

Merry looked from Simon to Santa's hand around her waist, then back again. "Yes, obviously. We have a very strict no fraternization policy. Can we please just eat? I'll make all the proper introductions inside."

Their whole party surged toward the door of poor, unsuspecting Ida June. For once, the three-year-old was the most well behaved.

Merry held back for a moment to wrap her arms around Santa's neck. "How pathetic will I be if I say I missed you?"

"Why would that be pathetic? I missed you so much." He kissed her again, then hefted the guitar in his hand. "And now I have the tools to compose a song about how lonely I was for the last eight hours while doing just enough work to appease the Fates."

She grinned up at him. "You won't hurt my feelings if you paint it green by the way. Or strip the paint off. I don't know if that's possible but do whatever you want."

He kissed her with the guitar between them. "Thank you, duckie.

Does this mean we're allowed to have instruments now? Joy said no because apparently, we are 'annoying' and 'easily distracted.'"

"Of course. I happen to love that you're annoying and distractible." She kissed him again to make sure he knew it was true. "Please be annoying and distractible with a guitar. It sounds hot."

He kissed the freezing tip of her nose. "I will play you every Willie Nelson song I know. Later. Right now, let's get you some coffee before you freeze."

She took his hand, unsure how to tell him that his offer of coffee was a lot sexier than the promise of being serenaded by "On The Road Again." It would be fine. She'd listened to a lot of teenage boys play "Wonderwall" around campfires; she could fake excitement over a few Willie songs.

CHAPTER 40

Inside the restaurant, they found Jeraltan with his arms wrapped around a large older woman in a floral print apron while the rest of their party stood crowded near the doorway.

"I love your hugs, Jeraltan, but they don't pay the bills. Show me that one of you has actual money and I'll give you my best table," Ida June said.

"I have money," Merry said, raising her credit card above her head for good measure since she was stuck behind Simon, Pari, and Rari—all of whom were at least half a foot taller than she was.

"Well, all right, then. Let's get Ms. Claus a table," Ida June said to one of her employees. They scampered to clear the dirty dishes and push tables together. In just a few moments, there was a long line of mix-matched antiques set with vintage dishes and warm cornbread.

"I love this place. Let's eat here every night," Merry said a few minutes later as she buttered her second piece of cornbread. Simon was on his third, but it wasn't a competition. Yet. "Oh right, I was supposed to be doing introductions. Everyone, this is Simon. He played football in college."

Dee and Graham laughed, knowing that Merry had stolen Simon's favorite fun fact about himself. Charli would have laughed too, but she'd skipped lunch to finish the website. Everyone else just looked confused. She made the rest of the introductions. The heads of all the departments were there, except accounting because no one wanted to spend time with Howard.

"So, Simon," Faye began. She looked even more intimidating than usual with thick black eyeliner accentuating her bright green eyes. The guitar case between her legs did nothing to undermine the authority in her tone or posture. "What are your qualifications for this position?"

Simon paused smearing apple butter over his fourth piece of cornbread and cleared his throat. "I double majored in Stats and Accounting for undergrad. Just Accounting for grad school. I'm a CPA. I've been a consultant for the last nine years and I was the youngest Junior Partner at Kline & Associates."

"For a week, until I was promoted," Merry muttered.

Santa chimed in, but not to Merry's defense as she'd expected. "We already have one ex-consultant, why do we need another one?"

Simon glanced at Merry. "I didn't realize we had a group interview planned."

"We don't," Merry said. She turned to Faye, "I already hired him."

"Then why are we here?" Faye asked. "You said you wanted us to be more involved in the business. Is helping choose new employees not what you had in mind?"

Her tone made it clear that there was only one right answer—a sincere and heartfelt apology. Unfortunately, Merry couldn't do that.

"What's your hesitation here? No one was upset when I hired Charli."

"We don't have to explain to Charli why we need new drawing pads, or why the pens we bought six months ago need to be replaced," Faye said.

"Or why we ran out of coffee two days early," Jeraltan added.

"Or the difference between matte and satin paint," Siofra added.

"Or explain why I can't make a six-inch toy out of a four-inch scrap of wood. I still can't believe I had to have that conversation," Santa said.

"Oh, I see the problem," Merry said, relaxing a fraction as it dawned on her. "Howard is an ass."

"Little ears," Dee reminded her.

"Sorry," she said. Luckily, Rosie was oblivious to the cursing, happily smashing cornbread against the arms of her highchair. "Expenditure approval is on my list of things to discuss with Simon today."

She glanced sideways at him, and he smirked. "I'm all yours 'til six. Then, don't bother me again until January 1st."

"That's fine, I'll just make all the decisions without you."

Simon sighed. "Only bother me virtually until January 1st," he amended.

"Excellent choice. Now, I'm sure you won't have a problem with this plan—"

Simon cut her off with a raised hand. It was even more annoying since he was still holding the cornbread. He turned to Faye. "Can you explain your current operating procedure and what about it is causing issues?"

Faye glared at Simon. Simon glared back.

Merry had hoped and prayed for this moment. It was even more satisfying than she expected when Simon added, "please."

Faye nodded and explained how every expenditure, no matter how small, went through Howard. And Howard, being the generally unbearable turd that he was, wanted all requests made in person so he could wield whatever modicum of power he was convinced he had.

Merry's enjoyment of the situation faded into anger as she heard that Faye was unwilling to subject herself or any of her employees to Howard's hour-long lectures, so she bought their supplies from her own money. Her anger burned hotter when Santa explained that he made requests on behalf of both the carving and painting departments, so Siofra didn't have to. Pari and Rari just shrugged and said they made a game of who could make Howard's face turn the reddest.

To no one's surprise that knew her, Dee was the one who jumped in and gave a very long, very loud description of every single thing that was wrong with the current system. She concluded by offering her HR expertise to help with an employee code of conduct while she was in town. Simon and Merry agreed at the same time.

While Dee was talking, their food was delivered. Ida June served everything family style so Merry quickly ran out of room on her plate with all the small piles of different foods and the much-needed border between them to prevent taste contamination.

She was half a second away from finding out whether the fried chicken tasted as good as it smelled when Simon said, "And your plan to fix the current process?"

Merry narrowed her eyes at his blatant power play. He just had to control every meeting, even ones where he was supposed to let her lead. Hiring him was definitely a mistake.

"It's a two-pronged plan," she said, forcing calm into her voice. She snuck in a bite of fried chicken between sentences and nearly died at the taste. It was divine. How had she not eaten here before? "Prong one, give Howard a boss so terrible that he quits. So, you know, just be yourself and we'll have that one squared away."

She ignored his eye roll and continued. "Prong two, give Santa a budget and a credit card."

"I've never had one of those!" The gleam in Santa's eye reminded her to set the spending cap on that credit card very, very low at first.

Simon nodded. "Yeah, I agree. The foreman should definitely be able to authorize purchases. I'll work with the procurement department to run an audit of last year's expenses and then we can set the budget. And Faye, if you'll send me any receipts you have for work expenses since January, we'll reimburse them."

If he thought they had a procurement department, he was going to be very unpleasantly surprised.

"I want an espresso maker!" Jeraltan cut in.

"Authorized!" Santa said immediately. "I'm great at this. Who else wants stuff?"

Merry pinched the bridge of her nose. "What Santa means is he will look at the *budget* and decide if we can *afford* an espresso maker without sacrificing any other important things."

"Ah, where's the budget?" Santa asked. His face fell. "It's in The Excel, isn't it?"

"Yeah, babe. It's in The Excel."

"But I'm still getting the espresso maker, right? It was authorized.

So, I get it." Jeraltan asked.

"Sure, whatever, just order it before the end of the year," Merry said. She turned to Faye, "Does that plan work for you?"

"I like espresso, so sure." She gave Merry a sharp smile, then nodded and answered the actual question. "Yes. And I will keep Santa on budget."

Thank you, Merry mouthed. Aloud, she said, "I'm sure he can handle it."

They fell silent as the waiter delivered dessert. Even to Merry, budgets paled in comparison to apple pie.

***

After lunch, she gave Simon a tour of the Claus Family Toys complex, introduced him to the rest of the employees, and ushered him as quickly as possible into a conference room. She checked her phone after closing the door. They had four hours to finalize the plan for the upcoming year.

Her nerves sang under her skin. The decisions they made that afternoon would determine if Santa and the others would be free from the bargain. Even under torture she would never admit how glad she was that Simon was there to keep her from making a mistake.

"We're doing divorced parent rules from now on," he said, plopping into one of the padded chairs and propping his bad leg on another. He rubbed the knee that had ended his football career.

Without conscious thought, Merry slid him a bottle of ibuprofen. "What does that mean?"

"Hate me all you want, but not in front of the kids."

"But I can still yell at you behind closed doors?" That was imperative.

Simon chuckled. "Yeah, Merry. We both know you can't think unless you're yelling. I'm assuming that's why you kicked your boyfriend out. He doesn't know how crazy you are yet?"

"No, and let's keep it that way. I made a presentation."

"Aw, you shouldn't have."

She flipped him the middle finger and set up her laptop. "We need to make a ten-million-dollar profit next year. And here's the plan to get us there."

They made it to slide two before they started yelling.

Simon was right. The rush of adrenaline that came from a tight deadline and an instinctive need to outsmart the most brilliant man she knew gave her the clarity she needed to see the flaws in her plan. This combative need to prove herself as his equal was what kept her at Kline through the tough times. It made her blood run hot and her head clear and her stomach go all fluttery. She'd missed it.

She'd barely gotten started when the conference room door opened and Santa strolled in, a cup of coffee in each hand.

"We're not done," she snapped.

He set a cup in front of her and rested an arm across the back of her chair. "Keep going. I have all day."

Merry struggled to find the words to get him to leave without hurting his feelings. "I—"

"Don't want me to see you angry. I understand. But I'm not scared and I'm not going anywhere. I let Joy keep me out of the decisions in the past. I'm not doing that again. So, yell all you want, duckie. Just don't try to make me leave."

It was Simon who made the final decision. "Divorced throuple rules."

Merry snorted and choked on a laugh. "Oh really?"

Simon shrugged.

"I don't like that," Santa said. "How about Merry and I are a couple, non-divorced, and you are her weird brother that I'm nice to for her sake."

They wasted another five minutes arguing about what to call the rules that meant they would be a united front in public before moving on to the actual problems at hand.

At exactly 5:59, Merry reached the end of her modified presentation flushed, tired, and deeply satisfied. True to his word, Santa hadn't balked at her temper or her methods for getting results. Even better, he'd proven to be just as opinionated and pig-headed as she and Simon.

Merry offered to be the one to tell the rest of the staff the plan but

Simon had just rolled his eyes and texted Nana that he would be late. Which is how Merry found herself on the wrong end of Faye's glare.

After careful explanations, all the department heads, Faye included, agreed with Merry's plan to cut the size of the catalog for the following year and focus all their attention on the toys that sold the quickest with the highest margin. They also agreed with her plan to add custom toys to their offerings with Santa handling those from start to finish.

The mood was subdued as Santa handed out new assignments for the design department since they wouldn't need to create any new toys the following year. It quickly turned when a harried-looking Charli pushed her way into the conference room with the announcement that the website was ready for prime time. Thankfully, Merry had warned her that products were likely to be cut, so she'd only uploaded a few of the most popular toys for her big reveal.

Simon sent another text to Nana but otherwise didn't complain that Merry had kept him two hours past the time he'd said he needed to leave. She felt guilty about that, but not guilty enough to reschedule. The website launch was vital to her plan, and she wanted it up and running by the start of the year.

Charli took over sharing her screen from Merry's mini projector and the homepage of the website popped up on the far wall to a chorus of excited squeals. Charli had outdone herself. As had the employees.

They were everywhere on the website. A short video of Pari and Rari showcasing the packaging department in the style of a cheesy commercial. Santa carving a toy at a speed no human could replicate. Melody singing as she sketched a new design in dizzying detail. And a series of pictures of Jeraltan that made Merry laugh out loud.

Under the heading *Contact Us. Jeraltan Is Waiting by The Phone.* was a photo of Jeraltan knitting while staring at an old-fashioned phone. It flipped to another image of him lying on the desk, staring upside down at the phone. Then, it changed to him sitting cross-legged on the desk wearing the sweater he'd been knitting in the first picture. Of course, it said *Call Me*.

Not only were the people perfect, but the photos Charli had taken of the toys showed their exquisite detail and coloring. She had created a masterpiece of a website that Merry would be proud to share. Unfortunately, there was one problem.

"We have to take off the pictures and videos of people," Merry said.

"What? Why?" Charli said.

"I'm sorry. I should have told you. But none of the employees can be on the website for their safety."

Her statement was met with a dozen variations of "it'll be fine," so she turned to Santa. His expression was shuttered for once.

After a long pause, he said, "Merry's right. It's not safe."

"I told you," Faye muttered. More loudly, she said, "I told all of you not to waste Charli's time."

"We can save the pictures and add them next year," Merry offered as a consolation. "Just not right now." Not while they were stuck in Poleton like sitting ducks. Yes, they were in human bodies, so it wasn't immediately obvious that they were Fae. But none of them looked particularly human either. Their odd combinations of colorings and unearthly beauty would catch more than a few eyes and Merry had no way of protecting them.

"I agree with Merry. Next year, when things are safer, we can add pictures of us," Santa said.

After the bargain was fulfilled, Merry would do everything in her power to make sure every employee was represented on the website and got to do what they enjoyed at work. Until then, though, she would have to keep making these tough decisions. It wasn't fun to diminish their joy, but it was necessary to keep them safe.

Simon spoke up. "I'll defer to you two on this one. I like the pictures and the website overall, but safety is non-negotiable."

He gave Merry a significant look and she nodded once, not sure if she was thanking him, confirming that this was cult-related, or apologizing for not consulting him privately before giving her opinion. If it was the latter, he would certainly let her know later.

"What about cartoons of people?" Charli said. "I have a room full of artists, surely someone can draw caricatures."

"That's a perfect solution," Merry said brightly. "Then you won't have to change the layout, and everyone can still get their jokes in there."

Simon and Santa agreed easily, and Faye's department took the lead on their last creative project for the next twelve months.

With the plan finally settled, the employees filed out and she handed Simon the keys to her dad's truck. He looked exhausted but she knew better than to suggest driving him to Nana's.

"I know you have plans, but we're going hiking tomorrow morning, then thrifting for Christmas gifts, then getting manicures."

Simon leveled a glare at her that usually heralded boundary-setting in the most annoying tone possible. "Schedule whatever bullshit bonding activity you want during work hours if you want me there."

There it was, frosty tone and all. "I was inviting you as a friend, you ass."

"Oh. In that case, still no. All that sounds miserable."

Merry snorted a laugh. "I didn't think you'd go for any of those activities. But there is a festival on Sunday if you want to bring Nana. We can look at houses after that if you want. I'm sure she'd like to see where you'll be living."

"Yeah, she'd like that. Text me the details." He went back to packing his laptop and charger then paused as he zipped up his bag. "You said hiking first just to get me to agree to the festival, didn't you."

"Of course," she said with a tired smile. It had been a long day, but she still knew how to get her way.

CHAPTER 41

Merry woke on Christmas Eve wrapped in Santa's arms and immediately knew it was how she wanted to spend every holiday for the rest of their lives. His would be considerably longer than hers if she didn't figure out the whole magic thing, but she pushed that thought aside to revisit on a less special day.

And yes, Christmas had begun to feel special to her. Not special in the sense that she hated it above all other days, but genuinely welcome.

She didn't have time to dwell on that fact, though. Ms. Claus was living up to her name and providing a special surprise for all the good boys and girls, even if it was a day early.

Santa broke out Christmas sweaters for them—courtesy of Jeraltan's knitting—and Merry laughed out loud when she saw them. Hers was navy with white cursive letters that said *I'm Santa's Favorite*. True to her wishes, there was no tree, ornaments, or Christmas iconography at all. Santa's was green, of course, and read *You're On My List* in a bold serif font.

"I wanted matching ones, but I'm ashamed to say I couldn't think of any good puns on the spot."

"There's always next year," Merry replied and instantly wished she could snatch the words back. They'd agreed to be a couple but hadn't discussed the future in detail.

Thankfully, he responded with a bright smile and a soft kiss to her forehead. "And all the years after that, if you'll have me."

Her smile was so wide it made her cheeks hurt. "You, I'm sure about.

Matching sweaters will take some convincing."

He captured her lips in a rough, claiming kiss that stole her breath. He tasted like peppermint and promises and Merry sank a hand into his freshly braided hair, pulling him closer.

When they finally broke apart, his lips were kiss-swollen and his eyes half-lidded and hazy. He was so beautiful she couldn't stand to have any space between them. "I'm still not convinced."

Santa brushed her lips in a brief, tender kiss. "I guess I'll have to try every day for the next year, then."

"Good plan," she replied, returning his kiss with a few playful pecks of her own. Those turned deeper, lingering and soon she'd forgotten all about the surprise, the festival, and the world outside of Santa's lips and wandering hands.

Charli's insistent knocking on their still-broken door brought her back to reality and she rushed Santa to the festivities.

They arrived just in time to see one hundred and three shivering Fae and one lawyer pile out of the cabs and beds of a dozen pickup trucks. Santa left Merry's side long enough to count his family like the chaperone of a field trip, then check every inch of his trucks for damage.

Graham and Jeraltan made their way through the crowd just in time to snatch Rosie before she darted into the throng of employees.

"We should have brought the Disney leash," Charli muttered, taking her squirming daughter from Graham.

"I still don't know how I feel about it," Deirdre said. "Our daughter needs to know we trust her."

"She's three. I do not trust her," Charli countered, which brought a scowl to Dee's face. "And I especially don't trust everyone else."

Faye wandered over and took Rosie from her mother, burying her button nose in Rosie's hair. It seemed that Charli trusted some people, which made Merry equal parts glad and wary. How would Charli react when she learned it was a pixie sniffing her daughter's curls?

As if sensing the direction her thoughts had taken, Graham wrapped an arm around her waist in what would look like a delayed greeting. He whispered, "I still feel guilty about not telling them."

"It's too late now. What would we even say? 'Merry Christmas, we got you a hundred magical beings. Surprise!'" she whispered back.

"Shouldn't you be hugging your dear sister who you plan to abandon in California? You'll have all the time in the world to hug Merry," Deirdre interrupted.

Graham was saved from making yet another apology to Dee by Santa's announcement that he was satisfied with the condition of his family and his trucks, and they could finally go inside.

Merry pulled Santa by the gloved hand and led him off to the side of their party so they could speak privately. "Please remember that I had good intentions and don't be mad at me."

"Sounds ominous, duckie. What did you do?"

"Do you remember making carvings of bears? They were about knee-high, and I found them in the reject room."

"Yes, I remember. Joy said they didn't count as toys."

Merry nodded, an uncomfortable twisting in her gut. She'd wanted it to be a surprise, but now she was worried she'd overstepped. "Right. Anyway, I was trying to decide what to get you for Christmas and I know how much you love your family so I thought the best gift I could give you was helping you give something to them."

He smiled down at her. "You know me well, love. But what does that have to do with bears?"

"Oh, I sold them on Etsy. Turns out people like sculptures of bears. A lot. And since they weren't toys, the money doesn't belong to the business. So, you paid for half of our joint gift to your family and had some money left over." She pressed a wad of cash into his hand.

He looked at the roll of bills, back at her, back at the money. "This is all mine?"

"Yes, there was five hundred and sixty dollars left."

Santa swallowed hard and when he finally looked at Merry, there were tears in his eyes. "Thank you. You don't know how much it has pained me not to be able to care for my people in the way they deserve. I've done my best, but…" He shook his head. "Just, thank you."

"You made the sculptures. All I did was take pictures and upload them. I'll show you how to do it later and you can sell whatever you want," Merry reminded him. "You're incredible. I have no doubt that your art will sell and will be able to take care of your family financially. You already take care of them in every other way."

He silenced her reassurances with a kiss. "I will let everyone know that this money is from both of us. They are your family, your people, too."

She stood on tiptoes to kiss him again. "Did you miss the part about the other joint gift?"

Merry led him and all their friends beyond the barriers that walled off the town square for the festival. There were dozens of booths bedecked in Christmas spirit selling everything from hot chocolate to last minute gifts.

In the center of the booths, was an ice-skating rink. A very expensive ice-skating rink considering she'd had to bribe the previous renter and pay triple for workers to set it up on short notice. The money didn't matter when she saw Jake and Jo—two members of the town council—ushering local children into rented skates with wide smiles on their faces. That joy extended to her employees, several of which took off at a sprint to be the first to hit the ice.

Santa swept her off her feet and ran, outpacing all but the trolls and ogres, to secure their spots on the crowded ice. She laughed as he playfully pushed Siofra out of the way and claimed the last pair of size 7 skates for her. "Since we are giving this gift, aren't we supposed to stand back and be happy to watch everyone else have fun?"

"I'm not a saint, duckie." He fitted the skates over her fuzzy socks.

"You're not very patient, either," she added. He didn't argue, just took her hand and led her onto the ice.

They made it one lap around the crowded rink in silence with Santa just grinning at her and everyone else. Skating wasn't as much fun with the ice crowded, but the happy faces all around her made up for the annoyance of bumping into people every five seconds.

When he'd finally regained his voice, he skated backwards to look into Merry's eyes while holding her gloved hands in his. "This is perfect, duckie. Tell me everything you did to make it happen."

She explained step by tedious step, and eventually agreed to include him in all future plans. He loved surprises but wanted to be a part of their joint gifts in the future. That was fine with Merry since it meant they had a future together.

***

Merry dragged Santa off the ice after fifteen minutes and passed her rented skates to Siofra. Deirdre and Charli were stepping onto the rink with a delighted Rosie between them, but she didn't see Graham and Jeraltan.

Santa took her hand, and they made their way through the growing crowd. She found the two missing members of their party behind a wooden table bedecked with various holiday decorations—some with the tags still on them. So, this was what the seven hundred and fifty dollar charge on her credit card had bought.

Jeraltan was offering cookies to passing festival goers with his usual enthusiasm wearing a sweater that said *Tis The Season For Queer Cardinals*. Graham stayed safely behind the table, helping Melody organize a display of hand painted wooden charms, and wearing a sweater with two red birds perched on a branch with a rainbow heart between them.

Santa proudly presented each of them with a crisp five-dollar bill from the proceeds of his toy sales and an offer to watch over their wares while they spent it. Both Fae quickly accepted and darted off in different directions.

Graham watched his boyfriend snake through the crowd, searching for the perfect place to spend his money while Merry took stock of the other boxes they'd brought. One was full of bourbon and jars of eggnog. She didn't know much about liquor licenses, so she left that one until Graham could weigh in and started unpacking wooden figurines instead.

A little while later, Santa had gone to hand out more spending money and Simon arrived with a tall, slender woman in a floral dress and orthopedic shoes on his arm. She was younger than Merry expected, and her eyes were a sharp brown below graying brows. If it wasn't for the oxygen tubes in her nose, Merry would have thought Simon was exaggerating his grandmother's health status.

Merry rushed forward to welcome her with all the enthusiasm of a teenager meeting their friend's parents and hoping to make a good impression.

The older woman took Merry's offered hand. "I'm Merry Claus, I worked with Simon at Kline, and we'll be working together at my family's company."

"May-ree," she pronounced the name in true Southern fashion, "nice to meet you. With a name like that, you must hate Christmas."

Merry's eyes widened. "I do!"

The older woman laughed; a rough, wet sound that forced Merry to remember the portable oxygen tank strapped to her hip. "My name's Iris. Couldn't tell you how many ugly flowers I've been given over the years. I had to tell my friends that it was my mother who loved 'em, not me."

Merry wrapped both her hands around the thin, wrinkled one. "You get me. Can you be my grandmother too?"

That drew another pained laugh. "Sorry, sugar. I've got my hands full with one grandkid. I won't be taking on anymore."

Merry laughed and turned to Simon to make a joke about him being a handful. His gaze was turned away from them, firmly planted on Faye fighting a tangled orange extension cord, attempting to bring it close enough to plug in Merry's old amplifier. The electric guitar was already hanging from one of her slender shoulders and she held a pink guitar pick between her teeth.

"You could help instead of staring, Simon."

He started at being caught, a hilarious thing for a six-foot-seven ex-football player. "Right. Yeah. I can help. Nana, will you be alright?"

"I've been standing on my own two feet for seventy-three years. I think I'll manage."

Simon rolled his eyes, flashed his dimples at Iris, and went to help Faye set up her new guitar.

"I've heard a lot about you," Simon's grandmother said, fixing

Merry with sharp brown eyes.

Merry winced. "All bad things, I assume."

"Some. Some good things. Some things that are not good or bad. I heard your name so often I was beginning to wonder if you would be the death of my boy or the mother of my great-grandchildren."

That startled a laugh out of Merry. Unfortunately, Santa chose that moment to reappear with his arms around Merry's waist. "Something I need to know, duckie?"

Merry kissed his cheek. "No. Simon and I were rivals and now hopefully friends. No murders or babymaking in our future."

"Don't speak so soon. He might kill you for sending him to help Faye when she doesn't want to be helped." Merry followed his gaze to where Simon was standing with both palms up while a red-faced Faye clearly preparing to prove that her ass-kicking boots were aptly named.

"Why is she yelling? Never mind, just save him. I need a CFO."

"On it," Santa replied with a kiss to her forehead.

As he walked away, Iris harrumphed. "Your boyfriend has a tight little rear."

"Nana!" Merry chastised, which only brought more of the older woman's gurgling laughter. After a moment, Merry joined her with a few giggles of her own. She swore Santa sashayed his hips even though he was too far away to hear the compliment. "But he does, doesn't he? And you should see his abs."

They ogled Santa like schoolgirls until he and Simon returned. Simon narrowed his eyes at her. "You did that on purpose."

"This time, I really didn't. What did you say to her?"

Simon shrugged. "Nothing, I just started helping. Then she was yelling that I was stealing her guitar."

Santa laughed. "It's nothing against you personally. I think you're the only person she's talked to all day who hasn't tried to take it."

Simon raised his eyebrows at the implication that Claus Family Toys—or maybe Poleton in general—was full of would-be guitar thieves, but let it go. They broke out the eggnog and bourbon—to drink, not to sell thanks to Graham's lecture on liquor licenses—and spent an hour wandering through the nearby booths and listening to Faye add gorgeous guitar to traditional Christmas carols.

By one o'clock, Santa had handed out all the money Merry had given him, Iris was leaning heavily on Simon's arm, and Deirdre and Charli had brought a screaming Rosie into the mix. It was still the best Christmas celebration Merry had ever been a part of.

CHAPTER 42

After lunch, Rosie needed a nap, so Dee and Charli took her back to the inn. Iris was still looking a little wan, so Merry suggested they leave the festival early and start the house hunt.

It had taken some convincing to get the only local realtor, Alvin, to work on Christmas Eve, but the fact that Merry made up most of his business pushed him to set his plans aside. She would feel bad about that later. Now, it was time to find a house to start her new life in Poleton.

Luckily Alvin had kids, so he also had an SUV with a third row. They settled Iris into the heated front seat and the rest of their party filled the remaining space. After much grumbling, Merry took the middle seat between Santa and Simon while Graham and Jeraltan took the seats in the very back.

Santa claimed he'd never heard of HGTV but did an excellent job impersonating the host of House Hunters. It was way too soon to think about moving in together but Merry still paid attention to which features he sought in a house. Unsurprisingly, those features mostly had to do with wood.

Merry owned twenty-seven unoccupied homes—a fact that made her squirm in progressive discomfort. The first available unit was a townhouse built in the nineties with faux cedar shakes, faux wood floors, and plastic blinds. None of them jumped at the chance to live there.

The next was a large craftsman last updated in the eighties. It had five bedrooms of shag carpet and peeling paint. Again, it didn't speak to any of the three people searching for their new place.

They saw a one-bedroom apartment above a shop on Main Street with exposed brick, scarred wide-plank flooring, and vaulted wooden ceilings. It was gorgeous, and Graham made three full loops of the small space before putting it on his 'maybe' list.

Out of respect for Iris, Merry directed them to a brand-new construction townhome next. It met almost all of Simon's criteria including a two-car garage, a gas stove, high ceilings, and a killer view. While it didn't have the fourth bedroom or the hot tub he wanted, he quickly agreed that it was the place for him.

With his new home chosen, Simon left to take Nana home while the rest of their party kept looking. They saw four more houses including a split-level home near Henry's house which Graham added to his 'maybe' list. They'd seen almost a dozen houses, but none of them felt like home to Merry. She was starting to feel discouraged when Alvin finally said he had something special up next.

They drove a few minutes toward the north edge of town and stopped in front of a cute stone cottage with multiple chimneys, a wide front porch, and over ten acres of land. Merry finally felt a twinge of longing. So, it seemed, did Graham.

They toured the house which had been built in 1905 and felt like it. The floors were wide plank hardwood, the ceilings were low and cozy, and the kitchen was adorably vintage. There was a fireplace in the main bedroom and a balcony overlooking the mountains. It was small but perfect.

Santa flitted around, informing everyone and no one of the types of wood used for the overhead beams and floors, the types of stone on the exterior and the chimneys, and the possibilities for gardening in the sprawling backyard. He clearly loved it as much as she did.

They finally made it outside to find half a dozen garages lined up against the edge of the property.

"Do you think we can steal the 'Santa's Workshop' sign from work?" she asked, pointing to the garages.

Santa went unnaturally still beside her. "You want me to have a workshop here?"

Her heart beat too quickly as she realized what she'd just asked. "And a toothbrush and at least one drawer if that's okay with you. If it's too soon..."

"It's not soon enough, duckie. Yes. I will leave all my stuff here."

That wasn't exactly what she'd said, but it was much better than a refusal. She grinned at him. "I want this one."

Graham looked up from a surprisingly heated conversation with Jeraltan and his shoulders slumped. Jeraltan's cheeks were splotched, and he looked dangerously close to tears. As much as she wanted the house, she wanted her friends to be happy even more.

"What's wrong, is this the one you wanted?"

"Of course it is," Graham snapped. "You've seen the other options. But we might not be ready to commit to a house yet."

"I can't." Jeraltan's voice was panicked. "I just know this isn't the right house. I'm sorry."

"Don't be sorry," Graham said, rubbing Jeraltan's arms through his coat. "If it's not right, then it's not right. Let's look at the last few houses and then decide."

Jeraltan nodded glumly and Merry was secretly a little glad she hadn't needed to fight over the house.

None of the other houses on their list spoke to Jeraltan either and Graham decided to take the apartment above the shop on Main Street until he and Jeraltan found the right house for the two of them.

Merry and Santa headed back to the festival for the final hour, walking through the dwindling crowd hand-in-hand and discussing all the furniture she had in California and what she would need to buy. He didn't mention moving in again, and that made her unreasonably sad. It was way too soon. But she couldn't picture the house without thinking of him there as well.

CHAPTER 43

Merry snuck out of Santa's bed before dawn on Christmas morning, which was not an easy feat since he was a light sleeper. She met Jeraltan already in the kitchen wearing a brand-new apron that said *Chop It Like It's Hot*.

He waved at his apron and whispered, "If Graham asks, tell him I love it. Between us, his puns need work."

Merry laughed and kissed his cheek. "Merry Christmas. And at least he tried."

Jeraltan responded with a kiss to her cheek and a heavy sigh. "I know he did. I hope I'm not saying the same to Santa after you exchange gifts."

"You won't be. I'm very confident in this one." She wasn't. Her stomach was a ball of nerves. "Did you have a chance…"

"Right here," Jeraltan said, holding out a basket of muffins covered by a red checked dish cloth.

"Thank you so much. I would have made them, but I couldn't sneak away last night."

"It's no problem! Go wake him up."

"You're the best."

Santa was already awake when Merry made it back to his bedroom. He looked almost human with his hair unbraided and his flannel pajama pants. Then he smiled and the illusion was shattered—no one that beautiful could be human.

"I need you to put a shirt on right this second," she said.

"Why is that, duckie?"

She ran her hands up over his sculpted abs to his defined pecs. "Otherwise, we won't be leaving this room, and all my morning plans will be ruined."

He tilted her face up with a finger under her chin and kissed her lightly. "If your plans are outside this room, I fail to see why they shouldn't be ruined."

Merry let out a little groan and sunk her teeth playfully into his pec. "Dressed. Now. I only have so much willpower."

He laughed and began gathering his clothes. Slowly. So torturously slowly.

He chose the exact moment he dropped his pajama pants revealing a biteable backside to wish her a Merry Christmas.

A half hour later, Merry rushed him out the front door and the icy morning air froze the sweat at her temples. Santa was also sweaty and looking quite proud of himself as he climbed into the passenger seat.

The streets were empty, homes lit with Christmas lights and laughter. She didn't know who lived where, but she mentally assigned townspeople to houses, imagining them in matching pajama sets with mugs of coffee surrounded by torn wrapping paper and children squealing with delight.

Those images made her feel warm and safe in Poleton, a homey feeling she'd been missing all the years she lived in California. And she had her own partner beside her, idly tracing her fingers with his while he fiddled with the radio.

She parked Santa's truck at the local playground, the only public space she knew in town, and brought the basket of muffins and two travel mugs of coffee out of the floorboard. "I wanted us to have breakfast together this morning, I hope that's okay. We can spend the rest of the day with your family, but I wanted you to myself for a little while."

"That's perfect, love." Santa kissed her, tender and unhurried. "I made you something."

"I made you something too!" she said.

Their muffins were quickly forgotten in the haste to exchange gifts. If she knew anything about Santa it was that he loved to receive presents.

The gift he gave her fit in the palm of her hand, a tiny parcel of green plaid paper. She opened it to reveal green tissue paper and had to laugh at his commitment to the color. Inside of that, was a snowflake. It was so delicate that she first thought it was real. She held it up by an equally intricate chain of tiny wooden links and the sunlight glinted through the white pendant.

"This is wood?" Her voice was full of awe. He'd captured every facet of an ice crystal including the fleeting feeling that it could melt at any time.

"Yes, I wanted to give you a real snowflake, but I couldn't work the spell."

"This is perfect. I love it. And I love you." She kissed him quickly and turned back to her necklace. The only one like it in the world.

"I love you too."

It took him returning the sentiment for her to realize that she'd finally said those three words aloud. She'd thought them so many times that they'd slipped off her tongue without conscious thought, but she couldn't be upset with the turn of events. Santa loved her. He *loved* her. *He loved her.* She would never get tired of reminding herself.

He took the gift from her and turned it so that she could see the clasp, a complicated little hook that blended perfectly with the rest of the chain. He was acting as if they hadn't just said the most important three words in the history of the world. Or at least her world.

But maybe the words weren't as important as the feeling – and she'd known his feelings long before this moment. She knew them in the gentle way he turned her head so that he could clasp the necklace for her. She knew it in his scent of pine and wood polish, as familiar as her childhood home. She knew it in his clear, deep voice as he explained, "There are a lot of mistranslations of Unseelie. It means 'dark' or 'unbright' which a lot of people take to mean in the metaphorical sense, but it's actually about the weather. Seasons don't change in Faerie like they do in the human lands.

285

Seelie is where the sun is bright for much of the day and Unseelie is where nights are long. 'Summer' and 'Winter' would be better translations."

"Does it snow in the Unseelie lands?" Merry asked.

"All the time. My magic is very attuned to snow and ice, so I wanted you to have a little piece of me with you always."

She flipped the sun visor down and looked at the beautiful pendant nestled between her collarbones. Her voice was thick with emotion as she teased, "How do you always one up me when it comes to romance? You're going to think my gift is shallow and silly compared to yours."

"I'm shallow and silly, duckie. It sounds perfect."

Merry gave a little snort of laughter. His jokes and ever-present smile made her a little more confident as she handed over the wrapped present. Santa tore it open with enthusiasm and turned an even wider grin in her direction. "You got me a tape?" He turned it over in his hand, showing the side she'd written on in ballpoint pen. "You *made* me a tape? A mixtape? Like in the movies?"

"Yep," Merry replied. "Not my most romantic moment, but I called it 'duets' since it's all the songs I want to sing with you while we drive."

"I love it. I love it so much. A mate to sing with is every Fae's dream."

Christmas morning was not the time to delve into the word 'mate' so Merry let it slide. Her boyfriend—not mate—liked her gift and that was all that mattered.

"Look at number seven," she said.

He read the paper list of songs again and looked up at her with wide, excited eyes, "'Santa Looks A Lot Like Daddy.' The Garth Brooks version? You put a Christmas song on here? And why have I never thought to put that on a sweater? Call Jeraltan and have him get started. No, wait. He won't have time to finish today. Next year!"

Merry stifled her giggles against his shoulder. "I love when you ramble."

"That's good to know since I ramble when I'm happy. The only way to shut me up is to put on music so I will stop talking and start singing. My mouth needs something to do."

Merry gave his mouth something to do before sliding the tape into the player. They ate their breakfast, drank their coffee, and sang all twelve duets sitting in the parking lot of the playground.

On their way back to the mansion, a few fat snowflakes landed on the windshield. The flurry passed quickly but painted the muddy landscape bright white.

***

The snow continued in short-lived flurries throughout the day, a magical backdrop that kept them all indoors and made their holiday movies seem more tangible. They stuck to cartoons for Rosie who'd arrived around lunchtime with her moms and all her new toys.

Between commentary on the movies and Jeraltan's thousand group votes on which phone Graham should buy him—which were more to rub the gift in everyone's face than to collect their opinions—there was no shortage of conversation.

Merry talked everyone into helping Jeraltan make Christmas dinner, but he was so particular that they ended up sitting in a big, talkative Fae heap on the floor and watching as he cooked. It was too loud and too warm and absolutely perfect.

They set the 'tables' under Jeraltan's watchful eye in the ballroom. They were actually boxes of Halloween decorations with long pieces of wood balanced on top, but once tablecloths and candles were added, they were surprisingly elegant.

Merry's favorite people sat down in the same room to share a meal, and she felt that, for the first time in her life, she understood why everyone was so fond of Christmas.

The doorbell rang throughout the house, and they all exchanged glances, searching for the person who was missing. Everyone was accounted for, so Merry followed Santa to the entryway to see what new addition they would be welcoming.

Her shriek of joy was reminiscent of an over-excited Jeraltan as she flung herself into her dad's arms. "You came!"

"Of course, pumpkin. Hell, high water, and nuclear outages couldn't keep me from spending Christmas with you."

She quickly realized that she had a gorgeous white-haired shadow and introduced him to her father.

Santa struck his hand out and directly into her father's belly, then backed up a step. "Hi-er, hello…sir. I'm Santerralesium."

Holy shit, was he nervous? It was the cutest thing she'd ever seen.

Merry stepped back to his side and wrapped a comforting arm around his waist. "My boyfriend. Everyone calls him Santa."

Her dad raised his eyebrows at the label but took it in stride. Merry ushered him out of the snow as he began his fatherly duty of interrogating her boyfriend. Luckily for Santa, there was a curious three-year old, three old friends, and a hundred welcoming Fae to distract him.

"You're adorable." Merry kissed Santa's cheek as he hurried behind her with a chair for her dad. "And you don't have to be nervous. He will love you."

"Fathers generally don't," Santa replied. But he took a deep breath, plastered on a smile, and tried his best to impress her dad.

Merry knew his efforts were wasted. Her dad already liked him because he so obviously made Merry happy.

Best of all, her father had used some of the vacation he'd been accumulating for years and offered to go with Merry to pack up her life in California. They would have ten full days to sightsee while driving her car across the country.

Between her boyfriend, her dad, and the rest of her family, she couldn't have asked for a better Christmas.

CHAPTER 44

Christmas ended without fanfare. Merry fell asleep on Santa's shoulder watching *Home Alone* on VHS in the old sitting room and woke the following morning in her bed at the inn. Santa was there, already packing her suitcase.

"If you miss your flight, you're just going to book another one, right? I can't keep you here by throwing your clothes out the window?"

Merry groaned sleepily against her pillow. She would have rather done so against Santa's chest, but he rarely slept through the night. "Don't throw my clothes anywhere. And yes, I would just book another flight after I finished yelling."

"Ah, yes. I'd like to avoid the yelling if possible. It's very early."

She snorted and snuggled further into her pillow. He seemed to have the packing under control.

An indeterminate period of time later, an efficient knock sounded on the door. "Merry Claus! Get out of bed. Our flight is in seven hours." She sat up with a start, as she had every morning when her father woke her from a too-long snooze before school. "And what happened to this doorknob? It looks like it exploded."

She chose to focus on the first statement rather than the question she didn't want to answer. "I'm coming. I'm coming. Give me five minutes."

Both airports were overcrowded with hungover people trying to get away from their in-laws, but they braved the masses and made it back to her apartment.

It took eighteen sleepless hours to throw her clothes and personal items into boxes and another three to find movers she trusted to ferry everything across the country.

The following morning, she returned her keycard to Kline & Associates and had a short exit interview with Deirdre's boss. It was all heartbreakingly efficient. Within two days, her life in California was over and she and her dad were driving her Porsche home. Because that's what Poleton was, home.

They missed New Year's and made it back just in time for the first Monday of the new year.

By the end of the week, the Amazon account was updated with fresh branding, photos, and intriguing descriptions and the website was live.

Merry trusted her gut and let Jeraltan lead the meetings with distributors to explain the new pricing model. It was a wise decision. Once she got them in a Zoom meeting, his big brown eyes and sunny personality did the rest.

By the end of the month, online sales were up five percent year-over-year, and the distributors had increased their orders by ten percent.

Merry was worried about the lack of warehouse space, but Pari and Rari exceeded her wildest expectations when handling Santa's custom orders and the select toys they'd made available for direct purchase. Once they learned to use technology to print shipping labels, they were a force to be reckoned with. There was little need for warehouse space because they were shipping as fast as the others could make the toys.

Santa was the biggest difference. His confidence grew along with their sales, and he was a king in the toy making domain. He set schedules, encouraged the staff, and picked up slack wherever he was needed. If the past records were anything to go by, they had never been this efficient.

Merry did away with rent for the mansion, much to the property manager's dismay, and the employees had to learn to manage money. At first, they spent every penny as soon as they got it. Merry read a thousand variations of the article *How to Teach Your Teenager to Manage Money* and tried every budgeting app she could think of. None of it helped.

Around the start of summer, however, they calmed down. It turned out that having no money at all for so many years had left them with a pent-up list of wants and no concept of saving for the future. Once they had a steady stream of income—still less than Merry would have liked, but she would fix that later—they relaxed.

They still spent way too much on candy and other frivolities, but they'd proven her grandmother wrong. They could learn to be responsible; they just needed a chance.

Graham officially moved into the apartment on Main Street but spent most of his time at the mansion with Jeraltan or in an empty office at Claus Family Toys studying for the bar. He had no luck getting Jeraltan to move but settled for taking over Santa's private bedroom with an attached bath. He wasn't happy about having a hundred roommates, but he put up with it for Jeraltan.

Where did that leave Santa? With Merry, of course.

She realized a month after officially moving to Poleton that waiting to ask him to move in was stupid. He'd rolled his eyes when she finally worked up the nerve and said, "Finally, duckie."

The second half of the year was a blur of paperwork and overtime, but the people made it all worthwhile. They sang while they worked like Snow White's hundred dwarves, and it made every day feel like a movie. And on the weekends, they had basketball games, picnics, and costume parties.

Her dad took advantage of the drivable distance between them and visited at least once a month. And, for an entire year, she never questioned her decision to move to the middle-of-nowhere North Carolina.

CHAPTER 45

One Year Later

Simon grumbled that he should have a lot more time and a lot less of an audience to finish the previous year's accounting. Merry ignored him, her nerves in a frenzy that even verbal sparring wouldn't calm.

He was right about one thing—his office was crowded. The mass of Fae spilled out into the hallway, all holding their collective breath as he manually input the day's orders and generated the financial statements.

Merry's hand was sweating where it gripped Santa's.

It would be close.

With marketing expenses and the growing pains of taking a paper business online, their profits would be damn close to the goal. Merry just prayed they were on the right side of it.

Santa squeezed her hand so tightly that the bones ground together. He was vibrating with barely contained energy. If Simon didn't hurry up, he was going to have a very annoyed Fae prince to deal with.

But Santa held it together and Simon worked quickly. At 8:02 PM, he turned the monitor around and Merry saw the "10" at the front of the "Net Profit" line. She cheered like a diehard fan whose team had won the Super Bowl.

Her cheer spread through the gathered employees like wildfire and champagne sprayed from somewhere behind them. She would have to buy

Simon a new computer, but that was next year's expense, and it didn't matter now.

All that mattered was that she'd done it. They'd done it. The bargain was fulfilled and in just four hours, Santa would be free.

Their nervous energy made for the most raucous, drunken party of Merry's life. She drank whatever Jeraltan put in her hand, smoked whatever Faye had been secretly growing, and danced with Santa until her bare feet bled.

The familiar New Year's countdown sounded through the trashed ballroom and Merry held her breath. Each second felt like an eternity. Santa had his arms around her, and they stood still in the middle of the dance floor.

"Two. One. Happy New Year!"

Santa kissed her. It's how they decided they wanted to greet the new year and their new life.

There was the familiar magic of his lips on hers, but nothing else. Those lips didn't change. It didn't snow indoors. His head was still very much covered in white hair and braids, no antlers in sight.

She waited. And waited.

But a glance around the room showed bewildered humans, not Fae.

"We did it, you Fate bastards! Let them go!" she shouted at the ceiling. Nothing happened. She shouted at nothing, cursing until her throat was sore and tears streamed down her face, but there was no answer. Nothing at all but her friends, still very much trapped in their human bodies.

Santa held her as she collapsed. The weight of a year's wasted work and several bottles of champagne were too much for her body to handle. His cheeks were wet as he tucked her head against his shoulder.

"No. Nonono," she sobbed into his shirt. "I don't understand."

"Neither do I, love," Santa said. "But right now I need you to get up. Tell our people that they will be okay. Tell them that we will fulfill the bargain next year. Or the year after. Tell them we won't give up. I can't do it, love. I need you."

She clung to his shoulders and cried. It felt impossible to say those things. It felt like a lie. But that's what Santa meant. He couldn't say it because he didn't believe that they could do it. That broke her heart all over again.

Merry stood and did what Santa couldn't. She lied through her tears. She told them that it would be okay. That they would figure it out. She looked into their faces streaked with glitter and tears and lied her ass off.

She didn't know what to do from here. She didn't know what else to try.

Graham broke out a case of whiskey, his own eyes as dull and broken as Merry felt. He'd come prepared in case the Fates decided against them. She wanted so badly to yell at him, to blame him for planning for their failure. But it wasn't Graham's fault. It wasn't any of their faults. And her grandmother wasn't here to scream at. So, Merry took the bottle from Graham's hand and drank until she couldn't remember the pain.

***

Her head felt like it contained a dozen jackhammers. Her mouth tasted like cotton balls soaked in antiseptic. But neither of those things had woken her.

The sky beyond the ballroom windows was just beginning to pinken, like the first blush after a compliment. Santa was wrapped around her on the cold marble floor, clinging to her, holding her. The dried tears on his cheeks made her stomach twist.

She touched his face, needing to let him know she was there, and she would be there no matter how long it took to fulfill the bargain. He woke with a start. And ran.

The wall of windows exploded in a shower of glass.

Someone screamed.

Someone else cried.

Merry whipped her head around, trying to take in the sights around her. Two beings with skin the color of forest moss grinned at each other, showing elongated fangs. Another with skin like terra cotta and tusks jutting from his lower lip lifted a smaller figure over his head.

A woman had one eye in the center of her forehead. A man had far too many arms. Those arms disappeared back inside his body like Stitch from the Disney movie.

Graham was there, thankfully looking normal, trying to undress Jeraltan. No, trying to keep Jeraltan from undressing. She focused on that. It was familiar. Jeraltan's hair had lost all the brown undertones and was pure sunshine gold, but he was otherwise the same.

"Let me go!" Jeraltan shouted. "I have to fix it. I have to fix my house."

Graham let him go and Jeraltan was naked in a heartbeat, shaking his limbs like a cat escaping a hug. The shattered glass rose in the air and fit itself back together like a puzzle.

Her mind took a long moment to rationalize what she was seeing. The green-skinned Fae were Pari and Rari. Trolls in their true form. The terra cotta man must have been Alastor, no one else was that big. And the Stitch-looking guy was…Addie. Silent, sweet Addie, who was a type of Fae Santa hadn't been able to name. Now, she understood why.

"What. The. Ever-loving…" Simon stared around the room, wide-eyed. Had he been there all night? What had she been thinking letting him stay? There was no time to coddle him now.

"Where's Santa?" she asked everyone and no one.

"Outside. He broke my window," Jeraltan said.

Merry looked through that window and saw a trail of dead flowers and discarded clothing heading away from the mansion. Not a good sign.

The window broke for a second time and a green and black blur darted through it. Faye.

Ignoring Jeraltan's pained scream, Merry followed the pixie out of the window and onto the icy grass. Santa's trail was obvious, tall brown flowers that had pushed up through the ice and then wilted. She ran past his boots, socks, shirt, pants, and more dead flowers.

The flowers were yellow further along the trail, then a promising but quickly wilting green. She followed those live flowers and found Santa kneeling in the snow, his back heaving with heavy, panting breaths.

He turned quickly. Too quickly. Panicked gold eyes met hers. They were different—like the irises had exploded and left his whole eye filled with molten gold. And jutting proudly from the top of his head were beautiful white antlers.

"Santa," she said, awed by his transformation. His already high cheekbones were higher, his jawline inhumanly sharp. He was the single most beautiful thing she'd ever seen. "It worked."

He didn't return her smile. Instead, he bent his head and bit an already bleeding wrist. Blood flowed freely, staining the ground red. Where his blood touched, flowers bloomed. And then died.

He couldn't bond.

She didn't know how she knew that's what he was trying to do or how she knew it wasn't working. But none of that mattered when his worst fear was coming true. His Fae nature couldn't bond to the human land.

He groaned, the sound more animalistic than human, and bit his wrist again. More blood. Too much blood.

Merry rushed to his side and dropped to her knees beside him. "Stop. You're hurting yourself."

He froze and turned slowly to face her. "You." His voice was familiar but *more*. More sweetness. More gravel. More emotion. More of everything that made him, him. "It's you."

"Yes, it's me. Merry," she said. Her hands waved around his shoulders in a futile attempt to find some way to help. She wanted to cover him, protect him from the cold, but he clearly didn't want clothes. She wanted to hold him and protect him from the world, but that wasn't what he needed either.

He shook his head once, slow and awkward with the added weight of his antlers. "You are why I am here. The Fates didn't bring me to the human lands to bond. They brought me to you. My mate."

He raised his bloody wrist in front of her face.

"I don't know how to heal you, baby. Can you do it?"

"Drink," a voice said from above them. "Accept the mate bond." Faye hovered there, naked with green and gold dragonfly wings beating so quickly they were a blur. Like Santa, her eyes had lost their whites and were wholly green with a starburst of black from the center.

"Drink his blood? You can't be serious."

Apparently, she was. Santa pressed his torn wrist to her lips, and, despite her reservations, she tasted the salty tang of blood. She really, really wanted to spit it out, but forced herself to swallow. It was a terrible time to worry about being rude, but Southern manners died hard.

Crashing sounded through the trees and more Fae appeared all around them. Some were clothed, the ones with stronger magic were naked. Was it the synthetic fabrics? She didn't have time to ask.

"Did she accept?" someone asked.

"Yes, but she has not reciprocated," Faye answered. "He is hers, but she is not his."

"Will someone tell me what is going on?" Merry shouted at the group. She didn't understand. Santa had never mentioned blood drinking. Just bonds. Bonds that he and the others would make. He'd never said she needed to do anything.

"I see now," Santa's voice sounded far away, like it was a struggle to get the words out. "You are Seelie and human. I am Unseelie and Lesser. Together, we are all things. We cannot bond the land separately, but we can together. It is Fated."

"We're Fated Mates? Like in the books?" Merry asked. He nodded slowly. It was not the great declaration of undying love that Fated Mates received in fiction. "Couldn't you have told me that before I drank your blood? Are we married now?"

He shook his head. "I am sorry. I should have said."

"Offer him your blood, Merry," Faye said.

"She doesn't have to marry someone she doesn't want to," Graham put in. "The Fates can't force her."

"No, they cannot. But I can already feel the magic fading. We are not replenishing as we should. We cannot pull magic from these lands without a bond and Santa says he cannot make the bond without her. So, you'll have to excuse my haste to assure my own survival," Faye replied.

"What does mated mean?" Merry asked.

"In this case, everything. You will be Fated and Chosen mates. You will be stronger together, sharing magic and a bond with the land. If we are lucky, the flood of his magic will overpower any other spell on you." Faye said. At Merry's skeptical look, she hurried to continue. "Despite what your books say, you can break a mate bond if either of you chooses to do so. But once you bond the land, you will be drawn back here, bound to care for these lands and your people."

That didn't sound bad. She was already drawn to Poleton, and she already wanted to take care of these people. And she had planned to marry Santa one day—

"Oh, what the hell." Merry tried to bite her wrist as Santa had but her human teeth were too dull.

Santa held her gaze as he slowly lifted her wrist to his mouth. "Yes, go ahead. Bite me and drink my blood." She shivered as the words left her mouth.

He opened his mouth to reveal canines much sharper than they were before. As gently as he could, he laid those sharp teeth against her wrist and bit until two drops of blood surfaced. Santa licked one away and she watched his throat bob as he swallowed.

Light, it was the only way to describe it, bloomed in her chest and spread along her limbs. She felt like a snake shedding its skin. The old Merry burned away, leaving something new and painfully raw in its wake. The cold felt colder, the air smelled cleaner. She heard heartbeats and shifting feet. She saw the veins on a leaf fluttering to the ground.

No wonder Santa wasn't himself. This magic was incredible. Overwhelming. It obliterated everything she thought she knew and replaced it with something sharper. More real.

Her mouth felt different and Merry ran her tongue along new teeth. Sharp canines, like Santa. Had she become Fae? Or had her Fae nature been revealed?

Santa turned her wrist so that another drop of blood fell, mixing with what he'd spilled from his own veins.

If she'd thought the mating bond was overwhelming, it was nothing compared to bonding the land. She was kneeling in the same place, but she was aware of the water running beneath the surface of the ground, the clouds above them, the critters darting through the trees and those curled safe in their burrows.

She felt the people around her, bright lights for Jeraltan and Faye, dimmer ones for the other Fae, a shadow that was Addie, and an earthy sort of feel where Graham stood. Another, similar feeling stood a few yards behind the group.

Alarmed, Merry focused on that human. She touched the leather of a football, smelled sweat and grass, felt the calm of numbers fitting into their assigned columns, and underneath all of that, loneliness. Simon. She relaxed. It was just Simon.

That extra awareness shrank until Merry was once again in her body, feeling and seeing things with only mildly heightened senses. Beside her, Santa's shoulders had lost their rigidity. He opened those strange gold eyes and smiled.

"Come," he said, his voice ringing with authority. As he spoke, greenery grew and twined up his body, shielding him like clothing. A flowering vine curled around his forehead. A crown. Merry was so awed by him that she barely felt a matching vine mark her own brow. "Accept the bond through us."

One by one, the Fae knelt in front of them and offered a drop of their blood. Santa responded with a drop of his own. Though Merry was, thankfully, not participating directly in the ritual, she felt the effects. A tether from herself to each person, and another through her to the land. Her tie to the land grew stronger with each new connection Santa forged.

She and Santa were the tree, sinking roots into the earth and offering a branch to each person inhabiting it. Through them, they could reach the well of magic beneath.

The bonding ritual also gave her the opportunity to study her people. They were still them, even with different colored skin, wings, scales, and the occasional extra appendage. They were still her family, and she would protect them with every bit of newfound strength.

The bonding was more tiring than Merry expected. Not that she'd expected to be a part of it at all, but that was semantics.

Addie knelt in front of them, looking exactly the same as he had in his human form, but Merry still remembered the extra arms that had appeared when the bargain was fulfilled. She also remembered the shadow she'd felt where his magical light should have been.

Santa didn't offer his wrist. "You have no need of a bond." Addie shook his head in agreement. He slowly reached forward and pressed a bloody finger to Santa's forehead, then hers. Marking them.

"Thank you," Santa said.

Merry didn't have time to question why Addie didn't need a bond or what he'd just done. Faye knelt before them and accepted a drop of Santa's blood, her wings stilling and her eyes rolling back. The tether that bound them together felt stronger than the others, and Merry was wary of that strength as she offered to go after Simon and ensure their secrets stayed secret. Santa agreed for both of them.

Faye's bond might have been strong, but it was nothing compared to Jeraltan's.

He was the last to accept the bond. Graham stood beside him with a comforting, or maybe cautious, hand on his shoulder. Merry smiled at the cherubic face with its luminous lavender eyes. He was even more beautiful in his brownie form and one look at Graham told her he agreed.

When he accepted the drop of blood from Santa's wrist, Merry gasped and pressed her hand to the center of her chest. The magic was elated. Hungry. It grabbed him with dozens of tendrils of power.

Santa's laugh broke her concentration. "Duckie, I think you just lost a house."

"What?" She blinked a few times, and her vision cleared. She was so tired, but Santa was smiling. He was focused on her, fully present. Her relief was instant. She'd been worried that he would be caught in the magic's thrall forever.

Instead of answering her, he stood and raised his arms. A true king addressing his tiny kingdom. "We have a bonded brownie!"

Cheers rose through the crowd, none louder than Jeraltan cheering for himself. "I did it! I bonded! At only one hundred and sixty. Eat your heart out, Aldric!"

"What does your brother have to do with this? What's going on?" Graham asked.

Jeraltan bounced on his toes, gripping Graham's arm. "Come back to my house and I'll show you."

"Your *house*? You bonded a place? Not a person. Not a person, right?" Graham couldn't have sounded more relieved if he tried.

"I did! The mansion is mine. You are all welcome...until I decide otherwise." His cackle was nothing short of devious and Merry briefly wondered what a pissed off brownie was capable of. She didn't want to find out.

She tried to stand, but her legs gave out. Santa was there, catching her before she hit the ground. "It was a lot, I know. You'll get used to the magic, though."

"I don't understand most of what just happened. I have part of your magic. And it changed my teeth?"

Santa leaned down and kissed the top of one of her ears. The movement was awkward, like he was still getting used to having antlers again. "Your ears too. But that wasn't my magic, it was yours being unbound. Our bond transcended your grandmother's magic. You're free, love."

"I don't feel free, I just feel tired," she complained. "And still confused."

He laughed his usual carefree chuckle, but it sounded lighter now. Like it took less effort. "I am sorry. I was trying to bond the land, and I was caught in that magic. I couldn't complete the bond, but it wouldn't let me go either. Then, you were there, and it all made sense. The push to come to the mortal lands, the nudge I felt to accept the bargain, even that pull toward you from the moment we met. We are Fated and Chosen, my darling queen."

"People keep saying that. You'll have to explain later," she said, snuggling against his chest. The mansion and all its newly freed inhabitants came into view. She tried to smile, but she ended up just sighing and leaning against Santa's chest. "Right now, I need a nap."

"I can arrange that. Then, we will…I don't know, duckie, what do you want to do?"

"Everything. I want to dance with you on the beach, I want to watch Faye fly over the Grand Canyon, I want to hear you complain about traffic in New York City. I want to do everything with you."

"Yes, let's do that. All of it. But maybe take me to dinner first." His wink was the last thing she saw before she fell asleep against his chest.

ABOUT THE AUTHOR

Sara writes high fantasy and contemporary romances with strong female characters.

She started her writing journey on a lime green Mac desktop in the "computer room" of her childhood home. Between illegally downloading the latest hits (and only a few viruses) on Limewire, she discovered the joy of creating exciting worlds and loveable characters. Then, she accepted the grave responsibility of every author—making those loveable characters squirm.

When she isn't writing, Sara knits (badly), plays tennis (also badly), and annoys her husband with plot ideas.

www.ingramcontent.com/pod-product-compliance
Lightning Source LLC
Chambersburg PA
CBHW021958130726
47903CB00014B/1903